Will Kingdom is a journalist who has specialized in the paranormal. He is married and lives at the foot of the Black Mountains.

THE COLD
CALLING

Will Kingdom

CORGI BOOKS

THE COLD CALLING
A CORGI BOOK : 0 552 14584 X

First publication in Great Britain

PRINTING HISTORY
Corgi edition published 1998

Set in 10pt Bembo by Kestrel Data, Exeter

Corgi Books are published by Transworld Publishers Ltd,
61–63 Uxbridge Road, London W5 5SA,
in Australia by Transworld Publishers (Australia) Pty Ltd,
15–25 Helles Avenue, Moorebank, NSW 2170
and in New Zealand by Transworld Publishers (NZ) Ltd,
3 William Pickering Drive, Albany, Auckland.

Reproduced, printed and bound in Great Britain by
Cox & Wyman Ltd, Reading, Berks.

For Graham Nown,
journalist, author, wit,
and the bloke who said
'You've really got to do the crime novel . . .'

Prologue

Sacrifice should not be equated with our modern
attitude to murder.

Aubrey Burl, *Rites of the Gods*.

i

May, 1994

He is invisible in the greenery.

The Green Man.

The very oldest Guardian of the Earth, whose face one sees carved in stone above church doorways, his hair luxuriant with leaves, the leaves bearing fruit – stone nuts and stone berries. More leaves sprouting whole from the grinning mouth, foliage gripped between stone teeth. The grin that says, I am the Earth.

The Green Man, who stands – or crouches, or squats – for the Old Energy which once sprang from hill to holy hilltop across a shimmering land – a force which could make the fields breathe visibly and bring the oldest and coldest of stones to squirming life and . . .

Stop. Listen. Watch.

This day, the Green Man, our Green Man, knows he is perceptible only as foliage – roots and branches, fungi and moss. He is of the Earth.

Utterly, utterly still, he listens to the Earth, his mother, his sister, his wife . . . her heart beating faster and fainter nowadays . . . most people have never heard it, will not leave their cars to walk on anything more responsive than tarmac or concrete.

And these people . . .

Even they, who consider themselves defenders of the land and Her creatures, are unaware of the Green Man as they slouch in the clearing, filling their senses with cigarette smoke, plotting.

* * *

'Hear what he said?'

The bearded man in the khaki anorak unknowingly crosses the energy line as he speaks.

'When they come out the pub, this colonel-type guy says, Oh, they won't show up today, Jeremy, it's raining. No fun in the rain. Haw haw. Arrogant bastard. They think we got no staying power.'

'Be a lovely surprise for them.'

The female.

She is about thirty. Could be quite pretty if she let her hair grow, took a few of the rings out of her nose. The rings imply some tribal affiliation. What utter nonsense. These people have no ethnic roots; they are outcasts.

The other two are shaven-haired teenage boys, possibly twins. They grin a lot and kick mindlessly at the Earth . . .

Kick at Her!

The Green Man hopes that one of these boys will be separated from the others and will cross the line alone at an opportune time.

As that first rabbit did. And the squirrels, and the fox. And once – at night – a badger. Whump! Speeding down the line, the Earth swelling with the energy of blood.

'OK,' the bearded man says. 'Here's how it works. I'll go to the top of the mound and when I see them leave the road I'll wave both hands. Like this, yeah? So you keep an eye on that mound, 'cause I'm not gonna get the chance to do it twice without one of 'em sees me. So when I wave . . . Maria, if you can count to thirty, then give a little toot.'

From the pocket of her waterproof jacket, the female pulls a hunting horn and shakes it. 'Hope it bloody works this time.' She gives a smoker's snort of laughter.

'Well don't fucking try it now. All right. Shaun, if you and Gary go down the dingle now, and open the metal gate . . . Idea is, the hounds'll come tearing this way and when they're through the gate, you shut it bloody fast and piss off quick 'cause they'll know what's happening by then and they'll be bloody mad enough to do you an injury.'

'See 'em try,' one of the boys mutters mutinously.

'You won't. You'll disappear, soon as that gate's shut. We're not here for aggro, this is about saving life.'

Listen to them.

Mindless, disconnected vermin. The badger was worth more. At least the badger knew the rules.

They think that by breaking the natural cycle they are saving life. They want to sit in their eleventh-floor flats watching the foxes and badgers scamper innocently on the neat, square lawns.

But foxes kill.

Badgers kill.

The Earth kills.

And so life goes on. The faint spark of life that flits from the small body is drawn back into the greater organism. Blood-fed, the Earth breathes more deeply . . . and She feeds us.

Because, you see, once, we all killed. Isn't it obvious? It is as natural as eating and sleeping. And as important. It invigorates and enhances us. It renews us.

And hunting . . . the very act of hunting . . . all the senses streamlined, focused, combined into a single electric impulse. In hunting, we are more aware, more open to revelation. Was not John Aubrey out hunting when, in 1648, he realized the significance of the great stones of Avebury?

And even as the Green Man is thinking this, there comes through the trees the distant baying of the hounds, a sound as natural and joyous as birdsong, but, of course, more focused. Hounds hunting in packs. Hounds and horses and men, a tight and yet gloriously ragged combination, a stream of pure, concerted energy.

As old as England. Older. A communion. Pure instinct. Fusion. The wild sound of the horn on the wind, the primeval bellow, tally ho, the ecstatic blooding after one's first hunt, licking it off, swallowing it. So much sweeter than human sex.

'They're away,' the female says.

'Right.' The bearded man throws down his cigarette. 'Let's do it.' He grins. 'Sab, sab, sab.'

*　　　*　　　*

Closing his eyes, the Green Man hears the man and the youths stumbling gracelessly between the trees. The swelling heart of the wood – an entity in itself – pounds loudly in his ears.

Only the female is left in the clearing. With the Green Man and the Earth.

He feels Her pulsing with anticipation against his groin, stiffening him. Stiffening his resolve. It isn't a major step, just a question of breaking a small, social convention.

Ideally, it should be the man, as he stands upon the mound.

Motte it says on the Ordnance Survey map, signifying an artificial mound where a Norman castle once stood. In fact, many of these castles were built on the so-called 'burial' mounds created as far back as the Bronze Age, when all men hunted and were instinctively aware of the needs of the Earth and the subtle patterns of Her energies.

The female lights another cigarette. It is raining steadily and strands of her short hair are gummed to her face. She waits, smoking.

When, then?

Watch. Listen to the Earth.

He wishes there was some way She could speak directly to him, make Her wishes known. The old shamans would go into trance, make their requests and receive their instructions. He doesn't have their skills. Not yet. One day, it will all be given to him. In the meantime he must rely on signs and signals.

The female has taken out the hunting horn. Suddenly, she disgusts him, with her sexless, shorn hair, the rings in her nose, her apathy, her negativity, her hatred and contempt for the upholders of tradition.

She moves forward to see the mound through the misty rain, and she steps into the line, which he can see clearly now, falling straight as a sunbeam, having travelled half a mile from St Agnes's Well and crossing another track leading to Salisbury Cathedral.

The Green Man rises slowly to his feet, parting the bushes. The sounds he makes are small, might be the bustling of nesting birds. And just as the female guides the false horn to her lips, she sees him.

In his glory.

Lowers the horn. 'Who the hell are you?'

'Oh,' he says dismissively. 'That doesn't matter at all to you. It's what I represent that matters.'

'What? You sabbing, too?' There's uncertainty in her eyes.

'Sabbing?'

'Watch my lips. Are You A Hunt Saboteur?'

He is silent for a moment. Then he says, disappointed, 'You wouldn't understand, would you? I'm afraid I'm wasting time.'

'We did say one-thirty at the pub. If you aren't organized about this you'll get nowhere.'

He makes no reply.

'You really stupid or what?'

He hefts the crossbow to his shoulder.

Her eyes widen. 'Shit,' the female whispers. 'Oh, God.'

Emotion! Energy. At last.

What can he see in her eyes? Fear perhaps. He sees that she's just a girl.

'You better bugger off. I've got mates over there.'

Her tone is bitter but her rain-bubbled skin is soft and fresh. And there glows within her . . . a kind of desire. A response from the underlayer of her consciousness – and this layer exists in all of us – which moves and bends to the rhythm of nature. She just doesn't know of it.

'Don't be stupid.' Her face muscles struggle for a contemptuous smile. 'Those things should be bloody banned,' says the surface part of her, bravely. But there are hairline cracks in her voice, for contempt swiftly withers in a moment such as this.

And respect arises.

The Green Man laughs. 'Brace yourself,' he says encouragingly. 'Let your spirit be released. Fly with it. Don't look back. Your energy will be redeemed.'

She isn't listening. He sees a fever boiling in her eyes, which flick frantically from side to side as she thrusts the hunting horn between her lips.

He shoots her then, with great calm, great precision, through the throat.

The spontaneous surge of pure energy is utterly magnificent and *brings him to his knees and then to his face on the forest floor. His heart is full, his head afloat on golden light, the forest around him brilliantly lit as the female also falls to her knees, as though in prayer, her fingers at her throat, the blood jetting down her wrists and into the sleeves of her waterproof coat, her attempt at a scream turning to gurgling liquid.*

Her eyes, at last, showing love. The earth-spirit in her has fallen in love with the bearer of such a fine death.

Her hands reach for him. Small, white fingers, imploring.

She cannot turn her head to follow him as he moves around her, fitting another bolt into the bow before shooting her – decently, he thinks – in the back of the neck and prodding her with a foot between the shoulder blades so that she topples forward and gives up her blood, at last, to the Earth.

Shivering with energy now, head filling with white light, he summons her newly released spirit, imagining her shade beside him, free now, liberated from its bitterness and constriction, its feeble pity for the hunted fox. Fulfilled now. Appreciative of her small role in the great rehabilitation.

Raising his arms to welcome the rain, dripping from his body to the Earth, he knows he has never felt so utterly alive. An almost blinding joy fills him as he raises the female's horn to his lips, tasting the rain and the blood on the mouthpiece, and blows a long, euphoric blast and falls to his knees, laughing.

But he dare not stop, and he dismantles the crossbow as he glides, slippery as an elf, through the slick greenery. He will drive fifteen miles to bury the bow in a badger's sett at the base of a tumulus called Alfred's Grave, and then climb to the top of the tumulus and stand beneath a broken pine, shedding his shirt and lifting his arms to the rain, feeling the glory.

Having broken the convention.

And wasn't it easy?

14

ii

'*Look at you,*' said Kelvyn. '*Coming apart, you are. Your jawline's gone, your cheeks are caving in . . .*'

Cindy peered in the mirror. The blasted bird wasn't entirely wrong.

'*As for your legs . . .*' Kelvyn cackled. '*Well, no wonder you have to wear black stockings. It'll be bloody surgical stockings before long, you mark my words, lovely, you mark my words.*'

'Shut it,' Cindy snapped, 'or I'll bang down the lid on your neck and leave your head hanging out all night again.'

'*You wouldn't.*'

'Try me, bach, you try me.'

'*Becoming a nasty old bag, you are. Not getting enough, is it?*'

'Enough what?'

'*You know what I mean. Laughs.*'

'That's it,' snarled Cindy. 'Back in the case. And think yourself lucky. You know what the props boy said to me this morning? He said, Here, Mr Mars, why do you have to keep carrying that thing back and—'

'*Thing?*'

'His precise word.'

'*He's a dead man.*'

'. . . why do you keep carrying that *thing* back and forth, back and forth? Why don't you leave it in the dressing room? Nobody'll mess with it.'

'*That's what they said in Blackpool, and next morning I'm dangling off the end of a flagpole with a pair of knickers in my beak.*'

15

'What are you moaning about? Got your picture in the *Daily Mirror*.'

'*It was humiliating.*'

'*No* publicity is humiliating. Come on . . . off we go, back to the digs.'

With no ceremony but perhaps the dregs of affection, Cindy dumped Kelvyn in his imitation-crocodile suitcase, the bird still rambling on in his muffled way as Cindy lugged the case to the dressing room door. '*Don't know why we can't get decent digs any more. I remember, I do, when we had a three-room suite in . . .*'

'Oh,' Cindy said. 'Good evening, ladies.'

The two cleaners giggled. Margot and Sarah. Been outside the door listening for a good five minutes. Cindy gave them a free show after the matinee every Friday. On a long summer season, it was important, for your general health, to keep the cleaners on your side.

'He's a card, isn't he, Mr Mars?'

'Irrepressible.'

'Does he sleep in your bedroom?'

'Perches on the curtain rail, he does,' said Cindy. 'Course, he's awake at first light, the bugger. Chatting up this little gull, he was, at six-thirty this morning. Six-thirty!'

'*Gotta get what you can these days, lovely. In Bournemouth, a red kite's worth ten points among your common seagulls, did you know that? Quite sexy, she was, this one, mind, so you never know how it might turn out. All together now, The bells are ringing, for me and my gull . . . haw, haw, haw.*'

'Shut up, or you won't get any of Mrs Capaldi's lasagne.'

'*Call that a threat?*'

'Oh,' said the younger cleaner, Sarah, paling.

'Oh God,' said the older cleaner, Margot.

They weren't laughing any more.

Sarah fiddled with her duster. 'I didn't know you were staying with Mrs Capaldi, Mr Mars.'

'We *always* stay with Mrs Capaldi in Bournemouth.

Forget all that posh hotel stuff, Kelvyn lies through his beak.'

'You haven't seen tonight's *Echo*, then?'

'It's just awful,' said Margot. 'Doesn't bear thinking about. She was a difficult enough girl, heaven knows, but nobody on this earth deserves that. Nobody.'

Dear *God*.

By the time he reached the Bella Vista Guesthouse, Cindy had read the *Echo* story twice.

Maria Capaldi? *Maria?*

Maria it was who had first called him Cindy, when she was quite small and couldn't get her lips around Sydney. Uncle Cindy.

The *Echo* had a photograph of her, from the days before she'd had her hair cut short, before the nose-rings. The photo from Mrs Capaldi's mantelpiece, taken on the girl's eighteenth birthday, when she was due to go to university – from which she would drop out a year later. Mrs Capaldi would have handed it willingly to the press, a beautiful memorial, the last picture of an unsullied, unembittered Maria.

Cindy had bewildered tears in his eyes as he turned the corner and saw – as if the report needed confirmation – a police car outside Bella Vista and another car behind it, both on the double yellows.

The VACANCIES sign had been replaced by an ominously crooked NO VACANCIES. The little, square lobby was deserted, the picture postcards hanging limply from their rack alongside the pink and blue poster announcing KELVYN KITE (with Cindy Mars) with a picture of both of them wearing mocking smiles.

'I'm sorry, sir, it's closed.' A policewoman had pushed through the bead curtain.

'I . . . er . . . I'm staying here.'

'What name is it?'

'Mars-Lewis. Sydney Mars-Lewis.'

The policewoman vanished into the chinking curtain. When she came back, she said, 'Sorry, Mr Lewis, but you might have been a reporter.' Lowered her voice. 'Know what's happened, do you?'

Cindy nodded, as there came a wail from within. 'Let 'im in! Let 'im in!' The policewoman shrugged and held back the beads for him, and Cindy went through into the artificial darkness and the real despair.

The curtains were drawn tight in the residents' lounge, a table lamp shone under a picture of Jesus. Mrs Capaldi was a tiny creature in a corner of the four-seater sofa. A teacup shivered in its saucer on her aproned knees. Her greying black hair was in stiff peaks. Fresh make-up plastered over tearstains.

'Cindy . . .' She held out both hands, like a drowning woman, and Cindy took one, kneeling on the carpet at the side of the sofa. 'What I do? What I ever do to anybody to deserve this 'appen to me?'

All the times he'd heard her ask this about Maria, alive.

'Mr Lewis.' A youngish man with thinning hair arose from a deep armchair. 'Peter Hatch, Detective Chief Inspector. I, er, brought my children to see your show a couple of years ago. Very, er . . .'

Cindy moved to shake hands, but Mrs Capaldi held on to him. The detective nodded, smiled briefly, sat down again. He spoke quietly.

'You have much to do with Maria, Mr Lewis?'

'Less lately than at one time,' Cindy said. 'Although we did have our discussions about blood sports. Which both of us deplored.'

'So you knew what she was doing in that wood?'

'Shamed me into going with them once, she did.'

'Oh God,' cried Mrs Capaldi. 'Oh, Cindy, why couldn't it be you with her today, instead of that stupid Martin?'

'Alas,' Cindy explained to the detective. 'Always been a little queasy about open confrontation, I have. Maria was

braver than me.' He sighed. 'Poor dab. Poor dab. Have you
. . . you know . . . ?'

'We're talking to a few people,' DCI Hatch said. 'I don't
anticipate a long investigation. What I'm trying to find out
from Mrs Capaldi is if it was well known that Maria was a
hunt saboteur. If she'd ever received any personal abuse or
threats as a result.'

'An' I say to 'im, even if she 'ad a threat to kill 'er, the
last person she ever tell about it is 'er own mother.'

Cindy squeezed Mrs Capaldi's hand as the tears spurted.
Yes, he'd known where Maria was going today. Even
wishing her luck last night. *Yeah*, she'd said, with a limp
good-night wave of the hand. *Tally ho, Cindy*. It wasn't
something she enjoyed any more; it was something she
had to do, like hospital visiting or donating blood.

He shivered. Shot. Shot dead in a clearing in the forest,
the paper said. The cleaner was right; it didn't bear thinking about.

'Like she was lying in a bed,' Mrs Capaldi said faintly. 'A
sheet tucked up around her chin.'

Cindy looked at Hatch.

'Mortuary,' Hatch mumbled. There was an uncomfortable silence. Hatch made eye contact with the policewoman. 'More tea, I think, Alison.'

Cindy said, 'What . . . kind of person are you looking
for?'

'This stage, we have to examine all the options. My
money's on some sixteen-year-old yobbo who, at this
moment, is a very frightened kid.'

'Or a hunt supporter?'

Hatch smiled thinly. 'Now you're being controversial,
Mr Lewis.'

'Pah!' said Mrs Capaldi. ''Unters! Big family, lotsa
money. You never gonna pin it on a 'unters.'

'Mrs Capaldi, I can assure you that, at this stage, nobody
has been ruled out.'

'Pah.' Mrs Capaldi's tear-glazed eyes rising to a lurid

Pre-Raphaelite madonna over the fireplace. 'She was a good girl, a lovely girl when she wanted. She got principles. More than me. Her father, 'e 'ad principles. Me, I like peace and quiet. She say, Mum, she say, you just a cucumber. Vegetable. Make me so mad sometime.'

'Maria had integrity,' Cindy said. 'She believed that everything had a right to life.'

Mrs Capaldi struggled to the edge of the sofa as the policewoman approached with a cup. 'I don' wan' more tea. I told you, I wan' see where my daughter die. It's my right. I wan' you take me, Cindy, in your car.'

'As I said, Mrs Capaldi,' Hatch said quickly, 'I wouldn't advise it. Not at the moment. There'll be press everywhere, and TV crews . . .'

'Wassa problem with TV an' a papers? I don' wan' 'ush this up. I wan' everybody know what these bastard do.'

Hatch shot an appeal at Cindy, but Cindy pretended not to notice; he said, 'Of course I'll take you, my love.'

'Mr Lewis—'

'Catharsis, inspector, catharsis. Don't you think?'

Hatch sighed. 'All right. In which case, perhaps we should all go with WPC Webber in the police car, or you might have trouble getting past our people.'

Cindy nodded, helping Mrs Capaldi to her feet.

In the event, there were no cameramen, as Hatch must have known. This part of the forest was sealed off by a police road block on the track.

The immediate area was taped. There were several police hanging around, although there didn't seem to be much for them to do, except to drive away photographers and sensation-seekers, and try not to look at Mrs Capaldi.

'As soon as you want to leave . . .' Hatch said.

She shook her head, waved him away.

'Peaceful,' she said. 'Such a beautiful place. Nowhere is safe any more.'

She'd put on a black hat and black gloves, dark glasses.

Being the centre of attention had calmed her, Cindy thought. The irony of it was that, if it hadn't been family, Mrs Capaldi, who read lurid magazines, would have derived a shivery excitement from being so close to a murder investigation. She crossed herself and walked alone into the trees. Hatch nodded to WPC Webber to follow her.

A soft, early-evening sun cast a pastel glaze on the forest; yes, it was a lovely spot. And yet, left alone, Cindy felt suddenly tense. If this outing was going to be cathartic for Mrs Capaldi, it was having quite the opposite effect on him. There was a sense of imbalance. Of the world itself horribly askew.

A young, bearded detective with a mobile phone came over. 'Bloody hell, sir, did you know there were no less than *four* crossbow clubs in the general vicinity? What's the world coming— Oh, sorry.'

Hatch hustled the detective away from Cindy.

Who was startled. A *crossbow*? In the paper, it had said simply that Maria had been shot. The police were obviously sitting on the crossbow angle for the moment. What else had they not yet disclosed?

Cindy stood motionless in the clearing. It was still an old woodland. Part of the prehistoric and medieval landscape he liked to walk on Sundays. Fordingbridge to the northwest . . . a castle mound beyond there . . . several tumuli . . . And, of course, as soon as they'd arrived, he'd spotted the motte and bailey nearby. Probably built on a prehistoric site. It would certainly have been here when William Rufus . . .

He closed his eyes, emptied his mind and at once felt a frigid trembling in his solar plexus and a powerful sense of residual evil around this soft-lit glade.

A *crossbow*.

An horrific flash-image of Maria with a steel bolt nailing her to the floor of the forest.

He turned away, his hands cold and tingling. He moved

21

to the edge of the tape and walked away along the track for a few yards.

'Has something occurred to you, Mr Lewis?' He turned sharply to find DCI Hatch right behind him.

'Yes,' he said, 'I suppose something has.'

'Do you want to tell me?'

'It's probably already occurred to you. Being a local man. Do you know the story of the death of William II? William Rufus, son of the Conqueror?'

'Shot in the forest, wasn't he? By a man with a . . . oh, right.'

'A crossbow,' Cindy said. 'In this very forest.'

'About eight hundred years ago, as I recall,' Hatch said. 'Unlikely we're looking for the same man, then.'

'No.'

'And no, it hadn't occurred to me,' Hatch said flatly, 'I'm afraid.'

'Perhaps not so much a *man*, Chief Inspector, as a tradition. We know who killed William. It was his own huntsman, Walter Tirel. During a hunting expedition, the king shot a stag, wounding it, following its flight and holding up his hand, ostensibly to protect his eyes from the brightness of the setting sun. At which signal, Tirel, purporting to aim at another stag, shot the king.'

Hatch said, 'Signal?' Showing he had, at least, been paying attention.

'Do you know the Margaret Murray theory? That William was a ritual sacrifice?'

'The only Margaret Murray I know,' Hatch said heavily, 'is a Labour councillor on the police committee.'

'This one was an academic. An historian. Dr Murray published her anthropological history of witchcraft and paganism in 1931. Her theory was that although William Rufus might have appeared to support the Church, it seems likely he was a lifelong pagan. As the king, he would have been regarded as a god incarnate, and he was growing old. Well, a god could never grow old or weak or feeble.

22

He must die for his people, to strengthen their attachment to this new land. And, of course, as the king, he was permitted to select the time and circumstances of his own ritual death.'

'Dubious privilege,' Hatch said. No doubt thinking, *Old Welsh queen's lost his marbles*.

Cindy walked into the centre of the clearing.

'The king had prepared himself for death, had eaten and drunk well and taken possession of six fresh bolts for his crossbow. Two of which he handed to Walter Tirel before they left. When he was shot, William then broke off the wooden shaft of the bolt and fell upon the stump.'

'Very interesting, sir,' Hatch said. 'But I'd be glad if you wouldn't mention crossbows to anyone at this stage. Probably be common knowledge by tomorrow, but by then we can've pinned down every crossbow-owning nutter between here and—'

Cindy said, 'Do you see the beauty of it? William let the Earth finish him.'

'To be honest, Mr Lewis, I don't see much of a link here. Two crossbow killings eight hundred years apart?'

'Just thought you should be aware of it, Chief Inspector.'

'Yes. Thank you very much, sir. Do you think we could persuade Mrs Capaldi to go home now?'

Part One

Stone with magnetic or radioactive properties
seems to have been incorporated into some
monuments. Certain parts of the brain are
sensitive to magnetic fields – particularly the
temporal lobe region which houses the organs
that process memory, dreams and feeling. There
is an archaic tradition of sleeping on stones
of power to achieve visions.

Paul Devereux, *Earth Memory*.

I

Autumn, 1997

The night he died, Bobby Maiden was drinking single malt, full of this smoky peat essence. Put you in mind of somewhere damp and lonely. Moorland meeting the sea, no visible horizon.

The whiskies were on the house, all five of them. Could be the same went for the woman. Who was starting to look more than OK, the arrangement of her too-black hair coming apart in a tumble, sexy as a bathrobe falling open. Face white, lipstick a luminous mauve, all very Gothic. When you hadn't been in this situation for quite a while, you tended to forget what an over-scented lady in a pasted-on black frock could do when she was concentrating.

'So, Bobby . . .' Shaking out a fresh cigarette. 'Your old man was one too, then.'

Five whiskies. About right for explaining how the old bastard shafted him.

'A real one,' Maiden said. 'Not many left. As he'd keep telling you. A Plod. Village copper, deepest Cheshire. I mean, there's nowhere very deep in Cheshire any more, but there was then. Police Sergeant Norman Maiden. Never Norman. Certainly never Norm. Not with the uniform on. Question of respect, madam.'

Well after midnight now. Just Maiden and this woman called . . . Susan? . . . in Tony Parker's nasty new club in the grim, concrete west end of Elham. How this had happened, he'd arranged to meet Percy Gilbert, Snout of the Year, 1979. *Be worth your time, Mr Maiden, no question.* No-one else in Elham CID had any time, never mind money, for Percy these days. But it was Bobby Maiden's weekend off, so nothing lost. Nothing at all. Sadly.

But the bugger hadn't shown. Maiden had ordered a Scotch, and the barman wouldn't take any money – *special introductory offer for new members, the drink'll be brought to your table, sir.* On these soiled streets, a police warrant card bought more drinks than American Express, but he didn't think the barman knew him. Next thing, the woman's arriving with a tray, claiming to be Parker's niece, from London.

By this time, the gears are whirring, cogs clicking into place. A nicely oiled mechanism starting up. The sound of Tony Parker making his move.

Mr Un-nickable. Mr Immunity.

Maiden deciding to roll with it, see where it led.

'. . . course, all the kids were terrified of this flesh-eating dinosaur in the tall hat. He had the human race divided into three: the police, the evil toerags and the Public who were grateful for your protection and showed a bit of respect. So there was only one role for a *real* man and, particularly, for Son of Plod. Thing was, Su . . .'

Suzanne. That was the name. But, remembering it, he'd forgotten what he was going to say.

Suzanne put down her vodka and orange, kind of thoughtful. What had she asked him, to start him off about Norman Plod? *What's a sensitive guy like you doing in the police?* Maybe. Couldn't remember.

One thing about Suzanne: she was professionally unknown to Maiden. That is, not one of Tony Parker's regular slags. Plus, she had a certain bizarre style.

'There was some poet, Bobby . . . wrote this really deep-down truthful line. Tennyson, Keats, one of those. I don't go much on poetry, but . . . "Your mum and dad, they always fuck you up . . ." Something like that. Wordsworth, would it be?'

28

Maiden ogled the ceiling. 'That would be before or after he wrote about the fucking daffs?'

'Nah, what I'm saying, a man like him . . .' Suzanne leaned her head back, blew out smoke. 'I can see, a man like your dad, why he wouldn't want you to be a painter or nothing like that.'

And then you get out of your nancified art college, what happens then, eh? Norman Plod, gardening in police boots and ragged old police shirts. *What you gonna do for readies then, with no government grant to prop yer up? Eh? Eh?*

Maiden realized he was doing his Norman Plod out loud.

Artists? Parasites, lad. Nobody wants 'em till they've snuffed it. Live off the State and sponging off their mates. Go bloody mad, cut their ears off.

'Cut their ears off.' Maiden shook his head. 'I'd forgotten about that.'

'Right. Yeah.' Suzanne's white face bobbing like a Japanese doll's. 'I think I heard of a guy that happened to.'

'Fancy.' Was this woman real?

Look, Norman said, back from the Conservative Club, flattening a tube of flake white with his size nines. *Do yourself a favour. Get rid of this nancy shit. Else they'll think you're a poof. Think you're a poof, lad!*

'What a bastard. Did you?'

'What?'

'Get rid of it.'

'No. Just went undercover.'

And still was. There were nights now when he was painting through till dawn: pale, minimal, imaginary landscapes, not much more than air and light. Paintings of the white noise in his head. Not, in fact, a long way from the cutting-off-the-ear stage, when you thought about it.

'What do you paint?'

'Places. Feelings. Usual crap. Never sold one. Never tried. Copper's little hobby, who needs it?' Me, I need it, he thought. There's nothing else. Isn't that terminally pathetic?

Suzanne smoked in silence for a few seconds, then she said, 'So you wanted to paint and he was determined you were going to trail in his big footsteps. Where was your mother all this time?'

Bobby Maiden stared into his glass.

'In heaven.'

You know what happens to them, coppers like Maiden, the sensitive ones . . . Two possible career projections. Either they go to the top faster than they deserve . . .

This was Martin Riggs, Divisional Super now, talking to veteran DI Barry Hutchins at the CID Christmas binge. Barry just loved to tell this story, especially loved telling Maiden, who – unforgivably – avoided the Christmas binge. Barry had taken a retirement deal, worked for Group Four Security now, so he could say what he liked.

. . . or else they crack up, Riggs tells Barry. Top themselves. Look at the situation. He's thirty-five, still a DI. Goes off to the Met, can't stand the heat, and he's back after a year. In this job, Barry, if you want to get on, you don't come back.

This was very true. You certainly don't come back when the new boss is someone you happened to run into in London, in circumstances that convinced you he was bent.

'You still got them, Bobby?'

'Huh?'

'Your paintings.' Her eyes were opaque.

'Oh.'

'Only I wouldn't mind seeing them,' Suzanne said.

He choked off a laugh into the whisky.

'Let me get this right. You're saying you would like to come up and see my etchings?'

'Whatever.' Suzanne ground her cigarette into the ashtray and reached across the table for her bag.

'You mean now?'

Got to think, got to think.

'All right then,' he said. 'I'll just pop to the bog.'

Alone in the gents', Maiden slapped cold water on his face.

OK. Think.

Owen Anthony Parker, entrepreneur. Fairly new in town. Cheery, beaming Londoner making a fresh start in the provincial leisure industry. Looks dodgy as hell, but no record. In no time at all, Parker has two clubs, one lowlife, one upmarket*ish*, and five pubs. Public figure, hosts charity evenings. Thanks to Mr Parker, Elham General Hospital has its long-battled-for new body-scanner.

Also, thanks indirectly to Mr Parker, the recently opened drug-dependency unit has a whole bunch of extra clients.

Tony Parker. Mr Immunity.

Why?

Well, several people have a good idea. And somebody in CID has to be *fully* in the picture.

Maiden dried his face on a paper towel. Too many whiskies for this, really.

Still. See what happens, then. Suzanne.

By the time the minicab dumped them outside the blackened Victorian block at the bottom of Old Church Street, where it meets the bypass, her perfume was everywhere. At first it was sexy, then it became nauseating. Maiden always got sick in the back of cars.

Thigh to thigh, they hadn't talked much. He hadn't made a move on her – he still had *some* style. Plus, there was the problem that the quiet, grizzled cabbie just might have been the father of a kid nicked for dealing crack three months back. A kid who'd sworn the bastards had planted the stuff. Clutton. Dean Clutton.

'This is nice, Bobby.'

'It's just a nice front door.' Sorting drunkenly through his keys. 'Not nice at all inside.'

Might not have been Clutton's dad; too dark to tell, really. He unlocked the communal door with the lacquered brass knocker and five illuminated bell pushes.

Dean Clutton had hanged himself in his cell while on remand, this was the thing. Before Maiden got a chance to talk to him.

'Sad, isn't it?' Suzanne said wistfully, long fingers playing with the collar of her black silk jacket.

'What?'

'You start your married life all fresh and clean, get yourself a nice, tidy little home together . . .'

'It was a little Georgian-style semi. In Baslow Road. Yeah, it was nice. For a while. And tidy.'

Except for the night Liz had impaled four canvases, one after the other, on the pointed newel post at the top of the stairs. One after the other, with a stiff, crackly, ripping sound. That was when he'd taken the chance of a transfer to the Met. A new start, somewhere neither of them had connections, where they'd need to rely on each other.

As it turned out, Liz had hated it. Hated her job at the huge, crazy London hospital. Liz wanted to come back. There was a vacancy for a DI in Elham Division; he'd walked into it. Back with the old crowd. Who resented him. Naturally.

'Baslow Road,' Suzanne mused. 'I wouldn't know where that is. Being a stranger.' She followed him inside and he felt for the light switches, flipped all three, but only one greasy yellow bulb came on.

'You're right.' Suzanne's nose wrinkling as she took in the state of the hallway. 'It *is* a bit of a shithole. You OK, Bobby? You're not going to throw up, are you?'

He said, 'You're not serious about this, are you?'

'Course I'm serious. Why I came,' Suzanne said. 'Come on, let's see them.'

'All right.' Despite the half-dozen whiskies, Bobby Maiden, on the last night of his life, was feeling almost shy as he propped the biggest canvas against the TV.

This was weird. He couldn't figure this out at all. Started out like a direct approach, now it was just very strange.

Just as coppers in the Met above a certain rank could expect an invitation to join the Masons, in Elham there'd be a friendly, innocent overture from the Tony Parker organization. It was like a recognition of status. Almost above board.

Because Maiden stayed off the police social circuit, it had been a long time coming. But now it was here, and it was strange.

'Little haven you've created here.' Suzanne ran a finger along the art books. Grinned. 'Bobby's burrow.'

Maiden propped the other pictures against the table legs. Acrylics. And some watercolours, because there was less mess and they were easier to conceal if anybody turned up. Nobody at the nick had ever known about it.

'Hey,' Suzanne said. 'Not what I was expecting. Where is it, Bobby? Morocco?'

The big canvas had a full moon like a lamp over sand dunes.

'Formby.'

'Where's that?'

'The Liverpool Riviera. Costa del Shite.'

'You make it look dead exotic. You're an imaginative guy, aren't you?'

'What the defence lawyers say to me. Look, you don't really want to see this crap. I thought we—'

'I like the way you've done the colours of the sandhills. Like you can see colours in places the rest of us can't.'

Her coat was off and her hair had come all the way down. It was cold, as usual, in here and she had her arms entwined around her, pushing her breasts together. He shuddered with an unsuppressible spasm of longing. All

33

wrong, of course. The very last thing you did was let them into your private life. If you could call this dump private, or what he had here a life.

'. . . or is it Wainwright?'

'What?'

'Guy who painted those night pictures,' Suzanne said. 'Greenish. With, like, full moons. They were Liverpool and industrial kind of places too, only he made them look dead romantic. Atkinson Wainwright? Tony's really into him. He's got three or four now. A couple, anyway.'

'Grimshaw,' Maiden said knowledgeably. Tony Parker was into Atkinson Grimshaw? As *well* as prostitution, gambling and drugs?

Suzanne said, 'Course, seeing this guy's dead, his pictures are worth a stack, like your dad said, and a good investment. Still, Tony buys new things as well. If he likes them.'

'And then he has the artist killed to make it worthwhile. You want some coffee? Wine?'

Suzanne smiled. 'He might like these. Might *well* like them.'

He went still.

'The moon and the sand,' Suzanne said. 'Tony'd go for that one, certainly.'

The moon in the painting wobbled in the deep, green sky. Maiden was gripping the edge of the table as a voice from somewhere said, *Careful. Be cool. Flush her out.*

'Forget the pictures,' he said. 'Let's go upstairs.' Which made no sense; it was a ground floor flat.

'No, I reckon . . .' Suzanne stood back from the moon picture, pursing her lips. 'I reckon, a picture like that, Tony would give . . . what? . . . seven grand? It's the moon that does it. Tony's ever so partial to a full moon.'

He saw, for the first time, the mocking intelligence in the smoky eyes.

'Cash, of course,' Suzanne said coolly.

*   *   *

34

He started to laugh.

'So Tony wants me on his wall.'

He couldn't decide whether it was ridiculously naive or totally brilliant. Five whiskies said brilliant.

'And what do I have to do?'

Suzanne sat down. She chose the wooden garden chair by the gas fire, maybe making a point about the unnecessary frugality of his lifestyle.

'You really his niece, Suzanne?'

'You really an artist? See, I'm authorized to negotiate with artists. Policemen . . . that might be open to misinterpretation.'

'What's he looking for?' His head felt as if it was floating away from his body. 'Bit new to this game.'

'Game, Bobby?'

'Blind eye? Friend at court?'

Seven grand . . . not a bad base. Seven grand could get you out of here. Seven grand could get you into a rented cottage somewhere damp and lonely. Seven grand could—

Christ, you can't help thinking about it, can you? Seven grand for a painting, take the money and run, run, run . . .

'And maybe in a couple of months' time,' Suzanne said blandly, 'if you were to come up with something else Tony wanted . . .'

'Like?'

'You're the artist.'

'Why don't you spell it out?' Maiden said easily. 'We're both grown-up people. Who else has he got on the wall? Biggish wall, is it?'

'Look.' She stood up, smiling at him, kindly, like an auntie. 'Been a long night, lovey. You must be completely shagged out. You have a nice think about it. You know where to find me.'

Picking up her silk jacket from the block pine coffee table, he moved towards her, knocking over the moon picture.

'Who else besides Mr Riggs?' he said.

Shit. Couldn't believe he'd said that. Too much to drink. Could feel it slipping through his hands like a fish, now, swimming away into the murk.

'I just wouldn't like to do anything the boss would seriously disapprove of.'

Disastrous.

'I'm not following you, Bobby.' Slinking into the jacket, tucking her hair down the collar, shouldering her bag.

He put his hand over hers on the door catch, noticing that the last light in the communal hall had finally expired, a dead bulb with a dark halo of cobwebs on a frayed wire.

'Night night, Bobby.' Suzanne's voice was lower and harder as she detached his hand from the door. 'All right?'

'No,' he said. 'The night is positively embryonic. And you are—'

Aw, forget it. You blew it. Worse still, you left yourself wide open.

Members of the jury, the defendant has claimed that he took this woman back to his flat 'to show her my paintings . . .'

Stupid.

The day before he retired from the Job, Barry Hutchins had said to Maiden, *Some divisions, you find being a tiny bit bent is strongly advisable. Just a spot of oil on the wheels, a tweak on the steering.*

Let's face it, most coppers are introduced to it not by villains but by other coppers. Starts in a small way, like being shown which cafés on your beat will give you a free coffee, which restaurants operate a twenty per cent police discount.

Problem I found is, you never quite know whose toes you might be treading on by not accepting a bung. Know what I mean? You're walking a tightrope in this town, now.

He stood inside the door, listening for the sound of her feet in the hall. She hadn't gone.

'Suzanne?'

He opened the door wide. No sound out there but his own voice dancing around the walls. But she hadn't gone.

'Suzanne?' Maiden called softly into the darkness of the lobby. 'Just confirm something for me, would you?'

No reply.

'Tell Tony thanks very much, but why would he need me when he's got Riggs?'

Once you'd soaked your boats in paraffin, you might as well apply the match.

Martin Riggs. Hotshot from the Met brought in to clean up seedy little Midland town. On a promise. Super's job if he does well, when old Stan White retires. And Riggs does extremely well, hoovering up a bunch of dealers, pimps, small-time hard men in no time at all.

'Suzanne . . . ?'

Nothing. But he felt an odd tingle in the dark air.

Always struck him as curiously coincidental that Riggs and Parker should arrive in town around the same time.

And what an amazing clean-up rate. The *Elham Messenger* loved it. STREET-CRIME DOWN AGAIN. Loved *him*. POLICE CHIEF'S DRUG WAR PAYS OFF.

'Everybody's happy, Suzanne. Dealers working for one boss. Job security, long as nobody gets too greedy. And the toms . . . better working conditions, more respectable pimps. Much healthier all round.'

'Not for everybody, Bobby. Not for you, the way you're going on.'

Even though it was still September, the lobby had a late autumnal damp-plaster smell.

'Listen, Bobby. Just listen.' Her voice was different. 'Do yourself a favour. Shut the fuck up and make yourself scarce. You're playing well out of your league. Can you—'

Silence.

Like she was afraid of being overheard.

He switched off the light in the flat and slipped outside, found a patch of shadow and snuggled into it.

Click, click of heels. Suzanne making for the front door. He slid after her, back to the wall.

Think.

Riggs will have confirmation now: Maiden knows. Maiden doesn't like it. Maiden's not up for a buy-off in regular instalments. Maiden's not one of the lads. Maiden is well under the feet.

'Bobby.' Suzanne's voice, very low. 'Look. Go back in your flat and lock the door. You know what I'm saying?'

He could see her shape now, in the doorway.

'Bobby?' From outside. 'I'm not kidding. I like you, OK? I like you, you stupid sod. Can't you get a transfer or something? Jesus, what a fucking mess.'

Footsteps fading.

Aye, go on, nancy, lock yourself in . . . go back to your painting.

Not any more, Norman.

Maiden came out quickly in a crouch. Didn't make for the steps, edged instead around the side of the building where a short passageway ended in an iron gate. Bad move if that was where they were waiting but unless they'd checked out the building by daylight they wouldn't be.

Nobody grabbed him. His relief came out as a rough sob. He stayed in the passage, breathing in its acrid stale-piss air, until he heard her heels moving down the steps.

At which he moved out into the overgrown, iron-railed garden.

Because, God help him, he wanted to know who was waiting for her.

He crept down the steps.

Seeing Suzanne for the last time when she passed beneath a sodium streetlamp, he felt a confusing pang. How could he possibly . . . ?

Without the Gothic make-up? In different circumstances? Just the two of them, somewhere damp and lonely?

The street was very still. Rundown Victorian villas turned into flats or boarded up. A derelict pub. No parked cars – double-yellow zone.

Maiden came quietly down to the pavement. The streetlamps shimmered in oily puddles, the tarmac still pitted from a laying of new drains. No sign of Suzanne. He stepped off the kerb to peer further up the street.

Out here his head was clearing. Pleasanter now. He began to stroll up the road, hands in his pockets, the essence of peat coming back to him. Damp and lonely. Funny thing, now Liz was gone, now he could go where he liked, he just hadn't. He'd stayed in Elham, sorting out burglaries and domestic murders, occasionally going out with unsuitable women, building up the Tony Parker file on his home computer.

Waiting for a break. Waiting for something to give. Wondering how it could all have gone so wrong. Thinking that if he could just nail Parker and Riggs he'd walk away from it.

After fifteen wasted years.

He stopped. There she was again. Across the street, under a dodgy streetlamp which kept flickering on and off, and even when it was on it wasn't *fully* on, so you could almost see the filament in the bulb, a worm of blue-white light. She was standing under the lamp and seemed to be going on and off like the light; you saw her and then you didn't.

There was a roar. Two flat discs of greasy yellow spinning out of Telford Avenue. Turning to blinding white when they came round the corner.

Suzanne screamed, and it was strange; her voice, *in extremis*, sounded bizarrely refined.

'*Oh Christ, Vic, no, for fuck's sake . . .*'

The voice diverted him for a moment.

The wrong moment.

In the very next moment, his last conscious moment, two tail lights like dirty red pimples wobbled and blurred before a great and welcome silence came over him like a big, soft blanket.

At 2.37 a.m., Detective Inspector Bobby Maiden died in hospital.

II

Guardi's Deli was just around the block from the *New York Courier*.

'I mean, Jesus,' Grayle said, making for the window table. 'You look at this realistically, *I'm* the one should be missing. Like, Ersula was always the intense, academic sister, and I'm the crazy bitch with the crystals and the Tarot cards and the Eye of Horus earrings.'

Before Lyndon could even sit down, she was dumping her bag on the table.

'Then she goes off to England.' Pulling out the leaflet. 'Then *this*.'

The University of the Earth

As we prepare to enter the Third Millennium, many of us feel the need for a deeper understanding of the land around us: how our distant ancestors related to their environment, and what that tells us about how *we* should respond to it.

The countryside of Britain remains a great enigma. We are surrounded by the mysterious monuments of antiquity: megalithic remains, prehistoric burial mounds and chambers . . . the holy places of the past.

In recent years, the study of such remains has

appeared to become the preserve of a 'New Age' fringe, whose theories about ley lines and 'earth-energies' have been scorned by the archaeological establishment.

The *University of the Earth* is the first serious attempt to bridge this gulf, by undertaking a formal but open-minded investigation of the mysteries in our landscape. The project is being steered by the eminent archaeologist and anthropologist Prof. Roger Falconer, presenter of the Channel Four programme *Diggers*.

To help fund the *University of the Earth* project, and allow for the involvement of interested amateurs, a select series of summer schools has been scheduled, to be based at Prof. Falconer's farm on the Welsh border, and involving lectures, practical work and expeditions to a number of key sites, including Stonehenge, Avebury, Silbury Hill and the Rollright Stones.

Prof. Falconer says, 'My twenty-five years of study have shown me that there are many lessons to be learned from our most remote ancestors. While I have little truck with nonsense about the Earth once being ruled by aliens or radiant beings from the lost continent of Atlantis, I do believe that the people of the Bronze Age in particular possessed certain skills, allied to a heightened perception of the natural world, of which most of us are no longer aware.

'It is one of the aims of the *University of the Earth* to study methods of working with the Earth and discover how effective they are in a scientific framework.

'Dowsing, for instance, not only for water but for archaeological remains, has been shown to be surprisingly successful, and we shall be putting its practitioners to the test under survey conditions, as well as giving our guests an opportunity to see if they themselves possess the ability.

'While I am personally convinced that some dowsers have an extraordinary ability, other schemes and theories I find considerably less convincing. However, the spirit of the *University of the Earth* is one of exploration and my younger colleagues, Magda Ring and Adrian Fraser-Hale, will be conducting experiments on what we might call the outer fringes . . . notably, the Dream Survey, in which volunteers will sleep at ancient sites and record their dreams in an attempt to discover whether human consciousness is influenced by the alleged electromagnetic properties of stone monuments.

'Although its aims are serious, those of us involved in the *University of the Earth* have had a great deal of fun. The inevitable arguments between the archaeological purists and the 'earth-mysteries' enthusiasts have been essentially good-natured and suggest that we share a common goal: to uncover the deepest secrets of the distant past and use them to develop a more harmonious relationship between the human race and its native planet.'

Early application for the *University of the Earth* summer schools is advisable, as places on the courses are strictly limited. Cost per head for one week is a basic . . .

Lyndon McAffrey, sitting stately as a Supreme Court judge, put down the leaflet and ordered up some doughnuts.

'Well,' he said. 'You gotta admire the guy's technique. Like, how we gonna persuade gullible rich folk to hand over megabucks for a week spent shovelling shit out of a trench? Hey, let's tell 'em they're helping a famous TV star unlock the secrets of the universe.'

Grayle thought this was a tad unfair. She'd called her father at Harvard, and he'd called up a friend at Oxford University about Professor Falconer and ascertained that, outside of television, the man was a respected academic with his name on about seventeen books.

'Just he has the popular touch. Nice-looking, charming, dates actresses . . . like that.'

'Uh-oh,' said Lyndon.

'This makes him a shyster, necessarily?'

'Well, no. It just don't win him instant sympathy from fat old guys such as myself. So your sister is – what?'

'*Not* one of your gullible rich folk. Ersula was on the staff for the summer. One of the expert research team. They had several archaeology graduates helping organize the field trips and stuff like that. Of course, they weren't paying her anything either, apart from expenses and accommodation, but she—'

'—was allowed to be part of the Great Experiment, too,' Lyndon said with a wry, fatcat smile. 'Educated people can be *soooooo* naive.'

'Nnn-nn.' Grayle shook her head. 'This woman is a believer in neither God nor spaceships. A sober, bookish person. Her father's daughter, you know?'

Five weeks ago, their mother, folding Ersula's last letter from England, had said lightly, 'Well . . . she's getting into some stimulating areas. She's having fun. In her own way. I guess.'

It was true that Ersula's official letter to Mom had been mostly about what fun she was having and how hospitable and kind the Brits were, not stiff and stuffy like you were led to expect. Her letter to their father, although more academically oriented, would likewise include nothing pertaining to nights spent under prehistoric stone monuments.

That Ersula's letter to Grayle was more revealing came as no big surprise. Since Mom went off with the younger lover and Dad locked himself in his Harvard tower, they'd become warily closer for the first time in years. The letter began, *You may be interested in some of this, but for Christ's sake, DSF!*

DSF: Don't Show the Folks.

Ersula's last letter. Before the silence.

'Run this past me one more time,' Lyndon said. 'Your younger but normally more balanced sister has been

43

sleeping in a Stone Age burial chamber. She lose her credit cards, or what?'

'If you aren't going to take this seriously—'

'Jesus,' said Lyndon, whose job at the *New York Courier* was all about knowing which stories to take seriously. The waitress arrived with the doughnuts and they helped themselves. The waitress stepped back, studying Grayle. She was a new waitress.

'No, see, the problem with Ersula . . .' Grayle inspected her doughnut then shrugged and took a bite. 'Balanced? Yeah, OK, in some ways. But also passionate. More than that, obsessive. She gets into something, it's like . . . whooosh.'

'Unlike you,' Lyndon McAffrey said heavily.

'Unlike me. Like, Ersula would not eat this doughnut. She doesn't do comfort-eating. Ersula is very controlled. Has concentration. Focus. All of that.'

'Dear God,' said Lyndon. 'We hired the wrong sister.'

'Also, as a committed academic, Ersula vaguely despises the inevitable superficiality of journalism.'

Lyndon McAffrey nodded moodily. Twenty-five years ago, he'd become the paper's first black deputy city editor. Since then there'd been three black city editors and Lyndon . . . well, he was still number two. He knew all about being vaguely despised.

'Hey!' The waitress suddenly screamed. 'You are! I saw you on TV. You're Grayle *Underhill*? Holy Grayle? For Crissakes, this is incredible, this is *fate*. I was gonna write to you. I need your help.'

The waitress pulled out a chair, flopped into it.

'See, my boyfriend, who most times is this real sweet guy, every few weeks he comes on kind of mean, and I noticed – this is true, I swear on my mother's grave – he has to shave twice . . . three times a day?'

Lyndon looked down at his plate, closed lips strained by an uh-huh kind of smile.

'Time of the full moon, huh?' Grayle said without enthusiasm.

'See, I tell this to people,' the waitress said, 'and they're like . . . oh, *sure*. Then I'm reading that thing you wrote about how men, they all have this werewolf element to a degree, and I'm going, *Right, shit, yes, this is the woman I have to talk with*. And now here you are. You tell me this isn't, like, karma or something . . . ?'

Grayle said, 'Listen, uh . . .'

'Marcia.'

'Marcia. Right. OK. The piece I wrote, Marcia, that was like an interview with the author of this book, *The Lycanthropic Virus*, which examines the effect of the full moon on society and blah, blah, blah. So if you have a problem in this area, the person you need to, uh, approach is the author, D. Harvey Baumer. Maybe if you wrote him through the publisher?'

'That would take forever,' Marcia said dubiously. 'See, the way you wrote the article, it was like you really had a handle on the whole thing.'

'Yeah, that's . . . that's part of the job, Marcia. Look, all I can suggest is maybe if I was to do an article on *your* situation.' Grayle pulled a pen from her bag. 'So your second name is . . . ?'

'Uh–uh . . .' Marcia was up on her feet and back behind the counter in a couple of seconds. 'I don't think so. I think I misunderstood. I mean, you sound like some kind of *journalist* . . .'

Lyndon started to chuckle, dusting sugar crystals from his big hands.

'This is not funny,' Grayle told him when Marcia, mercifully, had gone to wait on another table. 'I get this all the time. You write a New Age column, people think you must be a person of, like, higher dimensions.'

'You write a crime column, they think you're a sleazeball with Mob connections,' Lyndon said unsympathetically. 'What's your problem?'

'This is different. This is about spirituality. How do I know I'm not messing up someone's immortal soul? How do I know how much of what I'm publicizing is true or at least well intentioned and life-enhancing? Crime, you know who the bad guys are, New Age, you can never be quite sure.'

Grayle licked raspberry jam from her fingers. Nearly thirty years separated her and Lyndon, a sweet tooth glued them together. Journalism could be a hostile world, especially when most of your colleagues thought everything you wrote about was a piece of crap.

'Ersula thinks I just peck around things, like a chicken.'

'She thinks that, huh?' Lyndon's eyes widened. 'Imagine.'

'Yeah, yeah. Screw you too. Maybe she's right. Back when I was in college and she was still in school we were both heavily into New Age. Like, we'd talk about cosmic consciousness and read the Tarot and stuff in my room and have a lot of innocent fun. I should've realized that Ersula, even then, she only had *serious* fun. She would throw herself into something and then emerge the other side, dismissing it all as bullshit. When she was fourteen or fifteen and I was at college I found she'd been, you know . . . initiated? As a witch?'

'Eye of newt?' Lyndon was unfazed. 'Toe of frog?'

'As I recall, they were known as the Hermetic Sisterhood of Central Park West. I didn't look too closely at her altar. I think it was just candles and pentagrams, but she made sure and piled it all in the trash before the folks got home from vacation. It was OK; by then she'd concluded this was all phoney shit anyway. You wanted to get into the real, authentic stuff, you checked out True Ethnic Sources. It was a short hop from there to anthropology and related studies . . . and to despising her sister, her sister's crystals, her sister's amulets . . . OK, go ahead, read the letter . . .'

46

August 20

Dear Grayle,

First off, if you want the nice stuff about the accommodation and the scenery and all the wonderful people I'm meeting, you should read Mom's letter. I'm not doing that crap twice.

OK. You may be interested in some of this, but for Christ's sake, DSF!

As I may have indicated, I was frankly skeptical about the University of the Earth summer school. There is a lunatic fringe which has infiltrated archeology here in Britain (people who believe ancient sites were strung out in mystical straight lines, to follow the courses of some mysterious earth-power which they cannot define except to say it can give you a buzz) and I was less than enthusiastic at the thought of working with an organization which seeks to build bridges with these airheads.

However, in the absence of a better way of researching prehistoric remains in the British Isles and getting paid for it . . . here I am, in this tiny, comparatively isolated village on the border of England and Wales.

So . . . OK.

The dreaming experiment.

The airheads have been suggesting for some time that human consciousness can be altered or infiltrated by the 'energies' at ancient burial mounds, stone circles, whatever, and that this occurs most effectively during sleep.

Our distant ancestors were people whose day-to-day survival depended upon an intimacy with their environment, an understanding – which we today would consider inexplicably precognitive – of what the Earth was going to do and when. Dreams were considered to be an important way in which useful information was conveyed to them. In the Old Testament, wasn't it Jacob who slept on a pillow of stone and had prophetic *dreams? While in ancient China, the emperor would spend the whole night on stone before making some important decision. You get the idea.*

The University of the Earth Dream Survey aims to establish whether specific images or motifs occur in the dreams of people sleeping at particular 'sacred' sites. Individuals elect to spend the night in a sleeping bag inside a circle or a burial chamber with a helper or therapeute who, while they sleep, stays awake with a tape recorder, watching for the Rapid Eye Movement which will indicate they are dreaming. At which stage the dreamer is awoken and gives a full résumé of the dream into the recorder.

Off-the-wall? Yeah, I thought so when I was appointed therapeute to a middle-aged woman who talked about meeting fairies with which she frolicked naked under a waterfall! Then Roger suggested I should sleep at a site myself . . . and my mind was somewhat blown by an extraordinary vivid and lucid dream – one in which I was fully aware of dreaming and able to function on a mental level I would never have imagined possible.

I was, you might say, hooked.

Lyndon shook sugar from Ersula's letter. 'Looks like she's headed back your way.'

'Which is not good, for the reasons I already stated.'

'Whooosh?'

'As an academic, Ersula believes nowadays in the power of the mind over the power of the spirit. Well, OK, she has a good mind and I'm stupid, and when you're stupid all you got to fall back on most of the time is, like, the dream that some kind of spiritual earthquake will come along and get us out of all this shit.'

'This may be getting too heavy and West Coast for a poor Brooklyn boy,' Lyndon said.

Grayle stared at the river of blood seeping out of the half-eaten doughnut. For Ersula, nothing was an inexplicable phenomenon any more. So nothing was spiritually threatening.

She looked up, saw her own frustrated face in the mirror

across the counter, lumps of blond hair all over the place, the Eye of Horus earrings swinging. Crazy Grayle Underhill, New Age Sub-culture Columnist, widely syndicated.

'Huh?'

'I said, if there's some way I can help you,' Lyndon McAffrey said patiently, 'maybe you could just lay it out for me in moron-speak.'

'Finish the letter,' Grayle said. 'I'm delaying you. Your wife will think you're having an affair.'

'Haw,' said Lyndon. He picked up the second sheet of blue airmail paper and read it with obvious concentration before re-reading the first sheet.

'Hmm.' He grunted thoughtfully. 'I begin to see your point.'

At night, you discover, stone is always cold.

Sleeping on stone – that's not natural. You awake time after time, usually uncomfortable as hell and sometimes in a panic simply because of the stone all around you. Well, that's good – it shouldn't come easy, not at first. Without a challenge there can be no achievement.

Which is just as well because this particular burial chamber, where I slept last night, is fully exposed, the earthmound which once concealed it having long since eroded. It is like a long, low stone table on little, stubby legs. Or maybe a clump of big mushrooms fused together. Kind of weird-looking, but not what you would call spectacular. Indeed, without a large-scale map you would not find it at all except by accident.

Well, certainly not at night.

Under your head is an old gray stone which you can feel as though there was no sleeping bag there at all. What it makes you think of is those petrified pillows supporting marble effigies on tombs in old churches. Creepy, huh?

Hey, come on. This is a scientific experiment.

Anyway, like I said, when you sleep on stone, sometimes you awake but you're not awake, if this makes sense. You know you can't be, because the stone isn't cold, nor even hard; you're sinking into it – so damn grateful it isn't cold and hard any more that you just let yourself luxuriate in it. And down you go, quite painlessly, into the ground, into the earth. Your subconscious mind that is. Or whatever you want to call the part of you that admits the dreams.

You come to realize that the very easiest phase is the letting go. I say easy . . . it was hard for me at first. I am, as you can guess, the odd one out on this course, most of the others being half-assed pseudo-mystics who are just here for the buzz. (You will notice, Grayle, that I have been at pains not to say 'people like you'.)

They tell you not to think too hard before you go to sleep, so maybe it's just as well your main concern is to get comfortable. If you go into waking fantasies and your conscious mind influences your dreams, this is a bad thing, obviously.

Before you know it, you've been gently awoken and the therapeute is whispering, Did you dream? Tell me . . . describe it to me . . .

You feel wonderful then. You did it. You interacted.

The actual interacting, the dreaming, often becomes, well . . . kind of scary, if you want the truth. Not at all what you're expecting. Maybe it has occurred to you that this place where you're sleeping, when it comes down to it, when you get beyond all the screwball stuff about secret energies and the healing powers of Mother Earth . . .

. . . is a grave.

A repository for bodies. Flesh has rotted here, bones have crumbled.

The claustrophobia, at this point, can be intense. You start to scream inside. All you want is out of there. But, like I said, you have to stop your conscious mind getting a hold of you. What you are dealing with here is the unconscious and that must be left to find its own route to what you would probably call enlightenment.

In relation to this, OK, there is one small problem, I am told.

You know how, in nightmares, when you get into a very frightening situation – like, you're about to fall a thousand feet

onto rocks or you turn around to find the psycho with the ax was
behind the door all the time – you awake?

Well, sleeping in a prehistoric burial chamber, so they tell me,
you can't always count on this happening – implying that under
these physical conditions it is possible to reach a deeper level of
unconsciousness. This, I am convinced, is the first step to a
scientific explanation of so-called prophetic dreaming, as sup-
posedly experienced by Jacob and tribal shamans the world over,
and it excites me profoundly.

Before you say a word, sure I've heard that stuff about how,
if you weren't able to awake from a nightmare, when you got
into a terminally tight corner you'd just die.

Like I said, it's important that it isn't easy. That there are
risks. Nothing significant is ever achieved without risk.

'Your parents seen any of this?'

Lyndon McAffrey solemn now, maybe the old news-
man's antennae starting to vibrate.

Grayle shook her head. 'Don't Show the Folks. Pain of
death. We used to put it on cards and letters when we were
kids.'

'When you were kids is one thing—'

'Listen, it's bad enough we haven't had a letter or a
phone call in five weeks. No, I didn't show it to them then
and I don't plan to. My father would be acutely embarrassed on his younger child's behalf and blame it on my
mother's genes, like he does with me. Mom would be
spooked all the way to the cocaine cupboard. No, hell, this
is down to me. Time for Crazy Grayle to get her shit
together.'

'OK.' Lyndon leaned back. 'What are your own personal
conclusions here? That Ersula blew out her mind under
some old stone and went native? Among the primitive
Brits?'

'I know . . . you don't believe, any more than my father
would, that my sister could be psychically damaged by any
of this. You don't believe for one second that she's messing

with awesomely powerful cosmic forces. You think more likely she got laid inside a stone circle, fell in love, lost track of time . . .'

'OK,' Lyndon said. 'What do you plan to do about it?'

'Well . . . I already called this University of the Earth summer school. Spoke to a guy who was very helpful. Surprised we hadn't heard from Ersula, on account of the course ended a month ago and they presumed she'd flown home. He didn't *sound* like a fruitcake . . .'

Lyndon's expression said he wouldn't trust Grayle to identify a fruitcake at knife-swinging distance. She averted her eyes.

'So, I . . . I called the police department. I guess there'll be some kind of hook-up with the English cops. But . . .'

'The English police are very thorough,' Lyndon said. 'If there's anything wrong here, they'll find out.'

'You don't think I should fly over there?'

'How would that help?'

'Well . . . it would help me, I guess.'

'Grayle, you yourself admit that Ersula is the balanced one.'

'And, yeah, she went to Africa, just out of high school, and we didn't hear from her for close to two months. But that was when the folks split. Her way of coming to terms with all that. This is different. She's a grown woman. Also she knows that if the very last letter I get from her is as weird as this . . .'

'OK,' Lyndon said. 'You have a point. See what the cops come up with. They may not be too enthusiastic about finding a grown woman who's only been missing a few weeks, but being she's a professor's daughter and all . . . Leave it to the cops.'

'Right.' Grayle's voice a little too high. 'You're right. That's sensible.'

Lyndon nodded. He folded the blue airmail letter, tucked it under Grayle's coffee cup. He hadn't read the other pages.

Because she hadn't given them to him.

About Ersula's dream. The page with the disturbing details of Ersula's dream lying out on the burial chamber.

So Grayle went home to her windchimes and her crystals and her tree-of-life wallchart. Tried to meditate, gave up and half watched an old John Wayne movie on TV until she fell asleep and dreamed uneasily about dreaming.

III

Around two-thirty a.m., Sister Anderson, scenting smoke, slid quietly into the sluice room. The young Nigerian houseman, Jonathan, bounced off the wall like a scared squirrel, tossed his cigarette out of the window.

When he saw who it was, Jonathan looked no less intimidated. 'Sorry,' he muttered. 'I'm sorry.' His face no longer black but grey with fatigue in the white lights.

These kids. He'd have been hardly born when Sister Andy, red-haired then and vengeful, had first hunted down wee nurses and sprog docs who'd risked a ciggy in the sluice or the lavvies. Been a good while now since she last chewed the leg off a junior housie – no fun terrorizing some hollow-eyed kid at the end of a sixteen-hour shift. But reputations stuck.

'Jonathan,' Andy said wearily. 'Daft sod y'are, wasnae likely to be the chairman of the bloody hospital trust this time of night. Here . . . have yourself a replacement.'

Jonathan looked surprised and then smiled tentatively, still unsure whether it was a trap. Getting the cigarette to his mouth, his hand shook, poor wean. Twenty-six years old, veteran of three weeks in A and E, two on the slaughterhouse shift.

'Aw, come on, son.' Andy flashed the ancient Zippo. 'It happens. You did your best, no?'

'Is that what I am supposed to keep telling myself every night for the next forty years?'

'It's what I've been saying to young guys like you the last

thirty.' Andy sighed. 'Aye, you're right, it's a trite wee phrase.'

She lit up too, having a good idea what was coming next.

'I honestly don't think I am going to stick it,' Jonathan said bleakly. 'It's like working in some sort of meat-processing plant. By midnight, one gets so one doesn't want to go back out there.'

If she'd had twenty Silk Cut for every time an intern said that to her, she'd have gone down with nicotine poisoning years back. What the hell was she supposed to say? If she told him the truth of how bad it became, he'd just think she was stir-crazy. The truth was you grew to love it. The stink, the drips, the bedpans, the old guys who drooled – you loved it all and, when you took a holiday, your heart ached to get back.

This was how bad it became.

'But I mean,' Jonathan said, 'does anyone ever surprise you? You know, by suddenly responding to treatment? Does that happen any more? And is anybody ever, *ever* grateful?'

'Oh, thank you, thank you, doctor, you saved ma life.' Andy assuming a geriatric quaver. 'Stayed awake long enough to administer the right drugs in the right order. A credit to the hospital trust.' She sighed. 'Ah, Jonathan, in my own worst moments I figure if you manage to save a life you must've beaten the system, y'know?'

The same way you loved the whingeing patients and the underpaid nurses and the thirty-year-old doctors looking fifty, so you hated the suits, the admin guys, the caring, cut-glass quango ladies with their spectacles on gold chains and clipboards full of rationalization plans. It was all a business now and the last thing businesses were about was healing.

She became aware that Jonathan was looking down at her in some kind of awe.

'Sister Andy! My God, it's true, isn't it? You really *are* leaving us.'

'Where've you heard that?' Knowing – dammit – that with the sharpness of her tone she was confirming it. Although it wasn't certain, by no means.

'Well, I . . . somebody said you accepted a retirement package. But someone else said it was just a vicious rumour and they'd never get you out . . . out . . .'

'. . . alive? Never get me out of here alive? Bloody hell, Jonathan, I look that old and ruined?'

Jesus God, were the damn sprogs beginning to *pity* her? Maybe it was time to start dyeing the hair again. Bring back the old red. Fiery red and halfway down her back when she came down from Glasgow in sixty-five. Faded ginger seven years ago when she and Mick were divorced. Straggly grey now.

'Well, you know, a lot of people nowadays are taking early retirement,' Jonathan said, embarrassed. 'To do the things they always promised themselves. Travel the world . . .'

'Sod off,' said Andy. 'You're just digging yourself in deeper.'

'Sorry. Another job, then? It'll go no further, I promise. It's just that if even *you* are getting out—'

'Look, son.' Andy glared up, smoking no-hands, pushing the words out the side of the ciggie. 'If anybody wants to know, I'm gonny marry a brilliant heart surgeon and fly out to his private clinic on Paradise Island, OK?'

'Sorry. None of my business.'

'Right,' said Andy.

Paradise. Sure. Paradise stripped down to a stone and timbered village huddled under the Black Mountains, which were the lower vertebrae of the Welsh border. A paradise called St Mary's. A grand wee place, in its way, a haven, a sanctuary . . .

. . . and the nearest general hospital twenty rugged miles away. A clean break, right enough. Jesus God, was she really going through with it this time? Big hospitals, most people found them soulless and scary, but they gave Andy just a fantastic buzz, the smell of piss and disinfectant invigorating all her senses like ozone. Her element. *Was* her element. In the days before the suits. Before healing got deprioritized.

'OK,' Andy said. 'I'll tell you the truth. But it goes no further, right?'

Jonathan placed his hand over his heart.

'Only, I've been worried a while about the personal touch going out of health care. Like you said, a production line. I worry about the drug companies ruling the world, y'know?'

'Don't they?'

'I've been studying alternative healing,' Andy said. 'Y'know what I mean?'

Jonathan's eyes widened. 'Mumbo jumbo?'

'This is the question, Jonathan. *Is* it?'

'Well now, Sister Andy, that is a very profound question.'

'Glad you think so. I was a wee bit scared to mention witch doctors and such in case you took it as some kind of racist slur on the African health service. We're all treading eggshells these days, son.'

Jonathan grinned. 'It's all turned around again. Now, witch doctors are part of a great cultural tradition. And sometimes . . . unlike us . . . they still come up with the odd miracle. But Sister Andy – pardon me if this is racist – one is not aware of a similar tradition here in the UK.'

'Oh, it's there, right enough. Just buried deeper. OK. Couple of years ago, before you came, I developed what was turning into chronic ulcerative colitis, y'know?'

'Unpleasant.'

'And inconvenient. You cannae do this job efficiently when you're spending half the morning in and out of the lavvy. I was pretty desperate. Down to about eight stone. Eight Asacols a day. All I wanted was to sleep. Only it doesnae give you much sleep, the colitis. Your hair falls out, you develop big red lumps on your legs . . .'

Jonathan looked her up and down. 'You seem fine now. Surgery?'

Andy shook her head. 'Nor drugs. But it's cured. Ask me how it happened, we're talking serious mumbo—'

Jonathan's bleeper went off.

Shutters slamming down on personal issues, Sister Andy took his cigarette and held open the plastic door for him, like the grizzled old guy in the war movies who pushes the paras out of the hatch.

'Get your arse outa here, son,' Andy said. 'Never let the bastards see the fear, aye?'

'Bugger!' The paramedic sweating. 'I think he's bloody well arrested.'

The injured guy was still strapped to the stretcher, the red blanket wrenched back and the guy's chest bared. Big Nurse Debbie Barnes running alongside reaching for the carotid pulse.

'He's right, Sister. Nothing.'

'Oot the way, Debbie.' Andy's accent thickening the way it always did in crises. 'Come on, son,' she hissed at the patient, 'we're no havin' this.' Bringing her fist down like a hammer on his chest. 'Let's have him on the table, aye?'

'Car or something,' the ambulance driver said, helping Debbie attach the terminals. 'Or mugged maybe. Didn't just fall over, though he's had a few. Hit and run, I reckon. Thrown over the bonnet, comes down on his head. Nothing below seems to be broken, but—'

'Stuff the speculation,' Andy said briskly. 'No your problem, Michael. Defib. Come on, move it!'

Blood from left ear, left eye. Strong smell of whisky. Face . . . Jesus God, face familiar.

'Monitor flat,' Jonathan said, drab-voiced, as if it was a formality. 'How long has he been—?'

'No more than a minute,' the driver said. 'Still going OK in the van. Going strong. Must've stopped on the way in. Shock catching up.'

While the tube was going down, before the ambi-bag went on, Andy fitted a history to the face on the end of the neck brace, images clacking in like colour slides: young copper sitting on a stool drinking cocoa in the winter dawn, uniform flecked with snow and someone else's vomit. Waiting for some assault victim to get patched up. Ten years ago? Twelve?

A dead flat line on the monitor. Andy holding his head as Jonathan got going with the paddles, everyone else standing back.

Come *on*, son.

More like fifteen years ago, maybe more. The wee nurses collecting like starlings, Andy shooing them away, but she could sympathize; he was a nice-looking boy was Bobby Maiden.

Young coppers: one of the first things they learned as probationers was where they could grab a hot cocoa on the cold nights. And a wee nurse for the night off.

Those days, Bobby looked too young to be out at night on his own. Made his cocoa last. Didn't want to go back, you could tell, and always looked apprehensive. But, still, cute and bright some nights . . . and prey to Lizzie Turner. Clever, ambitious Lizzie. Not his type, but you never knew.

'Come on, Bobby.' Andy's hands either side of his head, fingers down the cold, mud-and-blood-flecked face. Backing off as the paddle threw another seismic shudder into his chest.

'We're not getting anywhere, Sister.'

'Go again, Jonathan.'

Lizzie Turner and, by then, *Detective* Constable Bobby Maiden. She'd missed the glittering wedding – somebody had to hold the fort. Down the pan now, anyway, Lizzie working in some BUPA clinic in Shrewsbury, they said, and living with one of the suits. A better cut of suit in a BUPA clinic.

'Jesus *God*, Bobby.' Andy closed her eyes, the big light

over the table making a warm orange globe inside her eyelids, like the sun at dawn. Like the morning when Marcus and Mrs Willis took her to Black Knoll, told her how the sun had come down for the wee girl after the First World War, Marcus saying craftily that it sounded like a classic UFO encounter to him and Mrs Willis smacking him on the arm.

'We're wasting our time, Sister Andy,' Jonathan said. 'Three minutes gone? Three and a half?'

'Keep going!' *Come on, Bobby, you cannae go out like this, son, covered in shit, stinking of whisky.* This was the routine that never became routine; each time it knocked you back like the bolts jolting the person having his death invaded.

Another electric punch. The shudders going up both of Andy's arms. It was a brutal business, but that was modern medicine: hit them with something mindless and powerful . . . drugs and violence, this was the modern manpower-saving Health Service – street-level stuff. Incredible she should be thinking like this, but Andy was remembering the laying-on of Mrs Willis's hands later that morning back at the farmhouse and for nine more days, on a diet of greens and windfall apples and water from the well. This was when, after thirty years faithfully wedded to a hospital, something came through that turned into an itch.

'Nothing.' Jonathan's voice as flat as the monitor. 'He's got to be over the vegetable threshold now anyway.'

'No. Don't stop, OK?' Taking it personally, as always, but tonight it was all the more intense because maybe there wouldn't be many more of them before Sister Andy dropped out to join the burgeoning ranks of the alternative healers, to dangle from the lunatic fringe, dispensing a laying-on of fragrant hands to well-heeled cranks who'd come to St Mary's because it was prettier than a rundown spare-part warehouse like this place. And what was the alternative health sector, what was it really, but another small business leeching off the soft in the head?

Jesus God, *which is right*?

'We've done all we can, Sister.' Jonathan's hands over Andy's, trying to detach them from Bobby's head. But the amber sun was rising behind her eyes and its heat rushing all the way down to her hands, to the tips of her fingers in the corpse's blood-stiffened hair.

'She's upset, Doctor.' Debbie Barnes sounding amazed at this, as if she was watching the *Titanic* going down.

Cold. The boy was long gone.

And the sun in her head turned suddenly black and she shuddered, head to foot.

'*No!*' Andy cried aloud, tears coming.

This was when the great roar went up.

IV

Once, just after dawn, the sun had come down for Annie Davies.

This phenomenon occurred in either 1920 or 1921, on Midsummer's Day, which happened to be her birthday.

It also took place on High Knoll.

Which was fair enough, as far as Marcus was concerned. Which actually, in fact, made *perfect bloody sense*.

However, what was upsetting was this: had it occurred almost anywhere else around the village, Annie Davies might, by now, have been some kind of saint. And the village a little Lourdes.

This was how Marcus Bacton saw it, anyway. Hoping, as he stepped out of the castle ruins and set off across the meadow, that the Knoll had a little inspiration to spare for *him*. That simply being there, in the energy of dawn, might somehow resolve the pressing question of what to do about Mrs Willis, his housekeeper, his best friend, his doctor.

Who, possibly, was dying.

Who might, in the end, require the nursing home she'd always sworn she'd never enter.

But who, if it came to it, he'd *carry* to the bloody Knoll.

It had taken Marcus years to piece together the story of young Annie Davies and the midsummer vision. Interesting, the way the village's collective memory had filed it away under Don't Quite Recall.

Bastards.

'Come on then.' Marcus walked more quickly, afraid the sun was going to beat him to the top. Getting on for seven a.m., and there was already a blush on the hill where the mist was thinning.

'Come *on*.'

About twenty yards away, Malcolm, the brindle and white bull terrier cross, raised his bucket head briefly and went back to whatever dead and rotting item he was sniffing. A couple of sheep watched him uneasily.

'All right, you bastard. Get your balls blown off, see if I care.'

Problem being that the Williams boy, who leased the grazing from the Jenkins brothers, could get difficult about dogs upsetting his flock. Even Malcolm, who despised sheep even more than he despised Marcus.

Eventually, the dog grudgingly ambled over and down they went, through the meadow and up the pitch towards the Knoll, until the already reddening field lay below them like a slice of toast tossed from the mountain.

And Marcus looked down, as he always did, and tried to see it as it must have looked to Annie Davies.

Wouldn't be able to, of course, because he was now sixty, and Annie had been thirteen – by just a few hours – on the morning of her vision, in a world still recovering from the Great War.

The unheralded marriage of Tommy Davies, a farmer well advanced in years, to the local schoolmistress, Edna Cadwallader, must have provided a year's worth of gossip for the drama-starved inhabitants of St Mary's.

Annie was Tommy and Edna's only child. Born 'prematurely', as they used to say in those days.

Amy Jenkins (related only by marriage to the Jenkins brothers, owners of the meadow, the Knoll and another hundred acres), who kept the oldest village pub, had told Marcus that her own mother used to say it was 'a bit of a funny family'. As schoolmistress, Edna had considered herself Village Intellectual. She was a parish councillor, too, and would spend most nights at one meeting or another, putting the community to rights. And so Annie had grown up closer to her aged father.

Marcus often imagined – as if it had really happened this way – a strange, still atmosphere on the night before the vision – Annie brewing a pot of strong tea for her dad and the two of them taking a mug each and wandering companionably down to Great Meadow, watching the hayfield turn almost white in the deep blue dusk.

Thirteen, is it now? The cooling mug must have looked like a thimble in Tommy Davies's huge, bark-brown hands. *Big age, that is, girl. Sure to be.*

Annie's father probably didn't talk a great deal. He would have been as old as most of the other village children's grandfathers. So when he made a pronouncement it would be charged, for Annie, with a glowing significance, like the words of an Old Testament prophet.

Thirteen. Marcus saw her grinning up at Tommy Davies, laying her mug on the grass and, with a rush of coltish energy, clambering over the wooden gate and dashing off down the track dividing Great Meadow, with the first breath of the night billowing her cotton frock almost over her head. The beginning of the parting, and Tommy too old and experienced not to accept it.

Perhaps the image of Annie had become inseparable now, for Marcus, with the last picture of his own daughter, Sally, who had died of leukaemia within months of her own thirteenth birthday. Perhaps this, in truth, was what had made him so determined to get Castle Farm: the feeling that something of Sally was here, too. That if he'd known about the vision when she was dying he would have brought her here. To the natural shrine which the Church had denied.

Soon, what seemed like all of south Herefordshire was at Marcus's feet, the crimson line of dawn drawn tight over the misty, wooded hills, cleft only by the stocky church tower of St Mary's.

The church was built on the site of a Celtic hermit's cell. It was probably older than the woods and the fields. For Marcus, the hills around the Golden Valley hid the lushest, richest, least-spoiled countryside in all of southern Britain. The villages had altered hardly at all, and St Mary's was probably not so very different from when Annie was here. In those days, it might even still have been known by its original Welsh name Llanfair-y-fynydd: St Mary's in the Mountains.

The village itself, viewed from above, seemed almost circular, in its nest of wooded slopes. From the churchyard, you could look up and see the long, dark ridge of the mountains, but the eye would always be drawn back towards a single promontory which seemed to punch the sky like a dark, gauntleted fist.

High Knoll. Or *Black* Knoll, as it was called in the village and now, to Marcus's disgust, even on the maps. When you got there, it wasn't so stark, although the grass was brown and rough around the stones.

The burial chamber on the Knoll was far older than the church and even older than the Celtic hermit's cell. Annie Davies would have been told (by her mother, at the village school) that it was where heathen folk once came to worship the sun. Ignorant people who thought the sun was a god.

Perhaps Annie had been dismayed. Perhaps, whenever she'd tried to imagine God, she, like Marcus, had thought at once of the sun, the brightest light in the sky. Wondering if that made her a heathen?

Perhaps, as she walked up to the big, broken table of stones, she'd decided that the prehistoric people couldn't have been so very ignorant if they could find such a perfect place to greet the day. And anyway, Jesus hadn't been born then, so how were they to know about the true God? They were worshipping the brightest light they knew; what was so wrong about that?

Tommy Davies, who wasn't well educated but was doubtless very wise, might have told her that the people who built the monument were his ancestors, the first farmers here. And that having the bits of old stones up there somehow kept the land in good heart.

The burial chamber had been partially collapsed for centuries. It was unlikely that even Annie would have been able to get inside. Perhaps, that morning, she had clambered on top of the chamber, the huge capstone, and turned to watch the daily miracle of the sun trickling out of the horizon. And lifted her face to the sky.

Was that when it had happened?

About a hundred yards from the Knoll, along the steepening track of stones and baked red mud, Marcus had his first tantalizing glimpse of the top of the capstone.

Just about make it in time for the dawn. Even more than three months after midsummer, the view of the dawn from High Knoll was never a disappointment.

And then he heard voices.

What?

On the Knoll? Voices on the *Knoll*? At *dawn*? Marcus felt violated. He stiffened, snatched hold of Malcolm's collar, clamped a hand over his muzzle.

Accepting he had no right to feel like this. Wasn't Castle land any more, although it was Marcus's ambition – if, for instance, there was a sudden upturn (ha!) in the fortunes of *The Phenomenologist* – to buy it back one day. However, the elderly, reclusive Jenkins brothers, whose father had acquired the Knoll as part of a land package in the late 1940s, seemed to accept the footpath as a right of way, for the owners of the Castle, at least. On this understanding, Marcus laboured up here at dawn twice a week, summer and winter. And in all that time he'd never met a soul, except for the intense American girl that one occasion, and at least she'd had the bloody decency to consult him first.

Because, at the Knoll, the dawn was *his* time. His and Annie's and Sally's.

There was a clump of rowan below the summit, and Marcus crept between the trees, marching Malcolm ahead of him, and waited and listened. A man's voice was drawling in that rhythmic up and down way that told you he wasn't really talking to anyone he could see.

'Now, this is a fairly unexceptional chambered tomb, dating back over four thousand years. We can't get into the chamber any more because, as you can see, it's collapsed in the middle. Of course, what we're looking at here are merely the *bones* of the structure. Originally, all this would have been concealed by tons of earth, and all you'd have been able to see was a huge mound, with an opening . . . just . . . *here*. Now I say it's unexceptional . . . except . . . for one aspect. The location.'

There was silence for about half a minute. Marcus seethed.

'How was that, Patrick? We could run some music under the bit where we open up to the dawn spectacle. Do you think? What's that da *da* thing from *2001*? Or is that a bit of a cliché?'

'No, it might work. Roger . . . Just another thought. When I pull back, but before I open it out, if you were to stand fractionally to the *left* . . .'

'How far? This?'

'And back a bit. Hold it there. Spot on. What I was thinking, if we time this right, do it just as it's breaking through, it'll look as if the sun's rising out of the top of your head. Nice effect. What do you think?'

'Hmm. Yes, OK. Why not? Worth a try.'

'Make a change,' Marcus said loudly, coming out of the trees, 'from it shining out of his fucking arse.'

He hauled himself up onto the small plateau of the Knoll. Where there was hardly bloody *room* for him. The molten orb in the east turning five faces florid as they all spun at him.

Young Fraser-Hale looked startled but otherwise unperturbed. The haughty Magda Ring said, 'Oh for heaven's *sake*,' and slapped her clipboard like a tambourine. The cameraman swung round, aiming his lens at Marcus like an assassin with a rifle. The sound man resentfully snatched off his headphones. And Falconer . . .

Falconer just smiled.

'Marcus,' he said.

Falconer. In his fur-trimmed motorcycle jacket and his ridiculously tight jeans. Falconer who strode the hills with his ponytail swinging, followed by a string of adoring acolytes: the old ladies he charmed, the young ones who – by all accounts – he shagged senseless.

'One realizes, old chap,' he said, 'how terribly fond you are of this place, but we are *working* and, as you see, space is somewhat limited.'

Falconer, with his weekly television audience of an estimated six million.

Marcus with his ailing private-subscription magazine, circulation just under eight hundred and slipping.

His aversion to the man couldn't be as simple as *that*, surely?

'If I could just point out . . .' the cameraman said, looking agitated, 'that we're going to have about four minutes, maximum, to get this shot before the sun goes behind a frigging cloud or something.'

'Don't worry,' Falconer said. 'Our friend just wandered up for a teensy snoop, and now he's leaving. Aren't you, Marcus? Old chap.'

Old chap. Always a slight emphasis on the *old*.

'As a matter of fact, no.' Marcus flicked back his heavy, grey hair and straightened his glasses. 'I don't think I am.'

Big problem was: most of the villagers seemed to love the bastard. The star-struck idiots on his damned courses taking all the rooms at the local hotels and pubs, filling up the holiday caravans on the mobile-home park; Jarman, the postmaster, claiming Falconer was the biggest boost to the local economy since they closed the bloody railway.

But look at the bloody *damage* he's doing, Marcus would protest, and they'd all stare at him, mystified. And Marcus would try to explain how the damned man was destroying the *ancient sanctity*. Because that was his *thing*: to demystify, unravel, explain, according to his own limited, prosaic criteria, the essentially inexplicable. Demolishing mythology, dispelling atmosphere, stealing the energy and giving nothing back.

Except money.

Marcus delivering his side of the argument in two successive issues of *The Phenomenologist*: why the ludicrous University of the Earth would ultimately be a bad thing for the area. Leaving copies lying around, pinning up the article on the village noticeboard. With the exception of Amy, at the Tup, the villagers didn't understand. They all thought he was out of his bloody tree. And jealous.

Falconer's perpetually tanned face flexed and he flashed his white crowns. A combative, buccaneering smile, often seen on his accursed TV programme: the informed sceptic challenging the gullible, hare-brained mystic.

Marcus released the dog and straightened up: six inches shorter than Falconer, two stones heavier, ten years older. Malcolm growled happily.

'You get hold of that bloody thing.' The soundman backed away, protecting his privates. He wouldn't know Malcolm was all mouth, no bite.

'Dog's got as much right to be here as you,' said Marcus. 'Probably more.'

'You couldn't be more wrong about that,' Falconer said smoothly.

'That animal touches me,' the soundman said, 'I'll have the police in. Have it picked up and put down and *you* up in court.' Turned on the cameraman. 'I hate the country. You never told me there'd be any of this shit. You said there was no need for personal injury insurance. I've got kids, Patrick.'

'Marcus,' Falconer said, 'did anyone ever tell you what an offensive little man you were? You've been here approximately half a minute, you've disrupted my shoot, upset my crew . . .'

'Falconer.' Marcus stared him in the eyes. 'You have lived here less than six bloody months. In that short time, you have offended every one of my most basic sensibilities.'

'Sensibilities?' Falconer shook his head pityingly. 'God preserve us.'

Marcus advanced on him. 'Turned the whole valley into a sodding *film set*. Everywhere I go, there you are doing one of your inane "pieces-to-camera" on the psychology of Neolithic *person* . . . as though the whole bloody Stone Age is your bloody backyard.'

'Well,' Falconer said. 'At least *my* version of pre-history is based on knowledge, as distinct from wishful thinking. But I really don't have the time to discuss the nonsense of ley lines with an old fart whose opinions are irrelevant anyway, so—'

'Bollocks! You don't really *know* any more than the rest of us. You're just a bloody academic vampire. A *leech*.'

Marcus stopped, knowing he was losing it. Falconer was laughing.

'Roger,' the cameraman said. He looked about twenty-two, and petulant. 'Just look at that sun, will you? We're missing *my shot*.'

'Oh *dear*!' Marcus snarled. 'You're missing the little turd's shot.'

Falconer stopped laughing. There was clearly a real possibility they wouldn't be able to video him with the sun beaming out of his head. Not today, anyway. *Oh* bloody *dear*.

'All right, old chap.' The great man stretched a stiff arm at Marcus. 'Run along. Out!'

'Out?' Marcus stood his ground. 'Out of the district? Out of the country? Who the fuck do you think you are?'

'All right, I'll tell you who I am.' Falconer's face hardened. 'I am the owner of Black Knoll.'

There was a moment of ghastly silence as the words hit Marcus like an anvil and all the breath went out of him. Before disbelief set in.

'Rubbish. That's . . . rubbish. Balls. You . . . you can't just buy an ancient monument. Even you.'

'Of course I can. *And* the land it stands on.'

'That's impossible.' Marcus felt weak. Couldn't be true. The Jenkins brothers knew how much he wanted the Knoll. Knew he'd get the money together one day.

'Contracts were exchanged yesterday at four p.m., in Hereford.' Falconer pausing to savour the reaction. 'The Jenkinses are very happy indeed at the thought of getting rid of a useless, scrubby little mound without having to sell the meadow as well. If you'd like to see the paperwork, Marcus, call in at my office at Cefn-y-bedd. On your way down.'

'But . . .' Marcus couldn't summon the breath; his chest felt tight as a bloody drum. Wait till he saw the Jenkins brothers, fucking traitorous bastards. '*Why* . . . ?'

'Because I *like* the bloody thing, Marcus. Because I want to study it in peace. Because the University of the Earth really ought to have its own ancient site, where my people can carry out their experiments uninterrupted by—'

'Their *experiments*? This is a bloody *shrine*!'

Falconer passed a hand across his eyes, tottered theatrically. 'Bacton, people like you astonish me. You have the credulity of small *children*. Anything bizarre, anything determinedly unscientific, like the fantasies of some deluded, pubescent brat back in the twenties—'

'It's people like you' – Marcus brandished a finger at him – 'who hounded that child out of the village.'

'And one can only be thankful, Marcus, that there weren't people like you around to canonize her.'

Marcus thought suddenly of Mrs Willis. Her recent, unprecedented tiredness, her headaches. His stomach went cold.

'You don't understand anything, do you? It's a *healing place*. That's why it was sited where it is. To channel solar energy.'

'Sure, sure. Just one of the theories we'll be putting to the test. Scientifically.'

'With a view to disproving it. And meanwhile, what about the people who come up to draw on the energy?' Marcus felt his lip tremble, picturing Mrs Willis making her way here in the dark, increasingly unsteady, but determined, knowing that the return journey would be so much lighter.

'Balls,' Falconer said. 'I've never heard such complete balls.'

'*Roger* . . .'

'I'll be right with you, Patrick. Marcus Bacton is leaving. And he's not coming back. In future – and I'm making this clear now, in front of witnesses – he'll not be welcome on this site.'

'Oh, I'm sure you'd bloody love to stop us coming here, but you know you can't, so—'

'Oh, I can, Marcus. It's not a public right of way. When we install our fence . . .'

'Fence? *Fence?*' He'd bring Mrs Willis up here in defiance of the bastard, but how could he lift her over a fence? 'You don't know what you're fucking *doing* . . .'

'I'm fully cognisant of my legal position. Anyone wishing to visit Black Knoll will require permission which, in most cases, if we're not working here, will be given. Between the hours of nine a.m. and six p.m.'

His narrow, allegedly handsome face flushed with triumph, Falconer waited for the significance of this to dawn, as it were, on Marcus.

'You bastard,' Marcus whispered. 'You utter, crass *bastard*.'

Falconer flicked a contemptuous hand at him, walked off and went to stand by the burial chamber. 'Too late, Patrick?'

'Not if we're quick,' said the cameraman.

Marcus turned abruptly away so they wouldn't see the tears in his eyes, his jaw quaking. Sensing his distress, Malcolm kept close to his legs as he made his way down from the Knoll.

'He can't,' Marcus told the dog. 'He fucking *can't.*'

The rising sun full in his face.

For Annie Davies, the sun had come down and appeared to roll along the ground, between the hills, a great, glowing ball. Just rolling, in total silence. But also vibrating . . . shimmering.

'And if that animal happens to shit on my land,' Falconer called after him, 'clean it up, would you? Old chap.'

V

The sky was boiling over.

A finger of lightning prodding almost languidly out of the deep, dark, sweating clouds as if it was attached to the arm of a vengeful god. There was a flock of sheep, several already struck down, a heavy tumble of bodies, milk-eyed heads flat to the plain.

A few yards away, the shepherd lay dead. His dog, back arched, howling a pitiful protest at the heavens.

Terror, death.

And only the great stones in their element. Whitened, as if they were lit from within by electric filaments, the stones exulted in the lightning.

Energy. The horrific energy of death.

The sky boiled over and yet it was cold. So cold.

All through the night, he cowered in terror on the plain as the frigid lightning struck and struck again, like a white snake.

Sister Andy had hardly slept, feeling close to feverish. And in the morning, when she ought to have been totally clapped-out, she felt stronger and years younger. There was a polish on the world. The colours were brighter.

Very much like the time when she herself was cured. What was this saying to her?

Don't dwell on it. At the best of times, Sister Andy was ever a fatalist. *It cannae last, hen.*

Coming on nightshift, she dumped her bags in the office and went straight to find Jonathan.

'So. How is *he* tonight?'

'Your miracle?' Jonathan beamed at her. 'He wakes up.

He looks bemused. He drinks half a cup of tea and he goes back to sleep. He's fine. He's restored all our faith.'

Andy shook her head, looked down at her hands. All worn and scoured, the texture of grade four sandpaper.

Something moved in mysterious ways.

'He saying much?'

'Not a great deal.'

'It's a bloody miracle he can even activate his lips. Four minutes gone? Jesus God.'

'Maybe it just seemed like four minutes,' Jonathan said. 'We were all a little . . .'

'Hysterical? I don't think so, Jonathan.'

They'd all be backtracking now, of course. The paramedics saying maybe we were wrong, maybe he was alive when we brought him in. Debbie Barnes saying maybe he *wasn't* flatlining three minutes plus. Well it couldn't have been that long could it, or he'd have come round as a cabbage; you could turn him into coleslaw and he wouldn't notice.

'*You* think it was mass hysteria, Jonathan?'

'I think it would be a black day for all of us if you were to leave, Sister Andy.'

'Aw.' Andy turned away, embarrassed. 'It really wasnae me, y'know?'

He was blinking at her with the undamaged right eye. The left eye would take a while to clear. It looked like the RAF symbol, circles of red, white and blue, but not necessarily in that sequence. She'd been there the first time the good eye opened. And there to hear the first word he'd spoken when, against all the medical precedents she could recall, his brain broke surface.

He'd said, *Cold*.

Which was how Andy had been feeling, entirely convinced they'd lost him, the way the sun turned black fast as a shutter coming down over a camera lens.

'How you feeling, Bobby?'

'Strange.' He blinked some more.

They had him in a side ward, on his own. There was always a small risk; something they might've missed, so Jonathan wanted to hold on to him until tomorrow, when they'd wheel him up to the men's ward for a few days' bedrest, observations, tests.

Andy touched her fingertips together in slightly cautious wonder. She couldn't let him go to the men's ward yet. Something very strange had happened here. It would never make it onto any report; the suits would see to that, but . . .

'Hang on,' Bobby said. 'It's Sister Andy, isn't it?'

She went to sit on the bed. His eyes were open again.

'Nothing wrong with the memory then, son.'

'I can still smell cocoa.' He smiled, all lopsided, a boxer's smile the day after the fight.

Some fight.

He fell asleep again and the smile died on his lips.

It had looked textbook, the way he'd come out of it: a long sleep, a few words, another long sleep. The usual questions. *Who's the Prime Minister, Bobby?* Neville Chamberlain, he'd said grumpily, and gone directly back to sleep. He'd seemed annoyed at being wakened. *Not* quite textbook.

Cold, he'd said, that first time, everybody amazed at his coming out of it enough to make a sound, let alone speak a recognizable word.

Then he'd coughed and rolled his head this way and that on the pillow, and there'd been a bit of a panic in case he was somehow choking on dust or something. He'd made small, dry spitting motions with his mouth before subsiding into an uneasy sleep.

Andy had hung around and watched and listened. Staying on for nearly two hours after her shift had finished, sitting beside his bed, talking to him softly, making notes of the things he said.

Concluding that something well outside the textbook parameters had happened to him during the minutes of his death.

Every word he'd spoken she'd written down more or less verbatim, in shorthand. Feeling it was important, somehow.

Rushing down cold tunnel.

Flushed into the street.

Everybody stuck in a smog. Don't care. Don't want to get out of it. Faces all squashed and smeary. Stocking masks.

Walking coma. Streets all grey and icy. People passing you either side, they don't see you. No feeling of being here, no feeling of being . . .

Bus tyres sucking at the slush. Slops over the kerb onto your shoes.

February. It's all February.

All February.

And once he'd woken up and said, quite lucidly, 'Don't let Riggs in.'

Shortly before midnight, Andy was finishing a cup of cocoa when Bobby Maiden appeared at the door of her office.

'Jesus God,' Andy said. 'Gave me the fright of ma life.'

He stood there, shaky, in just pyjama bottoms, sweat-shine on his face and chest, eyes all over the place.

'Let's go back to bed, shall we, Bobby?'

'Wha'm I doing here?' Slurring his words, as she led him back to bed. Brain-stem damage.

'You're in hospital. You were in an accident.' Telling him again because they forgot things very rapidly, head injury cases. Yesterday, he'd asked if Liz was OK, if she'd survived the accident, which ward was she on, could he go and see her? But the next time he woke up he knew well enough that they were divorced.

'Shouldn't be here,' Bobby said. 'Shouldn't *be* here.'

She held back the sheets for him. 'You can say that again, son.'

'It's cold,' he said and wouldn't get into bed. Stood there looking confused.

A warm enough night, but it was the first day of October and the autumn heating was on too, one economy the suits hadn't got round to yet.

'Look,' he said. 'Can you just answer me one question?'

'Do ma best, son.'

'Am I fully awake?'

'Looks that way to me,' Andy said.

'But you've got me on drugs, right? Sedatives.'

'Who told you that?'

'Nobody. I don't think. It just feels—'

'It's no true, Bobby. You're not on any kind of medication. Last thing we'd do in your state. All you need's sleep.'

He put a hand over his eyes. 'Somebody say I died? I dream that?'

'No.' She sat on the edge of the bed, patted it for him to sit down next to her. 'Wasnae a dream. You snuffed it, right enough. For four whole minutes. A long time. But you came back. That's a hell of a hold on life you got there, son.'

He seemed to find this momentarily amusing.

Andy said, 'Tell me, would you . . . Did you have any distinct kind of dreams?'

'How do you mean?'

'Like . . . lights? You see anything like that, Bobby? Bright lights at the end of a tunnel?'

'Not that I can remember.'

'Colours?'

'Too dark. Too cold for colours. Have I been to another hospital?'

'You havenae been anywhere, Bobby. As such.'

'Then why were they rushing me back?'

'That would be the night they brought you in? You remember that?'

'No, this was daytime. Thick fog, but it wasn't quite night. Frozen, mucky slush. Like February.'

'You said that soon after you came round. Maybe it was in your head when . . . whatever it was happened. You don't remember being anywhere . . . you know . . . warm?'

'No.' He looked puzzled.

This is not right.

'Bobby. Can you think back for me? What's the first thing you can remember when . . . I mean, do you remember the accident?'

'No.' Too quickly, but she decided not to push it.

'What do you remember before this slushy streets episode?'

His eyes flickered.

'Can you tell me, Bobby?'

He bit his bottom lip. 'Fear.'

'Did you say *fear*?'

'And cold. Cold fear.'

'What were you afraid of?'

He thought about it for a few seconds, like the fear was an entity in itself, didn't have to be *because of* anything.

Finally, he said, 'I think, not waking up. Never getting out.'

'Out of what?' Andy said gently. 'What were you in that you were scared of not getting out of? Was it, like . . . a claustrophobia type of feeling?'

She saw he was shivering. He put his hands to his eyes.

'I'm sorry, Bobby. Get into bed. I'll bring you some cocoa.'

But by the time she was back with the cocoa, he was asleep.

In the deep of the night, he awoke again and they sat side by side on the edge of the bed, with the bulb of the Anglepoise turned to the wall, and they drank cocoa, like old times.

She asked him if there was any pain. Only a kind of numbness, he said. Down the left side.

'Do I have a fractured skull, anything like that?'

'You'll have to see a neurologist to get it hard and fast. Might be a hairline, but I don't think so. There's some brain-stem damage.'

'What's that mean?'

'Neural. It's what causes the numbness, the way your voice is slurring. And why you won't be walking a straight line for a wee while. They'll repair themselves, the nerves, in time. Meantime, you'll keep forgetting things and you won't be able to think as fast as you'd like or do things as efficiently. So take a breath before you jump in and – no offence, I tell this to everybody – you need to watch your temper. Meantime, relax. You were luckier than I can tell you. You were gone a good long time. According to the rulebook, you shouldnae be back at all, no way, know what I'm saying?'

'I died?' He'd have forgotten their earlier chat; this was normal.

'Aye, you did. You were gone . . . quite a while. Lucky man, eh?'

'You think so?' Not sounding too convinced. Oh, this is all wrong, Andy thought. This is perversely wrong.

'How long am I going to be banged up in here?'

'Way you're coming along, you could be out in a week. Long as there's no complications. But we do need to watch you. All you have to do, Bobby, is rest, rest and rest. Anybody to look after you at home? Girlfriend? Mother?'

'Died when I was a little kid. Got knocked down in our lane.'

'Oh.'

'Runs in the family,' Bobby said. 'Getting knocked down.'

'I'm sorry. You . . . you still don't remember what happened to you?'

Bobby shook his head, with a wisp of a smile, then he pushed the heels of his hands into his eyes for a long moment. Something she'd seen him do several times before.

'Why you keep doing that with your hands?'

'It's . . .' He hesitated. Then talked about there being a kind of thick glass screen, between him and everything he perceived. 'A sense of . . . *separateness*.'

'Like you're not part of what's going on?'

Bobby Maiden looked at her out of his red white and blue eye. She was feeling her way here, going with the instincts, but she had his attention.

'And there's something you think you ought to be able to get through to? Because you have a feeling you could before? Don't look so surprised, Bobby. I've been in this game a good long time.'

'It's normal?'

'It's no exactly *normal*. I've known it before with patients who . . .'

'You had many like this? People who died and came back?'

'Aye. And people who came close to it and then came back. Most of them . . .' She looked into his eyes. '. . . most of them said it was the most wonderful thing ever happened to them.'

Thinking back to some of the patients she'd had who'd died, or almost, on the table and come back. Nothing as dramatic as Bobby, no more than a few seconds most of them. But, aye, the same story with a few variations. Maybe seeing themselves lying on the operating table. Then, often, a bright light, more glorious than anything they'd ever seen or imagined. Sometimes green fields and lovely gardens with fountains. And the famous long tunnel, the umbilicus, one end in this life, the other in . . .

Chemicals. Most neurologists were agreed that this was brain chemicals, the more optimistic of them suggesting there was obviously some shutdown mechanism in the brain that was triggered by the death process. The brain turning on the soft lights and sweet music. Departure lounge stuff.

And when they came out of it, the world could seem, for

a short while, a hard, bright and fairly brutal place – maybe Bobby's slushy, February streets had covered that aspect.

And yet, for almost all of them, there was this lingering memory of the glorious light, something they'd hold on to the rest of their lives. More than a hope . . . a certainty. That everything, in the end, would be very much OK.

While this guy, who'd had more opportunity than any of them to bask in the paradise vision . . .

'Bobby, are you religious at all?'

'Well . . .' He thought about it. 'Kind of knocks it out of you, being in the Job.'

'Was it ever there?'

He did it again with his hands, palms squashed into the eyes. Must surely hurt him to do that. Maybe that was what he wanted.

Pulling his hands away, he looked like a child waking up in the middle of the night and finding itself not in its cosy room but on some bare hillside.

'I was never that scared of death. Scared of dying, maybe. But that's how most people are I suppose.'

'Dying's usually no that bad, these days,' Andy said. 'Any nurse'll tell you that.'

'I am now.'

'What?'

'Scared. *Shit*-scared. Don't know where the hell you go, but I'm buggered if I'm going back. I mean, OK, I realize one day, but . . . Oh, *shit*.'

The tremble was so prolonged it was like his skin rippled.

'Bobby, let me get this right . . .'

Andy felt cold just looking at him. Got the feeling it was only the separateness, caused by the slight brain damage, that was stopping him from turning into a basket case.

'. . . this has left you with a *fear of death*?'

His face was so white, his bad eye was like a target in the snow.

'Listen,' he said. 'I don't even want to think about it.'

VI

Marcus couldn't face going back to the Castle, breaking the news to Mrs Willis, so he walked. Walking the rage out of his system, each step grinding Falconer's smug face into the tarmac, all the way to Ewyas Harold, damn near six miles.

Mrs Willis wouldn't be worried when he didn't turn up for breakfast. Used to his ways. Perhaps she'd go back to bed. Hope so.

On the way back, fatigue dragged Marcus into a field and he sat down under a tree, wiping the rain and sweat from his nose and his glasses, watching the clouds leak.

Malcolm wandered around, picking up the ghost trails of rabbits and foxes and badgers. Marcus leaned his head against the tree trunk. Nobody would understand what it would mean to him, not being able to walk to the Knoll, along that very obvious ley line from the Castle, to watch the sun rise over the distant Malverns. Feeling there a sense of *home* that he'd never experienced before, throughout his career as an English teacher in four different schools, Hartlepool to Truro. All through his marriage.

Not that there'd been anything wrong with *that*. Only wished there'd been more of it. But Celia had died not three years after Sally, following a bloody hysterectomy, and nobody would convince Marcus that one death hadn't led directly to the other. It should *not* have been fucking incurable.

Bloody doctors.

And bloody priests. And bloody politicians and professional academics. And bloody lawyers and judges and television pundits and all would-be shapers and organizers of other people's bloody lives.

And teachers? Yes, all right, bloody teachers too. When they'd offered early retirement, he'd snatched the money and run with it. Run away. Ending up, faintly bewildered, in Herefordshire, where he was born. Thinking there was still, in theory, time to *do* something, to push back the boundaries of life.

And yet depressingly aware that his life had actually shrunk.

After no more than a month, this melancholic and aimless existence in a rented cottage had been interrupted by news of the sudden death of the latest proprietor of *The Phenomenologist*. Putting the venerable periodical once more on the market.

Seemed like a sign. God knows, he needed one.

Been a contributor to *The Phenomenologist* for years. Smudgy, ill-printed rag, following him around the country, arriving four times a year, familiar hand-addressed buff envelope, like pornography. Editorial pages entirely self-generating, with unpaid correspondents submitting garbled accounts of mystical and paranormal events in their particular towns and villages. Appallingly written, most of them; but after thirty years as an English teacher, he'd sort *that* out.

Envisaging a new *Phenomenologist*. Better layout. Certain literary style. On sale in newsagents and bookshops.

Only after he'd bought the century-old title for a suspiciously reasonable four thousand seven hundred quid had Marcus discovered that contributors and subscribers were, broadly speaking, the same people. If you rejected or even rewrote some piece of crap, its author would immediately cancel his or her subscription.

Bloody nightmare. Only way to keep it going was to print every blasted thing and never ask questions. Very little of it bore serious scrutiny. You would never, for instance, have imagined so many elderly English spinsters manifesting stigmata.

And the circulation dropped as they died off.

But struggling with the magazine had, for a time, given him a purpose. Also a solid excuse to indulge his long-suppressed passion for the Unexplained. If he heard of a poltergeist-infested house or the sighting of baffling lights in the sky, he could wander along and investigate, presenting his credentials. No-one had ever heard of *The Phenomenologist*, of course, but it did sound rather impressive and few people would shut their doors in your face.

Marcus Bacton: crusader for the curious, defender of the irrational.

And Annie Davies had been his Bernadette, his Joan of Arc, Marcus realizing, from his own researches, that the circumstances of Annie's vision were remarkably similar to those of several famous sightings of the Virgin, notably at Fátima in Portugal in 1917 and Medjugorje in Yugoslavia, as recently as the 1980s.

He also subscribed to the theory that many so-called burial chambers, oriented as they were to the midsummer or midwinter sunrise, were not only Neolithic calendars but initiation chambers for the priests and shamans. They'd spend the night in meditation inside the chamber . . . and then dawn's first rays would enter like molten gold through a slit in the carefully positioned portal-stones. Out of the darkness, into the light. A supremely transcendent experience.

A time for visions. A time for miracles.

Should've been *Saint* Annie.

It was an obsession. And when the decrepit Castle Farm, the old home of Annie Davies, arrived on the market, it seemed like another sign. To buy it, Marcus Bacton had cleaned out his bank account and sold his car. At least it had a little cottage attached, which he could let out for holidays, enabling him to afford a series of cleaners, who had found him so exasperating that none lasted more than six months. Until, just over two years ago, the one who became a live-in housekeeper: the extraordinary Mrs Willis.

All a bit hand-to-mouth. But he'd always known that one day he'd raise the money to buy the Knoll, and he'd have a display case behind glass so that visitors would be able to read the story of Annie Davies and the vision which the Church denied.

Fucking Falconer.

Marcus smacked a fist into the ground and badly grazed a knuckle on a protruding tree root. His eyes watered. He bound the hand with his handkerchief, called Malcolm and trudged back to the Castle through the thickening rain.

The grey-pink ruins were draped around the farmhouse, which was built on the edge of the original motte. Half of a tower stood next to the house, like a smashed grain silo.

Most of the castles in the area were reduced to this. No great kudos to owning one, unless you were an outrageous self-publicist like Falconer. The Listed Buildings people were always on your back . . . and the tourists, idiots who simply couldn't believe that there could be medieval castle ruins *not* open to the public.

So when Marcus saw, from a distance, the vehicle parked in the shadow of the outer curtain wall, his hackles rose faster than Malcolm's. He was in no mood to explain to some cretinous family that no, there *wasn't* a bloody ice cream stand.

However, the vehicle under the wall turned out to be a Land Rover, which suggested a local person. Possibly a patient. The Castle was remote enough from the village for most of Mrs Willis's patients to come by car.

Or it could be the doctor. Well, God knows, he had

no time for these bloody state-registered drug-dealers, especially after their fumbling failure to save Celia. But the local fellow was less offensive than most and, after all, you didn't have to go along with what they prescribed.

Perhaps Mrs Willis had seen the sense of it. *Healer, heal thyself* wasn't always the best philosophy.

Stepping into the hall, he heard voices from the Healing Room. Must be a patient; Mrs Willis wouldn't embarrass the doctor by having him examine her amidst her pots and jars of natural potions. Dammit, she wasn't fit to see patients. But what could you do? What could you *do* with Mrs Willis?

Marcus tramped into the kitchen, dumped the kettle on the Rayburn. She'd laid out his mail in a neat pile on the old pine table. He hooked out a wooden chair with his foot. Phone bill and two letters from *Phenomenologist* correspondents. He recognized the cramped handwriting of Miss Pinder, the crazed spiritualist from Chiswick. The other was a foolscap envelope, postmarked Pembrokeshire. Sure he knew the writing, but he couldn't quite place it. He sighed and slit the envelope with a butter knife.

Dear Mr Bacton,

Well, it's been some months since you've heard from me, but I've been away. I trust you are staying out of trouble with the Ancient Monuments people over the state of your castle. Perhaps I shall see it one day. Now, I know you are a busy man, so I shall contain my Celtic urge to gabble on, and come straight to the point. There is a pressing matter with which I hope you may be able to assist me. We have a murderer in our midst.

What the bloody hell . . . ?

Now, there's melodramatic, isn't it?

But before you dismiss it, in that delightfully brusque way of yours, as delusion, please peruse the enclosed cutting.

Oh God. Marcus closed and opened his eyes. Cindy the bloody Shaman.

Reached for a mug with his left hand, holding the shelf in place with his right.

Insane theatrical biddy who lived in a caravan in Pembrokeshire.

Only the word *delusion* kept him reading. Falconer had used *deluded* in connection with the blessed Annie Davies. Hate to think that anyone – even Cindy the bloody Shaman – might have cause to consider Marcus Bacton as small-minded as Falconer.

. . . and so, naturally, I was most distressed by young Maria's death and would have been only too relieved if the police had identified some local yob as the perpetrator of the crime. Yet it was clear to me from the first that it was not going to be so easy. I could not stop thinking about the death of William Rufus, as explained so well by Dr Margaret Murray in her wonderful book, which I am sure you have on your shelves . . .

Of course. Classic work. Murray had identified William as the Divine Victim. A king dying for his country. The ultimate human sacrifice. But only Cindy the Shaman could equate the historic slaying with the murder of a hunt saboteur some eight hundred years later.

. . . here, I felt, was a killer with a strong sense of earth-ritual, and the only proof I required – for myself – was evidence that this person had struck again. I began to monitor the newspapers, searching for any death that could be strongly linked to its location . . . crimes committed in places of ancient significance. Wherever I travelled, I scoured the local papers for details that the national press would not have the space to include. I

came across the attached report in the west Wales edition of the Western Mail.

Marcus unfolded the cutting.

BIKE BOY MAIMED IN HORROR TRAP

A 14-year-old boy was in hospital with horrific facial injuries last night, after riding his motorcycle into a brutal, barbed-wire 'man trap' on a lonely mid-Wales hilltop.

A police investigation is under way to find out who stretched a double strand of the wire between a fence post and a tree across a track regularly used by motorcycle scramblers. Schoolboy scrambler Gareth Wigley rode round a blind bend and directly into the wire. Surgeons are fighting to save his left eye.

A Dyfed-Powys Police spokesman said, 'He is very lucky to have survived. This was a calculated attempt to maim or even kill.'

Some local people have protested that the ancient track, in the Elan Valley, near Rhayader, is being destroyed by weekend scramblers, and the injured boy's father, farmer Bryn Wigley, 48, said, 'Some of these so-called conservationists are completely insane.'

The track, said to have been used by medieval monks walking between the abbeys of Cymhir and Strata Florida . . .

The last lines were highlighted with what looked suspiciously like yellow greasepaint.

Between the text and a photograph of the angry father holding a strand of barbed wire, the *Western Mail* had provided a little map, showing the exact location of the trap, on the edge of an oak wood. A line had been drawn across it in black eyebrow pencil, and Cindy had scrawled, *Get out your OS maps, Mr Bacton. All right, nobody dead this time, but if it had been a grown man on that bike, the wire would have had his head off, no question.*

The tin kettle shrieked on the stove, just about echoing what was going on in Marcus's head. Was he really supposed to print this creepy woman's fantasies? The Miss Pinders would think *The Phenomenologist* had metamorphosed into the bloody *News of the World*.

With the noise of the kettle, he almost missed the discreet creak of the Healing Room door across the passage. Dived to the door just in time to spot the young chap with tousled, tawny hair – moving pretty damn silently for someone with such a hefty physique – trying to creep out unseen.

'Bloody *hell*.' Marcus was out of his chair, the schoolmaster in him exploding to the surface. 'You! *Boy!*'

The outgoing patient stopped.

'Come here,' Marcus demanded.

The face came round the kitchen door looking stupidly embarrassed.

'Ah. Mr Bacton. It's you.'

'Who the fuck you think it is? This is where I live.'

'Ah. Yes. Course it is. Sorry.'

'What the hell do you think you're doing in my house? Sent you to spy, has he?'

'Well, actually . . .' Adrian Fraser-Hale, Falconer's resident boy scout, shuffled about in the kitchen doorway. 'I came to consult Mrs Willis. I have this sort of skin problem, and the lady in the pub said—'

'Skin problem? Fucking *thick* skin problem, if you ask me!'

'No, it's a sort of psoriasis.' The boy turned sideways and pulled his collar down, revealing an area of pink and white blotches. 'From the ear to the top of the neck. Itches frightfully.'

'God save us.' Marcus raised his eyes to the worm-ridden oak beams. The rash was probably the remains of adolescence. Young Fraser-Hale had the body of a man and the air of a sixth-former – the sort who was a natural captain of the first fifteen but lacked the dignity to make head boy.

'Actually, Roger doesn't know I'm here. I don't suppose he'd be awfully pleased. I mean, I've been to the doctor and a couple of chemists, and they all go on about allergies and elimination tests which could take, you know, yonks. Meanwhile the thing just grows, like some sort of alien lichen, and, well, Roger wasn't too keen on me appearing on the box looking like this.'

'Oh good heavens, no, mustn't have anyone epidermically challenged on the *Roger Falconer* programme.'

'And the lady in the pub told me how Mrs Willis had cured her of a fairly vile rash, so . . .'

'Yes, all right, I get the picture.'

The boy was so painfully sincere it was hard to imagine how he managed to work with Falconer.

Fraser-Hale said, 'I didn't mean to be surreptitious or anything.'

'No, all right. Just the old girl gets tired. She's . . . not young, and while she might think she's pretty fit, I'm trying to discourage people from just turning up.'

Marcus stopped talking and waited for Fraser-Hale to go, but the boy just stood there, looking uncomfortable and fingering his psoriasis.

'Actually, Mr Bacton, if I could just say . . . I mean, what happened this morning, and the bad feeling between you and Roger. I'm really frightfully divided about all that. Because, you know, I'm rather more on your side of the fence than his. And I think you're absolutely right about Black Knoll . . .'

'*High* Knoll.'

'Yes, of course. I think it was probably the pivotal terrestrial power-centre for this whole area. I mean, one only has to spend time there, put one's hands on the stone. So I'm . . . well, I . . . I think Roger's wrong to fence it off and try to keep it for himself. I just wanted to tell you that.'

'Well, it's, er, good to know that you're not all tarred with the same brush over at Cefn-y-bedd.' A thought struck him. 'You didn't tell Mrs Willis about what happened this morning, did you?'

'Oh dear.' Adrian Fraser-Hale looked bereft. 'I'm so sorry, Mr Bacton. You see, I thought you'd have already told her.'

'No,' said Marcus, 'I'm afraid I was in a bit of a state. Wanted to walk off the er . . . before I broke the news.'

'I'm terribly sorry.'

'Not your fault. I suppose I was avoiding it.'

Fuck.

Mrs Willis liked to rest after a healing session, so Marcus waited half an hour before popping his head around the door.

'All right, old love?'

She was lying on her daybed, a copy of her beloved *People's Friend* by her side.

'Sorry,' he said inadequately. 'I mean, you know . . .'

'I knew there was something when you didn't come back.' Her face creasing, activating a thousand wrinkles. The old dear had started to look her age almost overnight. It was frightening.

'I really am sorry,' Marcus said. 'Perhaps it's all my fault. Perhaps if I'd got down on one knee to the fellow from the start. I'm going to talk to the County Council anyway. He can't bar that footpath, he doesn't own the meadow. And there must be some way we can stop him fencing it off.'

'It doesn't matter,' said Mrs Willis.

'It doesn't *matter*?'

This was how she'd been for nearly a week. Not bothered about anything. Pale, listless. Dried up. Etiolated. No-one who saw her now would even recognize the bustling widow who'd turned up at the door, having come by bus and walked over a mile after his advertisement for a cleaner.

Cleaner. Ha. Much later, Marcus had discovered that the crafty old soul had made a few inquiries about him, discovered that here was a retired man with no practical skills to speak of but an undying interest in the Mysterious. And a house that was far too big for him: lots of room for jars and potions.

'Don't do this to me, old love,' Marcus said. 'You know it matters like hell that you won't be able to go to the Knoll.'

Remembering how unutterably moved he'd been when he'd introduced her to the Knoll. When she'd stood by the burial chamber in silence, taking several long, slow breaths before declaring that he was right, it was special, it had a healing air. And, by God, she knew how to use it. How to focus it and channel it and pass it on. Look at the Anderson woman . . .

'I never told you,' Mrs Willis said in that dreamy way she sometimes had. 'But I saw a black light.'

'You saw *what*?'

What remained of the English teacher in him restrained itself from pointing out that you couldn't actually *have* a black light. This was no time for bloody semantics.

'Tell me, old love,' he said. 'When was this?'

'What's that?'

'When? When did you see this . . . ?'

'Last Thursday night, would it be?'

'You went at *night*? You shouldn't be going out at bloody night! I didn't see you go.'

Mrs Willis smiled the old sweet smile. 'You're a sound sleeper, boy.'

'At night? I don't understand.' Bewilderment and panic jostling one another in his chest. 'What's going on? Bloody *hell*, Mrs Willis, *that's* why you've been off colour, is it?'

'Not been much of a housekeeper, have I?'

'Forget *that*. Jesus Christ—'

'Marcus!'

'Sorry. Look. Just tell me. This black light. What d'you mean a "black light"? How can you see a black light at night? What are we talking about here? Was it some premonition about Falconer? Why did you see Fraser-Hale? What did he tell you? What's going on?'

Mrs Willis just sat there with her back to the matchboard wall and the rickety shelves supporting the old lady's herbs and potions in jam jars and ancient Marmite pots.

'Falling apart,' said Mrs Willis wryly, following his eyes.

'What did you do for young Fraser-Hale?'

'What's that?'

'Fraser-Hale. Falconer's lad.'

'That boy? I said I'd make him some ointment. I advised hot baths in Epsom salts and told him to boil his meat first. It's only a rash.'

'Pity you can't poison his bloody boss.'

'Never say that,' Mrs Willis said sternly. 'It'll come back on you, boy.'

'I'd swing for that man.'

She observed him shrewdly through her pebble glasses. 'You're saying I shouldn't treat that boy because he works for a man you don't like? I would treat Mr Falconer himself, if he was in need.'

'You're a bloody saint, Mrs Willis. And unfortunately I'm never going to reach your stage of spiritual development. I'd push the bastard off a cliff. I mean, why is he doing this to us? Is it just bloody spite, because I've been slagging him off in a little sodding rag nobody ever reads?'

'Perhaps you should be grateful to him for fencing it off.'

'What's that mean? What d'you mean by a black *light*? A sense of evil? For Christ's sake, old love, that's what the Church tried to say when the child had her vision. I've spent years trying to knock all that on the head. Is that what you mean?'

'I'm tired.' Mrs Willis picked up her *People's Friend*. 'I think I shall finish my story.'

VII

The minute she reached home, Grayle dived at the answering machine, as she did every night, in case there should be a message from Ersula.

God, Grayle, I'm so sorry. Time just goes so fast when you're absorbed in research. I looked at the calendar and I just couldn't believe it was six whole weeks since I wrote . . . Can you forgive me?

This never happened.

The only message tonight was a fax from her sometimes-friend, Rosita, New York's number one New Age public-relations consultant, scrawled around an invitation to the opening of a new store called The Crystals Cave . . .

. . . where our experts will unite you with the mystic gemstone that's been waiting for YOU, and YOU ALONE, since the beginning of time.

Grayle crumpled it.

There were crystals on the bookshelves, a crystal on the TV, two crystals by the phone. Quartz and amethyst for opening the psychic centres. Tiger's eye for confidence in health. Onyx for concentration.

There was the tree-of-life wallchart above the sofa, a poster of the Great Pyramid at sunset behind the TV. A small Buddha served as a doorstop. And under the window, a three-foot-tall plaster statue of the Egyptian dog-god Anubis wore a diamante poodle collar.

Hey, just because you believe in this stuff, Grayle would tell visitors, you don't have to be too *serious* about it. The principle difference between Grayle and Ersula, five years and several epochs apart.

Tonight the crystals looked dull, there was a chip out of the Buddha she hadn't noticed before. Also, Anubis looked so resentful in his poodle collar that she took it off.

Detective Olsen. Well screw *him*.

Grayle finished off half a bottle of Californian sparkling wine which had gone flat in the refrigerator, drinking it from the bottle, like beer. Figuring that, by now, the entire NYPD must have been officially notified that Holy Grayle Underhill was a doped-up neurotic who should be handled with iron tongs.

So the prime theory here, Ms Underhill, is that your sister's been kidnapped. Do we have any kind of ransom communication? No?

OK, let's consider the other option. Murder. Do we have a body? Let me, in the first instance, ease your mind on this score. I persuaded my lieutenant to allow me to call up three police forces around the area you say your sister was last seen. I faxed them all a description, plus the photograph you gave us, and none of them appears to have a Jane Doe bearing any physical resemblance whatsoever to this person.

So where does that leave us? It leaves us with a highly educated, independent and apparently headstrong twenty-five-year-old woman who, for reasons unknown, has failed to communicate with her family for a period of just over one month. Ms Underhill, do you have any idea how many women in this city have been on the missing persons register for over one year . . . ?

What Grayle, in her desperation, had done next, had been to show Detective Olsen the letter. Even the final pages, which Lyndon had not seen.

Big mistake.

Let me get this right. What we are suggesting now is that your sister has succumbed to an insidious, mind-possessing force emanating from some Stone Age burial chamber. Do I have this right, Ms Underhill? Tell me, have you discussed this with a priest? Have you attempted to contact your sister telepathically? Or, maybe, enlist the assistance of some of the people you're always writing about and like beam down into her next dream, tell her to come back home at once? Have you tried that, Ms Underhill?

In the refrigerator, Grayle found another bottle quarter full of stale sparkling wine and she drank that too.

On the old wine crate she used as a coffee table lay Ersula's last letter, creased up and stained with doughnut jam from Guardi's. Except for the last pages, which Lyndon hadn't handled.

> *. . . Grayle, do you have smells in dreams?*
>
> *Perhaps you do. Perhaps the olfactory element is common-place in the dreams of others. I just know I do not recall ever being aware of a smell before. Certainly nothing so horribly powerful as this stench, this nauseous, all-pervading stench of corruption that made my insides contract until I was sure I was going to throw up. Can you throw up in dreams? Probably. I didn't. I sure sweated, though . . .*

Grayle sighed. In all fairness, what else was the guy supposed to say about this? In a city drowning in drugs, a homicide every hour on the hour, he has to get the woman who disappeared into a dream. Even if he believed in this stuff, taking it any further would be putting his precinct credibility so far on the line as to seriously damage his career prospects for years to come.

It occurred to her that if she were an ordinary member of the public the next person she would probably turn to for advice would be the city's premier mystical agony aunt, Holy Grayle Underhill.

Just as, in a way, Ersula had done.

> *The events of the past few weeks have given me, I suppose, an insight into your continued need to explore the phenomena of the New Age.*
>
> *I still believe in psychological answers, that the truth lies not Out There, as they say on your beloved X-Files, but In Here. But I confess that my belief system has been sorely tested on this*

*trip. I keep telling myself how glad I am that you are not here,
but the truth is I often wish that you were. I suspect that none of
this would faze you. I recall how, some five years ago, both rather
drunk, we watched some stupid old late-night Dracula movie
together, and I saw an all too human sickness in it and was
repulsed. While you just shrieked with laughter at the gorier
excesses and delighted in the possibility of someone actually being
Undead.*

*Sober by then, we argued well into the night about the validity
and the morality of horror movies, most of which you kept
insisting were scary fun but also basically religious. Well, I still
do not believe in Dracula, or the possibility of being Undead.
Only in the power of the Unconscious.*

And you know something? That scares me a whole lot more.

*The dream experiments both excite and terrify me because,
while I am prepared to accept and be fired by the possibility that
the abnormally high incidence of lucid dreaming at ancient sites
may, in some part, be caused by external geophysical stimuli, I
know that the substance of those dreams still comes from within,
and that is what makes me afraid. I am afraid of what the
Unconscious can make us do. I am afraid of liberating aspects of
ourselves that we are unable to control . . .*

Grayle shivered in the damp heat of a September night
in New York City and thought about Dracula. Sure, vam-
pires were scary fun which also held out the promise of
some kind – OK, a very *degraded* kind – of immortality.
Like werewolf stories illustrated the possibility of human
transformation. *I swear on my mother's grave he has to shave
twice . . . three times . . .*

So many people who believed this stuff believed Grayle
Underhill had a hot line to the source. Seventy-three
letters last week. Grayle read them all; a few would always
lead to stories.

Stories. Scary fun.

Maybe this reflected her level of spiritual development:
keep an open mind, don't go too deep, have scary fun.

Grayle drained the bottle. Turned to the next page.

We're instructed not to discuss our dreams, for very sound, scientific reasons. All the recorded dream experiences, thousands of them, are being fed into a central database for future analysis. Only then will any correlations be considered. It is crucial to the experiment that any influences should be as a result of the geophysical properties of the sites themselves and not from each other's dreams.

As the place where this experience occurred was not one of the specific sites earmarked for the project, I approached Prof. Falconer and asked if I could discuss it with him. He was reluctant – he said a dream symbol could spread like a virus if not controlled – but eventually he agreed and we discussed it over dinner at a local pub. I was disappointed with his response but appreciated his reasoning. He said that because I went alone to the site – no therapeute – the experience was inadmissible. He also seemed angry that I had checked out the history of the site with a local historian (Marcus Bacton – I sent you a copy of his magazine) without his permission.

Nevertheless, I regard this dream as the most significant so far and have enclosed my description of it. As a connoisseur of Scary Fun, you will no doubt appreciate it, although rest assured that if it comes to my notice that any reference to this has made an appearance in your scurrilous column, I will toss sibling tolerance to the winds and sue your ass.

OK. What is remarkable about this dream is that it is the first which, for its entire duration, directly concerns the site itself.

The site is Black Knoll (also known as High Knoll) in the Black Mountains, just under a mile from the center. It is a Neolithic burial chamber in a modestly spectacular setting atop a promontory affording a wide view all the way to the Malvern Hills where the composer Elgar found his inspiration.

The only person recorded as having found inspiration here at Black Knoll, about three-quarters of a century ago, was a teenage girl called Annie Davies who claimed to have had a vision of the Virgin Mary. This vision accords with the published accounts of such experiences (see Seward: The Dancing Sun, 1993) in which the sun itself appears to gyrate or, in this case, to descend and resolve itself into a robed, female figure. The story was recounted to me by the aforementioned Marcus Bacton, publisher of that obscure journal The Phenomenologist, who lives at Ms Davies's former home, Castle Farm, and is in some respects a most alarming person.

However, I had found the tale of the unsophisticated country girl charming (I was surprised to hear that it had not been well received by the local people at the time) and determined to spend a night at Black Knoll, if possible, alone – for I have found that, having done this so many times, I now awake with a total recall of the dream experience.

I waited until two a.m., when the center was silent. Adrian, Magda and I – the scouts and guides as Roger somewhat patronizingly refers to us – sleep in small rooms converted out of the lofts above the old stables, so it was easy for me to creep out of the center and make my way along the ancient trackway to Black Knoll.

It was a three-quarter moon, so there was light enough, and I felt a pleasant sense of adventure as I approached the monument; it seemed more awesome by night, but I was not afraid, finding myself, as usual, attracted by the silence and loneliness of it. I wished, more than ever, to know its mysteries. It seemed to me that an obviously pagan site which could inspire a fundamentally Christian vision was a weighty argument for the theory that the hallucinatory experience was directly influenced by the geophysical nature of the site itself.

What did make my flesh crawl, I confess, was a scuffling beneath the capstone suggestive of rats – of which, as you know, I am not overfond. There was no way I was going inside after that – probably wouldn't have been able to squeeze in anyhow, the way the middle part of the monument has collapsed – so I spread my sleeping bag on top of the capstone. I was used, by now, to sleeping on stone and drifted off quite quickly.

THE DREAM.

I am walking to the Knoll. You have to cross a beautiful hay

*meadow. It is harvest time now and the bales are stacked in
the meadow like small skyscrapers. As I wander through the
stubbly canyons between the stacks of bales and find the footpath
which takes me up into the hills, into the sparse, ochre moorland
grass, I am aglow with anticipation. Will I, too, have a vision
of the Holy Mother? My dreamself, I have discovered, is a firm
believer; this shedding of normal academic skepticism I find
oddly refreshing, like a holiday, like becoming you for a while.
Jesus, never thought I'd say that.*

Grayle's eyes began to prickle. It was as if Ersula was
reaching out to her.

Automatically, she closed her eyes, pictured Ersula with
her efficiently cropped blond hair, more blond, more pure
than Grayle's, and her steady, watchful, almost cold blue
eyes.

Slowing her breathing, reaching out for Ersula.

Nothing. It never did work, did it? Especially when
your senses were swimming in three-quarters of a bottle
of stale Californian white wine.

*I am not aware of it for a while but the temperature must have
started to drop as soon as I left the meadow. Not only that
but, in what I would guess was direct proportion to this decline,
the colors are fading. Some people only ever dream in black
and white. I guess my noticing this means that I have always
dreamed in color.*

*Visibility is also declining because of a thickening mist
through which I can see the sun like a pale coin. Familiar
clumps of gorse sprout from the otherwise bare hillside. The
Offa's Dyke Path which more or less marks the boundary
between the countries of England and Wales is close, and, in my
dreamstate, I can sense a converging of separate energies; I don't
know how else to explain this.*

*I feel lonely. Suddenly isolated. A strange sensation, con-
sidering that the center itself is ten minutes' walk away, that
the towns of Abergavenny and Hay-on-Wye and the city of*

Hereford are all less than thirty minutes by car. And although my waking self relishes solitude, in my dream I wish someone were here with me, even that amiable buffoon Adrian Fraser-Hale, whose enthusiasms tend to be as nonsensical as your own.

Upon the Knoll, encircled by a muff of most unseasonal fog, it is alarmingly cold. English summers can be capricious, but this is not the cold of summer. I bend and touch the capstone; it has a patina, like a hoar frost. I am feeling depressed about this as I know it was on such a summer's day that Annie Davies had her vision and was enveloped in a kind of rosy warmth. There seems little prospect of warmth here now.

I lie down upon the capstone. A curious sensation. Let me try to explain it.

It is as if my dreamself is entering into my corporeal self, two aspects of me fusing together. There is a quite awesome sense of what I can only describe as hyper-reality. For example, when I touch the stone at my side I feel I am touching a living thing or, more exactly, putting my hand into a vortex of swirling, pulsing energy, as though I am being permitted to penetrate the stone's molecular structure. And it mine.

I open (in my dream) my eyes. My dream eyes. Oh yes, I am fully aware that I am dreaming.

The air is hard with cold. I am naked, by the way.

It is now that I sense the smell. It smells as if all the rats or whatever they are under the stone have died and rotted. It is a stench so utterly abhorrent that I push my nose into the crook of an elbow in disgust and revulsion.

Of what I saw, I am still uncertain. Although, as an archeologist, I have been present at the excavation of several graves, some no more than two hundred years old, this is outside my experience and I can hardly bear to think about it.

I wrote it down at once, describing in as much detail as I could what I thought I saw, but when I read it back it seemed stupid and nasty, and quite unbelievable, and I thought, what does this say about me, what kind of credibility would I ever have again? And I thought of you, the way you laughed and took it all so lightly when we were watching that filthy movie.

OK. Here goes.

Awakening (when you awake in a dream it becomes a lucid dream, remember?) with a stiff back. On the hardest mattress you can imagine.

Lying on my back. Neck stiff; can't move it.

Although, my God, how I want to. I just want to turn my head away from the suffocating stench.

The night sky is moonlit, but full of racing clouds. I want desperately to float up, into the wild, fresh night, chase the clouds rushing past the moon, torn like rags, lacy scarves of vapor. (Lift . . . lift . . . you can do anything in a dream. Lift . . . float.)

Can't move. Pain. Muscles knotted, twisted like old lead pipes.

Stench of decay, corruption. Turn away.

A night breeze gets in my hair and my stinking bedfellow rattles beside me.

Finally. I am allowed to turn my head. Turn it – oh Christ – his way, into the stink and it fills my throat, and we are looking at one another and he's grinning his savage grin. His gums have gone. His jaws are agape like a trap, strands of yellow skin overhang his green-filmed eye sockets and the white, flesh-less tip of his nose appears beaklike under the three-quarter moon.

And we lie there, side by side, shoulder to shoulder, his shoulder naked bone where it pokes through the ragged clothing ripped at by the buzzards and the breeze.

He's been dead a long time, I guess, my companion.

And I cannot wake up.

Presumably, the dream ends at some point but I do not wake up until morning and when I do I am trembling and drenched in a cold sweat so thick and glutinous it is almost like Jell-O, and I am virtually fused to that stone.

Scary fun, Grayle? You tell me.

Grayle found it more chilling each time she read it.

What was worst was that you would expect Ersula to offer a scientific explanation involving hypnagogic hallucinations or some such – Ersula's predictable answer to stories about people who woke up and saw ghosts in their bedrooms. There was no attempt to explain this away; its effect on her had been too corrosive.

Grayle picked up the copy of *The Phenomenologist* Ersula had sent. What a rag. Badly printed, cheap paper, no lay-outs to speak of. No wonder it was entirely unknown even to Holy Grayle.

Still, there had to be a phone number in there some-where. She'd call up this Marcus Backhouse or whatever he was called.

When she was sober.

VIII

Wiltshire

The Holy of Holies.
 Defiled.
 Yesterday evening, the Green Man stood before a six-foot sarsen as it was being examined by people from the National Trust, a dozen or so tourists and villagers looking on in horror and disgust.

He'd been alerted to the atrocity by the lunchtime radio news and driven at once to Wiltshire, the county of his birth. He drove between the fields where he'd hunted, learned to shoot, snare and gut. Where he'd learned, also, about the lines of ancient energy which gridded the fields, making Wiltshire probably the only county in England where all the ground was sacred.

But the holiest ground of all was Avebury.

Perhaps because he grew up in its shadow, Stonehenge never had the same power for him as the henge-village in the Kennet valley, encircled – except for the church – by a ditch and the remains of the greatest Stone Age temple in the world.

The stones of Avebury were shaped by the Earth Herself. Each is an individual organism – here a lion, here a human head, a fist, a gnarled penis, a woman's pocked and scarred torso and upper thighs with a tightly clenched vulva. One can almost see them all flexing, pulsing, breathing, and he wanted immediately to offer a sacrifice. However, the problem with Avebury is the modern community at its heart. And the tourists. With their children, dogs, cameras, ice creams.

Always people. Their vulgarity and their ignorance. Even at dead of night, when this act of sacrilege was, presumably, carried out.

The affected stones had been covered ignominiously in sacking by the National Trust people.

To hide the abomination.

Dozens of disgusting, pseudo-cabalistic symbols had been scrawled over two of the outlying sarsens, in white emulsion and black bitumen paint. The megaliths defaced from top to bottom, so that when the paint was cleaned off, the sensitive skin of mosses and lichens would also be scrubbed away, leaving the stones flayed and aching, as bald as housebricks.

Who was responsible?

So-called New Age travellers, perhaps, the itinerant vagrants who live on social security and consider ancient shrines to be their inheritance.

He was reminded yesterday of the eighteenth-century farmer who went around massacring megaliths and rejoiced – literally rejoiced – in the name 'Stonekiller' Robinson. The Green Man does not know how the stonekiller had died but he hopes it was a long and exceedingly painful death.

Through the sacking, he heard the stones calling out to him in their pain and, from beneath his feet, the Earth shrieking for revenge.

Knowing then that he had been sent for, that he was to be the instrument.

Parking his car for the night on the outskirts of Marlborough, he walked to the Ridgeway and joined a line from the Avebury circle and walked on until he found the place.

They always turn out to be marked in some way, these sacred sites, but sometimes the marker is far from obvious and takes time to discover. It might be a small stone hidden in a wood or obscured by tufts of moorland grass. Or lost among buildings, because sometimes the place will be in the middle of a village, even a large town.

For instance, earlier this year, the Green Man slept in a hollow in the ramparts around an Iron Age fort contoured into the summit of a holy hill. There were pine trees here, as well, and through his dreams galloped the spectral figure of the Knight of Swords, from the Tarot. The Knight was riding down from a hill with stark pines upon it. His sword was raised. He was on a mission of vengeance.

There was no denying the command.

At first light this day, the Green man followed an obvious alignment from the hill to a church steeple in the centre of the town below. The church was locked, the churchyard deserted. He walked on. The town was empty, there was very little traffic. Following the line, he arrived at the stump of an old market cross, a familiar marker. The line followed a paved, pedestrianized area into a small shopping arcade, where the frontage of one shop jutted out beyond its neighbours into the middle of the line.

The shop was . . . an ironmonger's.

The first sign.

In its doorway was a large cardboard box. Inside it was a young vagrant.

The box was not quite long enough to accommodate him, so he had protected his feet from the cold by encasing them in another, smaller box. On it was a line-drawing of a carving knife and one stencilled word.

MEATMASTER

All the confirmation the Green Man needed. Putting down his rucksack in the silent, newly cobbled arcade, he located the serrated-edged sheath knife he sometimes used to skin rabbits.

He remembers how the vagrant awoke with half his throat open, that soundless liquid scream again.

The remains of the Barber-Surgeon are on display in Avebury's small museum.

The skeleton was found under Stone Number Nine in the henge circle.

His profession was suggested by the implements discovered on the body – scissors and what was believed to be a medical probe. The dates on the coins he carried suggested he died in the early 1320s. Surgeons, in those days, needed no more qualifications than those required for cutting hair.

It seems likely that the Barber-Surgeon was involved in a medieval assault on the stones at the instigation of the Christian Church, attempting to stamp out pagan rituals still carried on there.

Tragically – ha – he appeared to have died when the stone toppled upon him.

This is possible. There are many tales of foolhardy country people who tried to dig up ancient menhirs provoking thunderstorms, even being struck by lightning.

During his dream below the pines last night, the Green Man learned the truth: that the Barber-Surgeon had been abducted by the guardians of the stones and given in sacrifice. Bludgeoned to death and placed beneath the stone.

In his dream, the Green Man was kneeling under the pines in a dense mist which sliced off the tops of the trees. He had held out his hands and into them was placed something grey and misty but quite heavy.

When he awoke, he found, not fifteen yards from where he'd slept, a single stone, about eight inches long and three to four inches wide.

This dawn arrives wearing a mist as fine as lace, the sun tossed carelessly in its loose folds.

Too bright. He will have to thicken the mist.

This is quite easy. Most people can learn to do it. However, most people would do it in reverse; they teach themselves to shift clouds and dissolve them by pure concentration. A simple example of the way human consciousness can learn to interact with nature. With practice, the clouds can almost be blown away in seconds. Pffft!

Actually, producing clouds, adding density to the atmosphere, is more interesting and far more powerful.

Close the eyes, imagine (create!) cold in the body. This is done, initially, through the feet, the cold drawn up from the dark places of the earth (best achieved when standing on stone) and sent to the base of the spine to form an icy ball around the spinal chakra. Slowly, the cold is drawn – through breathing – into each of the body's seven power-centres, and then projected into the aura. Finally, often in a fit of shivering, the command is given.

It is easier at dawn, when the sun is vulnerable and unsure of itself. From the pines, he watches it fade. The Earth senses the commitment and he feels radiant in Her trust.

The stand of pines, on its small hill, is surely as old as the great stones three miles to the south. This can be felt. These trees and generations of their ancestors, sturdy and aloof, taller than many a church steeple.

But the power of this site is probably unknown. Except to the Green Man.

They have been priming the place, he and the Earth, through the hours of the night, he lying supine under the harvest stars or sitting cross-legged and straight-backed in meditation among the needles and the brittle cones. The weight of anticipation kept him awake, the certainty that someone would be sent. And, of course, the special energy of the site itself. Once, there was sex: his penis summoned aloft by the thrusting pines, Earthen lips exquisitely cold around it.

And then came the dream. The dream of the Barber-Surgeon. The dream sent to him from the great stones of Avebury in their agony.

The one who has been sent comes in a straight line (of course) through the mist, following the green road between the fields.

It is almost nine o'clock, later than the Green Man expected.

Still, the longer the wait, the greater the accumulation of energy. He feels Her moving close to him and his whole body hardens as he stands, legs apart, among the ancient pines.

Actually, this person is not quite what he expected. He was envisaging a New Age traveller. Or two. Two would be a challenge, although not much of one when one takes into consideration that element of surprise.

The man wears a waterproof jacket, flat cap and new-looking walking boots. He has a small backpack, carries a pair of rubber-covered binoculars and an Ordnance Survey map in a plastic sleeve.

He looks very respectable, fairly intelligent. Not the sort of person you would expect to deface an ancient monument.

Not your decision . . . Not your place to question . . .

No. Of course not.

'Good morning,' the man says cheerfully. Panting slightly as he reaches the top of the little hill and turns to make a theatrical point of admiring the half-misted view. 'Wonderful!'

They share a smile. The Green Man wonders if he should tell the newcomer what is to happen. This would be even more powerful. Especially if he was able to understand the complexity of it. And be proud.

'You are with our lot, aren't you?' The man chuckles. 'Thought everybody was having a bit of a lie-in. After last night. By Jove, it doesn't take prisoners, that real ale, does it? Mind you, I find this is the best way to clear your head. Make yourself get out of bed. Let the country air get at it. Beats aspirin, does country air.'

'Our lot?'

'The t— Oh.' He peers at the Green Man. 'Bloody hell, you're not, are you? Sorry, sorry. Many apologies. There's a collection of us, you see, from clubs in the north Midlands. Twitchers – birdwatchers. Every year, we go to a different county for a long weekend. Only, the first night it always gets a bit convivial. Demob-happy, you see.'

A birdwatcher!

And one with the garrulous self-importance of a minor local autocrat – council official, bank manager or some such. A bird-watcher. No guts for the kill. He's not meant to know, he would never understand. He's crass, an idiot, unworthy of the honour of knowledge.

'Super day, though.' The birdwatcher sets down his pack and sits on it. 'Been camping?'

Also, a poor specimen. Not very big, not very young, not very fit and depressingly unaware.

'Used to go in for camping when I was younger. My wife and I, that is. Couldn't get her into a tent nowadays. Don't mean she wouldn't fit, although there'd not be much room for anyone else, I have to say. It's just . . .'

He takes off his cap, smooths down his hair, replaces the cap.

'. . . just that women seem to get older younger than we do, if you see what I mean. Lose their instinct for adventure. No spirit. On holiday, are you? Know the area well?'

'Yes.'

He sniffs. 'Call ourselves birdwatchers. Just an excuse really. To get away from the wives, get some fresh air, have a few pints in peace. Ah, well.'

He breathes deeply and closes his eyes. Sitting on his pack with his knees together, his hands clasped around them. And at that moment, the sun finds a hole in the mist and lays a white beam up to his feet.

Yes.

Feel it. Feel it rise through the soles of the feet, up the backs of the braced legs into the spine, out to the shoulders, rippling down the arms, the wrists, the gloved hands behind the back, gripping the stone.

'So what do you do,' the Green Man asks mildly, 'when you're not birdwatching?'

The eyes tip open. 'You'll laugh. I run a small chain of ladies' hairdressers in Wolverhampton.'

And the Green Man does laugh, with the sheer joy of the revelation, the fitting of the last segment of a perfect circle.

He sees a first flicker of uncertainty in the birdwatcher's colourless eyes as the little man attempts to rise, before the stone crunches his nose, like a red pepper. His eyes flicker rapidly through an amazing range of emotions: outrage, disbelief, terror . . . and, finally, pleading. He opens his mouth and the Green Man stops his scream with the stone, and the birdwatcher gags on blood and smashed teeth. Soon there is a quite terrific amount of blood, mixed with vomit, and it forms a warm delta between the exposed roots of the tallest pine.

IX

He woke up in a dark panic. Or didn't. Didn't wake *up* . . .
. . . woke *down*.

Dreams bunched and knotted behind his shuttered
eyes, and he couldn't open them. Couldn't move, couldn't
scream. *I'm paralysed*.

A whizzing, a flittering, snipping tearing.

As he awoke again, into the cold.

Lying on his back, the sky above him alive with dark
wings. Tried to hurl himself away, muscles wouldn't
respond. Locked. Everything inside him got behind a
scream, but his throat wouldn't process it. No lubrication.
All congealed inside, all the liquids in him had clotted and
dried when the blood stopped flowing.

Like a corpse. *Like a corpse*. Muscles rotted through.
Torn. Shredded bits of him pecked away, ripped away,
chewed away, blown away . . . and no eyes to see any of it.
Couldn't open his eyes because there weren't any eyes.
You couldn't open bone.

Whimpering. He heard whimpering, and it was his own.
Whimpering and the clatter of a morning trolley. A morning was happening somewhere out there, but he wasn't
part of it. He was out of it. He was two days dead.

He turned his head on the sweat-damp pillow and
opened his eyes. Third awakening. Always three; never
trust the first two.

God help me.

'Tea, Mr Maiden. Bobby?'

'Andy?'

He was fogged, muffled.

'No, it's Sister Andy's day off. I'll leave it on the side here. Then you can have another sleep, if you like, before breakfast.'

He sat up in panic.

The words *another sleep* terrified him.

No Sister Andy.

Who'd saved his life.

The African doctor, Jonathan, had told him. How they were all ready to give up and she'd stood there holding his head, demanding they keep going with the defibrillator. Jonathan describing it all so gleefully that Maiden was sure he could remember them coming in like the Drug Squad on a dawn raid.

All this down to Sister Andy. *Left to me, man*, Jonathan had said, with a frightening shrug, *they'd be putting you in the ground today*.

Recalling the words now with a sense of deep horror, he could clearly see himself from above, still and bluish, eyes closed against the earth coming down on him in spadefuls, the first particles of grit drumming on his screened eyeballs. Closing his mouth against it . . . but suddenly his eyes were opening into a brutal, hurting hail of soil and stones.

He could still taste the soil in the back of his throat; he drank all the tea and then two glasses of water from the carafe.

Lay back, breathing heavily, remembering what Andy had said about the patients who returned. The soft warmth and the gardens, the angelic voices, fountains. Well, yeah, you read all that stuff, saw people talking about it on TV, faces uplifted to the lights. All very comforting.

And all crap. It ended with the grave. That was the truth. Burial. In the earth. And death wielding the spade. You saw the face of death through fibres and roots and decaying matter and worms.

Still tasting it.

And, oh God, he needed to talk to Andy. You heard it said that saving someone's life created a bond, a mutual responsibility. Something was reaching out to this grim-faced Glaswegian nurse as if she was his long-lost mother. No, that wasn't exactly it. Close, though. Close.

Where was she? Jonathan might know but he wasn't here either. There was a different doctor in the unit, the tight-mouthed, officious kind, patrolling the beds like a rogue traffic warden, peering into the side ward and rasping over his clipboard, as though the guy lying there was deaf, mute and backward.

'Nurse, explain to me, would you . . . why is this patient still here?'

Nobody could explain it, and so, after breakfast, they pulled Bobby Maiden out of the sometimes-comforting chaos of Casualty and dumped him in Lower Severn Ward.

If the side ward in A and E was limbo, Lower Severn was authentic hell: continuous daytime TV – colours cranked up to lurid-plus – playing to two rows of probably nice enough guys with drips and tubes, one bloke pre-op and nervy, one post-op and demob-happy, one who read the *Sporting Life* and kept trying to persuade the nurses to place his bets, one who sat on the side of his bed and farted like a moped.

All these guys, Maiden saw them in cold, rubbery shades of grey, their faces squashed into stocking masks, a layer of dense depression banked over the beds like industrial smoke. Sunshine streamed through long windows, but the whole place was full of February, and there might never be a March.

According to the book, according to Andy, he should be feeling real joy, able to spread some comfort. Sitting up in bed and glowing with this kind of smug benevolence.

Having died, he ought to have been reborn. His spirit pulled out of his body and washed clean.

It felt soiled.

Soiled. Literally. All he experienced was a very tainted kind of relief every time he awoke. A temporary relief, because one day he'd have to die again, and death was a sour grave. There was an old man in a corner bed they kept pulling the curtains round – the *Sporting Life* reader shaking his head, saying, 'Can't be long now.' And Maiden wanting to leap out of bed and scream at the old man, *For Christ's sake, hold on to every last, fucking second . . .*

The rest of life was going to be tainted by the acrid taste of the grave.

Meanwhile, Riggs was coming.

Boss'll be in to see you.

Vaguely remembering, from when he first came round, someone leaning over the pillow with sanitized, spearmint breath.

Just give us a name. Somebody we can pull. A name, Bobby.

Don't remember anything. Remember going home, latish. Nothing after that. Sorry, Mike. Sorry.

Mike. Mike Beattie.

Maiden instinctively lying to Beattie – Riggs's man. Of course he remembered. Even in and out of consciousness, he remembered about black-eyed Suzanne and the pictures and the offer. And Parker and Riggs and the filigree of corruption stitched so tightly into the fabric of the town that undoing it would leave the fabric itself in shreds.

Parker and Riggs. Or was it, in fact, Riggs and Parker? Had Riggs simply sat back and thought about it and decided reliable old Tony was, on balance, the best man to handle drugs and other essential service industries in Elham? Was Riggs, in some way, the contractor?

Whatever, Maiden seemed to have been offered a ticket for the gravy train on a climb aboard or be found dead on the tracks basis.

Dead. Been there. Been into the big tunnel, come out the other side. Crawled out, sick and scared. What happens now, back down the slime-trails of downtown Elham?

After a while, Maiden let the whole mess – Lower Severn Ward, Suzanne, Parker, Riggs and the certainty of the grave – seep sluggishly out of his mind like dirty water down a drain, and went into his black, swampy sleep.

Awakening unable to move again. Convinced at first that he was on a trolley in the mortuary, his consciousness like a bird caged in his corpse and it would only be free when the electric saw took off his cranium.

Death again. He could only ever dream about aspects of death. Dead people, dead sheep. Violence. Brutality.

He actually sobbed with relief when the grey world babbled in.

'So you're a snooker man, Tom?' the TV said, some daytime quiz programme. 'And *how* many kids? Blimey, Sharon, he must keep his cue well chalked . . .'

Maiden jerked in the bed, wrapped the hard hospital pillow around his head.

'So you're awake, lad.' The voice coming down like an oak truncheon.

Maiden opened and closed and opened his eyes.

'Papers said you was in a bad way. Don't look that bad to me. Bloody sight better than I did, by God, the night I had Harry Skinner and his lads cornered in the old paint warehouse at Wilmslow. Heh. Tell you this much. They di'n't look so pretty neither, when I'd finished wi' 'em.'

'Hello, Dad,' Maiden said.

'Two trains it took, getting here. Had to change at Shrewsbury.'

Norman Plod, boots gleaming, fusewire hair Brylcreemed flat, stood in the centre of the ward, glaring up and down the lines of beds as if he was scouring a pub for under-age drinkers.

'Bugger of a place, Shrewsbury,' said the *Sporting Life* bloke.

'Had to get hisself transferred down here to get away from me,' Norman Plod said, dead accurate for once. 'Not fit to be let out, this lad. Heh. Can't be trusted to cross the bloody road without getting hisself flattened.'

As usual, it had taken Norman Plod less than a minute to collect an audience. Presence, he used to say. You have to have presence. Halfway to respect.

'Bet you didn't get his number either, did yer?'

'No, Dad,' Maiden said wearily. 'Busy dying. You know how it is.'

'Bloody detective, this,' Norman Plod told the ward. 'Bloody detective.'

He could have been a detective, could Norman. CID had been on their knees to him. But the public didn't have the same respect for detectives, slinking, nosing and drinking on duty. The public liked a policeman to *look* like a policeman. To have presence.

Maiden noted the absence of grapes, sweets, bottles of Lucozade. Not even a newspaper. His old man never saw the point of little gifts for the sick. Their duty to get well, back to work, stop the drip, drip, drip of taxpayers' money into their arms.

'Nice of you to come all this way, Dad.'

'I'm retired, lad. Garden's winding down for winter. Nowt else on the go. They got any leads, your clever colleagues? Poor bloody do, you ask me. Got to be a motor somewhere wi' a busted front end. Listen . . .'

Norman leaned in, just the way he'd always done, as if he was about to confide the Secret of Life.

'I don't know the background, don't know what villains you've put away lately, who's got a grudge. An' I don't want to. I'm retired. All I'm sayin', word to the wise . . .' Tapping his veiny nose. 'Just don't, whatever you do, don't let this one bloody well go. Don't ever write it off. Make sure the bugger gets nailed to the bloody wall. Eh? Know what I'm sayin'?'

Maiden said, before he could stop himself, 'You're thinking about Mum.'

'I'm thinkin' *nowt*!' Norman lurched back as if his only son had struck him. Amazing to see the old hostility in his eyes, the look that said, *You never got the car number then either, did you, lad?* Even though Bobby had been not yet three years old when he toddled off the kerb in his pyjamas, seven in the morning, pushing Bonzo, the dog on wheels.

He stared at his dad. Had Norman ever cried?

He'd told Maiden once, and once only, what must have happened that day while he was on the early shift and the road at the end of the garden was no more than a country lane – not much traffic, but no excuse for the paper lad or the milkman (although neither would put his hand up to it) to leave the gate open, so that the child could get out.

The inquest had decided the mother must have rushed into the road and pushed the kid out of the way. And the vehicle hit her instead, ran over her. Whoever it was never stopped. No other drivers in the area, until the farmer on his tractor who found the woman dead, the child sitting silent and white-faced in the road beside her, hugging a white dog on wheels.

His hands clenched under the bedclothes. Everything seemed interconnected. Two explosive moments in time, two hit-and-run incidents over thirty years apart, two deaths. *Runs in the family, getting knocked down.* As though the same impetus that took away his mother on the out-skirts of a scrappy village in Cheshire had carried on through time until another Maiden had crossed its path in Old Church Street.

He saw, blurred by sudden tears, the struggling colours of Norman Maiden pulsing through the stocking mask of February. Felt momentarily closer to the concrete-faced old cop than he could ever recall.

There'd been no pictures of his mum in the house; Norman got rid of them all. Nan, who looked after him until she died, would bring out a precious photo album when he was older. Maiden's mother had thin, brown hair around a pale, sweet face. Small and slender as a waif. Tiny bones, crushed under the wheels of . . . a van, it was speculated. She was ten years younger than Maiden was now.

They'd never caught the driver, which left only one person for Norman Plod to hang the blame on. Finally conveying, with his usual iron-bar subtlety, that joining the police was the least the lad could do for his mother. Too many other drivers out there ready to kill and speed away. Get 'em nailed.

The guilt factor. Bobby praying, at the age of eighteen, for something to get him out of this. Solitary kid, no good at team games. Down on his knees, *Please God, I don't want to be a copper. Don't want to be like him* . . .

Always the feeling that the old man also had some secret guilt. Something he had to make up to her but there was no chance now because the bloody kid ran out into the lane and got her killed.

'Dad, listen . . .' If any old mysteries were to be solved, if anything was going to be said, any healing process begun, it would have to be now.

'No, *you* listen, lad . . .'

The peace process was probably doomed, but it never got started anyway, because that was when Riggs walked in.

X

And it was wrong. It was so damn wrong. Everything was wrong.

Up early, her day off, Andy had hit the henna and when it was all done and dried off, damn if she didn't look totally ridiculous. Red hair was a statement; all she had was a string of questions.

She'd bought the stuff on her way home from work on that first morning . . . in the flush of the excitement over Bobby Maiden's diaphragm going gloriously up and down. It was a confirmation. Irrational though it seemed, the combination of a rising sun and an old lady's wisdom had brought out the healer in her.

Two miracles in her life now. She'd been just dying to ring Marcus Bacton.

Give it a couple of days, she'd decided in the end. Let the euphoria settle. *It cannae last, hen.* And it hadn't.

Something completely wrong. He'd come back sure enough. But did he act like he *wanted* to be back? Did he hell. He'd returned confused and unhappy and with a lingering fear of death which was outside Andy's experience. There should be a feeling of *triumph*. He'd been through it. The death experience. Been through it and out the other side with no more than a probably temporary brain-stem problem. He should, at the very least, be feeling vaguely relaxed about the idea of death.

So it has to be me. I blew it.

Maybe now was the time to call Marcus. Andy dragged

on her ancient housecoat, sat on a corner of her bed with the cordless.

The phone had that distant, rickety ring, what she thought of as a *rural* ring. It wasn't getting answered. Most likely, Mrs Willis was there on her own. She was going a wee bit deaf and didn't like to answer the phone even if she was aware of it ringing.

The snarl came as she about to hang up. 'Yes!'

'Marcus!' Andy coming on cheerful. 'Andy Anderson. How are you both today?'

'Bloody hell, woman, I'm trying to make an omelette! Soon as I break an egg into the bowl, some bastard rings.'

'Call back later, shall I? About two?'

'No . . . damn it, don't do that. No. Please. I'm sorry. Stay where you are. I was going to ring you anyway.'

'Is Mrs Willis no too well?' Marcus was no cook.

'Ah . . . not terribly.'

Andy said cautiously, 'What's wrong?'

'Oh. Spot of blood pressure. She has a day in bed now and then, quaffs a few potions. Oh Christ . . .' Lowering his voice to not much more than a hiss. 'I don't *know* what's fucking wrong. Well, I do.'

'Jesus God, Marcus.'

'Damnation! Hold on a minute, Anderson.'

Sounds of clanking pans, oaths. A sixty-year-old man fending, reluctantly, for himself. A force of nature, Marcus Bacton.

Nature was a real presence around the village of St Mary's. You were always aware of its closeness. And of the miraculous.

Lying awake after the Bobby-miracle, she'd relived the other one.

Feeling again the absolute rock-bottom weakness, the alarming weight loss, the cramps, the red lumps on her legs, the hair falling out and the endless, *endless* journeys to the lavatory to release more blood and mucus into the bowl. Four barium enemas in as many months and three different drugs. Stress, they said, as she herself had said to dozens of other colitis sufferers. The stress of the job and the finding out about Mick's fancy woman.

Then the drugs weren't working any more and X-rays showed her gut was in one hell of a mess.

Which was when this schoolmistressy lady had been brought into the General after falling from her bike. Andy, dealing less efficiently than usual with the sprained ankle, provoking the comment, 'You look as though you could do with a long rest, my dear.'

Before they wheeled the lady away, she'd pressed an address into Andy's hand, a holiday cottage in the Welsh Marches. 'Not terribly luxurious, but wonderfully peaceful.'

Except for Marcus Bacton rampaging around the place. But he was just one of the many forces of nature at work in the village of St Mary's.

When she arrived she was getting to the stage of hating her own body. Scared to go out, in case she disgraced herself. Finding herself explaining all this to the housekeeper, Mrs Willis, who'd knocked tentatively at the cottage door this particular afternoon. Everything coming out, all the self-pity. Mrs Willis just listening, never once mentioning alternative therapies, as if she knew instinctively how a nursing sister was going to react to *that* old rubbish.

But would Mrs Anderson perhaps like to come for a walk with her and Marcus one morning? Well, Mrs Willis, that would be nice, but I have this wee problem about leaving the vicinity of a working lavatory before eleven. What time were you thinking?

Five a.m.? *Five?* Jesus God, are you *mad?*

Mrs Willis was the kind that just nods and smiles but you know you've ruined her day. So that night Andy just didn't go to bed. Stayed up all night, drinking coffee, chain-smoking, going to the lavvy. Some days you could just live in the lavvy, head in your hands, a human sewer.

By four a.m. she was half delirious, aching all over. They were waiting outside. It was painful to pull on her coat and scarf. Outside, it was still dark. Marcus said, Don't bloody well blame me, Mrs Anderson. Whatever the old girl says, I don't question it these days.

They clambered over stiles, Marcus leading with his torch. On the edge of a big field, Andy was stricken with a leg cramp and fell down, rolling on the grass in her agony. Mrs Willis massaging the leg until the lump went down and then Marcus picking her up. Good God, woman, you're like a bundle of bloody twigs. And it occurred to Andy that there wasn't much weight left to go; she was a living husk, the disease finally draining the life out of her, and she couldn't even cry about it, on account of the parched body wouldn't produce tears any more.

Just before she passed out in Marcus's arms, she heard Mrs Willis saying, in a matter-of-fact kind of way, *Inside, Marcus. God knows, she's thin enough. Put her inside the tomb.*

'Falconer!' Marcus roared in her ear.

'What?'

'Fucking *Falconer*!'

Just one aspect that was *not* so peaceful, the old lady had said. But there was no harm in him.

'Know what the bastard's done? Four-strand barbed wire fence. Five feet high, no stiles! Fucking *cunt*.'

The degeneration of Marcus's language had roughly kept pace with the deterioration of Mrs Willis's hearing.

'I don't understand. What fence?'

'Around the *Knoll*!'

'He allowed to do that?'

'He owns it. He's bought the fucking Knoll!'

'Marcus, you're kid—'

'He wants his own little burial chamber like other people want a garden gnome. He's going to do lots of *filming* up there, for his bloody programme. His assistants will be doing their scientific *experiments*. They'll be *dowsing* it and *dreaming* on it . . . Oh, and it's closed to the public between – are you ready for this – between six p.m. and nine a.m.'

'You mean nobody can go there at sunrise? Jesus God, Marcus. What about Mrs . . . Oh no.'

'You wouldn't recognize her. She won't see a doctor, of course. But what would a doctor do? Give her blood-pressure pills?'

'How old is she?'

'That, Anderson, is one of the Big Mysteries.'

'Must be over eighty.'

'I was going to take her to the Knoll this morning. I was sure . . . Bloody hell, Andy, I *love* that place. I *believe* in it. I don't give a *shit* what anybody— Did I tell you about the lunatic American woman?'

Andy said, absently, 'Lunatic what?' She was thinking about Mrs Willis. *If I could bring down the sun for Bobby, why couldn't* . . .

'American woman,' Marcus said. 'This American woman rang me about half an hour ago. One of these who talks so fast you're lucky if you can answer one question in three. Trying to find her sister, last heard of working at Falconer's place. I met the girl, actually. Wanted to know about the Knoll. Told her about Annie.'

'Oh, aye?' *If I can bring the High Knoll sunrise to Elham General, why can't Mrs Willis fetch it to the bottom of the hill?*

'And, of course, she was involved in Falconer's stupid dream survey and so she wanted to sleep at the Knoll, and I said, you know, best of luck but don't expect a holy miracle. Now the girl's written to her sister describing this horrific nightmare and . . . Oh, I don't want to talk about it. I've had a bellyful today. She told me she saw a black light over the Knoll.'

'Americans are impressionable people, Marcus.'

'No . . . Mrs Willis!'

'A *what*?'

'A black light. Over the Knoll.'

Andy shivered, clutching the housecoat to her throat.

'I don't know what to do,' Marcus said. 'I'm at my wits' end.'

'OK, look. I'm coming down.'

'You?'

'I owe her everything, Marcus. I'll talk to the hospital. I'll get time off. I'll be there tonight, all right?'

'That's bloody good of you, Anderson.'

'Jesus God, it's the least— A *black light*?'

'I don't know what she meant either,' Marcus said. 'But it does have an ominous ring of death to it, doesn't it?'

XI

Riggs, the boss man, turned slowly and looked into space for a moment before inclining his head. He smiled with all the warmth of a polecat greeting a rabbit.

'This is my dad, sir,' Maiden said. 'Norman.'

Riggs had a thinner man's face. An oddly sensitive face with fine translucent skin; you could see tiny veins underneath, like the filaments in a light bulb. There was something extraterrestrial about Riggs; you always thought he could read your thoughts, and this struck you anew every time you saw him.

'Honoured to meet you, sir.' Norman hung around, like someone waiting to be called into the witness box. 'Reading about you the other week. Now what did I read?' He pretended to think for a second or two. 'Jarvis. You nailed Terry Jarvis. I nicked his dad, must've been four times. John Karl Jarvis. GBH mostly. Aggravated burglary, once. By, that were a hard bugger . . .'

'Family trait, Mr Maiden. Sit down. I'll fetch another chair.'

'I'll get it, sir,' Norman said, and he did.

Riggs sat. His narrow, bony face smiling at Norman with its full, genial mouth while its eyes remained cool, occasionally seeking out Norman's boy.

Who stayed glazed, focused on nothing, smiling inanely from his bed. Playing damaged. Brain in dry dock. Attention-span of a goldfish.

'You're looking a bit blurred, Bobby,' Riggs said. 'You were lucky.'

'So they tell me, sir.'

'Oh, before I forget . . . Roger Gibbs, managing editor of the *Messenger* group, was asking me about a picture of you, recovering as it were. Perhaps the two of us together. I wasn't too happy. Co-operate with the local press whenever you can, always been my motto as you know. But in this case, a wounded hero picture . . .' Riggs shrugged. 'Well . . . up to you, Bobby.'

It was also, when you were in his presence, impossible to believe Riggs was bent. He always looked fully at you; he was always calm. One day soon, Riggs would be promoted and leave Elham. Within three years, he'd be an ACC, maybe even a chief constable, living a chief constable's lifestyle and all of it paid for. A cottage here, a villa there and Tony Parker safely retired.

Face to face with Riggs, you knew he was never going to be nailed. He was direct, ruthless, efficient, had important friends; but he was also, oddly, a copper's copper. Got results but never pinched the credit; the lads liked working for him. Nobody Maiden knew would have wanted Riggs to go down.

'I was suggesting, sir,' Norman said, 'that he should make a list of all the toerags who had it in for him.'

'Oh.' Riggs lifted an eyebrow. 'You think it was like that, do you, Mr Maiden?'

'Copper gets knocked over, it's not usually a drink-driver, sir.'

'Not a drink-driver.' Riggs pinched his nose. 'What do you think about that, Bobby?'

'I wouldn't know, boss. Would I?'

'Obviously not. You don't remember anything, Mike Beattie tells me. Unless something's come through.'

'No. Not a thing.'

'How long before you're out?'

'Few days.'

'Some nerve damage, they're saying. You may be walking around in a bit of a fog for a while.'

'Should sort itself out, boss.'

'Have to see, won't we, Bobby?'

Norman looked at his watch. Maiden flashed him an imploring glance. *Shit, Dad, don't walk out on me. Whatever this bastard's really come to say, I don't want to hear it.*

'By heck,' Norman said. 'It's nearly five o'clock. Be missing me train.'

Surprisingly, Riggs stood up. 'Yes, I have an appointment, too. Speaking engagement.' He made a wry face. 'Magistrates' Association annual dinner. Just wanted to make sure the lad was all right before I went home. Can I give you a lift, Mr Maiden?'

'Very kind of you, sir, but I like to walk.' Patting his stomach. 'Don't let retirement get the better of me.'

'That's the spirit. Well, I'll see you again, Bobby.'

'Thanks for looking in,' said Maiden.

Watching the two of them, strolling companionably down the ward, smiling at other patients. The visit over almost before it had started.

What's he going to do to me?

Coincidence.

Riggs and Maiden had arrived in Elham the very same week, Maiden direct from the Met, Riggs after four months in Kent, taking over from a DCI who was facing allegations of corruption. (Yes, he was *that* hard-faced.) Never thought they'd see each other again after the Met, but here they were.

Suspicions.

Once, when Riggs was a DI, he'd sought DS Maiden's co-operation in fitting up this troublesome Animal Rights woman for an amateur parcel-bomb at a butcher's shop in Fulham. Naturally, if the fit-up had gone ahead, it would have been entirely down to Maiden – Riggs merely turning a blind eye; this was how it worked.

Or – to be honest – how Maiden *presumed* it still worked. He'd never stopped watching Riggs, and he hadn't got a thing that was rock-solid. Just the names of four small-timers fitted up by Parker's crew, nicked by Riggs. Three of them figured it was safer to let it go, do their eighteen months, flit to some safer town on release. The other was Dean Clutton who'd topped himself on remand.

'*You stupid little twat!*'

Maiden lurched; his eyes sprang open.

Norman Plod's familiar, leathery breath on his face. Norman Plod hissing in his ear.

'Dad? What about your train?'

'*Fuck* the train.'

Maiden struggled to sit up, but Norman was leaning over him as if he'd just brought him down after a chase.

'No bloody wonder you don't remember owt.' Voice loaded with contempt.

'What did he say to you, Dad?'

'Drink-driver. Drunk *driver*? Put me bloody size nines in it that time, didn't I? Heh. Drunk bloody pedestrian, more like.'

'Oh shit,' Maiden said.

'A good man, is Mr Riggs. A damn good senior officer. Better than *you* deserve. Telling me on the quiet. Copper to copper. Save me any more embarrassment.'

'All right,' Maiden said, 'I'd had a few drinks.'

'*A few drinks*. You bloody little toerag. Five Scotches and four pints. You were lucky you could bloody stand up.'

'That's not quite true, Dad. No beers.'

Norman looked down on him, breathing through his teeth. 'You were in a club called the Saint Moritz, that right?'

Maiden said nothing.

'Where you picked up a brass.'

'*Not* quite right.'

'And where you drank five Scotches and four pints. The barman remembers every one, lad, because he recognized you. Then you and the brass left, wi' your hand up her jumper.'

'No.'

'You got in a minicab and you went to your flat. About an hour later, a witness saw you come out chasing t'brass. What were up, lad? Wouldn't she take a credit card? By Christ, I always knew you weren't up to much. I were bloody amazed when you made DI. Bloody *amazed*.'

'Dad—'

'I thought you'd maybe sorted yourself out at one time. When you married Elizabeth. Bonny lass. Woman wi' a bit of go in her. Could you keep her? Could you buggery. You're a dead loss, lad. A bloody dead loss.'

Norman took his weight off Maiden's chest. Moved away, brushing at his jacket in case bits of his son had come off on him.

At the foot of the bed, he looked over his shoulder, *Sporting Life* and the farter both watching keenly.

'You left your front door open, son,' Norman said with a visible sneer. 'But it's all right. Nobody wanted to nick your pictures.'

The storeroom was full of boxes of paper towels and toilet rolls, cartons of soap, bleach, industrial cleaning fluids. All the non-human hospital smells began here.

Maiden stayed behind the door as someone went past with a trolley. He was sweating. His left side had shut down. The blue-white light from the fluorescent tube was squeezing his head like an accordion.

Sister Andy had told him, *You won't be walking a straight line for a wee while*.

Take it slowly. This was the furthest he'd been; taken himself to the lavatory and that was it. He looked down at his trousers. No bloodstains, anyway. Somebody had given the suit a brush. There was a hole in his grey jacket below the breast pocket. It would do.

Normal thing would have been for the suit to go to

forensic; always a small possibility of paint traces. Somebody obviously wasn't trying very hard to find the car that ran him down.

He still needed a sweater or a shirt. The crash team had obviously torn his off in a hurry to get at his chest. Maybe he could find some kind of surgeon's smock in here.

He had no watch. He opened the door a crack to look up at the clock at the end of the corridor. Five-thirty. Teatime. They'd be missing him soon. Checking out the toilets and the day rooms. Could have tried to sign himself out, but that would have led to arguments, drawn too much attention. Especially with the state he'd been in . . .

. . . when, not five minutes after Norman's final exit, there'd been this sudden activity down the ward and the screens went up again round the old man's bed, and there were murmurs, the ward darkening, the air clotting with death, a purple-grey cloud almost visible over that bed. Maiden's stomach had gone cold with dread. He had to get out of here. Out of the hospital, out of the town, out of the grey, out of the cold. The need stifling him.

. . . *take a breath before you jump in* . . .

No. He'd found his suit in the locker, rolled it up into a ball around his shoes. Made his exit before they removed the body.

He found the T-shirts wrapped in Cellophane in a box marked *Liquid Soap*.

The T-shirts were white, all one size. He held one up. Across the chest, it said, ELHAM GENERAL HOSPITAL LEAGUE OF FRIENDS FUN RUN 1997.

Maiden put one on, his jacket over the top. Switched off the light and relished the darkness, until he realized he was going to sleep, even though he'd spent most of the bloody day asleep.

All you have to do, Bobby, is rest, rest and rest.

Wondering if he could ever really rest again.

Anybody to look after you at home? Girlfriend? Mother?

Liz would have known how to look after him. Would've known all about the care of head injuries. But he knew that if he'd still been with Liz she'd have sent him straight back to the hospital in a taxi. Then told Riggs. Liz liked there to be a framework, structure, hierarchy, organization, rules, discipline . . .

He clutched his head, suffocating. No wonder Norman liked her.

When the lift let him out in the reception area, his legs felt weak. The place was full of visitors and cleaners and auxiliaries. There was a small shop selling tea and coffee and snacks, a few tables and chairs, and he sat down for a moment, eyes going at once to a framed print on the cream wall opposite.

He knew the painting. Turner. *Staffa: Fingal's Cave*. Skeletal ship in an angry, glowering maelstrom of sea and sky and rocks. Small, struggling sun. There was a sudden heaviness in his chest, a memory rolling around in there like an iron ball. It meant something, this picture. It had the essence of something. He felt its violence.

The picture was groaning with half-spent violence and the threat of more to come.

More to come. Maiden felt sick, as though he was on that ship among the black elements.

Couldn't look at it any more. Stood up. Didn't hang around, didn't look to either side until he was in the hospital car park, on the hillside overlooking the town and the dying sun.

XII

'*Shit!*'

Slamming the flat of his hand into his head.

An elderly man steered his wife away from the bus stop, throwing Maiden a glare of disgust. Bloody drunks, he'd be thinking. Bloody drunks on the street before seven o'clock, that's what you get with all-day opening.

Maiden rocked on the kerb, hands pushing at his eyes. So he was making an exhibition of himself. So what?

He'd only left his wallet in the hospital safe.

So no money. Not even a few coins for a cup of tea with three sugars – he needed the sugar, he felt as though his brain was floating out of his skull like a balloon on a string.

Made himself take three deep breaths. *Think.*

OK. It wasn't as if he was breaking gaol. It was only a hospital. He could go back and demand his wallet from the safe.

Except they'd probably know he was missing by now and, as he was a policeman, who would they tell?

Not worth the risk. He wanted to be well away before Riggs found out. Not that even Riggs could stop him; it wasn't a police hospital. And, as he was hardly fit for work, he could do what he liked, go where he wanted.

Anybody to look after you at home? Girlfriend? Mother?

Girlfriend, no. Mother, no. *Home.* Get back to the flat. Must be some money there, a spare chequebook. Pack a suitcase, take a bus out of town – don't even try to drive the car – find a hotel, sleep, sleep, sleep. Then consider stage two.

He wanted to *worry* Riggs, if that was possible. Make him lose some sleep about where Maiden might be, who he might be talking to. Worried people made mistakes. One day, Riggs would *have* to make a mistake; you could only hope somebody would be there to pick up on it.

Maiden started to walk, avoiding the town centre, slinking into the back streets like a vagrant, walking slowly, trying not to sway. Passing people were glancing sideways at him, as at some kind of downmarket street-theatre performer. The sneering sun hung like a cheap, copper medallion. He felt naked. He tried to run, but the pavement came up at him before he even realized he'd stumbled. Slow down; it was no more than half a mile to Old Church Street, he could manage that.

Oh no. Please, no. *Fuck.*

Now he was kicking a lamp-post. Again and again and again. *Fuck, fuck, fuck!*

Because his pockets were empty: not only no wallet, *but no bastard keys.*

He was supposed to break into his own flat?

Shit! Shit! Shit! Where had his mind *gone*? Not thinking like a copper any more. Not even like a human being. And he'd actually believed he was *putting it on*, for Riggs. Shit, he was half vegetable. Couldn't work out really, really simple things. He looked wildly around him. No money, no keys. Nowhere to go, now. Nowhere to go. Nowhere to sleep.

The street swayed. His left leg had gone dead. He wanted to smash his head into the lamp-post. Again and again and again. His useless, damaged head.

He gave the post a final kick. Its light began to flicker on; he backed away in alarm. Then saw that lights were coming on all down the street.

Because it was dusk.

He started to laugh, pushing away the memory of a woman under a sputtering lamp in Old Church Street only seconds before . . . and walked on towards a row of mostly darkened shops, resting his right shoulder against the windows as he passed from doorway to doorway. Only one shop was lit. Or, half lit, drably, around a window-display.

H. W. Worthy: monumental mason.

Mottled, grey, marble gravestone, with a glistening black flowerpot, empty, and a dark green, tangly wreath. No bright, beckoning lights, no flowers, no fountains. Worthy had it right. The dark and true nature of death.

Bobby Maiden rested his forehead against the cool of the plate-glass window, staring death in the face.

And the face of death stared back, from the drab wreath. The dark leaves framed it, a face made of compost and fibre, broken twigs clenched in its earth-blackened teeth, its deep-set eyes darkly glowing, its hair and beard writhing with voracious organic life.

The face of death grinned at Maiden; his stomach pulsed, an acrid bile rose into his throat. He was only vaguely aware of a grey car gliding to the kerb, the passenger door swinging open before it slid to a stop.

'You look lost, Bobby,' Suzanne said.

'We have a problem,' Jonathan said on the phone to Andy. 'Your friend has checked out of Lower Severn without leaving a forwarding address.'

'Bobby Maiden? What's he doing on Lower Severn?'

'Dr Connelly had him moved. Couldn't see why he was still in Accident and Emergency. Now he's gone.'

'Brian Connelly wouldnae see his own— He's *gone*?'

'Taken his clothes and left.'

'You mean you let him just *walk oot*?'

'It was before I came in, Sister Andy. He had visitors, apparently. His father and the Superintendent. Nobody liked to disturb them. Then they had a death on the ward and tea was delayed, and when they brought Mr Maiden's, he was gone. And his clothes from the locker. The man in the next bed says he simply got up and strolled out.'

'Staggered, more like. You checked around the building?'

'Virtually everywhere except the ventilation tunnels. We assume he became disoriented. Wandered off. Sister Fox has informed the police. I thought you'd want to know.'

'Taken his clothes? Aw hell. The boy's no fit to be out.'

'That's what I thought.'

'Like I havenae enough problems,' Andy said.

The half-packed suitcase lay on the bed. If she didn't leave soon she wouldn't make St Mary's before Mrs Willis was asleep.

'Just let me know, OK?'

She sat in the back with him. Thigh to thigh. Just like before.

'This is nice, Inspector.' She was luminous in the dimness of the car. Wearing an orangey sweatsuit, her hair down. A lot was different about her. 'This is *really* nice. In fact, when we spotted you I really couldn't believe it. We thought you'd be in hospital for a long, long time.'

He said nothing. Same driver too. Victor Clutton, father of the late Dean. No mistaking him this time.

The old Sierra rattling off into the twilit town centre. Suzanne gazing at him, looking genuinely, spontaneously happy. A glow about her that shone through the ubiquitous grey, kindling something half forgotten in the late Bobby Maiden.

Don't get fooled again.

'This the very same car, isn't it? Bit of a risk.'

'Not a dent on it, Bobby. You went whizzing over the bonnet, banged your head on the kerb. Jesus, I really can't believe this. In the papers, it was touch and go. Touch and gone, in fact. Inspector Lazarus, you might say. Pretty scary all round, Bobby. Especially as Vic was trying so hard to avoid you. As it was, in fact, all your own fault.'

'That's the story you've agreed, is it?'

'That's the truth.'

'Just like Tony's your uncle?'

'Well, yeah, that *was* a lie. I also know a Van Gogh from an Atkinson Grimshaw. *And* a Wordsworth from a Larkin. I was just having fun, Bobby. You know that. Hey, I'm not kidding.'

Suzanne crooked her head to peer directly into his eyes.

'Whether you remember or not, it was a genuine bloody accident. We just couldn't believe you didn't get out of the way.'

Vic Clutton said, 'Ask him why he was walking down the middle of the road, sorter thing. Ask him what he thought I was supposed to fucking do.'

'You did look awfully strange, Bobby. Like you'd been dropped out of a UFO.'

'I was walking towards *you*. You were under a streetlamp. You were waiting.'

'I was in the car, Bobby. I went straight back to the car. Vic'd been parked round the corner the whole time, hadn't you?'

'You were under the bloody—' The faulty streetlamp, coming on, going off, lighting the figure of the woman. Had he imagined her?

'Waste of bleedin' breath.' Clutton hit the accelerator to overshoot the junction with Old Church Street. 'Like I said. He'll either finger us or he won't.'

Suzanne said, 'Just do the driving, Vic.'

'He thinks we fitted up his son, isn't that right, Mr Clutton?'

'Don't be naive, Bobby. Vic knows Dean was dealing, freelance. He was a very silly boy, was Dean, God rest his poor, corrupt little soul. Had to prove he was smarter than his old man, didn't he, Vic?'

Vic said nothing, drove down towards the suburbs, the sun low over a horizon spiked with pylons.

'They were never close,' Suzanne said. 'But we won't open that particular can of worms.'

'OK.' Maiden leaned his head back until it was almost

on the parcel shelf. 'If it was an accident, why, not long before this . . . accident happened, did you advise me to go back in the flat and lock the door?'

Suzanne was silent for a long time.

'Oh yeah?' Vic said, suspicious. 'That's what you said to him, was it?'

'Look, there's a kids' playing field back there,' Suzanne said. 'I fancy a bit of a swing. You up to pushing me, Bobby?'

The playground was deserted in the dusk. Maiden wedged himself into a metal roundabout; Suzanne sat on the lip of a rusting slide. Maiden felt calmer than he could remember.

'What gets me, Bobby, is not so much why a halfway decent artist like you became a copper, as how you got so good at it. Putting two and two together and making seventeen.'

'I was pissed. Out of interest, though . . . purely out of interest . . . was seventeen the right answer?'

'You know it bloody was.'

Vic Clutton was leaning on his Sierra, parked fifty yards away. He was having a smoke, feigning unconcern.

'Look, I'm not saying Tony's a *good* man,' Suzanne said. 'He's a businessman. In the free market. First and foremost, a businessman is what he is. He can be, like, awkward, if anybody threatens his regular income, but he's never – and he wouldn't lie about this, not to me – he's never done anything *terminal*.'

'Terminal.' Maiden sighed. 'You're really into this vintage gangland vernacular, aren't you, Suzanne?'

'Look, Inspector, no bullshit . . . it would've upset him quite a bit if somebody'd suggested to him that the only way of removing a particular obstacle was that he might actually do something, like . . . I mean, cold . . .'

'You mean a wet job in cold blood.'

'Don't laugh. I didn't.'

Something close to anxiety in Suzanne's eyes. The eyes were dark but no longer black. She looked a little older, but softer. Her voice had softened too, the brittle edges planed off.

'Are you saying somebody *did* suggest something like that to Tony?'

She shrugged.

'I wonder who that could have been.'

'I haven't the faintest idea.' Suzanne looked him frankly in the eyes. 'But you could probably expect it to be somebody who might not find it so convenient to do it himself.'

'Or compatible with his chosen profession?'

Maiden thought about this for a while in his new state of calm. The double-glazing again; everything far below him, an insect world. Superintendent Martin Riggs had invited Tony Parker to help him decommission Bobby Maiden?

'So . . .' Closing his eyes to trap the thoughts. '. . . what I think you might be saying is that Tony thought . . . or was persuaded to think . . . before he went along with the suggestion of this *other person* . . . that he ought to have one attempt at dealing with the problem in an equally time-honoured but less drastic fashion. Based on Tony's usual philosophy of everybody having his price.'

'I wouldn't know about any of that.'

'Of course you wouldn't.'

'But someone else might've been strongly disapproving if he'd had it done. I mean the other thing.'

'Who?'

'Me, for a start.'

Suzanne stood up, smacking grass-cuttings from her trousers, as if she was brushing off extraneous lies.

'Stuff this.' Facing him, hands behind her back. 'If you hadn't worked it out. Emma Curtis. Née Parker.'

Maiden grabbed the bars of the roundabout, almost losing his balance.

'Oh,' he said.

Tony Parker was known to have a grown-up kid Elham had never seen. A kid raised at the house he'd given his former wife in the nice part of Essex, where a daughter might attend a good school, learn languages, have riding lessons, grow up respectable.

'Bugger me,' Maiden said.

Of course, she'd have loved it: doing herself up like a faintly sinister tart: white make-up, little black number to spill out of when she reached for her drink.

He grinned. Surely the first time since his previous life. 'Was that your idea? The pictures?'

'Not bad, I thought, Bobby, for a spur of the moment thing. I was quite proud of it. For a while. But then . . .'

Then, when it started to go badly wrong, the reality of her old man's world thrown in her face like a bucketful of ice.

After which, she might have been expected to wash off the white-face in a hurry, go running back to Essex to hide under the bedclothes, avoid reading the papers for a while.

Only she hadn't. A few coloured sparks started crackling across the drabness, the rippling electricity of sex.

'Tell me,' he said. 'What made Riggs decide drastic action was called for?'

'Oh,' she said. 'Well . . .' She lay back in the arms of the playground slide, looked up at the darkening sky. 'All right, what the hell? A guy called Percy Gilbert – I don't know these people, I don't spend much time up here – this guy's a police informer, right? They all know that, but it's tolerated because it works both ways, in his case, and these days he only grasses up the people they want grassed up.'

'The little turd,' Maiden said.

'So this Gilbert knows you've been asking questions about Tony. But it was the *Messenger* that did it.'

'The local rag?'

'You had a brief thing going, word has it – Percy's word, anyway – with a certain Siobhan Gallagher, journalist with the *Messenger*.'

'Oh no,' Maiden said weakly.

'Whose boss – Roger Gibbs, Gibson . . . ?'

'Gibbs.'

'. . . was informed by Laurie Argyle, the estate agent, who's a member of his lodge, something like that, that this Gallagher's been making inquiries about the unnamed names behind the Feeny Park development.'

Maiden moaned.

'Not getting anywhere, because the Riggs connection's buried much deeper. But it caused some anxiety. Not very bright, Bobby, if you don't mind me saying so, letting your pillow talk stray into areas this dangerous. Mr Gibbs gave Ms Gallagher a very serious talking to and she buggered off back to Belfast anyway. But this is when – I understand – your Mr Riggs suggested it might be better all round, knowing you as he did, if Pa were to have you popped before you did any damage.'

'You *understand*?'

'This isn't something I would normally ever learn about in a million years, because, as far as the little girl is concerned, her daddy is a *bona fide businessman*, a straight-down-the-line *plain dealer*. But I was up for the weekend and he was drinking like the proverbial. Worried? I've never *seen* him so worried. It's not his thing, really it isn't. The reason he moved up here in the first place was he was winding down. "It's nothing but drugs," he kept saying. "Drugs are taking over. It's all hard kids now. I'm too old." '

'Somebody send for a violinist,' Maiden said.

She scowled, sat up in the slide. 'I'll deny all this, of course.'

'Of course.'

'I said, Have you never tried . . . you know? "Nah," he says, "the geezer don't do the circuit. Stays at home on his days off, apparently, painting pictures, you believe that?" Well, I thought you sounded interesting. I said, I want to meet him. Then I get all this "you're staying out of it,

141

princess, and that's final" stuff. But I could always get round him.'

'You surprise me.'

'Honest to God, Bobby . . .' Emma Curtis stood up. 'I know when I've blown it. I was ready to go crawling back shamefaced that night. Then you just walked into us. Like you couldn't give a toss. What the fuck came over you?'

'I don't know.'

'I made Vic stop. I sent him to phone for an ambulance. I ran back. I thought you were dead. I didn't know what to do. Vic came back. He'd parked down near the main road. When we heard the ambulance, he dragged me away. I'm sorry. I couldn't be more sorry.'

He saw tears in her eyes. He believed her. She went to sit on a swing, kicked at the ground to get it moving.

'What happens now, then, guv? They call you guv up here? I'm only *au fait* with the London vernacular, as you know.' She found a shallow smile. 'Life gets complicated, don't it?'

'Ain't got nothing on death.'

'Really?'

'Never mind.'

The other side of the playground, Vic Clutton coughed impatiently, stamping on his cigarette end, sparks flying up.

'He your regular chauffeur?'

'Pa thinks I need a good, strong minder.'

'You don't live with Tony, then?'

'I'm in one of his single-person's apartments for the moment. In the, er, Feeny Park development. It's quite nice, actually. For Elham.'

'Has it got a bed?'

She stopped swinging. Her eyes widened, but not very much.

'Bobby, pardon me for saying this, and I don't wish to sound unflattered or anything, but quite frankly, at this moment, you don't look like you could screw the cap off a bottle of Ribena.'

'I meant a spare bed, actually. I've got a problem. Just for tonight?'

She bit down on a smile.

XIII

Vic Clutton drove them back towards the town centre. It was dark. Maiden hadn't thought about death for nearly ten minutes. It was a start.

'Your poor eye.' She stroked his hair back, put her fingers on his forehead. 'State of the health service. A few years ago, they wouldn't have discharged you like this.'

'Where's *Mr* Curtis?' He leaned his head back on the parcel shelf, closed his eyes under her hand.

'Everybody's allowed one mistake.'

'Only one?'

'Mr Curtis was a commodities broker.'

'And you got tired of being a commodity.'

'He liked to handle a *variety* of commodities.'

'What a loser,' Maiden said.

'Thank you.'

They turned into Old Church Street and then left into Telford Avenue.

'Here?' Vic Clutton said. It was Suz— Emma's idea that Vic should assist Maiden to gain access to his flat to pack some clothes, spare chequebook, whatever.

'Fine.' Maiden didn't want to move. Possibly ever.

'Let's not hang about.' Vic slid the Sierra into the kerb. 'Em, you keep a serious eye open. Any problems, honk twice, all right? Little short ones, bip, bip. Not just a police car, *any* car.'

'Especially any car,' Maiden said. 'Especially if it's a biggish Rover.'

'Whatever he says,' Vic said. 'Shake yourself, Mr Maiden, let's get this sorted.'

From the glove compartment, Vic took gloves. Soft leather motoring gloves which he put on. Plus a small tool kit in a canvas pouch. Plus a little torch.

'When we get in we *don't* put lights on, all right, Mr Maiden? And don't take too much out. One suitcase. Otherwise it looks like a bleeding robbery.'

Maiden got out, noticed Emma doing a little smirk. 'Nothing criminal, Bobby. It's just like hiring a lock-smith.'

Maiden still felt about five feet from his brain.

'Bump on the head's a funny thing,' Vic said conversationally, not whispering, as they let themselves into the yard behind the flat. 'You read about people, their whole personality changes, sorter thing. Previous to this, I've never seen it at first hand.'

'You don't know what I was like before.'

'I know you were a copper. This ain't the way a copper does it, he loses his keys.'

'Wasn't my idea.'

'No. Full of ideas, little Em. Well.' Vic lowered his voice. 'Seems like you're in trouble, Mr Maiden. Somebody wants your balls on a saucer. Where you gonna go? I mean after tomorrow.'

'Somewhere at least fifty miles away. Maybe more.'

Vic shut the yard gate behind them, screwed the latch back. It was very dark in the yard. There was one light above them on the third and top floor. Curtains drawn. Vic stood with his back to the gate.

'Look, Mr Maiden. Something I want to get out the way, sorter thing.' Lowering his voice considerably. 'The boy. It was me planted the stuff on the boy.'

'Dean?'

'He was dealing, he was using . . . He wouldn't listen. I put the stuff in his motorbike. Smack. A lot. Enough to get him off the streets. I give him to Beattie. For Riggs. Only regret it wasn't soon enough. As it turned out.'

'I'm sorry,' Maiden said. 'How it turned out . . .'

'Yeah, well, remand centres are bad places. They can get you that way. If you're already jittery. I just didn't see no alternative at the time. Could've worked for Tony, he didn't wanna know. Wouldn't listen to me. Big man, you know?'

'As I recall,' Maiden said, 'three other mavericks got lifted not long after Dean. Cowan . . . Sharpe . . . Tommy Singh?'

Vic looked momentarily uncomfortable.

'All *very* surprised to find they had a few ounces around the house, in their cars, wherever. No surprise to Parker, though. No surprise to Riggs.'

'If you had any proof, Mr Maiden, we wouldn't be discussing it.'

'And not a protest from any of them. Especially not after what happened to Dean.'

'Now look. Don't think I never considered it. Don't think the issue was never raised with Tony.'

'And Tony said?'

'Tony said it was bollocks.'

'Maybe Tony doesn't know. Wouldn't be the first time somebody on remand got an assisted passage. Screws don't earn a fortune.'

'You're suggesting Riggs had him waxed?'

'I'm suggesting nothing, Vic.'

'All right, I don't *like* Riggs. Too clever. Cut above. Important friends. One day he'll dump Tony in the shit, walk away clean as a whistle like one of them bent Tory MPs. Yeah, like I said, I thought about it, but in the end I'm not buying.'

'So you wouldn't consider giving evidence.'

'Oh, Mr Maiden, ever the humorist.' Clutton walked up a couple of steps to the back door. 'Right then. Good job you're ground floor. Mortice, I take it.'

'Three lever.'

'Not very clever, area like this.'

'I never cared enough.'

'What they say about you. Wild card. Loose cannon. Not one of the lads. No-one likes a copper who's not one of the lads. 'Specially if he's good at his job. Very dicey combination, that. Beats me what she sees in you.'

'You're fond of her, aren't you?'

'Like an uncle. Smart kid. University, the whole bit. Understands about her dad, what he does, don't try to change him. But clean. Tony's seen to it she's clean.'

'What a parent.'

'She fancies you rotten, that's the problem. In my view, a very serious problem. Comes over dead cool and street-smart, as you know, but the night we run you down, she's all over the place. Beating her lovely breast, sorter thing. What I'm saying, Mr Maiden, I would hate any harm to come to that girl. I lost my boy. Lost him a couple of years before he did for hisself, that's by the by. But if anything happens to that girl, you really are a dead man, you get the subtlety of what I'm saying?'

'Victor,' Maiden said, 'all I want out of Emma is somewhere to sleep for one night, no complications. Then I'm gone.'

'Make sure you are.' Vic bent over the lock, feeling his way with his gloved hands. 'Hello. Well, well.'

'Problem?'

'Saves us a job. In one respect.'

He stepped back, flicked his torch briefly at the lock and then off again. Long enough for Maiden to see splintered wood.

'Somebody must've read about you being indisposed, sorter thing. I don't know what society's coming to.'

'Hardly worth going in now, then.'

Surprised at himself. There was no feeling of anger or violation. The flat had belonged to someone else. Someone who was dead, so it didn't matter. Bobby Maiden felt very strange. An image floated into his head of a streetlamp going on and off; he heard the buzzing sound it made.

He shivered.

'You want to go in, anyway, Mr Maiden?'

He didn't want to. 'OK. I'll grab a few clothes. No burglar would bother with my clothes.'

'After you, then.' Vic pushed back the door. Maiden went into his tiny kitchen, where the only lights were the ones you could see through the small, high window. It smelled musty. It smelled of cigarette smoke. Suzanne's perhaps. Except she couldn't have had more than one, and that was . . . how many nights ago? No, somebody had been in here for some time.

He decided he ought to make the effort.

'I think I'll put a light on after all, Vic.'

'Make it quick, then. *Shit!*'

Maiden's hand hadn't reached the switch before *all* the lights came on, the room flooded with glare and movement.

He saw flat eyes in a shaven head. Denims. The guy kicking a table out of his way as he advanced on Maiden. Fat hands around a crowbar. Another one behind him.

'*That him?*'

'*Yeah.*'

The crowbar went back, knocking cups off the shelf over the drainer.

'*Do it.*'

Maiden raised an arm, but not fast enough and the crowbar smashed into the side of his head and he fell, seeing the bar going back for another one, before a steel toecap took away his sight.

XIV

Norah picked up, sounding relieved. Said it was real thoughtful of Grayle to call and she would be only too happy to prise Lyndon out the tub before he cut his wrists.

Huh?

'No, hey, listen, I'll call back . . .' Grayle yelled.

Knowing that if she put down the phone she'd do no such thing, that once the effect of the final half-bottle of California Flat had worn off she'd change her mind about this. But Norah had already gone and Grayle waited, biting her lip.

She found her voice also was shaking, when Lyndon McAffrey arrived on the line, sounding just as dry as usual, and she just said it, the words spurting out.

'Lyndon, I'm going crazy. I have to quit.'

'Uh huh.'

'You're surprised, right?'

Lyndon said, 'Uh huh.'

'See, I'm nearly thirty years old . . .'

'Mm-mmm.'

'And all I do is write about other people's searches for answers to what it's all about.'

'I think that's called journalism, Grayle.'

'And I've been doing this going on four years now, the New Age column, and at first I felt it was, you know, really important, like in a kind of *evangelical* way. Making people aware of . . . of *more*. I have like tens of thousands of readers, and most of them write to me, and I used to reply to all of them, but now when the guy comes in hauling this huge sack, I'm like, *Take it away, take it away*. The whole thing is way out of control. I'm just not . . . not *big* enough. All these poor, perplexed people who obviously think I'm this major guru-person when really my life's more screwed up than theirs, in most cases, and I'm just serving up spiritual junk food.'

'This is your sister brought all this on, right?'

'Well, I just wonder whether this whole thing's like conveying a message to me, that I need to get away. Find . . . I don't know . . . spiritual first base. That what I need to discover is not so much Ersula as me. Find out if there's really anything underneath the shlocky façade, and . . . and if you say . . . if you say *uh huh* one more fucking time . . .'

Silence.

'But you can, you know, say *something*.'

'You know,' Lyndon said, 'I thought at first you were going to say it was because of me. That you couldn't face life on the paper without someone to share nauseous doughnuts with.' He chuckled mirthlessly. 'Ah, how we overestimate our own status.'

'Lyndon, what are we talking about here?'

'I'm forced to conclude no-one on the *Courier* saw fit to inform you that our masters have formally requested my retirement.'

'*Whhaaat?*'

The god-collar fell to the carpet.

'Shouldn't have been a surprise. I'm fifty-six years old. Couple days ago I was telling myself, Hell, Lyndon, you're only fifty-six. I guess I was looking at it from the wrong end. Young guys been walking over me for years like there's a white line down my back.'

'Goddamn cult of youth. Oh, this makes me so mad, Lyndon. I'm so *sorry*.'

Lyndon found another arid chuckle. 'The editor is thirty-eight. He thinks he's already kind of old for the job. What he told me today, he said, Lyndon, I give myself five more years at the sharp end. So you see, Grayle, I am a fortunate man indeed to have survived so long.'

She was in tears. The column would have lasted about two weeks but for Lyndon. He'd pull off-the-wall snippets from the news mush, pass them on to Grayle who, in the early days, with only student and underground newspaper experience, was, frankly, floundering. Lyndon was a great newspaperman.

'Of course, after more than a quarter of a century, the payoff, as you would guess, is considerable. We could retire to Florida, Norah and I. Play a little golf. Maybe edit the senior citizens' community newsletter.'

'Without you there . . . I wouldn't want to stay anyway.'

'You don't need me any more. You're established. Why, you're almost . . . never figured I'd say this . . . almost a pro.'

'That's the kindest thing I ever heard you say to anybody. But even if I really was a pro, it would make no difference. It wouldn't be the same paper.'

'You know,' Lyndon said, 'I was just lying in the tub thinking, this is how a life goes. Leastways, the years between sunup and sundown. Just wish I'd realized twenty years ago that the higher you go the thinner the air gets. What I mean is, yesterday, I would have been trying to talk you out of this. Now . . . Well, nearly thirty . . . In the novelty-column department, you could be close to peaking, Grayle. Close to peaking. How important's the money?'

'The money never was important. Money just holds you down. I have enough to get by. I could always sublet the apartment.'

'You plan to go find Ersula in her Neolithic sanctuary?'

'I think we could talk now, for the first time, on something like level ground. I think we *need* to talk. Because, in some ways, *she's* been the big sister. You know?'

'You could take a vacation, do it that way.'

'I may find Ersula in a couple weeks; finding myself

could take a little longer. Holy Grayle carries a lot of excess baggage.'

'You'll go to England?'

'Wherever.'

'Beats Florida. Climate excepted.'

'You won't go to Florida, Lyndon. You will *never* go to Florida.'

'That a firm psychic prediction, Grayle?'

The wine all gone. The decision made. A decision made, if truth be told, some while back.

She'd give in her notice tomorrow. Maybe she'd tell them it was a protest thing, about Lyndon McAffrey and the cult of youth. Holy Grayle was through with cults.

She'd have to tell the parents. Mom, who read the column avidly, would be sorry to see it go but she'd understand all the stuff about finding yourself, having found a whole new (and arguably monstrous) self at the age of fifty-eight. Dad, who hated the column and all it stood for but believed in the need for a firm career structure, would come on like she was one of his more valued students planning to drop out before next semester. If things became difficult she would have to show him Ersula's letter, the whole bit.

He ought then to understand why she needed to be pulled out of this before she went as crazy as Grayle.

Grayle's eyes began to prickle. It was as if Ersula was reaching out to her. As if, thousands of miles apart, they were seeking a common bond.

Automatically, she closed her eyes, pictured Ersula with her blond hair and her steady, watchful, almost cold blue eyes.

Slowing her breathing, reaching out for Ersula.

Nothing. It never did work, did it? Especially when your senses were swimming in stale wine.

XV

'OK. Mr Lazarus. Where is he?'

'My flat.' Good-looking girl with very dark hair, dressed for aerobics. She kept biting her thumb, looked scared half to death but doing her best not to show it.

She'd been waiting for Andy in the lobby, where there was a uniformed doorman, who must be the only one in Elham. A digital wall clock showed 20.30.

She ought to be miles from here by now. She ought to be *there*. So no time for formalities.

The doorman lifted Andy's beaten-up holdall after them into the lift. Jesus God, but this place had changed. Not so long ago, the Edwardian building overlooking the park used to be full of old-established solicitors' and insurance brokers' offices and dentists' surgeries. Brass plates and steps up. Then, some consortium headed by Tony Parker, the 'leisure operator', had somehow acquired the building, and now it was very expensive luxury apartments – *not* flats – and it was all cream walls and concealed lighting.

She didn't recognize the woman. One of Elham's fortunates, then: never crashed the car, attempted suicide, got mugged, burned, battered by the husband.

Half an hour ago, she'd phoned the hospital, sounding panicky, demanding to talk to Sister Anderson. The night sister, Sharon Fox, had refused – as was customary – to give out Andy's home number, but the woman had left her own and her name – Suzanne – and a message: *It's about Mr Lazarus.*

Andy had called her back in seconds.

It was one of those lifts you couldn't even tell when it was moving. The girl leaned against the doors, breathed out. 'Thank Christ. I owe you one, Mrs Anderson. I'm useless in these situations.'

'You're Suzanne?'

'Emma. Em. Forget Suzanne. Bobby said *you* could be trusted. But not the hospital.'

'Aye. Maybe so.'

The lift doors opened. Directly across was a fancy, dark-wood apartment door with a brass 7 on it. The girl banged the panels with her fists. 'Me, Vic.'

No problem recognizing the grizzled guy who let them in. *Not* one of Elham's fortunates, Andy having glued him together more than twice in the bloodied hour after closing time.

'Could be a messy one, Sister,' Vic Clutton said, and Andy's heart sank, because if even he thought it was messy then it was very messy.

Big picture window in the bedroom. The lights of Elham, but it might have been Paris; distance, the night and the trees hiding all the scars and cavities and bruised, smashed people. The wee lights making it look pretty and contented.

'Peas,' Andy demanded.

Em said, 'Sorry?'

'Frozen peas. Soft packet. Beans. Sweetcorn. Anything like that.'

'I'll get it,' Vic said. Aye, he'd been down this alleyway before. 'I'll check the freezer.'

They'd put Bobby Maiden on the bed. Blood was soaking into the cream duvet where it had poured down from the eye to join another river from a long cut under the jaw. As for the eye itself . . . Jesus God. How could this happen . . . again? Tonight, of all nights.

'Put the big light on. OK, son, look up. And open it. I need it open.'

It would have to be the left eye again. He tried his best to open it, but she had to do it for him, which was like getting into a walnut. If this turned out the way she feared, it was going to be 999, no messing. And prayers.

Holding his head. It felt familiar, in an awfully disturbing way, but no time for that now. 'Keep still. Good boy.'

The woman, Em, standing with her back to the picture window, biting her thumbnail.

Andy peered into Bobby Maiden's left eye.

'Jesus God.'

'What?' Em sprang up. '*What?*'

'It moved. Shit.' Andy sagged. 'The damn pupil contracted in the light.'

'What's that mean?'

'Calm down, hen. It's a good sign. If the pupil wouldnae move we'd have big trouble. This is the eye that took it last time. I was convinced the pupil wasnae gonny contract, but it did, so we breathe again. You got pain anywhere else, son? *No*, don't shake your head, you daft sod! Jesus God.'

'Can I get you some tea, Mrs Anderson?'

'No time, hen . . . Aye, OK.'

Vic Clutton came back with the frozen peas, and she arranged the bag over the eye, instructing Bobby not to move. 'Any numbness?'

'Nothing I didn't have before,' he said thickly. 'I'm sorry. I'm really sorry about this.'

'Save it. How about the other eye? Can you see out of that OK?'

Bobby fumbled a deathly smile. 'What've you done to your hair?'

'Good.' She rummaged in her holdall, dug out a packet of lightweight gauze. 'You got any Sellotape, hen?'

'Drawer over the bookcase, Vic. Would you mind? I'll make some tea. Can you . . . I mean, is he going to be all right?'

'A hospital would tell you better than me. And a hospital's what he needs, I kid you not.'

'Forget it,' Bobby said. 'Really.'

'Shut up, you.' Andy turned to Em. 'All right. Forget the tea. No bullshit. How'd this happen?'

'We took him back to his flat to get some things,' Em said. 'Vic—?'

'These two blokes was already in the flat, Sister. In the dark. Dead quiet. Suddenly all the lights go on, no warning, and they come for him. With these iron bars. Crowbars.'

'Jesus God. Burglars?'

'What I thought. At first.' Vic looked at Em.

'Tell her,' she said, biting a thumbnail. 'Tell her the lot. I don't care who goes down for this.'

Vic shuffled. 'Well, it was . . . It wasn't burglars. You surprise a burglar, he might go for you in a panic, sorter thing. Not these two. It was what they'd come for. They was waiting for him. Give him a beating.'

'With iron *bars*?'

'A *big* beating,' Vic said.

'Say it,' the girl said. 'A *final* beating.'

'Yeah,' Vic said. 'Looked like it was gonna be a final beating. Sorter thing.'

'You mean . . .' Seen-it-all Andy knowing she'd gone white. '. . . they were waiting to *kill* him?'

'Would've looked like he'd interrupted a burglary. When they found him.'

'God above, what's he *into*?'

Vic looked across at the bed then at Em. Em said, 'Bobby?'

'Sure,' he said. 'You can say what you want in front of Andy. We go back.'

Vic rubbed his jaw. 'What a bleeding mess.' He sat on a corner of the bed. 'Course, they never thought there'd be two of us. And I had me little tool kit.'

Andy said, 'Against iron *bars*?'

'I threw the tools at the window, Sister. Well, it's a quiet street, in spite of the bypass. Em hears the glass go, thinks it couldn't be me, and starts on the car hooter. Course, they've no way of telling, these lads, how many of us was out there. Could've been we was mob-handed, for all they know. They piss off smartish, the front way. Self-preservation cooling their aggression, sorter thing.'

'You told the police?'

Em and Vic looked at one another.

'That's a problem, is it?' Andy starting to wonder who these people were, how they connected with Inspector Maiden. Like, were he and the girl an item?

'It's one hell . . .' Bobby tried to sit up, moaned, fell back on the bed. '. . . of a problem.'

'I told you to stay still,' Andy snapped. 'Don't you dislodge those peas.'

'We do have a problem with the police,' he said. 'Though not *all* the police.'

'There are policemen and policemen in this town,' Em said. 'Like everywhere, I suppose.'

'After they'd gone, we didn't hang around,' Vic said. 'We're practically dragging him back to the car. He's half out of it, as you can imagine. I know we shouldn't've moved him, sister, but if them guys came back . . . Which was a possibility. Be quite an earner for them. You know?'

'Listen, I don't *want* to know. The less I know the better. What I do know is you ought to be in hospital, Bobby. You ought never to've come out. This is some kind of madness.'

He didn't reply. He was looking deathly.

'Look, I'll make him an eyepatch with Sellotape, but he needs a proper one, Long John Silver job. No pressure's the thing to remember. Ice packs till then.' She stood back. 'Could look worse than it is, but we cannae be sure. There'll be bad bruises where they hit him with the bar. Could still be internal injuries. He needs constant attention. Any change for the worse, any change at all that isnae for the better, you get on to a bloody doctor pronto, y'hear? Can he bide here a while?'

'No way,' Maiden said. 'Not now.'

'You be quiet, son,' Andy said. 'You make too many of your own decisions. Did I no tell you to think first?'

'I think he might be right, Mrs Anderson. It sounds ridiculous to say he wouldn't be safe here . . .'

'But that's what you're saying, is it, hen?'

'Maybe. We knew things were difficult, we didn't realize how difficult.'

'Those lads,' Vic said. 'Not local. They was of an age I'd know them if they was local. Well, you think about it. You don't just hire complete strangers, half an hour's notice, to go and beat somebody to death. They was on a retainer. They was just waiting for the word.'

'If this is Pa, I'll bloody kill him.'

'I'd say not. I'd say somebody lost patience with your old man. It's getting less difficult to find people who'll do for somebody for a couple of grand. Plus, there's a lot of very discreet middlemen about, so it don't get traced back.'

Andy said, as calmly as she could manage, 'They're gonny try again, are they not?'

Vic shrugged.

There was an answer to this situation. Andy closed her eyes momentarily and saw a pale red sun against the lids. Oh aye, a very obvious answer here. So obvious, she wanted to resist it.

'I hear your *daddy* was at the hospital, Bobby. Is there no chance—?'

'Don't even ask.'

'Like that, eh? You got a problem, then, son.'

Andy walked over to the window. Saw her own grim-faced reflection hologrammed over the lights of Elham. She should've been in St Mary's by now.

'So what did you have in mind to do about this, Bobby?'

'Get out of town. Book into a hotel somewhere for a few days. Except my wallet's in the hospital safe. Cash. Credit cards. Looking like this is going to be another problem. You book into a hotel with a face like this, they do a courtesy check with the local police. I'm a bit buggered, really.'

'We can sort out the money. Jonathan'll get that. Bobby, listen, there's a place you could go. Well out of it. Where nobody's gonny find you. Where you could have the time to heal, son. You need to heal. Physically, mentally and . . .'

It was as if, when she'd placed her hands on his head, bringing up High Knoll, she'd made a connection, plugged into a live circuit and it wasn't going to be broken; the current was strengthening. It was the right thing to do.

'. . . and spiritually.' Andy looked at him, blood all over his Elham Hospital Fun Run T-shirt. 'There are some places you heal quick. Some places heal parts of you you didnae know were sick.'

'I'm sure there are,' he said, 'but it's not your problem, Andy. We're really grateful for what you've done. Don't get involved any further. Not many laughs in this.'

'Hey!' Andy walked to the foot of the bed. 'Don't you tell me what's no my problem, Bobby Maiden. They're gonny kill you, son, you hang around here, and then you'll die and go back to the nasty grey place, am I right?'

She regretted it at once. His whole body went rigid.

'I'm sorry, son,' she said.

She rang Jonathan and told him as much of everything as she could pack into four minutes.

'What a colourful life you lead, Sister Andy,' Jonathan said. 'How long will you need?'

'Well, I already begged two days. I'll try and stick to it, but if it takes longer, it takes longer.'

'Don't put your pension on the line,' Jonathan warned, 'for a bit of mumbo jumbo.'

She made the eyepatch.

She told Bobby Maiden to get some sleep. He said, no way. He lay there staring at the ceiling. He seemed to be glad of the pain.

She thought she understood.

Emma Curtis took her into another room. 'Where are you taking him?'

'I'm no sure you need to know that, hen.'

'Nobody's going to bloody torture me, Sister. And if he can't visit *me*, I want to visit *him*.'

'You sure you're good for each other, hen?'

The dark eyes didn't move. 'What's that got to do with the price of eggs?'

'OK.' Andy smiled. 'Let me have your phone number again. I'll call you when he can see what he's doing.'

'Thanks,' Emma said. 'And . . . thanks.'

At two a.m., an ambulance arrived. 'Apologies, sister,' the paramedic said, 'earliest I could make it.' Giving Andy the envelope containing Bobby Maiden's wallet and his keys. 'Dr Jonathan says good luck. With the, er, mumbo jumbo.'

XVI

Three-fifteen a.m., Andy driving as if she could read Bobby Maiden's mind. Grim-faced under the fluffed-up red hair, clogging the pedal as though they were breaking bail – all mobiles alert for a ten-year-old powder-blue Golf with a Greenpeace sticker.

Slowing only whenever she spotted a police car. But it wasn't police, as such, that Maiden was worried about. He was seeing a dark vehicle blocking a country road. Two men in balaclavas. Tooled up. Silencers. No small talk, no prelims. Maiden, then Andy. The Golf driven into a wood with the bodies.

But, then, Maiden was as paranoid as you can get.

They were a good ten miles out of Elham before Andy spoke.

'Who's Emma, then?'

'Mmm. Well . . .' He told her about the hit-and-run car which had first brought him to her attention.

'Aw, you're no serious . . .'

'Plus – in case you missed the references back there – her old man's Tony Parker.'

Andy shook her head, laughing her comfortable, smoker's laugh. 'Jesus God, Bobby. And I thought I was mixing with lowlife the day they called me into a meeting of the hospital trust.'

'She's OK. Didn't you think?'

Andy thought about it. 'Aye. Genes aren't everything. And the last person she'll ever harm is you. But you'll know that. Are you no awfully knackered, Bobby?'

'Long past knackered. Knackered was yesterday.'

She'd tilted the passenger seat for him, but he'd pulled it back up, even further, so it was almost a right angle. He concentrated hard on the lights through the windscreen, but with half his vision blocked by the makeshift patch it was hard to keep his good eye open.

'But you're no gonny let yourself sleep, right?'

'No.'

'Bobby, you need—'

'Sleep, sleep and sleep.'

'You're no gonny *die*, Bobby. Not again. I mean like not yet. Not *imminently*.'

They were at a brightly lit motorway intersection, big blue signs. When they hit the motorway itself, it felt safer: a no man's land.

'I was wondering. Got anything in your bag to kind of *ward off* sleep?'

'Speed? In your condition? Christ, you *would* be bloody dead. There's chocolate biscuits in the glove compartment, and that's your lot.'

'Should have asked Clutton.'

'I don't like the way you're talking.' Andy leaned back in her seat, hands loosening around the wheel. 'Look, I'm no shrink . . . But maybe what we're looking at here is your subconscious manufacturing a smokescreen, setting up a block to shield you from some trauma. Images of bleakness, this cold, soulless place. Cold neutralizes pain. Like when we put the frozen peas on your eye.'

'Yes . . . but . . . Well, OK . . . Suppose you wake up dead?'

'Is that no a wee bit contradictory?'

'With all your bodily juices drying up. Your muscles dead weight. Veins clogged.'

'Oh.'

'And being aware of decaying. Tasting the soil.'

'Shit,' Andy said.

'Twice that's happened. How normal is that?'

'Aw, hell . . .' She hesitated. 'You know what this says to me? I mean, this is just off the top of my head, I havenae thought it out, but it's as if when . . . after we brought you round . . . some part of you stayed dead. It's as though something down there in your mind doesnae know we got your body to come back.'

He saw her hands tighten on the wheel.

'It's like you're carrying around your own corpse, Bobby.'

'Well, thanks,' Maiden said. 'That's very encouraging.'

They kept on talking after that. There was a flask of black coffee Em had made, and chocolate biscuits. They were through Spaghetti Junction, so little traffic this time in the morning that the great concrete snakepit looked like a major overspend.

She was telling him about this guy called Marcus Bacton, a schoolteacher for over thirty years, though he claimed to hate kids worse than the flu. Took early retirement after his wife's death, and bought himself this run-down farmhouse on the Welsh border, to start a new career as a magazine editor.

'Kind of Learned Gentleman's Journal of the Unexplained. Printed on the kind of paper you wouldnae wipe your arse on in case your fingers went through. So . . . he's stuck out in the sticks, losing money hand over fist on this awful rag, and having to pay a housekeeper on account of he cannae tie his own shoes. Lucky to land one who didnae ask for much other than a roof over her. Mrs Willis. The healer.'

Andy pulled off the motorway, giving two fingers to the driver of an Escort who'd zipped in from the fast lane and cut in front.

'Dickhead. Listen, I never went for this baloney. Laying on of hands. Sending healing vibes. I'm a professional. Like, if it works, what we doin' spending billions on hospitals and clinics? And yet . . .'

Healing vibes. He was remembering Jonathan telling him about Andy's hands either side of his head as he lay dead, Andy's eyes closed. *It was as if she was somewhere else. She was concentrating so hard on bringing you back, it was as though nothing else in the world mattered or ever would again if she failed. When you started to breathe, she just sagged. And we thought . . .*

Maiden jerked in his seat. He'd almost slipped away. It was like waking up on the edge of a sheer cliff. He swallowed a lot of air and laid his cheek against the window, for the coolness of it.

'. . . burial chamber,' Andy was saying. 'Part of it had collapsed, and there was a sign telling you not to go inside. But me – all six and a half stone of me – I fitted under the capstone, no trouble. I was that weak, you know? When you said that about being dried out like a corpse, that was how it was for me, with the colitis. You're just crapping all the moisture out of your system. You're a husk. Tired the whole time, and weary as hell, and you'll try anything. And so I'm lying there, in this burial chamber, until the dawn comes. You like the dawn, Bobby?'

'When the world's all quiet and fresh and sparkly.'

'This was a dawn like I never knew – and I've seen a few thousand, end of a shift. It's like . . . very dark in this wee chamber. I must've fallen asleep straight away. Just lying there on the hard earth. These huge stones all around me. A really dense sleep. And then, the next thing, I become aware of my hand . . . I must've been lying with my arms under my head and my hands are out in front, and this hand . . . it's like it's on fire.'

The car slowed, her hands on the wheel lit by red light from traffic signals.

'But it's . . . it's like the fire's *inside*. The hand glowing in the darkness. Just this hand. Not the stone, not the earth. Just the hand, like there's fire inside. So I reach out with the other hand to touch it, and that lights up too.'

The lights changed to green and Andy pulled away. Maiden saw she was smiling.

'What it was, it was the midsummer sun coming in through the slit, in this really focused beam. They were warm, too, the hands.'

They were coming into Worcester city centre and by its lights Maiden could see the girl in Andy's rugged face.

'Found I was breathing very, very slowly, aware of each breath as it came in. And it was like each breath was going further into my body. And while this happened, it was getting progressively lighter and warmer inside the chamber. The sunlight coming between these big stones like . . . molten gold from a what-you-call-it? Crucible. I can feel it now.'

Maiden smiled at hard-bitten Andy, all poetic. But he was impressed.

'Afterwards, walking back to the cottage, it was like, you know, walking on the golden clouds. It was Midsummer's Day. They told me how this wee girl, years back, she had this vision of the Virgin Mary in this very same place, on Midsummer's Morning. Jesus, it's enough tae give you religion.'

He noticed how her accent would ebb – the result of thirty years in England – and then roll back in a wave with the powerful memories.

'They wouldnae take any more money for the cottage, though Mrs W fed me for days. Fresh fruit, homemade veggie soup. And weird stuff from bottles with stoppers. Miracles. Magic. When I left, I was about a stone heavier but . . . light. Inside, you know? And before I go, she says, *You* can do this now. If you want to. So when I get back to work, I'm signing on for every healing course advertised on the back wall of Elham Healthfoods. Acupuncture, homoeopathy, cranial osteopathy, Reiki.'

Maiden said cautiously, 'You're saying you used this on me?'

Andy shook her head. 'I wouldnae claim credit. I'm a

convert to alternative medicine, but . . . powerful enough to kick-start the dead? I don't dare think. The Holy Mother? Bobby, I was raised a Presbyterian. All I'm saying, there's something remarkable about that place, and I cannae explain it in any scientific terms. Whether it's some kind of magnetic thing, some property of the place, like Lourdes and such, I wouldnae have any idea about that. All I know is, when you were lying stone dead on that table in A and E, I was holding the image in ma head of the rising sun at High Knoll and willing it to come into ma hands and to come into you.'

. . . we thought, for a second, that she was going to drop dead, Jonathan had said.

'Maybe I blacked out for a split second. And the next thing, the whole team's jumpin' up and down and whooping and everybody's hugging me and stuff. I . . . couldnae . . . I couldnae go home. I was too high. Couldnae sleep that night.'

They were through the city now, back in the dark country.

'So why didn't *you* feel like that, Bobby? Breaks ma heart.'

The other side of Hereford, small signs were saying Michaelchurch, Craswall, Longtown. Tiny, scattered lights from windows in the sky. Hill country.

'I feel I've been ungrateful,' Maiden said. 'You wasted your . . . light.'

'Get lost. There's always a reason for things. Did I ask you what you believed, Bobby? If you ever believed there was stuff out there?'

'Yeah, well . . .' Through the windscreen, Maiden saw a church steeple greyly smoke-ringed with low night cloud. 'I used to believe all kinds of stuff. Once.'

'When you were gonny be a painter?'

'Yeah. Not many coppers believe. Like doctors. Like how can any kind of a just God allow this shit . . . ?'

'I'm a cynic, Bobby. And a sceptic. I take a lot of convincing. Years of seeing good human beings die prematurely and bad human beings keep on recovering. I have no answers. And yet . . .'

'Truth is I'd love to believe all that,' Maiden said. 'Be nice to be that kind of person. New Age cop. But my experience of being dead ties in only too well with the kind of deaths I've been seeing for years. Cold, ugly . . . to be avoided.' He sighed. 'To be avoided.'

At the end of the village street, a muddied sign said: *Capel-y-ffin. Mountain road, unsuitable for heavy vehicles*.

'Nearly there, son,' Andy said. She was thinking of how, when she talked to Marcus yesterday, he said Mrs Willis told him she had seen a black light. Over the Knoll.

That would make sense to Bobby, all right. With his experience. Black light.

In the headlights, the whitened bone-branches of two half-dead trees locked horns over the road.

XVII

Never needed an alarm; he awoke at six, precisely, to the bloody second. *Always* woke at six, from the days when he was employed to force-feed Shakespeare sonnets to glue-sniffing thugs.

So, when Marcus fumbled on his glasses and the luminous clock said 4.55, he knew there was a problem.

Had hardly any sleep. Didn't get to bed until half past one. Sitting around waiting for the Anderson woman – seriously, who *could* you rely on these days? – and worrying about Mrs Willis, who'd gone to bed early after two hours sitting alone in her Healing Room and not – here was the clincher – not even coming out for *The Archers*.

Another crash. Thunderous but familiar. An October gust thrusting at the barn door, slamming it back and forth – what happened to the new padlock and chain? One day that door would blow off and there'd have to be a gaping hole for the duration, because he couldn't afford to replace it. Whole bloody fabric was coming apart, rot setting in, and the farmhouse would collapse a bloody sight faster than the original castle.

Felt he was under siege in his own ruins, the motte a tiny island in a Falconer sea, foundations eroding. The whole of the western world turning into a Falconer society: glib, superficial, arrogant, narcissistic.

Bastards.

The barn door went again, this time with a faint splintering coda, as though it had been hit by a team of men with a battering ram and they were backing off for another go. It must have sprung completely open.

In the dark, Marcus pulled his trousers from the bedpost (*never* be caught without your trousers) and his tweed jacket from the bedroom door, hauling it on over his string vest. Creeping in his socks down the stone stairs – although there was little danger of awakening Mrs Willis, state of her hearing these days – and stepping into his wellies by the back door, Malcolm ambling through to join him.

The cold hit him with a surprisingly vicious punch. Be winter before you knew it. Seemed no bloody time at all since *last* winter, the way the years just flashed by. But, then, why shouldn't they? A year was nothing. *Sixty* years were nothing; what could you learn in sixty bloody years? What had Marcus Bacton learned?

Bugger all of any real significance. 'Just has to be more than this,' he told the dog. Grabbing his torch from the hook in the porch, stumbling into the yard.

The barn door blew out at him as he reached it, almost knocking him over. Bastard. Looked like the bloody chain had snapped. But when he pointed his torch at it, he saw the chain hanging loose from the hasp, the padlock still dangling from the chain . . . and the bloody padlock was *open*.

What the hell? Couldn't be a burglar or a tramp looking for a bed, unless it was a tramp with the skill and patience to pick locks, and the door was so rotten anyway that he could have kicked his way in quicker, and . . . Good God!

Marcus saw that the key was still in the padlock.

The keys to the buildings were all kept in an old coffee tin on the kitchen window ledge.

Oh my God.

Mrs Willis.

Andy swung the car sharply right into a bumpy track, between outstretched arms of stone.

'What's that?'

'It's a castle, Bobby. Did I no tell you he lived in a castle?'

Something huge and tubular was pushing out of a bushy mound into the charcoal-grey pre-dawn. Half of a stone tower.

'Well, he lives in it inasmuch as the walls are all round the house,' Andy said. 'More a liability than anything, with the upkeep and the official inspections.'

Behind the ruins, the headlights had found a low house, heavy with oak timbers, small, irregular black windows. Andy parked about fifty yards away. 'We'll bide here a while. Don't want to set the dog off. Marcus'll be about soon enough.'

'Get some air, I think.' Maiden pulled down his eyepatch, levered himself out of the car. It was chilly, the darkness rattling and squeaking. His body aching. There were no visible lights, apart from a fading moon and a single star.

Andy joined him. 'How you feeling?'

'OK.'

'*I* bet.'

'No, really. Better.'

'You'll sleep fine here. Air's like rough cider. Listen. I have a thought. This may be stupid.'

'Go on.'

'It'll take us no more than twenty minutes to walk to the Knoll.'

'You don't think that's stupid at all,' Maiden said. 'You've been planning it all along.'

Only a barn owl shrieked in reply. He found himself losing touch with the reality of it, the scene receding into a small screen of pebble-glass, the kind you saw in front of vintage TV sets from the 1950s.

He saw a sliver of gold in the east. In the west, behind the castle's bush-bristled mound, dark hills.

* * *

Halfway up the rise, he turned to look back into the east. Saw the dawn like an estuary in the sky: flat banks of cool sand and spreading turquoise pools. But he knew there was something wrong: it was just a pretty picture, he wasn't *feeling* it.

'You OK, Bobby?' Andy moving briskly through the dew-damp field, looking back at him. He was out of breath; she wasn't.

'I'm OK.' He could feel the excitement in her. Couldn't believe that she believed his survival was down to some kind of prehistoric magic.

Andy shook her head over the view. 'Will you look at that?' She had on a blue nylon jacket, pink jeans and a pair of walking boots she kept in the car. She looked loosened up, very much at home here. 'I mean, isn't that just amazing?'

'It's very nice.'

'*Very nice?*' She stared at him. 'Jesus, Bobby, I thought you were supposed to be an artist. You're talking like a guy with no poetry in him.'

'Sorry.'

'You think I'm mad, don't you? I mean, come on, if you think I'm out of it, you bloody well say so.'

'I think you're an optimist,' he said.

'Let's just try it, huh? You stand on the Knoll and you let the sun rise over you, and if you think it's still February . . . Just try it, huh?'

Ahead of them, in the west, the land rose steeply towards what were either high hills or low mountains, hard to separate them from the still-night sky. Andy tugged at the sprung bar on a metal gate.

'Not far. Just we'll need to go careful. Don't wanny get arrested for trespass. Guy who owns the land – this TV archaeologist, Falconer?'

'*He* owns this land?'

'He does now. He and Marcus are, ah . . .' Andy dragged the gate across the tufted grass. '. . . not over-friendly. He's apparently fenced off the Knoll. If he found Marcus climbing over the wire, he'd be pressing charges. We'd probably get off wi' a warning, but he's no gonny see us anyway, this early.' She lowered her voice. 'With any luck.'

Andy closed the gate behind them and crackled confidently through a patch of dry bracken. Did she really imagine she was going to have him skipping back down the hillside, praising God, the Virgin Mary, the Mother Goddess?

'What happened to the girl who had the vision?'

'Aw, it becomes less inspiring. Child tells her mother, gets the strap for being late to school. And lying. When she keeps on about it, Ma summons the vicar. No friend of the Roman Church. Plus the local people are saying any vision at a pagan site has got to be the work of the evil one. They kind of ostracized her.'

'Christians,' Maiden said.

'Cause célèbre for *The Phenomenologist* and Marcus. Hates religious prejudice, though, God knows, he has enough of his own. Look . . .'

She stopped, took his arm. About a hundred yards away, at the summit of the slope, something squatted like a massive, stone toad.

'Most people find them kind of weird, these old sites, wouldnae want to go up alone. Now it's like . . . approaching a cathedral.'

She turned her face into the dawn. There were channels of crimson under the lightening sandscape in the sky, chips of glittering cloud. Andy's skin was ambered in the morning glow, her eyes shining, red hair alight.

'Supposed to be a chambered tomb, that's what the books say, but this . . . this is no to do with *death*. Jesus, how can you ever turn your face into the sunrise and contemplate dying?'

Maiden looked down at the dirty yellow grass. He felt cold.

'These people,' Andy said. 'The old guys. They

positioned it to grab the earliest daylight. So it's all about rebirth. New life, healing the body, healing the mind, healing the spirit. It's everything we've forgotten. As a race, y'know? Like . . . Hey . . . you OK?'

'Nothing.' His mouth dry. 'Someone walking over my grave.'

He looked down at his hands, saw they were trembling. Never before, in his whole life, could he remember his hands trembling.

'You've gone pale, Bobby.'

The stone toad crouched over him.

'OK, listen to me.' Andy put her hands on his shoulders. 'C'mon now, what are you feeling? Right this second.'

'I don't know.'

'Yes you do. Give me a word.'

'All right, dread.'

'*Dread?* Son, this place saved your life.'

'You saved my life.'

'Aw.' Andy dropped her arms, walked away from him, shaking her head.

'Sorry. Wrong thing to say, huh?'

'Bobby, *everything* you say's wrong. Walked on your grave. You said grave. This is no to do with *graves*.'

'You're taking it personally.'

'Damn right I am. All the way down here I'm thinking this was gonny bring you out of it. Out of all this grey stuff, this fear of death, all this *February* shite.'

'It doesn't change what you did. You wanted to think it was linked to your own recovery and whatever happened to you up here. I don't know why you don't just accept that it was you . . . *your* instincts, *your* experience . . .'

He risked another look up at the stone toad on the mound, vaguely hoping it might have acquired a halo, turned to gold.

He shuddered. He could almost smell it. Like the worst smell he'd ever known: when he was with the Met, called out to this house in Islington, this well-to-do suicide couple sitting naked on the sofa, holding hands, dead for three weeks, their heads fallen together. Pills and whisky and hundreds of flies and, on the coffee table, a photo album full of pictures of naked children.

He turned his back on High Knoll. The colours of the eastern sky were flat as a fresco; the dawn didn't want him.

'All seemed so *meant*, Bobby.'

Maiden hated himself. For her, the place was sacred. Why couldn't he feel it?

But she wasn't even looking at him any more.

'Jesus God.'

A short, plump man was shambling and flapping towards them, down the Knoll.

'Anderson?' The man slipped and stumbled to his knees. 'Is it *you*?' He was grey-haired, late middle-age. Blinking up through heavy spectacles and a film of sweat. 'It really is you?'

Andy reached for his hand and he stood up shakily. He was wearing baggy trousers and, bizarrely, a string vest. He clasped her hand to his chest, as if to make sure she was flesh and blood.

'I'm sorry, Marcus. Unforeseen circumstances. Everything OK?'

'No.' Pulling from his trouser pocket a chequered handkerchief the size of a small pillowcase. 'No, it's fucking not.'

'What's happened? Marcus?'

'I'm sorry, it . . .' Snatching off his glasses, wiping his eyes. 'Andy, oh God, I think she's dying on me.'

They heard the noise before they saw her. It was suddenly sickeningly familiar to Andy. Like very loud snoring.

She ran ahead. About six feet back from the monument, there was a low, wooden stockade-type fence, several rows of barbed wire strung over the top. But the wire was cut and hanging like briars. They climbed over the fence.

'You brought her up here, Marcus?'

'Course not. She bloody well brought herself up. Oh God, can you do something?'

'OK. Just . . . you know . . . keep calm.'

'Woke up early, knew something was wrong. She'd come down in the night, let herself into the barn and pinched these . . . look.' Holding up a pair of rubber-handled wire-cutters. 'She cut the fence. Can you believe it?'

Close up, the burial chamber looked like a huge, collapsed crab, the shell split as if someone had stood on it. The old woman was laid out along the damaged capstone like . . .

. . . *like a sacrifice* . . . Andy smothered the image.

Mrs Willis wore a bright green coat and a yellow woollen scarf. Her hair in a tight, white bun. The volume of her breathing sounding perversely healthy.

'It's a stroke,' Andy said. 'No question. I'm sorry.'

'What I feared. Fuck.' Marcus sighed. 'Blood pressure. Why wouldn't she see someone? Someone *else*.'

The old woman's head was pillowed by Marcus's folded tweed jacket. Eyes were closed, mouth open, tongue protruding. Spittle and mucus all round her lips and her chin.

'Do we get her down, that's the question, Marcus? Maybe not. She up here when you found her?'

'Just as she is now.'

'OK.' Andy removed Mrs Willis's glasses, handed them to Marcus. 'We need to get her in the recovery position. Don't want her choking, swallowing her tongue. Bobby, can you take . . . this is Bobby Maiden, Marcus, patient of mine. Easy now. On her side.'

She stepped back. Bars of bright crimson had appeared in the eastern sky like the elements in an electric fire. Marcus said, 'Look . . . Anderson . . . can't you . . . you know . . . *do* anything?'

'Limited amount you can do for a stroke. We need to keep her still. Then we need an ambulance.'

'How the hell's an ambulance going to get up here?'

'That's their problem. You just go back to the house and call them, I'll stay here.'

'When I said *do* anything . . .' Marcus stood up. 'Look, you know what I meant . . .'

The sun had come out, full and round and red.

'Aye, I know.' Andy went to sit behind the old woman in the shelter of the stones, wiped her mouth with a tissue. Took the white head gently between her hands. 'Come on, Annie, you can hold on.'

The sun was turning to gold. Andy lifted her face to it, closing her eyes, waiting for the warmth to enter through the centre of her forehead, travel down through the chakras, until her hands were burning.

Marcus said, '*What* did you call her?'

'Oh, Marcus,' Andy said softly. 'Old fool that y'are. You telling me it never occurred to you? The natural feeling she had for this place?'

'Her name's Joan,' Marcus said stupidly. 'Yes. Yes, it *did* occur to me, the way she just arrived, out of the blue. But Annie would be at least ninety. Mrs Willis can't be that old. Can she?'

'If she'd told you she was pushing ninety when she first came, would you have even considered taking her on?'

'If she'd said she was Annie Davies, I'd have given her the Earth.'

'You wouldnae have been able to keep it to yourself. Not for a day. And you'd've been on at her about it non-stop, questions, questions, questions. She didnae want the Earth.'

'Oh my God.' Marcus sat in his string vest, the sweat drying on his arms, staring down at Mrs Willis then up at the sun, his glasses misted. 'She came here to die.'

'She came to heal.'

'No, I mean . . . here. She came up here to die at the Knoll. In the dawn.'

'Aw, Marcus . . .' Andy flexed her fingers in Mrs Willis's hair. 'How do we know what was going through her head?'

Andy's hands still weren't warm. She saw that Bobby Maiden had stepped between her and the sun. His face was deeply shadowed, but she could see the Sellotape was peeling away from his skin and he was holding the eyepatch in place.

He said, 'How about we get her down from there?'

'Bobby?'

'Get her off the stone.'

'Why?'

'I don't *know* why.'

'He doesn't understand,' Marcus said. 'She loves this place.'

Bobby turned away from them and the stones. He was trembling. He walked away down the side of the Knoll.

Andy said, 'Go phone for an ambulance, Marcus. Please?'

'Yes, of course. Yes. Sorry.' Marcus scrambled to his feet. Behind him, the sun was full and round and red, like a bubble of blood. He looked down at Mrs Willis. 'Oh God.'

'Marcus . . . go.'

He didn't look back. When he reached the bottom of the mound, Andy called out, surprised at the tremor in her voice.

'Bobby, come here. Talk to me.'

He came over reluctantly, not looking at the stone, left hand clamped over his eyepatch.

'I'm sorry. I don't know why I said that. What do I know?'

'Never mind what you know,' Andy said. 'This is no the damn crown court, what do you *feel*?'

'Cold. Sick.' Gauze from the eyepatch was hanging down his cheek. 'Frightened.'

'Give me a hand with her. Take her legs.'

They lifted her. Bobby Maiden wouldn't touch the

stone. They laid her on the grass, Marcus's jacket still under her head.

The sun was on the old woman's face. Her eyes were open.

'Annie? Can you hear what I'm saying?'

The eyes glared up at her.

'Blink. Blink if you can hear me.'

Mrs Willis's eyelids moved a fraction. Her skin was translucent, like tissue.

'Annie,' Andy said softly. 'You feel better now? Off the stone? You feel better where you are?'

The blink was a long time coming, but when it came it was more pronounced, as if she'd been concentrating her energy.

Andy looked up at Bobby Maiden. Then across at the sun.

Her hands were feeling cold.

The sun was a lantern of hope, the land aglow. In the valley, the spire of St Mary's church was tipped with gold. The birds were singing. And her hands felt cold.

Part Two

The world of prehistoric man was a complete one, wondrous and awful, and to survive in it he needed the protection that shamans could give.

Aubrey Burl, *Rites of the Gods*.

One of the least understood aspects of shamanic work is soul-retrieval, in which the shaman journeys to retrieve the soul of a sick person, who may be near to death. It relates to the phenomenon of 'soul loss' experienced by so many people today.

John Matthews, *The Celtic Shaman: a handbook*.

Part Two

XVIII

Inside the body of the Old One, the Green Man awakes.

His muscles are stiffened and numbed after his long, foetal sleep. A rich, resinous, ancient life soaks his senses. It is a while before he understands where he is.

Above him, all around him, dawn birds sing. Birds rattling in the branches, their twittering lives come and gone in a heartbeat.

The Green Man feels the silence of the Old One. Who watched them build the church. Who stood here while the bones of the Barber-Surgeon were crushed beneath an Avebury megalith. Who thrived before Rufus died on Walter Tirel's bolt in the New Forest.

And still lives.

Awaiting, perhaps, his third millennium.

Because of its size, the oak is more honoured, but the yew has more mystery. It is often referred to as the Death Tree because of its ubiquity in and around graveyards. Few realize that the yews were here long before the graves . . . that the churches were only built on these sites because they were already sacred, with the yew tree a symbol of that sanctity. Our oldest symbol of immortality.

The sign in this churchyard says, ALTHOUGH YEW TREES ARE DIFFICULT TO DATE, THIS VENERABLE SPECIMEN IS BELIEVED TO BE WELL OVER A THOUSAND YEARS OLD. THE WOODEN BENCH INSIDE THE HOLLOW TRUNK WILL SEAT UP TO TEN ADULTS SIDE BY SIDE.

Or one man sleeping.

It has been an experiment. How will a night in an ancient sacred tree differ from one atop a burial chamber or inside a circle of ritual stones?

The living yew might be expected to record stories, impressions and dreams in a different way from stone, and so it transpires. When he rises from the bench, the Green Man's dream is still alive and vibrating in colours in his head. He sees clearly what he must do, as if in a film. As if it has already taken place.

Not in or around the yew, but inside the church.

While many centuries younger than the yew, the church is medieval. It stands a hundred yards outside this Worcestershire village, screened from the nearest houses – on an ugly council estate – by a dense copse. He tried the two doors last night and found both locked.

Someone, at some time, will have to let him in.

No-one has passed through in the night. No-one disturbed the Green Man where he lay, his back arched into the yew. He steps outside the tree now, stretches. Goes to release his morning water among the bushes.

And scarcely has he sheathed his tool than he hears the click of the wicket gate in the churchyard wall.

It is not yet seven a.m.

Never has a sacrifice been delivered so promptly.

The Green Man slides to his knees in the bushes. The visitor walks along the gravelled path and into his place in the Green Man's living dream.

He is elderly, perhaps in his seventies, and slight of build with a bald, bony head and spectacles. He does not appear to be a clergyman, perhaps a verger or sexton. A ring of keys rattles loosely from his right hand.

Big keys. Church keys.

His keys to the afterlife.

The old man whistles as he enters the porch. The Green Man hears him fitting a key into the lock, jiggling it about.

He rises from the bushes.

He strides towards the porch, unarmed. No knife, no crossbow, no gun, no sharp-edged rock.

Just inside the porch is a stone baptismal font, the church's oldest artefact.

At the end of his living dream, the bowl of the font is glistening with blood and bone and brains.

The verger whistles a tune from some old musical as the church door swings open.

XIX

Cindy Mars-Lewis made it three, possibly four, dead, plus one near-miss.

The near-miss was the boy motorcyclist in mid-Wales. The possible was a sixteen-year-old schoolgirl found strangled, but not sexually assaulted, last January, in a bus shelter not far from Harold's Stones at Trellech in Monmouthshire. This was still only a possible because the bus shelter, as Cindy had confirmed on a site visit, was on a very dubious alignment.

But, then – Cindy watched a boat far out in St Bride's Bay – there was no evidence this murderer was a perfectionist.

Take the killing of the Midlands businessman on a bird-watching weekend in Wiltshire. The man had been savagely and inexplicably battered to death at the foot of a *small hill*, in the middle of field a couple of miles from *Avebury*.

He could almost sense them now, but it would be necessary to visit the actual murder site to be certain, and he was rather unwilling to do this so soon after the event, with police all over the place. Cindy had discovered he was not terribly popular with the police.

In particular, that mild-mannered family man, DCI Hatch, in Bournemouth. Cindy had telephoned Mrs Carlotta Capaldi from Liverpool where he was playing Third Witch in a rather downmarket touring production of the Scottish play, to discover that Hatch would appreciate a word with him.

'I've had an inquiry about you, Mr Lewis. From the West Mercia Regional Crime Squad.'

Suspecting something of the kind, Cindy had waited until he was home before telephoning Bournemouth CID on his mobile.

'What the holy hell are you playing at?' Hatch demanded. 'You just won't take piss off for an answer, will you? You know there's absolutely nothing to connect these killings – nothing admissible, anyway – and as for ringing bloody *Crimewatch* . . . '

A mistake, Cindy would agree. But the TV programme had run such a detailed reconstruction of the killing of the poor homeless boy in a shop doorway, showing *precisely* the location of the shop, close to the ancient market cross, and . . .

'An impulse, I'm afraid, Chief Inspector. They did appeal for anyone with information.'

'You didn't *have* information. You wasted police time with a crackpot, semi-mystical theory which even I can't entirely grasp, about so-called ley lines – which I understand the experts say do not even *exist* – linking a bunch of crimes which simply have *nothing in common*.'

'With all respect, Peter,' said Cindy, 'that's what they said about the Yorkshire Ripper.'

'Not my area,' Hatch snapped.

'Oh, no, you don't want to talk about that, do you? Why Sutcliffe kept walking in and out of the police net because he didn't fit the profile? And because they were conned by a hoax tape into looking for the wrong type of man entirely.'

'I don't see where this—'

'Still several unsolved murders out there, that might be down to him. And why were they rejected by the Ripper squad? Because they weren't prostitutes, and the profile said the Yorkshire Ripper Only Kills Prostitutes.'

'Mr Lewis, we are not looking for a serial killer.'

'Psychos make their own patterns, see. Sometimes, the police are just so *simplistic*.'

'That,' Hatch said icily, 'is because, at the end of the day, we have to make it stand up in court. Now look, Mr Lewis, I was very patient. I accepted your desire to do all you could for Mrs Capaldi and I answered your curious questions on three separate occasions. But public relations has its limits, and telling West Mercia you were a friend of mine has, quite frankly, done my career no good at all.'

'Is the file on Maria still open?'

There was a pause.

'You know it is,' Hatch said bitterly.

'There you are, then, lovely. Your ideas were no better than mine.'

'We'll get him, Mr Lewis, I promise you. Meanwhile, if I could give you a word of advice, some senior policemen get rather suspicious of people who hang around murder investigations. It isn't healthy, if you know what I mean.'

'No,' said Cindy, nettled. 'I do not.'

'Think about it. *I* know you're harmless, relatively speaking, and that your only crime is an attempt to generate some self-publicity to revive a flagging career, but less tolerant officers . . .'

'How dare you!'

'Sorry,' said Hatch. 'That was probably uncalled for. But you would do well to remember that, while we welcome all the information we can get from the public, we do tend to prefer it if you leave the interpretation to us, because *we've* been there before.'

But had they? *Had* they been here before? Would Hatch have been able to say that when, for instance, his Hampshire colleagues had discovered, not so very long ago, that a particularly brutal stabbing was down to a twelve-year-old girl who received *sexual gratification* from killing? The youngest potential serial murderer in history, dealt with at Winchester Crown Court in March, 1997.

The end of the millennium was continually pushing back the parameters of human experience.

The British police had simply never encountered a killer who walked the ancient tracks, in the footsteps of his prehistoric ancestors, and committed ritual murders – he would perhaps regard them as sacrifices – which were identifiable as such only by the nature of their locations. No connection at all, except to someone educated in the arcane mysteries of the landscape.

'There are more crimes in heaven and earth than are dreamt of in *your* philosophy, my friend.'

Cindy watched the clouds formation-dancing over the bay.

'*Bananas, you are, Cindy.*'

The eyes of Kelvyn Kite bulged from the shadows in his corner beside the sink.

'*Why do you bother, you old fool?*'

The bird had a point. Why *did* he bother?

Hatch's barb about self-publicity had stung only briefly. The stage was his career, but not his life. And he didn't need the money. His lifestyle was humble. He followed the work around Britain and returned periodically to this very pretty fairground caravan on a tiny plot, which he owned, in a sheltered spot on the most beautiful part of the Pembrokeshire coast. His earthly life was neatly boxed, the corners of the box pleasantly scuffed and rounded.

As for his inner life . . . Well, sometimes it seemed to be getting richer, more complex. One day, he would have to retire and embark upon the final stage of the great quest, in preparation for his transition. But that was probably years ahead. He couldn't help feeling there should be an interim stage. The idea that one should live one's spiritual life solely in preparation for what was to follow did seem unnecessarily self-indulgent. There ought to be a way of using the incidental abilities one inevitably acquired along the way for the greater good of the community at large.

To fight earthly evils?

Perhaps.

Cindy gathered all the press cuttings into a pile. On top was the one from the *Shropshire Star* he'd picked up last week, during the two nights the Transit Theatre Company's *Macbeth* had been playing the Ludlow Assembly Rooms. It was the kind of news story which, for Hatch, would be a complete joke but, to Cindy, was confirmation.

MURDER SHOP 'HAUNTED' CLAIM.

The story was written in a way that indicated nobody on the paper believed it either. It referred to the butchering of the homeless boy in the shop doorway, the case which had brought Cindy to the notice of the West Mercia CID. Now a local youth leader was claiming attendance at his club was falling off because youngsters didn't like to go past this particular shop at night.

'Two of the girls told me they had felt a sudden drop in the temperature as they passed the doorway, and one is convinced she saw a trail of blood dripping from the step to the gutter.

'These are decent girls, not, in my view, the kind to be prone to fantasies,' said Mr Ruscoe, who is calling for the area to be exorcised.

However, the owner of the hardware shop, Chamber of Trade chairman Mr James Mills, has condemned the scare. 'This was a terrible incident, which most people in this town just want to try to forget,' he said.

'Fairy stories like this are not good for trade or local morale, and Ted Ruscoe should have more sense than to encourage them.'

'Fairy stories,' said Cindy scornfully. 'Fairy stories!'

The man would, of course, have to be the chairman of the Chamber of Trade. Cindy was continually amazed at the arrogance of small-time local officials, who considered their particular field of commercial endeavour to be of supreme importance in the great scheme of things.

The police, in most cases, were exactly the same. If you couldn't explain it to the Crown Prosecution Service they wouldn't even consider it.

Cindy swept the pile of press cuttings into a box file and went back to work on the magazines. Wherever he went, he sought out the local dealers in publications devoted to paganism and earth-magic, some of them, like *Fortean Times*, *Kindred Spirit* and *Chalice*, high-quality glossies; some, like *The Ley Hunter*, quite specialized, and others little more than photocopied pages stapled together. At least one of these, surely, was read – and possibly contributed to – by the killer. Cindy saw this individual as someone with very definite and fixed ideas – ideas which he would want to disseminate. Also, like most killers, he would want his acts to be noticed.

The letters pages were a very likely source of clues. Cindy flicked open an issue of *Pagan Quest*.

Dear Sir, I have been a worshipper of Thor for over nine years and have recently moved to Basingstoke, where I am anxious to contact fellow pagans . . .

Most of them, unfortunately, were on this level. Cindy wondered if there were any submitted letters that the editors of these magazines considered too extreme for publication. He'd had no reply from Marcus Bacton at *The Phenomenologist*. But perhaps that had not been such a great idea. The journal only came out at three- monthly intervals, so even if its staid and ageing readers had any ideas, it might be Christmas before they appeared.

'Kelvyn, who was that boy we met in Gloucester who wanted to interview me? Long, red hair.'

'Jasper somebody, wasn't it?'

'His mag was called . . . No, it wasn't Jasper, you stupid bird, it was Gareth, Gareth Milburn, and the mag was called Cauldron . . . *Crucible!*'

Cindy leafed through a copy of a pagan magazine in which other, smaller pagan magazines tended to place small ads.

'Here we are, Kelvyn . . . *Crucible*! Oh, and a phone number, there's unusual.'

Cindy prodded out the number on his mobile.

'*Blessed be! You're through to Crucible. Leave a message and we'll get back to you . . . one way or another, ha, ha, ha.*'

'Gareth, it's Cindy Mars-Lewis, the humble thespian you were so determined to out as a pagan earlier this year . . .'

Cindy hung up, unsatisfied, restless. There must be something else he could do.

'*What's your hurry, old fool?*'

'I don't know. I feel . . .'

Cindy picked up his pendulum, slipped a middle finger through the loop.

' . . . I feel it's getting closer.'

When held over the maps at each of the murder spots, the pendulum reacted in exactly the same way: a furious anti-clockwise spin. What would Hatch say to that?

You're making it do that, he'd say scornfully. Even if you're not doing it consciously, something inside you wants it to happen.

Of all the extra-sensory disciplines, dowsing was the most widely accepted. It began with the practical skill of water-divining, but no-one knew where it ended, how deep it would go in its search for hidden truths. Sometimes, it seemed to be simply a way of communicating to your conscious mind something that you already subconsciously knew. Other times, as the great T. C. Lethbridge had first demonstrated, it could be your link with different levels of existence and, perhaps, with some great cosmic database from which information could be gathered.

Sometimes, as Cindy had found, the pendulum would spin like a propeller, a preliminary to shamanic flight . . . as when he'd held it over the spot in the Elan Valley in mid-Wales where the barbed-wire trap had been laid.

On a whim, Cindy spread out the pagan and earth-magic magazines in a circular fan formation and held the pendulum over the table.

He closed his eyes. 'Now,' he said, 'tell me. Which one of these, if any, will guide me towards the person who killed Maria Capaldi?'

Emptying his mind, letting conscious thoughts blow away like leaves.

Knowing, before he opened his eyes, that the pendulum was spinning furiously.

But over *The Phenomenologist*?

Cindy was sceptical. He was fond of the archaic publication, although under the editorship of this man Bacton it had become a little political, even angry sometimes. Still, there was always some message to be gleaned from the action of the pendulum. Perhaps it was time to telephone Bacton.

But what about the big question? He collected up all the magazines, put them in a pile on the floor and opened up his map of Britain on the tabletop. He sat upright, a hand on each knee, the pendulum under his right hand. He rotated his head a few times to relax the neck muscles, did some brief tensing and relaxation on the arms and legs, stomach and back, and followed this with some chakra-breathing, three times round the seven points, until he felt light and separated and glowing.

Then he began to visualize the islands from afar. The sound of the sea and the gulls through the open window lifting him. Feeling the air currents under his wings.

Flying.

Over the New Forest to the glade where a girl lay impaled . . .

. . . across the scrubbed mid-Wales hills to the flooded valleys, following the line of the oakwood, faster and faster, into the sudden whiplash snap and twang of barbed wire . . .

. . . spinning back across the English border, the tension of Offa's Dyke . . . the flash of rivers, the bulging of hills, the bright, hot grille of the ley lines . . .

. . . towards Clee Hill and the timber-framed market town . . . above a cobbled street to a doorway, bloodied cardboard in the pink dawn . . . and up again and down the border until he felt . . .

. . . three twitches from Harold's Stones and the choking terror of a girl, thumbs in her larynx . . .

. . . Across the Marlborough Downs, over old crop circles, feeling the magnetic, goose-pimpling pull of the still-pulsing Avebury henge, hovering over a field he did not know where a faceless man lay under a mask of blood . . .

. . . and then . . . and then . . .

Cindy felt his hand rising from his knee and the weight of the pendulum as it began to swing over the map. He closed his eyes.

Now.

Where will it happen next?

Later, unnerved, Cindy telephoned Marcus Bacton, editor of *The Phenomenologist*.

'Marsh-*what*?'

'Mars-Lewis. We've never spoken before, but I pen the occasional piece for you under the name Cindy the Shaman.'

'Oh my God. Look here, Mrs, er, Lewis, we're a trifle old-fashioned at *The Phenomenologist*. Correspondents who wish to communicate with us tend to put it in writing.'

'Just wondering, I was, Mr Bacton, if you had perused my letter regarding the murders.'

'Oh, hell, Look, er, Lewis. One doesn't want to bring down the heavy editorial hand, but – much as we value your contributions on Celtic shaman practices – this is not bloody True Crime Monthly.'

'No, indeed, I understand. But I have personal reasons

for continuing my investigations and it has occurred to me that you may be able to help me.'

'Very much doubt that. Look, I'm rather up to the bloody eyes—'

'I suspect the person I'm looking for, see – the murderer – may well, at some point, have been in communication with your periodical.'

'Oh, right. You're saying one of our chaps is a bloody psycho. I see. Well, what about Miss Pinder, the ectoplasm lady from Chiswick? I can just imagine her striding across the Welsh moors with a fifty-foot roll of barbed wire . . .'

'Always this receptive, are you, Mr Bacton?'

'What?'

'No wonder your circulation is sinking so rapidly.'

'Bloody hell! Look, Lewis. I can do without this. Things are bloody fraught enough just at the moment. For a start, we've had a rather difficult death . . .'

The phone seemed to freeze in Cindy's hand.

'Death?'

It took nearly twenty minutes and several attempts by Bacton to get him off the line, but when Cindy finally put down the phone he had learned how and where the house-keeper, Mrs Willis, had died. And that she had been a very good woman, a herbalist and a spiritual healer.

Cindy retired to bed with several back numbers of *The Phenomenologist* and Franklin and Job's *Guide to Prehistoric Remains on the Welsh Borders*.

He already had his suitcase packed.

XX

Marcus Bacton raged quite a bit.

His way of dealing with grief, Bobby Maiden decided. Obviously a huge hole in Marcus's life now, and the farmhouse seemed as much of a shell as the castle outside. Yet he never spoke of Mrs Willis as anyone more than the woman who had kept his home together. And his only show of emotion was rage.

Maiden had kept well out of the way while the paramedics were around, leaving Andy as the sole official witness to the old woman's death.

If they hadn't taken her off the stone, it would have looked suspicious; as it was – an experienced nurse with her when she died – it was just another case of an elderly woman wandering away, the way some elderly women did, and collapsing from a stroke.

The day after Mrs Willis's death, Andy had gone back to Elham, telling Marcus she'd return for the funeral. Examining Maiden's eye one more time, ordering him to get a good night's sleep.

And he had. No dreams, no sweat.

And again. *Two* good nights. He wanted to believe he was coming out of it; he didn't dare. Death still hung over him but its shadow was less defined.

Andy had bathed and repatched his eye with more gauze and tape. The second day, a small parcel arrived containing a black plastic eyeshield.

Maiden put on the patch, laid low, blanked out. The holiday cottage was a good place for it, a former dairy with only three rooms and all the walls of whitewashed stone. There was a small kitchen with a hotplate and grill, and Andy had left bread and soup and fruit. He didn't see too much of Marcus, who was making funeral arrangements, raging at the vicar, who claimed his churchyard was full and Mrs Willis wasn't local anyway. 'Fat bastard,' Marcus fumed. 'Know where *he's* from? Fucking *Croydon*.'

'Why don't you tell him who she was?'

'Because I don't *know* who she was. And that's official.'

Marcus shoved at him a letter from Mrs Willis's solicitors, in Hereford. She'd left him five thousand pounds and requested that he should make no inquiries into her past, nor in any way speculate publicly about her.

'Bloody typical. Unassuming to an almost perverse degree. Didn't even like being called a healer. Less than a year ago, she cured Amy, at the pub, of bloody skin cancer. *Amy* knew what it was, the bloody *doctors* knew what it was . . . Mrs Willis said it was *just a rash*. And you've heard about Anderson, of course. If you can't take the word of a trained nurse . . .'

And me? Maiden wondered. Did she bring *me* back, by proxy?

Relaxed enough, now, to consider the possibility. Almost dispassionately. He felt sorry about Mrs Willis, of course he did, just like the last hundred deaths, the accidents, the suicides, the murders. But in the end, it wasn't his tragedy.

Or was it? Why had he urged Andy to get the old girl off the stone? He didn't know, then or now. Why had he felt so uncomfortable at the place you had to be careful, in front of Marcus, not to call *Black* Knoll?

'So no-one's going to know she was Annie Davies?'

Marcus held up the letter in frustration. 'Bastards,' he said.

Maiden wasn't quite sure who he meant. Perhaps he meant everybody.

★   ★   ★

Even though they'd agreed that he was Bobby Wilson, Marcus's nephew, over for the funeral of a woman he'd come to regard as a granny figure, Maiden never went down to the village. Instead, he took long, uneven walks among the hills around St Mary's, across this strange no man's land between England and Wales – pink soil and stone, autumn fires on the fields under the dark mantelpiece of the mountains.

Lying down in the grass, a west wind on his face, he thought about the kind of things he *wanted* to respond to. He thought about painting again. And he thought about Emma Curtis.

The second night, Marcus banged on the cottage door to say Andy was on the phone for him. Police had been waiting for her at home. Wondering if she had any idea of the whereabouts of their missing colleague, about whom they were a little worried.

Also wondering where she'd been, perhaps.

Maiden took the call in Marcus's study. 'How did you handle it?'

'Told them – Jesus God – told 'em I'd spent the night wi' a man friend. Refusing to disclose his name on account of he was a doctor and married.'

'Nice one,' Maiden said.

'Aw, sure. Like they were gonny believe there was any doctor still young enough to work who'd take up wi' an old bat like me.'

'Or that you'd take up with a doctor, knowing how tired they always are.'

'Cheeky sod. You're sounding better, Bobby.'

'Two nights now.'

'Did I no tell you about the air? Anyway, I told this guy I had absolutely no idea where you might be and if they found you to bring you back at once, on account we hadn't yet given your head the all-clear.'

Maiden gazed into the flames jetting between flaking

logs in Marcus's woodstove. 'Who was this?'

'CID guy. Sergeant. Said he was a friend of yours.'

'Mike Beattie?'

'Aye. Trust him at all?'

'No.'

'Well, I did say you'd been very mixed up and restless and it was no big surprise to learn you'd skipped out. That all right for you?'

'That's fine. Just one thing. Maybe you could avoid ringing here from home. Call boxes are best.'

'Aw, hey, come on . . . they wouldnae—'

'They might,' Maiden said. 'They just might. I mean, if they already are doing, we're stuffed. But these things can take time to fiddle.'

Amid the clutter on Marcus's desk of beaten-up mahogany lay a new hardback book with a dark cover and big, silver lettering: *Beyond Roswell: The Paranoid Decades*.

'And maybe . . . I don't like to ask this, but is there any way you could avoid coming down for the funeral?'

'They could follow me?'

'It's possible.'

'Well,' Andy said bitterly, 'if you explain to Marcus. Don't imagine I'd be missed. I'm no bloody good to her now, am I?'

When he put down the phone, Marcus was furiously polishing his glasses. He put them on and glared through them.

'Maiden, what kind of shit have you got that woman into?'

Putting himself between Maiden and the stove. He had on what seemed to be his usual leisurewear, which included a long blue cardigan and a mustard bow tie. It had grown dark outside and the fire accounted for most of the light in the room.

'If you're going to use my house as some sort of bunker,

you can at least tell me precisely why. Am I going to wake up to find the place surrounded by some fucking task force with loud hailers and automatic rifles?'

'I think we can rule out the armed response unit,' Maiden said. 'But that's probably all we can rule out.'

'Going to sit down, are we, Maiden?' Marcus smiled threateningly. 'Have a drink?'

'No thanks. No good for head injuries, apparently.'

He found a sofa. Marcus dragged a bottle of Teachers' whisky and a tumbler from his desk and slumped with them into an easy chair by the stove, white stuffing spurting out of the seat as though the chair was frothing at the mouth.

'Entertain me,' he said. 'Remembering that I spent thirty years interrogating schoolboys. World's most convincing liar, the schoolboy.'

'Well . . .' Maiden sank into a dusty, brocaded cushion. 'The bottom line is, I suspect my superior officer would like me out of the picture.'

'You *are* out of the picture. You're eighty miles away. If you mean dead, Maiden, say it.'

'Dead, then.'

'Why, precisely?'

Maiden said, 'For being possibly the only copper in Elham division who hasn't at some time, to some extent, been on the take.'

Yes, he thought. It *is* that simple.

Marcus leaned forward, firelight gleaming fiercely in his heavy spectacles. Then he poured himself a Scotch.

'That's it, then, is it?' he said. 'I mean, do forgive me, Maiden, but I was rather expecting something to test the imagination.'

Only later, when Marcus was too drunk and maudlin to handle and he was trudging across the yard to the cottage, did Maiden realize this hadn't been sarcasm.

'Correct me if I'm wrong, Maiden.' Marcus holding out

his tumbler and gazing into the whisky as if it was the true elixir of life. 'But you snuffed it, didn't you?'

'Apparently.'

'And dear old Anderson coaxed you back from the Other Place when everybody was ready to pull the plug, have you bagged up and put in a big drawer or whatever they do. Doesn't that make you think? I mean, you now *know* that there's something beyond death. Does that not change your whole life, utterly and completely? Doesn't it blow your mind? Doesn't it make you think, here I am, a snivelling little detective getting all worked up about a bunch of bent coppers, when there are *real* mysteries all around. Mysteries so close, so damned *intimate* . . . that most people, especially policemen, never even focus on them. *Big* mysteries. Don't you ever feel overwhelmingly excited? Humble, even?'

He didn't want to answer that. Didn't want to confess to feeling, in what was supposed to be his soul, a coldness and a bleakness and a complete absence of hope.

Marcus sank a quantity of whisky. 'I was a teacher, Maiden.'

'Never have guessed.'

'Something happened to you. Like the thing that happened to Mrs Willis on High Knoll on her thirteenth birthday. Now, in all of the six decades of my life on Planet Earth, while the way we live has changed and worsened out of all recognition, I have never had anything that could be described as a vaguely mystical or paranormal experience. Which is why I run a spotty little magazine devoted to it. If I *had* had any kind of experience, I'd be out there *living* it . . . doing things, making things *happen*. But, then, you know what they say about teachers.'

Maiden said, after a barely respectful pause, 'Them as can do, them as can't . . . teach.'

'Which is why people like you make me sick. You *died*, Maiden. You died. And you came back. *And what the holy fuck are you doing about it?*'

XXI

Folklore. There was a whole lot of it around the Rollright Stones, Matthew Lyall said, and most of it was pretty sinister stuff.

The circle sure looked sinister today, with a black cloud the shape of a bathtub hanging over it, and these stalky pines; Grayle never had liked pines, they were too aloof, blocked out the sun but never seemed to offer you shelter. Pines didn't care.

In contrast to some of the ruined stone circles she'd seen in pictures, the Rollrights looked like a true circle. Almost too complete, the stones packed in tight, so it was like a wall in places. Matthew's girlfriend, Janny Oates, said it was part of the folklore of the site that if you counted the stones, you would never get the same number twice.

'The circle's known as the King's Men,' Matthew said. 'That stone over there is the King Stone, and across there is a group of stones that used to be a burial chamber, only it's caved in, and that's called the Whispering Knights.'

The stones were weird. The King Stone was like a twisted tree stump, and there were metal railings around it, like it might break out. The smaller stones, in the circle, were eroded, like lumps of rotting cheese.

This site should have been surrounded by miles of forest and swamps and stuff, and yet here it was, among well-tended fields, barely a half-hour out of Oxford.

'Ersula was here?' she said.

'We wanted her to spend the night,' Matthew said. 'In the stones. I said I'd be her therapeute.'

'But she wouldn't,' Janny said.

'Which we thought was unusual,' Matthew said, 'considering how enthusiastic she'd been, you know, in the end, about the whole experiment.'

Janny and Matthew were kind of cute. They were very early twenties and engaged. Both scrubbed and shiny, real childhood sweetheart types. They wore identical Shetland sweaters and finished off one another's sentences as if they'd been married for years.

'When was this?' Grayle asked. 'When was she here? When did you last see her?'

They'd both been on a University of the Earth course when Ersula was there. Now they were working weekends with something called the Dragon Project, which was a long-term inquiry into anomalous levels of radiation and electromagnetism at selected ancient sites. The Rollrights was its main base, which was fine for Janny and Matthew, who lived nearby, in the town of Chipping Camden.

'Three weeks.' Janny flicked back her fine, light-brown hair. 'Where did she say she was going then, Matthew?'

'Actually,' Matthew said, 'she seemed a little confused. I think she'd had what my father would call a mind-blowing experience. That was back at Cefn-y-bedd. When we first met her, Ersula was very much the scientist, and she was sort of pooh-poohing all this stuff about earth-energies that Janny and I *knew* existed.'

'Because we'd spent all our holidays going to hundreds of sites, and you can just tell after a while. You just walk into a circle and . . . and . . .'

'Whoosh,' Grayle said sadly.

'Absolutely. That's exactly it, isn't it, Matthew? I think – well, I'm certain – that Ersula came round to our way of thinking. And that can be quite a shock to the system when you start off by not believing.'

'She was sort of wandering around the stones,' Matthew said. 'Looking a bit starved.'

'As though she had a cold coming on, or a chill. I offered

her some tea from our flask, but she shook her head. She was wearing this enormous parka, with the hood up, though it wasn't a bad day, was it?'

'Not like today,' Matthew said. 'I don't think we'll be sleeping out tonight, Jan.'

Grayle thought, Jeez, I sure wouldn't like to sleep here. She stepped out of the circle, turned away. Just being near these grim, broken stones solidified all her fears for Ersula. It was clear she hadn't told anyone on the course about her awful dream at Black Knoll, the full details of which she couldn't even tell her own sister.

'Look.' Matthew patted her arm. 'I wouldn't worry about her, you know. I mean, compared with . . . well, some of the people involved in earth-mysteries are a bit bonkers, to be honest. But Ersula really had her feet on the ground.'

Grayle's father had said, *Be careful*.

Not what she'd expected. She'd imagined something like, *I never openly said this to you, Grayle, but I hated that column. I found it gross. It gives me enormous pleasure that you outgrew it finally*.

No, nothing like that. Dr Erlend Underhill had never once mentioned the column. He'd copied out the addresses and phone numbers of two professors he knew, history guys in Oxford, said he would call them to put them in the picture, tell them she was on her way. Grayle said, Why? Because, right now, prehistoric studies in England was attracting a large number of crazies, her father said; you needed some back-up, a point of reference.

'Dad, I'm an official, badge-wearing weirdo. I can *bond* with crazies.'

'Humour me,' her father said humourlessly. And insisted on giving her five thousand dollars for airfares and accommodation. 'This is family business. Keep me informed.'

Next, she'd gone to tough it out with the editor. Who,

to her dismay, seemed entirely undisturbed at his unique New Age columnist's wanting to quit. 'Yeah,' he said nonchalantly. 'I agree the column's been a mite tired of late.' (*What?*) 'We can handle it in-house, maybe. I got a couple new kids in the city room, maybe we can give it a new slant.' He meant save money. Asshole.

All right, she hadn't expected Burton to plead, but it still wasn't the exit she'd imagined. So she'd had her last doughnut with Lyndon (you were right, maybe I peaked), held back the tears, and took the first daytime flight out of JFK with a small suitcase and a strange lightness in the head.

The next night she was in Woodstock, the one Jimi Hendrix never played, outside of Oxford, at the home of her father's one-time associate, a sixty-year-old ancient history professor called Duncan Murphy, and his Australian partner, Nancy Chad, a poet.

'Oh yes, we know Roger Falconer,' Duncan Murphy said. 'People tend to sneer these days because he's big on the box and making the most of it, but that's us Brits for you. Can't stand other people's success. Of course, we'd all be doing pretty much the same in his place and he knows it. And he does actually know his stuff. These rather lucrative courses he runs, he may have let the ley-liners in, but that doesn't mean he accepts what they have to say. He *listens*, that's all. On the box, and during the courses too, no doubt, he appears more liberal than he actually is, which tends to be the best policy, long-term-careerwise, I've found.'

Grayle remembered the issue of *The Phenomenologist*, the almost unreadably dense journal which Ersula had enclosed with her last letter. The one with the front-page editorial which read:

Professor Falconer boasts of his 'open-minded' approach to the paranormal. In fact, all his books show him to be a sneering sceptic, and the 'exciting new venture' at Cefn-y-bedd promises to be merely a cynical exploitation of genuine seekers – people who, unlike Falconer, are unafraid to venture into battle without their academic armour.

'I was at a dinner party with him a couple of years ago,' Nancy Chad said, 'and that actually wasn't my impression. I thought he had a great *passion* for prehistoric people. That seems a strange way of putting it, but I can't think of a better one. He'll talk at length about the abilities we've lost that they possessed in abundance. He's quite magnetic when he gets going. I reckon he's closer to the ley-liners than he admits.'

How close to Ersula? Grayle wondered. Ersula, for whom knowledge could also be a great passion. *Unlike me, I just get crushes.*

'Women always claim to know him better,' Duncan Murphy said disapprovingly. 'Anyway, you can judge for yourself. I got you a videotape of a couple of his programmes. You won't mind if we don't watch it tonight?'

The video cassette had a picture on the box of a lean, suntanned man in denims and Ray-Bans, his back to the Great Pyramid of Giza.

'That's good of you,' Grayle said. 'Thanks.'

'Your father's done me many favours. He's very proud of Ersula, you know. I'm sorry, that's not to say—'

Grayle smiled. 'How old is Falconer?'

'Fifty-five going on twenty-five. Keeps himself fit, has to be said. Swims, rides, pilots his own chopper.'

'Ah yes,' Nancy Chad said archly. 'That as well. Some of my friends figure the guy's biggest claim to fame is the one he can't keep in his pants for too long.'

Raising the question of casual sex. The Ersula that Grayle knew didn't do casual anything. *For me*, she'd say loftily, if unoriginally, *the most erogenous zone is the mind.* Oh sure, Grayle had said. Until it happens.

'Look,' Duncan said. 'I feel I'm not doing enough.'

'Oh, hey, come on—'

'You probably need a more . . . radical viewpoint than ours. I didn't know whether to mention this, but some of our neighbours, their son and his girlfriend were on one of Falconer's courses. They spend most weekends down at the Rollrights, messing about with magnetometers and things. Won't take you long to get there and it'll give you a taste of what it's all about.'

'You know what I think?' Janny's face glowing with the need to be kind. 'I think she needed to go away by herself and think everything through. Everything that happened to her.'

'I can see her in some Oxford library,' Matthew said, 'hunched up with a laptop computer, feeding everything, puzzling it all out. I can imagine her getting a book out of this.'

'Not Oxford, Matt. More like Hereford library. I think she'll have gone back to the Welsh border. She was obsessed with the dolmen at Black Knoll, though, personally, I never thought it had much going for it. Not compared to Avebury and, well, here . . .'

'Why did she come here?' Grayle asked.

'Oh.' Janny looked as though she hadn't given this much thought. 'Well, I suppose . . . I mean, she knew we were here most weekends, and we'd said to her, you know, please come over when your next course is finished and you've got some free time. She just wanted to hang around and talk, I suppose, sort of loosen up.'

'The way you described her, she doesn't sound at all loosened up. She tell you much about her experiences with the dreaming thing?'

'Well,' said Matthew, 'she asked us a lot of questions about *our* experiences.'

'Like what?'

'Whether we'd ever been . . .'

'. . . frightened,' Janny said. 'I mean, we weren't

supposed to talk about our dreams or that would defeat the object of the exercise if someone was thinking about another person's dream and had the same one. The idea is to find out what influence *the site* has on our subconscious.'

'And have you?' Grayle said. 'Have you ever been scared?'

Matthew folded his arms. 'Not *scared*. Some of it's sort of . . . challenging.'

'In what way?'

'Oh, I can't tell you without . . . Should I tell her, Janny? I mean, it's not as if she . . .'

'. . . is actually involved. Go on, then.'

'I met the guardian once. That was here. At least I presume it was the guardian. Every site has one, you know. In my dream, I was over by the Whispering Knights, and this old lady was there . . .'

'Old . . . *lady*?' Janny spluttered.

'Oh well, a hag. She was pretty revolting, actually. She was wearing a sort of ragged cloak and she had terrible staring eyes, and she . . . um . . . smelled pretty awful. Oh, look, I'm not sure I should be telling you this . . . not here.'

Grayle said, 'Smelled?'

'I think it's OK,' Janny said. 'I think she was supposed to be off-putting. Guardians are. You've got to demonstrate your resolve, your intensity of purpose, by standing up to them. And you did, didn't you, Matt?'

'Well, I didn't run away. I just sort of tried to meet her eyes. And then she sort of dissolved, and that was when Janny woke me to get it down on tape.'

'You still have the tape?' Grayle said.

'No, this was a Dragon Project thing. We did a transcript and then . . . I don't know where it is.'

'So what's the difference between the Dragon Project and Falconer's stuff?'

'Well, the Dragon Project started it off, the national dream survey thing. It's all going into a computer in California or somewhere, to see if there are any correlations. I suppose Professor Falconer sort of picked up on it.'

'What happened,' said Janny, 'is a chap called Adrian Fraser-Hale, who was involved with the Dragon Project, went to work for Falconer, as an expert on the sort of earth-mysteries stuff . . .'

'And Roger thought it was a good idea,' Matthew said.

'You mean . . .' Grayle said carefully, 'he thought it would attract people to his courses.'

'He isn't like that!' the kids said almost in unison.

Matthew added, 'I really think he's going to be the best thing that ever happened to the earth-mysteries movement. Because he's part of the Establishment. I mean, in archaeology, he *is* the Establishment. If people like Adrian can convince him that there's really another dimension to prehistoric science, it could be the start of changing the whole of human thought.'

'Right,' Grayle said. Thinking, I was here before; everyone's on the point of a major breakthrough. 'So, uh, what conclusions do you draw from this guardian thing?'

'Well . . .' Matthew looked over his shoulder as though he thought this hag might be eyeing him from the edge of the circle. 'I suppose this is a bit obvious, but the legend of the Rollrights is about this king – not any specific king, just a sort of regional chief – who encountered the witch who controlled the land and – it's a bit like Macbeth really – the witch said to him that if he took seven long strides from here . . .'

At this point, Matthew and Janny looked at each other, held hands, said together, *'If Long Compton thou canst see, King of England thou shalt be!'* bringing their joined hands up and down to the rhythm.

'Well,' Matthew said, 'the king thought this was going to be a pushover, because he knew the village of Long Compton would come into view as soon as he reached the top of the rise. Only problem was, when he got there, this mound had arisen on the horizon and completely blocked his view.'

'Screwed, huh?'

'Turned to stone, actually. The witch turned the king into what is now the King's Stone, over there, and these are his men.'

Grayle looked around the cheesy circle, planning to smile, but it got overtaken by a shudder.

'She offer you anything, Matthew?'

'If she ever did, I hope I wouldn't be arrogant, like the king. I think, actually, she was telling me – us – that it was OK. Giving us her blessing.'

'We're going to be married next week,' Janny said.

'Well, uh, congratulations.' Grayle was suddenly feeling very old.

'We love it here, as you can imagine. It's our part of the world. The most mysterious part of our part of the world. Earth-mysteries is about discovering your own heritage, and this is ours. That's why we're doing it here.'

'There's a church out here?' Grayle looked around. No village visible, no spire, no tower, but presumably Long Compton was just over the next mound.

'No, *here*, silly. In the circle.'

'Jesus,' Grayle said. 'You guys are, like, witches?'

'Oh, good God, no. We've not gone pagan or anything.'

'Though we've nothing against that, obviously,' Matthew said hurriedly. 'But this is going to be a proper Christian service. There's a chap we know who was ordained and practised as a curate before he sort of . . . dropped out.'

'As your father would say.' Janny giggled.

'Actually, he was a friend of my father's. Used to turn up and camp on our sofa for days at a time, and the old man got a bit annoyed, but he is a real clergyman. Sort of.'

Grayle shook her head, mystified.

'My mother's a bit disgusted with us, actually,' Matthew said. 'Wanted the full church bit. But they don't realize these places were the original churches. I mean, the number of churches actually built inside stone circles or in places where there used to be circles or on top of Bronze Age mounds . . . I mean, a holy place is a holy place. Energy is energy.'

'And something really joyous like a wedding is really giving some energy back to the earth.'

The stones were all around Janny and Matthew like an open mouth full of decaying teeth. Grayle couldn't imagine there being joy here.

'It'd be lovely if you could come, if you're still around,' Janny said. 'We did invite Ersula, but . . .'

'Right,' Grayle said dismally.

XXII

On an evening like this, the village was made of stone and smoke.

The first fires had been lit on the cottage hearths – lit with abandon because the log-piles were high. The first amber lights were showing in the cottages, and an ice-blue fluorescence stuttered from the deep freeze in the village shop.

Easing the elderly Morris Minor across the stone bridge over the young but apparently seldom rebellious river Monnow and into the core of the village, Cindy felt unexpectedly nervous and stopped a while, with the windows cranked down, to watch and listen. And perhaps absorb, through secret pores, the essence.

An overcast sky. October, that most mysterious and numinous of months, was really beginning to *be* October, the land vibrating with the subtle lights of *nearness*.

The warped sign of the Ram's Head creaked in the breeze – perhaps it would be best to stay there tonight, if there was a room available – and, above it all, the warm clangour of bell practice was there to sustain and protect the ancient spirit, like cupped hands over a candle.

It was a night to drink cider and drowse by the inglenook in the pub, to the mellow thud of darts and the rumble of country laughter.

But not for Cindy, who was here to investigate a death.

No wonder that, when he had asked the pendulum *Where will it happen next?* it had not responded to the Welsh border. Because *it had already happened*.

And this time there was nothing particularly suspicious. An old lady had wandered away, disoriented no doubt, and died of a stroke. No intensive police investigation, no forensics, no scenes of crime people, no orange tape. Cindy would be free to examine Marcus Bacton's beloved High Knoll burial chamber without either being interrupted or the risk of further falling foul of the constabulary.

Perhaps an hour of daylight remained. He would go at once.

To find out, if he could, how a place of light had become a place of death.

'For you.' Marcus thrust the phone through a morass of books and typescript. 'Some woman.'

With Mrs Willis gone, the study was a mess. Unwashed teacups, and biscuit crumbs stuck to used whisky glasses. Verging on the squalid. Even worse than Maiden's flat, but his offer to help clean the place up had led to a brusque invitation to fuck off back to the cottage and keep his nose out.

The inquest had been opened and adjourned very rapidly, no uncomfortable questions – everyone apparently accepting, as Maiden had thought they would, that old dears sometimes died in unusual places. So the body was available for burial, throwing Marcus into a state about how the hell you organized a funeral, who you invited, all this sort of bloody palaver.

'A woman asking, somewhat coyly in my view, for a Mr Lazarus,' Marcus said.

For Maiden, the squalor instantly mellowed to somewhere around cosily chaotic.

'Still alive, then,' Emma Curtis said.

Now he was alive. 'Where you calling from?'

'Yeah, don't worry, I got that message. Your fairy godmother, the Rottweiler of Elham General . . . we've had coffee a couple of times. She thought you were being paranoid. Not me, baby, I know these reptiles too well. Hence, I'm in the phone booth inside the public bloody library. Late night opening. Listen, I just popped into the reading room for a glance at the *Elham Messenger*, just out. It says . . . hang on, let me fold the thing . . . it says your condition is giving cause for concern and you're believed to have been transferred to some specialist neurological unit in Brum. Unnamed, naturally.'

'I'm a *cabbage*?'

'Also, the paper suggests the police are having second thoughts about a hit-and-run. It's *believed* there is a real possibility that no third party was involved. Looks like you fell off the kerb, Bobby. Pissed again, I expect.'

'Bloody Riggs. Who's that guy he knows at the *Messenger*?'

'Roger Gibbs. What it is, Gibbs is next in line for Grand Worshipful thingy at the Lodge. Simple as that. Or so Vic says. Vic knows these things. Hey, you sound better.'

'All the better, as they say, for hearing you. Perhaps, er, perhaps we need to meet. Do you think? Discuss the whole situation in greater depth.'

'The *whole* situation? Are you up to discussing the whole situation?'

'In depth,' Maiden said.

'Really. Oh, well . . . No, hang on, there's a bloke outside. Just a bloke, I think, but we can't be too careful. Well, yes, I thought I could come down. Take you for a little outing. Uncle.'

'That would be very nice, my dear. When might one expect to be exposed to your delightful company?'

'Tomorrow?'

'Ah. We do have a funeral tomorrow.'

'Well, maybe you might need cheering up after that. Change of scene. What if I were to make a reservation for you and a friend at some primitive but homely B and B for tomorrow night? Would that help your recovery? Hey, the good Sister said she'd sent you a black eyepatch. Why do we find black eyepatches dead sexy, Bobby, can you tell me? I mean, Long John *Silver*?'

Down the steep lane went the intrepid Morris Minor, *putter, putter, putter*.

It was like going down a rabbit hole, the banks high each side, trees growing from the tops of the banks and tangling overhead, filtering the already meagre light through a dark green grille. At the bottom, you could almost miss the house, the way the single-track road swung round to the right, and the house was down a short track on the left, tree-screened.

Cindy stepped on the brakes and backed up. Ornate gold lettering on a black board read, *Cefn-y-bedd. The University of the Earth*.

Cindy saw lights coming on in the house behind the trees; what were they up to there?

The University of the Earth. Most of what he knew about this enterprise had been gleaned from the obviously biased pages of *The Phenomenologist*. It did, though, sound more than a little irresponsible, offering to connect students and holidaymakers to the inner mind of the planet. It would seem entirely innocuous, of course, to Falconer, an academic, a sceptic, a man who apparently believed there was nothing *out there* more powerful than his own intellect.

How could these people know so much and yet so little? Cindy had read some of the man's learned articles but not seen his apparently more populist television programme. Life was too short to spend in the company of sceptics.

Round the corner, past Falconer's farmhouse went the venerable car, and onto a track of stone and dirt, emerging into an open field, sheep nibbling around the fringes. It was bisected by a rough path, which began as a sheep-track, a narrow, muddied depression, and then turned to concrete before widening into a big, flat apron.

From the sky, this would look like a giant frying pan. Like a landing area for UFOs. A big new shed had gone up, too, and the whole damn thing across not only the path, but the Path – the principal ley line itself, leading through two dinky little round barrows and a standing stone to Dore Abbey itself. How utterly crass of the man.

But the concrete apron was out of sight of the house, so Cindy parked on the edge of it and set off on foot, with his little case. It was important, in a situation like this, to weave in and out of the path of power, the spirit-way. If you followed it directly, you were advertising yourself to the denizens of other planes, and might therefore attract all manner of unnecessary hangers-on.

How fortunate little Annie Davies had been on *that* morning. Just the right side of adolescence, the innocent side, and – due also, no doubt, to a rare and fortuitous pattern of circumstance – exposed to only the right, the very *rightest* elements.

And so her young life was blessed.

Marcus Bacton had written that each time he walked to the Knoll, it was a kind of pilgrimage. He believed it was a naturally blessed place. But of course there was no such thing. Some points on the earth, because of their geophysical properties and their positioning in relation to the sun and the stars, might be termed places of power. But power was not holiness . . . and holiness was not an inherent quality. It could be visited upon a place but it required maintenance.

And there was certainly no sense of holiness here this evening.

Senses racing ahead of him, Cindy followed the path up the side of High Knoll – or Black Knoll as it was called on the map. Why was that? Why *black*? A reference to the Black Mountains, or something more sinister?

Under a wind-blasted hawthorn tree was a small, staked sign.

Black Knoll.
Once a long barrow, this chambered tomb dates from

at least 3000 BC and appears to have been oriented to the midsummer sunrise. A monumental feat of Neolithic engineering, its capstone, now damaged, has been estimated to weigh nearly thirty tons. Evidence of several burials was found during an excavation in 1895.

No mention, naturally, of the vision of Annie Davies.

The stones were on a small, exposed plateau, like an island now in the misty rain. Cindy stopped. He could see the huge capstone, unbalanced and yawning like the open mouth of an alligator.

Where Mrs Willis had lain to die.

The stones glistening with damp and ancient magic.

There was a stout new fence and barbed wire. A gate in the fence was padlocked, but someone had cut the wire, and two of the horizontals had been taken out. Was this before or after the tragic death of Mrs Willis?

Cindy crouched in the damp, yellowed grass and went into the Quiet for a moment, wondering how best to approach.

No birds sang. The grey sky hung low and heavy, like a giant mattress.

A stroke was such a convenient way to go. It was rarely possibly to diagnose how, precisely, the stroke had been brought on. Had Mrs Willis overexerted herself getting here? Or had she been badly frightened by something or someone?

Cindy hitched up his tweed skirt and climbed over the damaged fence and walked, with undeniable trepidation, towards the burial chamber.

Was this, like, primitive, or was this *primitive*?

OK, there was no sawdust on the floor (Grayle had heard some English pubs still had sawdust on the floor), but the Waldorf it was not. The bedroom had a bed with an iron frame and a washbasin you could see the pipes coming out of and then snaking down this hole

215

in the floor. It did not, of course, have a bathroom en suite.

And no phone, on which to call room service and have them bring up a selection of the sweating pork pies and potato chips on sale in the saloon bar (it actually said *saloon bar* on the frosted glass door) or call a doctor to treat your food poisoning and your insomnia.

Grayle had been to Britain twice before in her life. That is, she'd stayed in London and Bath and Stratford-upon-Avon, and all these places were overcrowded but elegantly civilized, as you might expect.

But civilization seemed to end at Hereford. Even the roads. She'd hired this small Rover car in Oxford, spent some time getting over the problems of driving on the left. But most of the roads hereabouts, those problems didn't arise; they were so narrow you just drove right down the middle and closed your eyes and headed for the hedgerow when someone came the other way.

Scared she was going to trash the hire car, Grayle had parked outside the first building resembling a hotel she came to after crossing the St Mary sign and checked in for two nights. The Ram's Head. Maybe a mistake.

Grayle rested her ass on the edge of the bed – which was like a goddamn *girder* – and hoped it would take no longer than a day to establish if anyone in the village or the course centre, Cefn-y-bedd (however the hell you pronounced that), knew of Ersula's present location.

First thing she'd done, on arrival, was to use the phone. Gave the landlady a ten-pound note and called up her dad at the ivory tower.

And no. No, his favourite daughter had not arrived home. Or written. Or phoned. He sounded busy.

Grayle looked out of the window at the stone houses, the church tower. Ancient, beautiful, serene. But the cottages had TV aerials, a couple had satellite dishes, the village shop would rent out videos of Tarantino movies . . . and St Mary's was doubtless full of people with cute country accents thinking, God, I could really've made something of myself if I lived in . . . *the States*.

Feeling suddenly terribly lonely, Grayle keeled over on the bed, clutching her favourite quartz crystal. What if spirituality was just a human fabrication and life's real peaks were getting drunk and getting laid? What if it was like that?

Cindy straightened his tweed skirt and opened his case.

Meeting the gaze of Kelvyn Kite, the bird's glass eyes glittering malevolently. *Silly old tart.*

He scowled at Kelvyn and felt beneath the feathers for his drum, his beautiful *bodhran*, made with deerhide, stretched and patterned, dubbed and tightened, until the skin was a membrane . . . the membrane between worlds.

He decided not to bother with the feathered cloak. Too ostentatious. What he was wearing would surely suffice.

Cindy had come in his female aspect. Arising this morning, on the seaward side of the bed, to bathe in St Bride's Bay. Softening the body with powder and lavender water. Shaving his legs before dressing in sensible country-woman's clothing. Leaving Wales as a woman, entering England as a woman; if High Knoll were to be coaxed into giving up her secrets, there was no other way.

For this was where Annie Davies had been granted a vision of the highest female divinity. A feminine place, a goddess site. The Lady of Light – it didn't matter who she was, Holy Virgin, sun-goddess or alien being – was a symbol of *rightness* of the moment: the time, the person, the location.

Cindy sat upon the earth, in the passageway of open stones leading to the chamber. And began, with his fingers and the heel of his hand, to drum himself into *separation*.

This was the meeting place, the place of the confluence of many paths.

He began to chant, to the hollow, rhythmic resonance of the old drum.

Meeting place.
Meeting place.
Here the sky.
Here the earth.
Here the mountain,
Here the valley.
Here Albion,
Here Cymru.
Meeting place.

Time passed. The chant died. Cindy listened to the evening breeze, to the birds in the distance (the only birds were distant), to the waving of the grass.

He felt the weight of the capstone on the uprights and the strength of the Earth which bore the stones.

He collected all the sounds inside himself, in his head and in his breast and in his solar plexus. He breathed the sounds into his chakras, carried them around his inner circuit and let them go. And began another chant.

Here the sky.
Here the earth.
Here the mountain,
Here the valley.
Here Cindy.
Here Annie?
Here . . . Mrs Willis?

Time passed. Cindy was aware only of a faraway longing and an ache in his stomach. When his eyes opened again, for an agonizing second the sky was very nearly black and the stones were the colour of candlewax.

He didn't move. He took it calmly at first. It had happened before, a whole scene changing into a photographic negative, clouds becoming smoke, muddy rivers running like double cream, green grass turning pink as watered blood.

It had happened before. But never with a smell.

The smell was rank and feral. Of pond slime and decayed leaves with a smear of faeces. Cindy was deeply shaken. His hands felt as if they'd been in cold water. The woman in him felt violated. Holiness, a tender and vulnerable quality, could also be negated, reversed. All too easily. *All* too easily.

Beside the stone, three yards away, a figure stood in green-black smoke and looked down on Cindy, whose fingers fell from the drum, who sprang up in fear.

Stumbling away down the side of the Knoll, coughing into a handkerchief soaked this morning in lavender water.

Fleeing in terror from High Knoll, where little Annie Davies had been granted a vision of the highest female divinity.

High Knoll was a feminine place! A goddess site! Was . . .

XXIII

Amy Jenkins, whose name was over the door of the Ram's Head, was very neat, very dark and very Valleys – Cindy could tell by the little black Juliette Greco dress and all the gold bangles and necklaces. So he shook out his own bangles and stripped down to his glittery high-necked top, and it was as if they'd known each other years.

'Quaker's Yard, I am, born and bred,' Amy said.

'Abercynon,' Cindy lied.

'Never! Don't know Dusty Morgan, do you? He haven't lived there, mind, for thirty years, poor old Dusty. Tegwyn Bogart? Well, that wasn't his real name, but he could curl his lip brilliant, Tegwyn could . . .'

And it went on like this, in the not-very-busy saloon bar of the Tup, as it was known, Cindy having played enough of the South Wales clubs to busk it. *Needing* this . . . needing to be frivolously female for an hour or so to clean out his system after the dark green, malodorous, male evil of the Knoll.

He learned that Amy Jenkins had been in St Mary's less than two years, after half a lifetime in the licensing trade around Merthyr and nearly half a lifetime being married to someone called *That Bastard*. Always wanted a little country pub, she had, and she was going to turn this place into something more like it, soon as her Settlement came through.

Cindy adjusted scatter-cushions on the old oak settle, feeling a little calmer after a couple of rum and peps.

'Come across Marcus Bacton, have you?'

'Marcus?' said Amy. 'You know Marcus?'

'Friend of a friend,' said Cindy. 'Said I'd look him up, see. Only I didn't like to just walk in, things being as they are. The bereavement.'

'*Terrible!*' Amy shook her head, vigorously polishing a pint glass. 'A wonderful lady, Mrs Willis. *Wonderful.*' She leaned over the bar, whispered loud enough to be heard in the street. 'Had *the gift.*'

'Clairvoyance?' Cindy said innocently.

'Healing. Two years ago, had a rash, I did. On my back. Too much sunbathing, see – well, you never think *that's* going to happen, do you? Doctors gave me up for Cheltenham, so I went to see Mrs Willis – because you hear things, running a pub. She says, I'll promise nothing, Mrs Jenkins. Well!'

'Cured?'

'Not a speck.'

'Remarkable,' said Cindy. 'And she was his housekeeper?'

'Well . . . you know.' Amy did the big whisper again. 'There was something *strange* there. Some folk said she was his mother. Well, no family resemblance at all, from where I stood, but she obviously *meant* something to Marcus. More than a housekeeper. More than that.'

Cindy, having been aware for a minute or so of being listened to, half turned on his barstool and saw a pretty, blonde girl sitting alone in the very corner of the bar, her head bent over a book. But she wasn't reading; she was listening to every word they said.

Amy was talking about Marcus Bacton's feud with the famous archaeologist, Professor Falconer. 'Wouldn't kick him out of *my* trench, but him and Marcus . . . daggers drawn . . . worse, it is, since Falconer bought some more land, and now he owns the ancient monument up on Black Knoll.'

'He's bought the *Knoll*?'

'And he didn't want Marcus keep messing about up

there, so he fenced it off, see. And then Mrs Willis, poor old thing . . . Pint of Tankard, is it, Colin?'

Cindy noticed the book the blonde girl was reading. It was a new copy of *Lines on the Landscape* by Devereux and Pennick. Well, well, what was this? He looked pointedly at the girl. 'Good book, is it?'

She looked up from her book. She looked momentarily scared. Big eyes.

'Ley lines?' Cindy said. 'You believe in all that? Come to the right place, you have. Old Alfred Watkins of Hereford, he used to walk these hills, spotting how the stones aligned with the mounds and the old churches.'

'I, uh, I only just started it.' An American accent. 'I bought it on the way here. I don't know much about ley lines and stuff. We, uh, we don't have them in New York.'

'As far as you know,' Cindy said mysteriously. 'As far as you know.'

'Well, uh, we have like straight roads. But I guess straight roads don't qualify by virtue of just being, uh, straight.'

'Well.' Cindy put on his famous twinkle. 'There are, I hear, many strange energies in New York. Who knows how many new leys might have been created?'

'You think that's possible?'

'Anything,' said Cindy, 'is possible. It's a very strange world.'

'Gee,' the girl said. 'Do all you people talk like this?'

Cindy laughed. 'Sadly, very few of us talk like this. Can I buy you a drink? Cindy, my name. Cindy Mars-Lewis.'

'Grayle. Underhill.'

'Grail? How interesting. As in . . . ?'

'Kind of,' she said.

You died. And you came back. And what the holy fuck are you doing about it?

222

Marcus's outraged voice asked the question in Maiden's head at least a couple of times a day.

I'm trying to forget about it, that's what I'm doing, Marcus.

'What did you say?' Marcus threw a log on the stove.

'Nothing.'

It seemed to Maiden that, unless he managed to push the experience right to the back of his mind, he was never going to have a normal life. There'd be no pressure to go back to work. Maybe he could crawl back to Elham General in a few days' time and persuade some specialist that the brain damage was irreparable and would affect his equilibrium in some problematic fashion demanding early, *early* retirement. And making him, to the satisfaction of Riggs, a very unreliable witness. Would Riggs feel safe, then? Would Maiden feel safe?

Safe to go to art college, finally? Did he even want to do that any more?

Marcus sat down with his whisky. 'You'll be there tomorrow, Maiden?'

'Sure.'

'Don't have to, you know. If there's a problem.'

'I can't avoid death for ever, can I? Besides, I was there when she . . .'

'Yes.' Marcus swallowed some whisky. 'I've been thinking about that. Thinking back to when Mrs Willis was lying on the stone and you said, Take her down, get her down. Why did you say that?'

'I don't know.'

And the statement scared him because it was so completely true. There was an area of himself that he really didn't know. It was like carrying around a locked briefcase to which you didn't have the key, and you couldn't put it down because there might be a bomb inside.

'Perhaps something's reaching you, Maiden. When Anderson brought you back from the dead, she was imagining on the Knoll at sunrise. That sets up a connection.

Not only between her and you but between you and the Knoll. Now don't look at me like that, you cynical bastard!'

Maiden shook his head. He wasn't going for this.

'Did you know that *burial chamber* is a serious misnomer?' Marcus said. 'They were really *initiation* chambers. Yes, all right, the remains of the dead – funerary urns and things – were put in there, but that was part of it. The trainee shaman or whoever would spend the night inside the chamber and then, when the light came through, directly through the slit at midsummer, they would literally be enlightened, their consciousness raised.'

'Andy told me.'

'Did she also tell you how similar that was to the near-death experience? Hmm? The shaft of light out of complete darkness? That's what they see, isn't it?'

'Not me, Marcus.'

'Quite. If you saw only darkness and you felt only cold, that would account for your reaction to the Knoll, wouldn't it?'

'Possibly. I'm not qualified—'

'Not long before she died, the old girl told me she was seeing black lights up there.'

'Can you *have* black lights?'

'Like to talk in metaphors, your psychics. She was saying something's gone wrong. Perhaps Falconer's fucked it up with his bloody experiments. Perhaps the light that came into you from the Knoll was *black* light.'

'Don't do this to me, Marcus.'

'I'm trying to help you, you ungrateful bastard. Have a drink, you look completely shot at.'

'Do you know why it's called Black Knoll?'

'Local name for it.'

'But why exactly?'

'Some bollocks. It's irrelevant.'

'You going to tell me?'

'Just have a drink,' Marcus said.

★　　★　　★

'Missing?' this Cindy said. 'What do you mean, missing?'

'I mean she never came home. Or, if she did, she didn't make contact. Either way, that's missing, isn't it? Like, she's missing out of my life.'

It wasn't alcohol making her talk; Grayle was drinking Coke, or something that passed for it. Just she was getting past the stage of keeping quiet about who she was and what she was doing here. How many woman tourists travelled alone anyway?

The strange old dame – dressed like out of Agatha Christie, only more glitter – took in everything she said. Spoke in this light, flippant voice with a bizarre up-and-down accent and yet struck Grayle as being kind of heavy underneath.

What did I walk into here? Did she find me or did I find her?

Grayle swallowed an ice cube from the bottom of her Coke. Told this Cindy all about the dreaming. After a while, they bought more drinks and took them to a table at the back of the bar, and Grayle pulled out the sheaf of airmail paper.

'See, my sister, she's intense and hard-nosed, not easily fooled. But the dream thing had become like a personal obsession.'

'Yes,' Cindy said after she read the letter, except for the pages Grayle always held back. 'No matter how analytical you are, experiments with the subconscious can be rather like putting a needle into a vein. The subconscious demands more. Ancient-site-dreaming is dangerously addictive.'

Grayle looked into Cindy's still, green eyes. 'How do you know this?'

'Ah.' Cindy sighed. 'Ten, fifteen years ago, before it was fashionable, I decided to spend a night on the fabled slopes of Cader Idris.'

'Cader . . . ? What is that?'

'It's a mountain in North Wales where there's a legend

that if you spend a whole night there you will wake up either a poet or mad.'

'Sounds kind of like Greenwich Village.'

Cindy smiled. 'Gave me the taste for it. I slept around. Once dreamed for seven nights, either side of the full moon, under one of the trilithons at Stonehenge – that was in the days when you were still allowed inside. Oh yes, positively promiscuous, I was.'

'Wow,' Grayle said faintly.

'It does change you. Most of my dreams became *lucid* dreams – the ones where you know you're dreaming. Where you seem to have an element of control.'

'Sure. Dream control. I did a column on it.'

'And, of course, that's when it becomes risky. You think you're in control, but in fact your subconscious mind is starting to influence your conscious mind to an alarming degree. You think you're drawing inspiration from God, or the Earth Mother, the mind of Gaia, depending on your religious or your scientific persuasion.'

'Like with acid trips.'

'Indeed. And it can send you quite mad. I wasn't happy about it, so I stopped doing it. A shaman must, above all, have discipline. Be able to count on precision.'

Cindy smiled regretfully. Grayle sat back in her chair, against the ancient, grimy panelling. Through the brown, smoky air, she examined the weird old broad, from the purple hair to the chiffon scarf to the tweed skirt and the black-stockinged legs.

'Hold on just one moment,' Grayle said. 'You said *shaman*?'

'The tribal shaman was the witch doctor, the priest, the counsellor, the psychiatrist, the one who interceded with the spirit world.'

'Yeah, we have them. Collect Native American hand drums and feathers. Supervise sweat-lodges for overweight executives.'

'We all have to make a living, Grayle. An actor, I am, by

profession. Not a terribly successful one, but I've had my moments. Quite well known, I was at one time, on children's television. Straight man to the more famous Kelvyn Kite. We never crossed the Atlantic, sadly. But, then, perhaps a four-foot-tall, talking bird of prey would have been a little esoteric for the American market.'

Holy Jesus, Grayle thought. Would somebody wake me up?

'Always good with animals, I was,' Cindy said wistfully. 'Made Kelvyn myself, I did.'

'So you . . . You're a shaman, right? An English shaman.'

'*Celtic* shaman, if you don't mind. Our oral tradition goes back to Taliesin, the bard, in the sixth century. And, further, to the builders of the dolmens and the stone circles. As for me, I trained for three years, on and off, with Dilwyn Fychan, of Machynlleth, and other individuals too private to be mentioned. It was a calling. Some of us are called. Some of us are aware, from an early age, that we are . . . different.'

Cindy crossed his legs.

'The shaman, traditionally, has a foot in two worlds. Flits about. Passes from one sphere of existence to another. A condition usually reflected in his personal life and mode of dress. Neither one thing nor the other.'

Cindy smiled. Grayle stared.

'Oh,' she said. 'You're, uh . . . like, a guy, right?'

'Prehistoric sites were often misused,' Marcus said. 'Still are – satanic rites and all that nonsense. But this was nothing like that. This was a social thing. Ultimate degradation for an executed criminal. Making an example.'

Maiden drank some whisky, his first since the last night of his old life.

'Used to do something similar with highwaymen,' Marcus said. 'Gibbets by the roadside. Nothing so romantic on the Welsh border. These were sheep-thieves. Or domestic murderers. Chap comes home drunk, clobbers his wife with a bottle. Seedy stuff. That's what makes it worse, really – shows a contempt for the site.'

'So what did they do?'

'You all right, Maiden?'

'Just . . . carry on. Go on.'

'There's a fairly honourable tradition – a prehistoric tradition – known as excarnation. Laying out of corpses on some hillside to free the spirit to the natural elements. This was different, obviously. You cold, Maiden? You're shivering.'

Marcus gathered up a log, opened the door of the wood-stove. Orange splinters flew up when he tossed in the new log. Maiden didn't feel any warmer.

'They laid the body of the executed criminal on its back on the capstone. For the crows and buzzards to pick clean. The foxes to plunder the bones.'

'When was this?'

'I don't know when it started. It went on, amazingly, until early in the nineteenth century. This was a harsh place, Maiden.'

Maiden drained his glass, reached for the bottle, but Marcus took it.

'That's what *Black* Knoll recalls. I hated it. That's why they all rejected Annie's vision. Because it was a place of the rotting dead.'

'Marcus—'

'But she *purified* it, Maiden. What happened to her restored the sacredness. The locals had been desecrating it for centuries. It was a bad place, a diseased place, some-where you didn't go, that parents warned their children about. And this child . . . she restored this ancient site to what it was intended to be. A place of light.'

'Marcus, don't make too much of this, but I think I dreamt about it.'

'What?' Marcus shook back his heavy, grey hair, pushed his glasses into place. 'When?'

'Hospital. I thought I was waking up, but it was another

dream. It was like an open tomb. I was the corpse. Decaying. I had no eyes. I could feel the birds plucking . . . Oh, shit, Marcus, I don't—'

Marcus took Maiden's glass and poured him more whisky.

XXIV

Around midnight, the bulb in the bedside lamp began to sing. Close to one a.m., it blew, leaving Cindy to sit in the darkness, in his dressing gown, and ponder the vexed question of whether or not he was, as Kelvyn Kite had often stated, simply a stupid old tart.

The American girl had made an excuse and fled fairly rapidly after discovering that the person to whom she had unburdened herself was not only old enough to be her mother but also old enough to be her father, as it were.

He hadn't meant to startle her; he wanted to help her. What if her poor sister had been . . . No! Don't even think of it!

What if? All those *what ifs*?

What if the good and patient Chief Inspector Peter Hatch had been right all along, and there were simply several common or garden, sad, uncomplicated killers out there, rather than one person harbouring a warped and lethal obsession with earth-magic?

What if his own exercise in pendulum dowsing over the maps and the journals had been as spurious as the 'shamanic powers' of which he was so pathetically proud?

What if tonight's paranormal 'experience' at the High Knoll burial chamber was no more than a perverse and futile combination of paranoia and wishful thinking?

What if Sydney Mars-Lewis was no more than an old humbug of the most ludicrous kind, trying to make something significant out of his sexual ambivalence and social inadequacy, unable to face up to his reduced status as a failed actor relegated to the end of the pier with a stuffed bird?

Well, these were hardly new questions. Indeed, one night, in a dressing room in Scarborough, about seven years ago, he had almost given way to an impulse to hang himself by his dressing-gown cord from an overhead heating pipe.

Wearily, he climbed out of bed and switched on the central light, which was half smothered by grimy beams.

'An old manic-depressive, you are, boy. That's the only certainty.'

From his suitcase, he took the fax he'd received, just before leaving the caravan, from Gareth Milburn at *Crucible*, the pagan magazine. He'd asked the boy for information about the readers' letters he didn't print. (Modern pagans, ever anxious to promote a positive image of their faith as a pure and caring nature-religion, would almost invariably reject the propaganda received from the darker practitioners.)

Gareth's fax said:

We get fairly regular letters from something called the Black Temple of Set, with a Milton Keynes postmark, accusing us of being wimps who are scared to discover where the 'real power' lies. There's a crank who just calls himself the Green Man – postmarks from all over the country, so it could actually be a bunch of people – who reckons the Pagan Federation lost its way when it turned its back on blood sacrifice, and claims blood sports are a vital part of our heritage. There's also – this is really sick – a woman with an Omen fixation offering to have babies for use in satanic rites at very competitive rates. If I can find any on the spike, I'll fax them.

The Green Man was the one which lingered. There must be a dozen black temples of Set; their adherents also attended heavy metal concerts. The Green Man's enthusiasm for blood sports – unfashionable, reactionary and anathema to modern pagans – would certainly provide a motive for the ritual killing of Maria Capaldi.

And motive, Cindy thought, was important here. These were not entirely psychotic killings; behind them was a belief structure, however warped. Gareth's theory that the Green Man might be a group of people was interesting. This would account for the different methods of slaughter.

The Green Man seemed promising from the start. And that was the problem: the Green Man had been in Cindy's thoughts from the moment he left home to drive across Wales to the Black Mountains. The image of the archetypal gargoyle, with foliage foaming from his mouth and nose and sap in his veins, had nested in Cindy's mind.

Which would explain, for sure, the dark and frightening image he had seen on the periphery of his vision at the height of his shamanic ritual at the Knoll. He had conjured in his head the smoky form. A thought-form, nothing more. A message from himself to himself. Utterly terrifying, but completely unreliable.

There came a tapping at the door. Cindy jumped in alarm and dropped the fax paper.

'Who is it?' Shocked at the elderly quaver in his shrunken voice.

'Cindy?' An even smaller voice. 'It's me. Grayle. I saw the light under your door. Tell me to go away if this is inconvenient.'

Cindy smiled in relief and went to open the door. 'No, my love. An old insomniac, I am.'

The American girl stood there in jeans and an overlong sweatshirt. With her hair loose, she looked all of nineteen and somewhat waif-like. A mistake, it was, to assume that all Americans were brimming with self-confidence.

'I'm sorry,' she said. 'All that shaman stuff, and then finding out you were a guy and all, it kind of . . . fazed me out.'

'No, me, it is, who should be sorry. Just an old misfit, I

am, really. But I do have a kettle. Would you care for a cup of tea?'

Grayle found a grin from somewhere. Also, a small sheaf of folded airmail paper.

'I thought about what you said about dreams and ancient sites turning people crazy. This, uh, this is the rest of the letter from my sister. The part I don't show people.'

Maiden awoke not breathing.

His mouth was full of solid, gritty darkness. When he tried to breathe, the air couldn't get through; his throat was also tight-packed and bulging and when he tried to cough he just took more of it into his lungs, and there was a meagre wheezing sound.

Fighting for the cough tautened his muscles and made his body curl and jerk, as if he was struggling inside a straitjacket, but the cough wouldn't come out, just built up and locked, and he went into a blind panic and rolled out of bed, over and over on the floor, numbed fingers tearing at his throat.

Cindy made some tea on the dressing table and, while it was brewing, read the last pages from Ersula Underhill, in which the girl described her dream of lying on the stone, shoulder to shoulder with a decaying body. *Scary fun, Grayle?* Oh dear.

Grayle sat at the foot of the bed, hands clasped between her knees, clearly unsure of quite how seriously to take all this. Reading the letter had told Cindy a lot about the two sisters, how they differed in their beliefs and perceptions. Grayle was the insecure one, the scatty one; it must have taken a great deal of determination for her to come here. And a deal of anxiety, too.

She looked up at him. 'I met some people . . . at the Rollright Stones?'

'Oh yes?'

'This guy, he said sometimes you would encounter – in

233

your dreams – what he called guardians. Is that what I think it is?'

'The *genius loci*. Sometimes. But many guardians have been created by people using these places for worship. Elemental spirits. Ritual stones are like computers. Spiritual entities are stored there. For centuries sometimes, even millennia, to deter robbers and vandals.'

'Right.'

'And so anyone sleeping at an ancient site should not be surprised to encounter one. The deliberate act of dreaming is an invasion, and the guardian would be programmed, as it were, to react. The guardian, by nature, is a fearsome apparition which can be dangerous. Strong nerves are called for.'

'Well, sure, Ersula has strong nerves, but . . .'

'However,' Cindy said, 'this doesn't sound like a guardian to me. More of a trace-image. An ancient site usually holds more than one strand of history, see. For instance, in the Dark Ages, we have old shrines taken over by somewhat degenerate Druidic cults, not averse to human sacrifice. This could very well be a flash-image from some sort of blood sacrifice.'

Grayle said, 'You know what really scares me about this country? It's all so close, so near the surface.'

'It's near the surface in many parts of the Earth.' Cindy poured tea. 'It's just that here, so little has altered visually over the centuries that our imaginations do not have to work so hard.'

'My imagination is kind of like an untrained Dobermann. Most of the time you have to forcibly restrain it.'

Cindy smiled. 'Look, lovely, you trusted me, I shall trust you. This particular site is referred to by two names – High Knoll and Black Knoll, and they seem to reflect two sides of it.'

'Good and evil?'

'Possibly as simple as that, probably not. The concepts of good and evil seldom apply in this sphere. I was thinking more of male and female. The female side represented by the vision of the Virgin Mary, itself re-establishing a link with the earliest sun-worship at the site. And then we have the male element. Linked, perhaps, to the bloodier aspect.'

'Right.' Grayle accepted a cup of tea and held it on her knees. 'But where is this headed? Are we saying that Ersula – who we know was charmed by the idea of the Virgin appearing at this Stone Age site – are we saying she inadvertently let herself in for something . . . old and bad?'

'This letter was the last you heard? You don't know when she left here?'

'I know that some time after she wrote this, she was wandering around in a kind of dislocated state. She met these people at the Rollright Stones. They're nice. The people, not the stones.'

'No. Those stones have their problems. Why did she go there?'

'I guess she had something on her mind. Maybe she was looking for friends. Someone to confide in. But maybe, if something bad happened to you in connection with pre-historic remains, these people, Matthew and Janny, maybe they're not the kind of people to help you. They're real friendly, obliging, all of that, but a little, uh, enthusiastic. Kind of naive, I guess. Anything bad, they'd tell you you had it wrong.'

'Have you been yet . . . to see Mr Falconer?'

'I figured I'd go tomorrow. I wanted to gather as much background as I could before I confronted the guy. He sounds kind of formidable.'

'So I believe.'

'Actually, I was given a videotape of his TV programme which I hoped to view before I went over there, on account I don't even know what he looks like, but this place doesn't appear to be equipped with the necessary hardware.'

'I should quite like to view that, too,' Cindy said

thoughtfully. 'I travel around too much to see much television. I wonder if Marcus Bacton has a video machine.'

'Marcus *Bacton*. Yeah. I need to talk with him too. Maybe I need to spend another day here. Look . . . OK . . .' Grayle focused on Cindy over the rim of her white teacup. 'You know why I'm here. Why are *you* here?'

'Ah.' Cindy needed time to think. 'It would take too long. We'll talk tomorrow. After I see Mr Bacton.'

'Oh. OK.' Grayle put her cup on the floor. 'Uh, this . . . guardian . . . trace-image, whatever. I mean, they can't harm you, these things, can they?'

'Not . . . not physically. No. Probably not physically.'

'But they can fuck up your head?'

'I suppose . . . Yes, as you so charmingly put it, I suppose they can fuck up your head.'

But that's not what really worries you, is it?

Cindy lay in bed again, with the light out. It would be dawn soon. No matter; he didn't need much sleep these days.

The Green Man.

The oldest guardian. Stern defender of the Earth. Just talking it out with Grayle Underhill had made it so much clearer in his mind. He could almost feel the Green Man writhing there.

And Grayle's sister was missing.

Am I quite mad? Cindy wondered before sleep consented to take him. *Please God, let me be mad.*

XXV

This is how it goes, Grayle thought, struggling with the zipper on her jeans. This is how it happens.

Outside the window, morning rinsed the pink stone of the village.

So you do something rash and you wind up in a strange place. You're lonely and anxious and it all seems so futile. This is when you're at your most vulnerable. This is how rich, empty widows wind up backing half-assed business deals and homeless kids get sucked into fruitcake religious sects.

Somebody is kind to you, is how it starts. Deep into the night, somebody wants to listen.

Just that, by daylight, the whole idea of a cross-dressing actor-ventriloquist who believed he was into a mystical tradition with a direct line to the megalith-builders seemed a whole lot less convincing than it had last night.

Plus, why should Cindy suddenly pick up on her in a bar? What was he doing here anyway and why had he not wanted to tell her last night? If he was looking up his old friend Marcus Bacton, why was he staying at the inn, and why was he alone?

Grayle felt calmer and stronger this morning. She would investigate the University of the Earth. She would do it objectively and efficiently. She would find out what it was that had so seduced Ersula, but she would resist its allure. And Cindy's.

Get wise. Grayle moved down the dark, twisty stairs to

chase up a small breakfast before seeking out Cefn-y-bedd. Put some distance.

'What's up with you, Maiden?' Marcus dangerously dug a fork into the toaster to retrieve a fractured slice. 'I mean, what the bloody hell is *up*? You look like you haven't slept.'

'That's because I haven't slept.'

'Oh . . . shit!' Marcus held the toaster upside down and a million dry crumbs came out on the stone worktop. At the sight of the blackened heap, Maiden erupted into dry coughs and stumbled to his feet to run himself a glass of water. Marcus brushed the debris to the floor and carried the toast to the table on the end of a fork.

'That's it.' He sat down. 'That is fucking *it*.'

Malcolm, the dog, ambled over, checked out the ancient crumbs, sniffed and turned away. Maiden drank the water slowly.

'Had a piece for the magazine yesterday.' Marcus unwrapped a pack of hard, chilled butter. 'Woman in Norfolk claims actual fairies have been performing scenes from *A Midsummer-Night's Dream* in her bloody greenhouse. Been a subscriber since 1952. What do I do with *that*?'

'Offer her the editorship?'

Marcus stared at him. 'You may be right. I'll bury Mrs Willis today, full honours, be as nice as I can to the relatives, if any turn up. And then—'

'She have any children?'

'Niece in Hay. Another in Allensmore. One of them, I can't remember which, thinks she *might* make it to the funeral.'

'But if Mrs Willis was Annie Davies . . .'

'Then there'll be a few cousins and second cousins in the village. But did they know? And if they did, will they admit it? Old prejudices die hard, places like this. I'll bury her, and then that's it.'

'What is?'

238

'Get out. Piss off. Surrender *The Phenomenologist* to the mad biddies. Put this place on the market. Must be some appeal in a castle, even if the house is disintegrating.'

Maiden filled the kettle, set it down on the stove. 'Maybe Falconer would buy it.'

'Thank you, Maiden. Over my dead, fucking body. Rather flog it as an outward-bound centre for your ten-year-old car-thieves.'

Marcus was suddenly sunk into profound misery, bloodhound eyes blurring behind his glasses.

'Went into the bloody Healing Room late last night. Core of the house for the past year. All those bottles and jars, with Mrs Willis around, they were full of mystery. Potions and elixirs. All drawing energy from *her*. Full of a sort of condensed life-force. And at the same time you'd feel this overwhelming peace and calm in there. Now it's just old bottles full of dead and rotting gunge. Have to put them all in bin bags, take them to the tip.'

'I'll do it, if you like.'

Marcus shook his head, splattering butter on a fragment of brittle toast. 'If there's a message in those bottles, Maiden, it's for me. I look at my life . . . I mean is that fucking *it*? Standing in a desert, surrounded by graves. Celia. Little Sally. Mrs Willis. Possibility of seeing them again's about all there is to look forward to, you get to my age.'

'You're *sixty*,' Maiden protested.

'Unless, of course, your own version of the Other Side is the truth of it,' Marcus said. 'In which case we're all stuffed, aren't we?'

There was the sound of tyres on the forecourt. Marcus dropped his burnt toast.

Maiden saw someone getting out of a very old but beautifully polished black Morris Minor. 'Woman. Late middle-age, mauvy hair? Tweed skirt, kind of mohair sweater with white woolly lambs on the front. Gold earrings, necklaces, bangles.'

'Sounds hellish,' Marcus said. 'If we keep quiet maybe it'll go away.'

'Might be one of Mrs Willis's nieces.'

It certainly wasn't a policeman, so Maiden made for the front door and dragged it open before the woman had time to knock. It was a strange moment. She just stood there looking at him for several seconds. She was as tall as he was. She had the small, glittering eyes of a bird of prey.

'Well,' she said at last. 'You're not Marcus Bacton, are you, lovely?'

A long, flat-topped hill. Like a bed, with a pillow of trees at one end. Grayle headed toward the trees, as directed by Amy Jenkins, the landlady. Remembering what Ersula had written about the curious magic of this place.

She came to a plain farm gate and it was open. Walked through, and suddenly – like . . . *wow* – there was, below her, this unbelievably beautiful, rambling, mellow stone house spread out like a sleeping lion. The kind of country house they tried to clone in Beverly Hills and failed because the result was just too movie-set perfect. High walls suggested gardens with fishpools and stuff.

Typically – because the house was irrelevant to what went on there – Ersula had never referred to it, except as 'the center'. It looked more of a home than an educational establishment, which explained why Ersula and the others had had apartments over the stables, and why folks on the courses needed accommodation in the village. Couldn't be more than five or six bedrooms in the house itself.

And just one car parked in front, a rebuilt VW beetle, pink. A squirrel scampered past, otherwise no sign of life.

Clouds were gathering, and it looked like more than a gesture. She should've come in the car, but walking a couple of miles gave you a handle on a place. Fall was setting in, the first dead leaves curling together on the brown gravel as she tried – because there were no other options – the huge, solid, iron-studded door.

Tugging a bell pull on a black chain, she stepped back in alarm when it responded with this deep, churchy tolling, way back into the house. And Grayle thought, in a kind of terror, *Suppose the door opens and it's Ersula. Ersula in a bathrobe, hair mussed and smelling of recent sex?*

But there was no Ersula. No answer at all. And no use in ringing again, there was no way anyone in the house would have failed to hear.

Grayle was curious. Emboldened by the likelihood of there being no-one here at all, she wandered around the side of the house to peer over the stone wall. It was too high, around nine feet. But it had a door in it. A smaller replica of the front door, going to a Gothic point. There was a ring handle; she turned it.

Waited, holding her breath. Nobody came out with a shotgun or two snarling mastiffs on a chain. She pushed her head through the opening. 'Hullo?'

Expecting a stately Elizabethan knot-garden or something of that order, but it was just a gravelled yard with two white Portakabins. This noise coming out of one. A slow, cavernous noise, like a giant flute deep underground.

She stood and listened a while. There was an artificial quality to it. She padded across the yard. The Portakabin windows had Venetian blinds. One was open; you could just about see inside. She saw two tall speakers, computer monitors, a tape deck with a green pilot light. Whole setup looked like a recording studio, maybe for making those ambient, New Age tapes – whales talking to one another kind of stuff.

'Yes?' From close behind her.

'*OhmyGod.*' Grayle spun.

Found herself facing one of those people you just knew weren't going to be helpful. She was about Grayle's own age, good-looking and so sure of it she could wear an old wax jacket and baggy cords, harness her abundant hair in a rubber band.

'What are you doing here?' Authoritative voice, very

English, well bred; kind of voice that spurned Hugh Grant until the last reel.

'I . . .'

'No, don't tell me,' the woman said with a flick of a wrist. 'You're a bloody journalist, aren't you?'

'Well, uh, as it happens, yeah, but—'

'God al*mighty*. Don't you people *ever* get the message? *All* visits by journalists, interviews, etcetera, etcetera, are absolutely strictly by appointment *only*. So I suggest you go back to your office and attempt to *make* one. I mean, would that be so terribly difficult for you?'

'Listen, I don't even know what authority you have to say that.' No way was she going to identify herself, pour it all out to some superior being from the planet Arrogant. 'I'd prefer to hear it from Professor Falconer.'

'I speak for him.'

'And you are?'

'Magda. I run this place. Now look, I don't have time for this. We have a course next week, a dozen people, we're mega-busy, so please get back in your car—'

'I never heard of you. I believe my editor spoke to someone called Ersula Underhill.'

Magda blinked. 'That makes no sense. Ersula's ancient history.'

The words pushed a cold skewer into Grayle, who was just imagining Ersula, in a white lab-coat, messing with tapes and stuff and taking no shit whatsoever from this woman.

'Anyway,' Magda said, 'Ersula Underhill wasn't authorized to arrange for journalists or anybody else to come here.'

'You say she's gone? Like, where?' Grayle noticed that, in the Portakabin behind her, the giant flute had ceased. She watched Magda's eyes.

'Look.' Magda had her hands aggressively on her hips. 'What *is* this?'

'Could I *please* speak with Professor Falconer?'

'No. Go away.'

'Well, actually . . .' a man's voice said, and Grayle, half expecting this, turned towards the door of the Portakabin.

He was lean and he wore leather cowboy boots, his greying hair pulled back into a ponytail. He had an easy smile. He carried two small cassette tapes. She remembered his face from the front of the videotape package Duncan Murphy had given her in Oxford.

Magda shrugged, expressionless, and walked away towards the house without giving Grayle another glance.

'And *which* publication do you write for?' Roger Falconer said lightly.

Grayle suddenly started feeling nervous as hell.

The atmosphere had settled around Cindy the second he was inside. Dark little hall, smell of damp. An acute tang of despair in the chaos its occupant called a study.

It enclosed Marcus Bacton like a fog. His hair was lank, the purplish bags under his eyes blown up by his glasses. He looked like a man in need of help, but it was never wise to suggest this to anyone. Always better to turn it the other way round.

'Come for your help, I have, Mr Bacton.'

Marcus Bacton grunted. 'Better sit down then.' He tossed two telephone directories from the sofa and about a dozen pieces of paper flew out. 'Fuck it,' he said, but he seemed too weary to pick them up.

The dark-haired young man came into the study. He must be over twenty years younger than Bacton. Somehow, he looked even less healthy. His face was pale and blotched, his eyes clouded. This made no sense to Cindy; *Phenomenologist* editorials had been full of references to the wonderful healing ambience.

'I have to say, Lewis,' Marcus Bacton said, 'I'm totally nonplussed. Are you actually telling me you've come all this way to talk about this bloody serial-killer nonsense?'

Cindy saw the younger man stiffen, his eyes still.

'Er, this is my, er, nephew. Maid—'

'Wilson,' the young man said. 'Bobby Wilson.'

'How are you, Bobby? Yes, I'm afraid I *have* come to talk about this serial killer nonsense.'

Bobby leaned against a wall, his arms folded. 'You see?' Marcus Bacton said to him. Bobby didn't look at him.

'What does he mean?' Cindy said.

Bobby sighed. 'He had a letter from one of his readers who suffers from fairies in the greenhouse. That's not you, is it?'

Cindy was furious but contained it. 'No, lovely,' he said. 'That's not me.'

He paused. Marcus scowled at Bobby.

'I'm the one who wants to know who killed his house-keeper,' Cindy said.

XXVI

Corn-haired, apple-cheeked Adrian pushed the play button and the big noise wafted out of wall-mounted speakers. This close, it didn't sound so much like a flute as the sound you made when you blew down a seashell or maybe across the open top of a wine bottle.

'Adrian and various students spent three weeks inside Neolithic underground chambers recording this stuff,' Roger Falconer said. 'Different times of day, different weather conditions. Quite impressive, isn't it?'

'What does it mean?' Grayle wondered.

'Quite significant, actually.' Falconer wore a frayed denim shirt. Nestling in his greying chest hair was what looked like a flint arrowhead on a leather thong. His smile wanted to eat you up. 'It supports the theory that what we know as burial chambers served other purposes, perhaps initiatory. Yes?'

'Mmm.' Grayle nodded. Coming on like a journalist, as this now seemed acceptable. 'The Native Americans had something similar, right? The Hopi?'

'Exactly. Not so apparent now as it probably was when they were built, but the suggestion is that these sub-terranean cells were constructed as much for auditory as visual effect. To provide a sensory experience for the person inside.'

'To condition their consciousness,' Adrian said, his voice brisk with enthusiasm and private schooling. 'To make them accessible to Higher Influences.'

'Yes, well,' said Falconer. 'For Adrian, I'm afraid, it's only the beginning.'

'Oh gosh, yes.' Adrian stopped the machine and exchanged cassettes. 'If you listen to this, you'll hear . . . hold on, I'll wind back about ten seconds . . . now listen very carefully.'

Adrian pushed the button and stood aside from the machine, like a stage magician, looking, at the same time, too rough-hewn and honest for that line of work.

'OK?'

'Sure.' Grayle was feeling more relaxed and quite interested. After the cool, edgy reception from Magda, the whole atmosphere had changed, Roger and Adrian both up-front, friendly, charming.

'There,' Adrian said. 'Did you hear it?'

'Huh?' The Portakabin was divided into white-partitioned sections. It looked cool and modern, charts on the walls.

'OK, I'll run it again. In fact I'll turn it up a little, if your ears can stand it. You have to realize, of course, that all this is hugely amplified anyway, although we've managed to filter out much of the hiss.'

The hoarse, hollow whistling came rushing out of both the speakers like a gathering storm.

'Now,' Adrian said. 'There it goes. Hear it? Sort of like *atcha-ka, atcha-ka*.'

'Probably a bird,' said Falconer.

'Roger, it was at *night*.'

'Hedgehog, then.'

Adrian didn't look deflated. His face glowed with excitement.

'What do *you* think it is?' Grayle asked him.

'Well, I think . . . I believe . . . we're listening to a chant. Possibly the remains of a chant. Of course, it's obviously deteriorated over thousands of years.'

Falconer smiled indulgently at Adrian and shook his head.

'Hold on,' Grayle said. 'You're saying this is . . . like a prehistoric voice?'

'Stone records sound,' Adrian said. 'It's infused with magnetism. Stone records voices and images too, and one day I'm going to prove it.'

Roger laughed and clapped him on the shoulder. 'If only you could, old chap. Be enormously illuminating, because we really have no idea what kind of language these Neolithic people employed. You see, Grayle, that's what the University of the Earth's really all about. While I'm not convinced, not by a *very* long way, that there's anything to this EVP . . .'

'Electronic Voice Phenomena,' Adrian explained.

'. . . we're giving Adrian a chance to experiment under scientific conditions. And we're letting interested members of the public share in that experience, which makes for a rather exciting, memorable holiday for them and helps fund our continuing research. Science should *never* be rarefied or elitist.'

Grayle nodded, wondering if Ersula would agree.

'We do make a bit of a show of the arguments between us,' Adrian admitted. 'It all adds to the fun. I mean, you know, don't put that in your article. Which paper was it? Sorry. In one ear, out the other.'

'Story of his life,' said Roger.

'The *New York Courier*,' Grayle said, hoping to God they wouldn't check. Cautiously, she'd called herself Grayle Turner. Feeling she just might learn more if she didn't come out as Ersula's sister until it was absolutely necessary. 'It's, uh, it's a tabloid.'

'Don't be ashamed of that.' Roger laughed. 'We had an enormously successful season after the *People* featured us.'

'Kept asking me how many women had dreams about being seduced by hairy cavemen.' Adrian produced that peculiar English laugh you could only call a chortle.

'We have people sleeping at ancient sites under supervision,' Roger said. 'And recording their dreams. Adrian's convinced that the very nature of the dreams are conditioned by magnetic and radioactive forces and who knows what else.'

'And you're not?'

'I'm interested. But convinced only by evidence.'

'We're giving you evidence all the time.' Adrian sounding almost exasperated. 'We're *bombarding* you with evidence.'

'My place,' Roger said firmly, 'is on the fence. Until, perhaps, we have something *really* big to announce.'

Bobby Maiden was startled and on his guard. What *was* this?

The woman called Cindy – a woman Marcus had apparently never seen before – was sitting in the study, jingling her bangles and expounding some crazy theory linking together a series of apparently unconnected killings spread over half of southern Britain.

'Some of them, see,' this Cindy said, 'make perfect sense. Or at least they respond to this person's warped logic. A hunt saboteur? *Yes*. Because he—or she, though I think not – supports blood sports. A motorcyclist who churns up and pollutes an ancient track? *Yes*. A warning to the despoilers.'

'God preserve us.' Marcus raised his eyes, in disgust, to the yellowed ceiling.

'But the others . . . well, it's as if the victim was simply in the wrong place at the wrong time. The boy in the doorway, the birdwatcher . . . you've seen that one in the papers? The man who was battered to death near Avebury?'

Cindy had brought out a file of notes and maps and press cuttings. Maiden imagined her arriving at some police station with this stuff, the task of getting rid of her being delegated down and down to the most junior DC. The DC wondering if there might possibly be something in this that would make his name and his boss saying,

Look, son, you'll get used to people like this . . . be pleasant, give her a cup of tea and get her the hell out of here.

'I haven't been in person to the birdwatcher site,' Cindy said. 'But I'd be very surprised if it wasn't just like the others.'

'In what way?' Maiden was sitting at the other end of the sofa, trying not to show any professional interest. Marcus was polishing his glasses, always a danger sign.

'On a ley,' Cindy said. 'All the murders have been on leys. You do know what I mean, I suppose?'

'Remind me?'

'My,' said Cindy. 'You can't have spent much time with your uncle. Leys are straight lines – sometimes visible as ancient tracks, but mostly not – which have been found to connect prehistoric sites and some more modern build-ings, like churches, which were built upon them. They appear to mark channels of spiritual energy.'

Marcus rammed on his glasses. 'And more recently it's been suggested that the original tracks were reserved by our remote ancestors, expressly for the passage of the spirits. So you're trying to tell us you actually—'

'Indeed.' Cindy picked up two cuttings which had fallen to the floor and also a KitKat wrapper. Like she was just itching to tidy this place up.

'You actually believe . . .' Marcus tipped his chair back against the wall, Cindy's eyes going at once to the dirty scuffmark. '. . . that someone is *killing* people . . . on *leys*? *Deliberately*?'

'Obvious to me, it was, from the moment I arrived at the spot where Maria Capaldi died, in the manner of William Rufus. Now known to have been a ritual death. Did you read up on that, Marcus, as I suggested?'

'God almighty, woman, I haven't even had the bloody time to think about it. We've had a *death*, in case you—'

'Yes, I'm sorry. I was just pointing out that when the king's body was put upon a cart and taken to Salisbury, his blood was said – this is in the account by William of Malmesbury – to have dripped to the ground the whole way.'

'So?'

'A line of blood, Marcus. Murray, in her book, points out that this was obviously an impossibility but that it is consistent with the belief that the blood of the Divine Victim must fall to the ground to fertilize it.'

'So how do the others fit into this pattern? Nobody else was shot with a damned crossbow.'

Cindy shrugged. 'Perhaps it wasn't appropriate. My feeling is that he works intuitively. For instance, there would, to him, have been a poetic justice, a *holistic* justice, in the gory death of one of the motorcyclists who destroyed the Monks' Trod in mid-Wales. Decapitated as his machine is rushing along the sacred road, spraying out a line of blood in the slipstream. The fact that it didn't work out like that—'

'Equally,' Maiden said, 'it could·have been some mind-less rural vigilante. Or a farmer fed up with the noise. Or an angry rambler . . .'

Cindy tossed him a curious glance. 'You remind me of a friend of mine, a certain Chief Inspector Hatch.'

'Ha!' Marcus said.

'Look,' Maiden said carefully, 'The police are not thick. But when manpower and money are tight, they tend to stick to procedure. If there's anything in this idea, they'll get around to it.'

'After a few more deaths.' An edge to Cindy's voice now. 'When he's killed again and again and become care-less. The problem with the police is they always look for the prosaic solution first.'

'That's because ninety-nine per cent of crimes are not committed by subtle people.'

'A serial murderer's mind is never a simple mechanism, Bobby. They are open to strange influences, see, especially now, approaching the millennium. Psychological profiling is primitive and hopelessly inadequate. Think how many apparently motiveless murders are later accounted for by the perpetrator *hearing voices.*'

'Most of them only remember the voices after they've been nicked. At which stage, a psychiatric hospital often seems strangely preferable to the lifers' wing.'

'Never mind all this psychological bollocks,' Marcus said irritably. 'What I'm totally failing to bloody see is how you can conceivably link this nonsense with the natural – certified *natural* – death of the old lady we're about to bury.'

Maiden shuddered.

'Yes . . .' Cindy leaned back into the sofa cushions and sighed. 'The truth is I can't. Not yet. That's why I'm here. I suppose that any death linked to an ancient site is, for me, at the moment, a suspicious death, and when you told me on the telephone . . . Well, a few things fell together.'

'What bloody business is it of yours anyway?'

'Perhaps I, too, am hearing voices,' Cindy said sadly, and Marcus finally lost patience and leapt up from his chair.

'You're bloody mad! You've just come here to try and *make* something out of the tragically natural death of a bloody good woman! You're as half-baked as Miss Pinder and her bloody ectoplasm! You're as unhinged as the old bat from Diss with the fairies in the fucking greenhouse!' Marcus's hands clenched. 'Excuse me.'

'He's had a lot to cope with,' Maiden said, as the study door slammed.

'So have you, by the look of it, lovely. Still got an eye under there, I hope. What is it you do, Bobby?'

'Painter. Pictures.'

'Well, there's interesting. Make a living at it?'

'One day, maybe.'

'Otherwise, you're between jobs, is it?'

'On the sick,' Maiden said. 'Road accident. What do *you* do, Cindy? When you're not investigating serious crime.'

'Oh, a jobbing thespian, I am. When I can get the work. And an entertainer when I can't. Comedy.'

'And this is all part of your routine, is it?'

Cindy's piercing eyes glittered. 'Don't believe any of it, do you, lovely? You think I'm an old stirrer.'

'I just think all you've got is a theory. You've no evidence at all. You don't seem to have any possibility of *getting* evidence. Also, there's the problem that ley lines haven't been proved to exist.'

'Ah, so you do have some knowledge of these things, then.'

'We're not all thick and prosaic.'

'Artists?' Cindy said blandly. 'I never thought they were.'

Damn.

'Well,' Cindy said, 'you may argue that the existence of leys has not been proved to the satisfaction of scientists, but I, in turn, would argue that this is irrelevant. All that matters, see, is that *he* believes. He is killing people on what the maps and his own intuition tell him are lines of earth-energy.'

'Why?'

'Oh, Bobby, I could give you a dozen convincing explanations, each one dependent on the killer's own conception of earth-lines and the uses of ancient sites. If he believes leys are spirit-paths, perhaps he feels he is releasing the spirits of his victims to stimulate the energy-flow. Perhaps he sees them as sacrifices. Perhaps he feels he is himself absorbing the energy of his victims.'

'I just can't hear it in court, somehow.'

Cindy leaned towards him, with a waft of lavender. 'I tell you, Bobby, compared with the rippers who hear voices and Charles Manson, who believed he was in psychic contact with the Beatles, this person is utterly and coldly rational, according to his beliefs.'

More wheels in the yard brought Maiden to his feet.

A coffin passed across the window. He recoiled. The

inside of his mouth felt instantly dry and rough. The hearse reversed and three-point-turned in the yard, under the broken castle walls.

He was aware of Cindy watching his reaction with great interest.

'You're trembling. Don't like funerals, is it?'

'Who does?'

'Love them, we do, in Wales. You fascinate me, Bobby. You must've seen any number of corpses in your line of work.'

'I'm not that kind of painter,' Maiden said.

Cindy laughed. 'Oh, Bobby, so cautious. Talk to me, lovely, you know you want to.'

The hearse waited under the window, a man in a black suit got out. Cindy stood up and moved to the door. 'Shall we bring the old lady in for a moment? Lay the coffin on that oak table in the hall?' Cindy looked back at Maiden from the doorway and raised a surprisingly heavy eyebrow.

Maiden flinched.

'I just have dreams. Since this road accident. About what it's like to be dead.'

'Oh?'

'After the accident, I was dead for over four minutes. They brought me back.'

'My,' said Cindy.

'That's all it is.'

'All? That's a very big thing to happen.'

'Not as big as murder,' Maiden said. 'How could the old girl possibly have been murdered?'

'What brought on the stroke?' Cindy said. 'That's what we should be asking.'

Maiden thought about black light and said nothing.

'There are more crimes in heaven and earth,' said Cindy, 'than will ever be recorded on police computers.'

XXVII

Cindy's vague sense of unease about the funeral was reflected in the brittle smile of the vicar, who greeted Marcus with a perfunctory handshake.

Big and red-faced, the vicar was the country-parson type you rarely seemed to find any more; you imagined him drinking copious amounts of port, going off hunting with the nobs.

This vicar would like it here. A nice, discreet little church. Set back from the centre of the village on a small, grassy mound, possibly prehistoric, it had a strong, ancient resonance in its rusty pink stone, its squat tower glistening in the slow rain. You wouldn't prise this vicar out of here; any guilty feeling that he really ought to be helping to rehabilitate drug addicts in Brixton would be very firmly sat on.

Marcus looked ill at ease in a creased grey suit and a floppy black bow tie. And Bobby . . .

Bobby was turned away from the mourners under their umbrellas. Bobby was gazing up at some sort of gargoyle set into the gable of the church porch. There was a sudden heaviness around him. He was very still.

A strange boy. Two things apparent: he was not the nephew of Marcus Bacton. And he was, or had been, connected with the police.

Cindy, who had replaced his red beret with a black one and wore a black suede jacket buttoned over the lambs on his jumper, wandered over and followed the boy's gaze. At once, his unease became solid; breath piled into his chest so hard he choked.

'Sorry.' Pulling a handkerchief from his sleeve. *Oh lord. Oh heavens.* Chipped and pockmarked he might be, but there was no mistaking him. Old foliage-face himself.

'What's that, Cindy?'

'A Green Man, Bobby. It's a Green Man.'

'Which is . . .' His voice cracked. '. . . what?'

'He isn't anybody in particular. Simply the Green Man. A symbol often found on ancient churches. No-one knows what he signifies. Fertility, perhaps. Quite . . . quite terrifying, isn't he? Why does he bother you?'

'I don't know.'

'But you've seen him before.'

He breathed out, didn't reply.

'In a dream, perhaps? In one of your dreams?'

He closed his eyes. He shook. His face was grey. He looked as if he might pass out. Several of the thirty or so mourners had noticed his discomfort. The locals. The ones with farmer-faces, red-veined and weathered.

The mourners began to filter into the church, a few likely relatives pausing to speak to Marcus, the locals avoiding him as you would a cranky old bull.

'Go home, Bobby,' Cindy said gently. 'Not your day for a funeral. You'll only upset people.'

Roger Falconer had apologized that he had a commitment this afternoon. Anxious, however, that Grayle's article should be a true reflection of his work and his ideas, he'd invited her to dinner.

Grayle had thought uh-oh. Thanked him but pointed out she had some people to see tonight. Maybe some other time . . .

'Wise decision, probably,' Adrian said, seeing her out. 'Bit of a ladies' man, old Roger. I mean, not that . . . you know . . .'

Grayle smiled. Adrian was just about the most English person she'd ever met. He'd shown her round the centre, which essentially was confined to the outbuildings and

Portakabins. She'd seen the Geiger counters and magneto-meters they used to measure radiation and electro-magnetism in old stones, the infrared cameras and video equipment for capturing anomalous light effects and related phenomena.

'I will admit,' Adrian said, 'that it's become rather an obsession with me to show that our so-called primitive ancestors had an instinctive grasp of scientific principles our society is only just starting to reach. And to show that, compared with Neolithic people, we're hardly alive any more. We're just not in touch with our surroundings. Roger understands this very well, he just likes to play devil's advocate.'

'I'm just glad he agreed to speak to me without an appointment,' Grayle said now.

'That's because he overheard your accent. He's very keen on attracting Americans to the courses. They're more open-minded and they often leave donations as well. Oh, gosh, I keep forgetting who I'm talking to . . . you won't use this, will you?'

'Adrian, most American tabloids aren't at all like your British tabloids. I'm a, you know, a very straight person.'

'Oh. Right. That's all right then. Sorry to seem, you know . . .'

But he'd given her an opening and Grayle moved into it. 'Though I'd be lying if I said I wasn't kind of hoping for an American angle. When my paper called, they spoke to an Ersula . . . Underhill?'

'Oh. Yes.'

'I figured maybe we could nose off the piece on her, but, uh, Magda said she'd gone.'

'Yes. She's gone. Some weeks ago.'

'Would you know where? Maybe I could catch up with her, talk about the stuff she did here.'

'No, I'm sorry.' Adrian shook his head. 'I don't know really where she's gone. She left in rather a hurry. I think. We all assumed she'd gone back home to the States.'

'Did she say she was going home? I mean, you know, I don't want to cause any trouble. Like, if she was fired or something—'

Adrian looked shocked. 'Oh, no. People don't get *sacked*. Ersula was just a temporary person, anyway. She was studying the subject and so it was convenient for all of us.'

'It's just . . .' Grayle figured she could go further with Adrian than she'd have dared to with Falconer, without arousing suspicions. '. . . just that Ersula Underhill was building quite a reputation in the States as an archaeologist and when our guy spoke to her on the phone, she seemed so blown away by what was happening here.'

'Blown away?' Adrian frowned. 'I don't really think she was that type. In our debates she tended to take Roger's side.'

'Right.' Grayle took a deep breath. 'Maybe it was Roger?'

'Roger?'

'That she was blown away with? He's a . . . charismatic guy.'

'Oh, now, look.' Adrian's shoulders went back; he looked stern. 'It's not going to be that sort of article, is it? When the *People* came, they were sort of sniffing around, you know, whether Roger was sleeping with his students, that sort of thing. Really not on.'

Grayle assured him again that she didn't write that kind of stuff and swiftly spread some balm by telling him about the real nice people she'd met at the Rollright Stones.

'Oh, they're *awfully* good news,' Adrian said earnestly. 'Matthew and Janny are just the sort of people I'd like to see more of on the courses. Committed. Absolutely.'

'Got to be committed if they're even getting married in the stones.'

'This weekend, in fact! Are you going? I am. I think it's a really positive thing to do. All the times they've slept in that circle, committing their inner selves to the Earth.

257

That's what a wedding should be . . . a joining of a man and a woman with the Earth.'

And that was the moment – man . . . woman . . . Earth – when Grayle got the feeling. Like she'd swallowed a whole ice cube.

Adrian's face shone with honest fervour. She thought, These guys have no real idea what they're messing with. It's like Cindy and his shamanic stuff; these stones are magnetic, all right, they attract airheads and fruitcakes like iron filings.

'Well, thanks,' she said. 'You've been real helpful. Perhaps I will go.'

It'd be lovely if you could come, if you're still around, Janny had said. *We did invite Ersula, but . . .*

'To the wedding? Terrific!' Adrian said. 'We could go together.'

'Yeah . . . well . . . maybe. Just one thing before I leave here . . .'

One last attempt to get close to whatever Ersula's become.

'Any way I can help . . .' Adrian spread his arms. He looked simple and healthy, the least complicated of them.

'Is there some kind of ancient site locally where I could maybe get a feel for the kind of thing you do?'

'Oh. Nothing spectacular. Nothing like the Rollrights. There's the Knoll, of course. Sort of collapsed cromlech. Shall I take you?'

'No, please . . . I already took up too much of your time. Also, I'd kind of like to take in the atmosphere, make some notes. If you could just, like, point me in the right direction?'

'Perhaps *we* could have dinner some time,' Adrian said. 'Just, you know, the two of us.'

Cindy heard Marcus hiss, at nobody in particular,

'. . . fuck's *he* doing here?'

A lean man with a greying ponytail peeled himself away from a tweedy clot of local-looking people in the churchyard and clapped Marcus on the arm. 'Had to come, Marcus. Had to pay tribute to a remarkable lady.'

Cindy recognized Roger Falconer, respected television archaeologist and the educated, mature woman's hunk. Even if he hadn't known who it was, he would have realized that this was a TV personality. They had a way of projecting themselves from the crowd that was almost mystical; they made themselves shine.

'You never even met her!' Marcus clearly thrown off balance.

'To my eternal regret I didn't. But there are several people in this village who've testified to her remarkable abilities.'

'Oh bollocks, Falconer. Anybody who's read any of your crappy books knows you don't give a toss for spiritual healing.'

Falconer smiled. 'There's a difference, I think, between spiritual healing and natural healing and Mrs Willis appears to have had an instinctive gift for plucking cures literally out of the hedgerows. My young colleague Adrian, for instance . . . We were kidding him about his psoriasis, saying he couldn't possibly be seen on telly like that, and so he came, without even telling me, to see Mrs Willis and . . . gone. Gone in under a week. Flaked clean away. Now that's remarkable.'

Falconer was speaking loudly, in his television voice. As if they were filming him. He wanted the entire village, Cindy thought, to know what a magnanimous person he was, not one to bear a grudge. And it sounded not in the least patronizing. Oh, a clever man.

Unlike Marcus, reddening.

'Potent to the end, obviously.' Falconer's smile opening up two deep grooves in his lean, mobile face, from the edges of the eyes down to the wide mouth. 'Sliced through my fence without much trouble.'

'I'll pay for it,' Marcus growled, backing away.

'I didn't mean that, old chap. I realize she had a great

affinity with Black Knoll, and it was wrong of me—'

'*High* Knoll.'

'Sorry, sorry!' Falconer held up his hands in mock defence against a shorter, fatter, older man with glasses. 'Look, Marcus . . . I know this isn't the best time to go into all this . . . or maybe it is, I don't know . . . but things have been said that perhaps both of us regret.'

'Speak for your bloody self . . .'

'What I want to say . . .' Falconer squeezed his chin, apparently reaching a decision. 'In cutting that fence – her last act – Mrs Willis was making a point that I'm . . . well, that I'm ready to take on board. I shouldn't have installed the bloody thing. It was a stupid . . . high-handed gesture. No ancient monument should be considered private property. They belong to all of us. Anyway, it's all gone now, the fence, the wire, everything. So' – spading a hand through the air – 'go up there whenever you like. If it stands as a kind of shrine to Mrs Willis . . .'

A small crowd had gathered. Marcus's face was plum-coloured now.

'Another thing,' Falconer said. 'We may be approaching the same subjects from different angles and we're never going to agree fully, any more than I agree with young Adrian and his cronies. But we do have a common cause. Which is human enlightenment.'

Marcus spluttered something that even the good churchgoing folk of St Mary's would discern as *fucking hell*.

'I do recognize, Marcus – and Adrian *certainly* does – your vast knowledge of the unexplained, your passion for the paranormal. Your perhaps eccentric, rural mysticism. And so I'd like to talk . . . just *talk* . . . about the possibility . . . of your giving the odd lecture to our students at Cefn-y-bedd. Fee negotiable, of course.'

Marcus's lips moved; no words passed between them.

'All right,' Falconer said. 'I'm not going to push my luck. Just give it some thought.' He opened a long hand towards the church door. 'After you, chum . . .'

Under a very faint rain, Grayle picked up the track above what Adrian said was the helicopter shed, noticing how straight the path was, following a direct line into the shelf of low mountains.

She tried to see it as Ersula might have seen it: an ancient land, a portal to the past. Could this be a traditional English Old Straight Track connecting a string of pre-historic sites? To the Ersula she knew, that idea would be a turn-off. Ersula always maintained there was no evidence at all for the existence of ley lines. Ley lines were Grayle-stuff.

But all this was before the University of the Earth.

Grayle went on following the track to the end of the field. She found a stile there. Hesitated. Should she? The sky was a deep, shiny, all-over grey. She was wearing a light sweatshirt, jeans and sneakers. The blond clumps shoved into a baseball cap, the Eye of Horus earrings in her pocket.

She'd conceived this stupid, New Age idea of sitting by the old stones, closing her eyes and willing Ersula to come through to her. Ersula looking cross. *You asshole, Grayle, this is the last time I do this, right?*

Grayle forced a grin, climbed over the stile.

The church was even smaller than it looked from the outside. Mellow stone, quite cosy. And easily filled. But even so . . .

Packed, it was. *More* than packed. People were standing in the aisles, in the porch, some still outside, perhaps, in the rain. Stoical locals in their well-worn funeral-wear.

For an outsider? A woman who had been merely *employed* here, and for quite a short time? All right, a healer. But she hadn't healed them all, had she?

Mrs Willis lay in her coffin on a wooden-framed bier pointed at the altar rails.

This was no outsider.

Cindy sat with Marcus on a front-row pew under dusty red and blue rays from a stained glass window showing Jesus praying in the Garden of Gethsemane. It was all quite extraordinarily obvious.

Little Annie Davies, this was.

And they knew. They all *knew*.

But why had Marcus never *said*? For heaven's sake, what was going on here? Cindy scanned the faces, and they told him nothing, absolutely nothing. A shadow of sorrow over some of them, but mostly it was the famous British funeral face, and it told you nothing.

Cindy stared at the coffin. Annie Davies, the unsung visionary of St Mary's. Who had returned, most discreetly, to die. Who had quietly proved, by demonstrating the gift of healing, the validity of her experience. And who had surrendered her life-force at High Knoll, now a grim and tainted place again.

He felt a profound sadness now, an aching regret that he had not known Annie Davies while she was alive. The things she could have told him!

When the congregation rose for the first hymn, Cindy went into the Silence and, feeling suddenly quite inadequate for the occasion, called softly and tentatively, from the underside of his mind.

Annie.

Before they left for the church, he had found his way to what Marcus called the Healing Room and stood amidst the bottles and jars. In order to communicate with the spirit, the shaman must find the Sanctuary of the Essence. Why was it not here, among the remedies, in the room where Mrs Willis had healed and meditated upon her experiences?

Or indeed, despite the enormous congregation, here in the church? For there was no response from within the oaken casket or from the damp, steaming atmosphere in the little nave. As the congregation began to sing, the hymn underpinned by tuneless baritones and frilled by elderly, fractured sopranos, Cindy tried again.

Where are you?

A sudden, sharp breeze made the rain rattle on the stained glass.

Out there?

No audible, tangible, or in any way perceptible answer.

Why won't you come in?

Cindy looked at Marcus, singing quietly and out of tune, Marcus whose public humiliation had been accomplished with consummate, professional skill, leaving him looking peevish and curmudgeonly and Falconer tolerant and generous.

The hymn ended; the congregation sat. Cindy spotted Falconer across the aisle, between two village ladies, Women's Institute types, who kept glancing at him with undisguised awe.

What a vindictive man he must be. Here he was, with his wealth, his fame and his academic credibility, going to the trouble of attending a small, village funeral for, it would appear, the sole purpose of publicly crushing an elderly nobody who had dared to question his motives in a publication he'd probably never previously even heard of.

Ah, there was more to it. There had to be more to it.

'It was a long life,' the red-faced vicar said, his voice rising and falling as if he was still leading prayers, 'and, in the most traditional sense, a *good* life. And although most of it was spent away from here, although most of us only knew Joan when she was already advanced in years, I'm sure I speak for the village when I say . . .'

And so went the eloquent but mindless eulogy to Mrs Willis. How popular she had been in the village. How she'd belonged to the WI, supported local charitable events, was caring towards the sick, always cheerful when you met her, had – quite remarkably – continued to work into her ninetieth year.

Ninety? She was as old as that?

Well, of course she would be.

And caring towards the sick? Surely, even if her true identity was not revealed, the man was going to mention the healing?

But the vicar's high, fruity voice intoned not a word to suggest that Mrs Willis had been any more than an averagely dedicated parishioner. He expressed sympathy for her nieces, named, and for her employer, unnamed.

And suddenly Cindy saw the interior of the church as perhaps Bobby might have seen it: the rose-tinted wall hardening to a flinty grey and the members of the congregation rigid as stones. A conspiracy of silence.

The stained glass rattled with rain. In his phoney, bloated baritone, the vicar said, 'And so, before we go into the churchyard for the interment . . . we will sing hymn number . . .'

A shuffling of hymn books. But Marcus Bacton was on his feet ahead of the rest of the congregation.

Oh no. '*Marcus!*' Cindy hissed.

Marcus's shoulders were shaking with rage, his hands gripped the prayer-book shelf until his knuckles blanched, and when he spoke it was in a voice rather louder and certainly more resonant than the vicar's.

'You hypocritical *fuck!*'

Black Knoll.

Jesus.

An avenue of stones no more than two or three feet high on either side. An open passageway, curving towards the caved-in chamber.

There was a fine, discreet English rain which very politely soaked you to the skin inside a couple of minutes. I could shelter, Grayle thought. I could shelter under the big stone.

And then she thought, *Are you kidding?*

Standing, dismayed, at the entrance to what had once

been a covered passageway, the whole thing once concealed inside an earthmound, but now bleakly exposed, like the abandoned skeleton of a whale.

She wanted to cry.

This was it? She crossed an ocean for this? Like, she was supposed to believe the stark, ruined shell held some kind of key to the transformation of Ersula?

It was nothing. It had no grandeur at all. Maybe it was impressive at sunrise but now, on this damp, cooling October afternoon under low, spongy cloud, it was just . . . derelict . . . meaningless.

She strained to see the green and yellow in the grass, the pink in the soil and the little plants growing on the small stones of the passageway.

The Offa's Dyke Path which more or less marks the boundary between England and Wales is close . . . I can sense a converging of separate energies.

Energies?

This place just sapped you.

Was that the path, that bare track behind the bushes? Was this the boundary? Between waking and dreaming, the known and the unknown, sanity and madness?

Scary fun, Grayle?

Was she missing something?

She tried to picture Ersula, in her sky-blue ski-jacket, making notes on a clipboard, lining up a picture with her Canon Sureshot – no sky on it, no flowers, no people; all Ersula's pictures were for reference only – *Oh, Grayle, what is the point of piling up pictures of people you see every day?*

For when they're not there, Ersula. When they're not there any more.

A curtain of rain separated her from the big stones. She told herself, *If I go through that fine curtain, she'll be there. She'll be waiting for me.*

'Aw come *on*!' she howled aloud. 'You're fucking crazy!'

Crazy as Cindy the goddamned Celtic shaman. Crazy as Adrian Fraser-Hale with his cassette tapes of the number one Neolithic rap band. Like, what the hell are you *doing* here? You know where Ersula is? She's back home with some guy, is where. You read stuff into her letters that was never there. You created a mystery because you're still Holy Grayle and you're never gonna change!

She sobbed. She looked at her watch. It was nearly three p.m. She would go back to the crappy hotel and she would call up her father and he would say, *Sure she's back in town, hell, your planes probably passed each other over the Atlantic. Hey, never mind, Grayle, at least it pushed you out of that cruddy little tabloid job.*

She stared at the wet, grey stones and she sobbed again, and soon the air was full of sobs, heavy and soggy like the goddamned English clouds. She felt weak and walked through the curtain of rain to sit on one of the flat stones; she couldn't get any wetter.

Which was when she realized they weren't her sobs. That she wasn't alone up here.

This figure was coming towards her off the stones, a figure in blue. 'Ersula?' she whispered, in spite of herself, although she knew it couldn't be.

And yet she had to know. She tried to move forward but it was as if her sneakers were stuck in the red mud. '*Ersula!*' she screamed into the rain.

And then – *ohmygod* – the girl was running towards her, in a skimpy cotton dress with blue flowers on it. The girl had braided hair and she was running hard, although the distance between Grayle and the stones was no more than a couple of yards, so it was as though the girl was running on a treadmill and the stones were some kind of back-projection.

Which was not possible, and Grayle was disbelieving and confused and then scared, more scared than she'd ever been in her whole life, and she started to hyperventilate.

A vivid distress vibrating in the grey air. The girl was a

blur of threshing, graceless child-limbs. Running hard at Grayle.

Yet not reaching her. Never quite reaching her, but always coming on in a bumpy, flashing pattern, like those picture books you flipped through quickly with your thumb and the picture moved, only sometimes you flipped several pages at once and the image jerked. Rushing in tears through the rain. *In* the rain; the girl was *part* of the rain, like a rainbow, but only dowdy colours: the faded blue flowers on the dress, the dry, mousy brown of the plaited hair. And she was flinging out her arms to Grayle, blown towards her, light as the husk of a dead flower, her face in flux, forming and reforming, each time a little closer until Grayle could see her sagging, flaccid lips and her eyes, white and wet and dead.

'Oh God,' Grayle whispered. 'Oh . . . *God*.'

XXVIII

Nobody said a word; that was the odd thing. No murmurings, no rustlings, no echoes from the rafters. The village was letting him have his say.

'Nothing's changed, has it?' Marcus stormed. 'Nothing's bloody changed in nearly eighty years!'

Cindy sat and watched him explode like a series of firecrackers. Powerless to stop it, not sure he ought to try. Falconer watched too, a tiny smile plucking at a corner of his wide, professional mouth.

Leaning out of the pew, Marcus was, a wave of grey hair banging against his forehead, glasses misted, so he couldn't, probably, even see the vicar. Who was just standing there, lips set into a typically ecclesiastical, turning-the-other-cheek pout. *He* knew what this was about; they all knew; they'd probably inherited the silence from their parents and grandparents.

'Are you all bloody dumb?' Marcus whirled on the congregation. 'Is it really possible to sit on something for the best part of a frigging century? You really are a bunch of *medieval* bastards. She'd have had a better bloody deal growing up in the fucking East End!'

His voice bounced back at him off the stones. Nobody spoke, but Cindy saw compassion on the face of Amy Jenkins, an outsider who was clearly in the know. He'd persuade the truth out of her later.

'I did say,' the vicar said in the nearest he could manage to an undertone, 'that you might be better advised burying her elsewhere.'

'Oh yes, that's a *classic* Anglican tactic,' Marcus roared. 'If in doubt, don't get involved.'

The undertakers moved imperturbably into position around the coffin on its wooden bier.

'You're a very offensive man,' observed the vicar. 'I can tolerate only so much of this in the House of God.'

'Before *what*?' Marcus lunged out of the pew as if he was about to grab the vicar by the surplice and bang his head on the side of his oak pulpit.

'Marcus . . .' Cindy murmured.

'You just stay out of this, Lewis . . .'

'Come on. Let's get some air. You're upsetting Mrs Willis.'

'And that,' said Marcus, 'is the sort of bloody thing you *would* say.'

As they followed the coffin and the vicar out of the church, Cindy could almost hear a communal sigh of relief and a closing of frayed curtains over the St Mary's Silence.

She was soaked, hair matted to her face, and when Bobby Maiden found her she was stumbling around the castle walls like someone coming down from a bad acid trip or maybe a mugging. Maybe even a rape.

'God damn it,' she said, 'can't anybody around here answer a simple question?'

'Sorry,' Maiden said. 'You're about a mile and a half out of St Mary's.'

'Am I anywhere near, uh, Cefn-y-bedd? I say that right?'

'That's the University of the Earth place?'

'Uh huh.' She snatched off her baseball cap and shook her hair like a dog. It was blond and it came down in a wet heap.

'I don't know,' Maiden said. 'I've never been.'

'Terrific.'

'You're on a course there?'

'Visiting. I took a walk over . . .' She shuddered and it turned into a shiver that looked like it wasn't going to stop.

'See, I must've come down the wrong way. I saw the rooftop, figured this must be Cefn-y-bedd. And then . . . is this some kind of castle?'

'Some kind.'

'Weird.'

'You need a drink.'

'I do,' she said gratefully. 'Jesus, do I need a drink.'

'Well, that's it, isn't it? I'm finished. And I'm not sorry. Couldn't give a flying fart.'

Mrs Willis had been buried in virtual silence, Marcus tossing in his clod of earth and turning away, avoiding eyes, almost running out of the churchyard. Cindy had caught up with him in the lane, under a dripping horse chestnut.

'Like to buy a serious, parapsychological quarterly, Lewis? Christ, you can have the bastard. Change it to *Shamanic Times*. Have the fucking castle, too. I'll get a council flat. They still have council flats or did Thatcher flog them all to slum landlords?'

'This isn't helping anyone, Marcus.'

'Why should I want to help anyone? Mrs Willis helped people, and where did that get her? Perhaps you were right. Perhaps she was murdered. Perhaps the village murdered her with three-quarters of a century of indifference.'

'Aren't you coming back to the pub?'

'What do *you* think?'

'You've paid for the funeral tea. That gives you the right to watch them all eating it and feeling uncomfortable. I think they owe you an explanation.'

'Then you don't know the people of St Mary's.'

'And I think you owe *me* one.'

Marcus stopped. 'What?'

'Why did you keep it to yourself?'

'What?'

'About Annie Davies.'

'I don't know anything about Annie Davies.'

'Did she tell you to keep it quiet?'

'She didn't tell me anything. We never discussed it. Piss off. Go and find your serial killer. I'm tired.'

'OK. If you must know,' Grayle said, 'it's not that kind of shivering.'

Maybe finding the guy easy to talk to because he looked kind of like she felt. Beat-up. Exhausted. That eyepatch. And with this air of apprehension – it was maybe an illusion, maybe she needed to feel there were other people around like this, after Roger and Adrian and the mad Cindy, who were all so sure of everything, but she felt the guy didn't trust anybody any more.

He opened up the woodstove and tried to position a couple of logs. Not looking at her as she talked.

'Like . . . things . . . things you see. Jesus, this doesn't *happen* in my part of New York. We *say* it does. We love to *think* it does. We have a million psychics and people claiming they talk to the spirits, see the future, read stuff in the Tarot, purify your aura . . .'

Hearing her own voice going higher and higher, as if she'd taken a hit from a helium balloon.

'Have another drop of Marcus's whisky. I'll make some tea in a minute. Go on, Miss . . .'

'Underhill. G . . . Grayle.' Feeling her shoulders shaking, like an apartment block about to collapse, under the sweatshirt he'd left out in the bathroom for her.

'You weren't attacked or anything, were you?'

'I, uh . . .' Grayle took a big swallow of whisky and coughed, tears and stuff smeared all over her face. 'I just had to get outa there.'

'This is Cefn-y-bedd?'

'What? Oh hell, no, this is . . . this was . . . Black Knoll? The prehistoric . . . whatever you wanna call it.'

'What were you doing there?' His eyes going a mite watchful.

'That place is . . . I mean, seriously . . .' Grayle shuddered a breath down, like the dregs of a glass of milk gurgling through a straw. '. . . haunted. Right?'

Haunted. Just saying the word . . . it was a whole *different* word now.

'Are you saying you saw something? At Black Knoll?'

'Would you think I was real crazy? Would you think, like, here's this insane American tourist, she's only been here like a couple hours and she's already going around seeing—'

Another word. Another key player from the Holy Grayle thesaurus. *Ghost. Phantom. Apparition. Spook. Revenant . . .*

'What was it you saw?'

'You're gonna think I'm crazy.'

'I'm not. Honest.'

'OK.' Grayle pushed her hands through her still-damp hair. 'A girl. A young girl. In a blue dress? With flowers on it? Like billowed out, kind of Alice in Wonderland? She had also . . . she had like, pigtails. And she was, you know, majorly upset. Like she was as scared of me as I . . . Or scared of *something*. A frightened ghost, Jesus, how can you have a frightened ghost?'

Grayle gulped down the rest of the Scotch.

'This is crazy. They can't harm you. In my column – I had this column – I was always quoting people who say, Oh they can't harm you. Like all aliens are good aliens out of *Close Encounters*, never *Independence Day*. I mean, how the fuck do they *know*? You're supposed to stand there, and like, Hey, this thing can't harm me, maybe it needs my *help*? Are there people who could *do* that? I don't believe it. I listen to all these assholes talk about communion with the spirit world, and now I know the truth, and the truth is it never happened to them. Never . . . happened. To them. Or else they'd know it is not nice, not good. We shouldn't have to see them. It is truly terrifying, even when you think you understand. It is . . .'

This could send you terminally crazy. Was this how it started for Ersula? Any wonder she got the hell out?

'Oh boy.' Grayle started to shiver again, held on to the fat dog with uneven eyes. 'Oh Jesus.'

No more than two dozen villagers had arrived at the Tup for the tea and sandwiches paid for by Marcus. Amy Jenkins let them get on with it and joined Cindy at his table in the deepest corner.

'It's a can of worms, love,' she said. 'Fair play, if it was happening today, I don't think there'd be a problem. But the church doesn't have that hold any more, see.'

'A good thing,' Cindy said. 'But also a bad thing. So, let me get this right, the Church said, well, visions of the Virgin Mary, that's a *Catholic* thing, so we don't want to know.'

'Got to remember there was a big chapel influence, too.'

'All hellfire and damnation. And at vision at a pagan place. Devil's work?'

'Well, it destroyed her family, isn't it? That was the thing. Annie's dad, Tommy Davies, he was never much of a churchgoer, apparently. Real old farmer, the kind you don't get much nowadays, knew everything about the weather and the . . . you know . . . the land.'

'Moods of the land?'

'That sort of thing. Black Knoll was a forbidden place because of the bodies of hanged criminals they used to put there. Be people then could still remember it. But Tommy Davies, he wasn't afraid. He'd say they put up these stones to help the old-time farmers. So he'd take Annie up the Knoll on the quiet and that's why *she* was never afraid. Wouldn't have got any other village girls going up there before sunrise.'

'Does Marcus know about this?'

Amy snorted. 'Nobody'd tell *Marcus*. Fair play to him, but he'd write it all down for his magazine, and nobody wanted that.'

Cindy bit into a cream cheese and celery vol-au-vent. 'What do you mean, it destroyed her family?'

'Because Annie's mam, Edna, she was all for the Church. Headmistress of the school, ran the Women's Institute, the Parish Council. Tells Annie she'd better forget this nonsense and pray for forgiveness, and when she won't drop it, out comes the strap. Have the social services on to her now, see, but then . . .'

'Didn't her dad do anything to stop it?'

'Edna was the dominant one. A Cadwallader. So it was a long time, see, before Tommy Davies did what he did.'

Cindy noticed they were getting some attention, now. A big woman in a hat giving Amy daggers.

'Don't you go looking at me like that, Ruthie Walters,' Amy said. 'Or I'll tell him how much Owen and Ron took Falconer for, for that land.'

'Careless talk . . .' said the big woman.

'The bloody war's over,' Amy snapped. 'You don't like it, tell your Edgar to get hisself a slate at the Crown.'

Ruthie Walters scowled. Amy said, 'Owen and Ron Jenkins are That Bastard's cousins who used to own Black Knoll. Till they found out how badly Falconer wanted it. That's the sort of dealing goes on in this village. Like a dog with two dicks, Owen is. Where was I?'

'You said it was a while before Tommy Davies did what he did,' said Cindy.

'Well.' Amy lowered her voice. 'He've snatched that strap off Edna and he've nailed it to the side of the barn. If that leather ever comes off its nail, Tommy says, he's going to use the strap on Edna till her arse is blue.'

Cindy smiled and helped himself to another vol-au-vent.

'Well, nobody ever spoke to Edna Cadwallader like that before. A headmistress commanded respect, see. So the strap never came off the nail, but Edna never spoke to Tommy again for the rest of his life. The farmhouse was divided into two. They say you can still feel the change in the atmosphere to this day when you walk from Tommy's half into Edna's half.'

'Well, well,' Cindy said. No need to guess which half Mrs Willis's Healing Room was in. Or was it? Perhaps she'd healed the house too.

'And the two halves . . . well, that happened in the village as well. Those who supported Tommy . . . and the so-called God-fearing half who were on Edna's side. Or didn't dare not to be. It was like a feud. A silent feud. A . . . what's the word?'

'Schism?'

'Prob'ly, aye. Family against family. Hard to credit, but this is a tiny little village.' Amy looked up. 'Are you trying to threaten me, Ruthie Walters?'

'Get out of it, woman,' an old man in a flat cap said. 'It was somethin' an' nothin'.'

'Oh, there was a truce,' Amy told Cindy. 'And the terms were that the whole thing was forgotten. So, to this day, nobody mentions Annie Davies's vision.'

'Weren't *her* fault, though,' the old man said.

'That's why there was such a turn-out this afternoon,' Amy said. 'No hard feelings, Annie.'

'Now, you can say *that*, Fred,' Ruthie Walters said. 'But whatever powers that old woman had, I'm telling you, it wasn't Christian.'

'Course it was Christian, woman. Look at Lettie Pritchard's shingles. You go an' ask her if it wasn't Christian to have her shingles took from her, her as sung in the church choir for forty-five year.'

'See,' Amy said. 'Can of worms.'

'No!' Marcus said. 'Whatever it is . . . no! I'm going to get pissed in my study and then I'm going to bed. The only person I want to speak to is a bloody decent estate agent, and as that's probably a contradiction in terms it doesn't arise.'

Maiden blocked his way to the study. 'I just think

you should speak to this person. Big Mysteries are involved.'

'I'm sure,' Marcus said sourly.

'Her name's Grayle Underhill. She's from New York. She—'

'York?'

'*New* York.'

'A bloody American. Had a bloody American woman on the phone last week. Insane. Gabbled.'

'That was me, Mr Bacton.' Grayle Underhill came out of the study, carrying a tumbler with an inch of Scotch, looking very small inside the borrowed sweatshirt. 'I called you about my sister. In the dreaming experiment? At Black Knoll?'

'*High* Knoll.' Marcus glared at her. 'Is that my fucking whisky?'

When Marcus Bacton pulled out this leather-bound photo album, Grayle got cold feet.

'Listen, say I . . . Just say I *do* recognize her. I could be lying. How would you know I'm not lying?'

'*I'll* know if you're lying,' Marcus said. 'Thirty years of interrogating bastard schoolboys. World's most adroit liar, the schoolboy.'

It was nearly six p.m., going dark early. In the lamplight, Marcus's study was like something out of *The Wind in the Willows*. Flames in the glass-fronted woodstove. Shadows leaping up columns of books and everything misshapen and kind of organic, as if the furniture had grown out of the thick walls.

She took the album onto her knees. Part of her didn't want to do this.

'OK.' She opened the album.

'Fortunately' – Marcus poured himself more whisky – 'the pictures aren't captioned or anything, and there are a lot of little kids in there, as you'll see.'

'I'm kinda scared to look.'

'Where did you get this?' said the guy with the eyepatch Marcus called Maiden.

'Mrs Willis's. To be honest, I pinched it in case any of the relatives tried to claim it. It's all we have, you see. The only picture.'

'I can't believe I'm doing this,' Grayle said. 'All these years of writing about people claiming they saw ghosts. I just can't believe I saw . . . Did you ever? Mr Bacton?'

'Sore point,' Maiden said.

'I mean, I read hundreds of books, interviewed all these psychics and mediums. I knew if ever I saw a ghost, no way was I gonna be scared because of course a ghost is just a trick of the atmosphere, a memory imprint. Like, you see an old movie on TV and it's Errol Flynn and you know he's dead, you don't go, *Waaaah! That's a dead guy!* Because although I personally cannot *imagine* how a plastic box can bring a dead guy into my apartment, I know there are people who can, so that's all right. And so I think . . . I think I lost the point. Am I burbling here? Am I *gabbling*?'

Turning the stiff card pages, peering back down a sepia century. Past men in wing collars, ladies in droopy hats. Men in baggy pants tied up with string, standing under haystacks. A line-up of small children.

Both of them watching her. Marcus with his soft bow tie and his glasses on the end of his nose. The comical dog called Malcolm watching too, through misaligned eyes. Everything completely still except for her hands turning the pages.

'If you don't find her,' Marcus said, 'it doesn't invalidate your experience. If any of this was simple . . .'

But she could tell his tone was forced; Marcus was trying to keep emotion out of his voice. And Grayle was scared to look into the eyes of the children in the album. Although she knew, anyway, that the eyes were unlikely to help her, on account of none of them would be either wet with tears or flat and dead.

Lights shone in the window. Car sounds outside. Maiden stood up.

'Probably bloody Lewis back,' Marcus said. 'Don't let her in.'

And just then Grayle turned over a page and her hands sprang back from the album.

'Red BMW. Oh my God, it's . . . Oh, Christ.'

'Oh God,' Grayle said.

'Underhill . . . ?' Marcus leaning urgently towards her.

'Oh Jesus. I can't believe this. This is, like . . .'

Marcus staring hard at her, searching her face for any sign that she was lying.

XXIX

Below them, St Mary's was a smudge on the bronze evening sky. How could he possibly have forgotten about this?

'I can't believe you're living in a place like this,' the blonde said.

Not having rushed out to embrace him or anything like that. Or left the car at all. Hardly looked at him, in fact, as the red BMW spurted dirt getting them out of the farmyard.

'Well, I like places like this,' Bobby Maiden said. 'Quiet, lonely places.'

'Very weird.' She relaxed, checked her speed. 'Wouldn't want to get stopped by your little Welsh colleagues.'

'We're still in England.'

'Not for long. Always safer to go abroad, I tend to think.' She pulled up at the junction outside the pub. 'I'm confused now. How do I get back on the main road?'

'Just carry on through the village, turn left, keep going. This is possibly a naive question, but what's with the blond wig?'

'You don't like it? A bit Marilyn, maybe? Nah. Maybe not. Truth of it is, I've been tailed, Bobby.'

'You sure?'

'Of course I'm bloody sure.'

'Who?'

'Well, it didn't have a blue light, but . . .'

'Bastards.'

'Pa would've gone berserk. Straight to Riggs. That

would never do. So I didn't tell him. Anyway, you start taking this seriously, you lose your bloody marbles.'

'Too late,' Maiden said.

'For you maybe. Nothing wrong with me, sunshine.' Emma Curtis drove slowly down into the village. 'Gawd, you forget there are still places like this. That a Black Cat cigarette sign over the shop? This is not my car either, by the way. Hired. Mate of Vic's. A gem, that guy. Takes an almost paternal interest.'

'Good,' Maiden said.

A silence. Nightfall nuzzled the high hedges on either side.

Em put the headlights on. 'It's not good, actually, is it, Bobby?'

'Shows they're worried, not sure which way to jump. What's Tony's position?'

'Saying nothing. But I suspect, in the blackness of his heart of hearts, even *he* wants you popped now.'

'*Popped?*'

'Killed, then. *Killed*. All right?'

'Absolutely fine.'

'You know what I really wish? I wish he'd retire to Spain like any normal . . . businessman. He's looking old. Not well.'

'That an option? Some contingency plan there?'

'Not for me to say, Bobby.'

'You can say what you like to me, love, I'm out of it now.'

'Or perhaps,' Em said, 'just biding your time until you can come back with enough to screw down Riggs and Pa in the same coffin and cover yourself with commendations?'

'You'd like that?'

'Riggs? Sure. Stake through the heart, whatever. Pa – retirement, don't you think? I mean, he hasn't done anything really *bad*.'

'*What?*'

'Well, he hasn't!'

'So, *you'll* tell the junkies, then. And the dead junkies' parents. And the small-timers who were fitted up to get them out of the picture. How they all seriously misjudged Father Tony of Calcutta Street. Em, you ever think maybe your old man lies to you a lot?'

She trod on the brakes so hard the BMW stalled and a Land Rover coming up behind had to swerve into the hedge.

'All right.' Hands flying off the wheel. 'No more. Change of subject.'

'You want us to be ordinary people?'

'We can do that, can't we? One night?'

He saw her face in the headlights of the Land Rover behind.

In the silly blonde wig.

'Course we can,' Maiden said.

Almost believing it.

Confirmation.

Even the goddamn dress was the same, with the print flowers. Looked faded, worn—not blue, sepia in the picture, obviously, but it was the goddamn *same dress*. The hair wasn't in plaits, but it looked like the *same hair*, and the eyes . . .

The eyes weren't dead, but they weren't laughing either. Weren't laughing, even then.

Grayle felt as if she'd been attached to some kind of emotional vacuum pump.

'Listen,' she said earnestly, straw-clutching. 'This could be a delusion. Like that explanation they have for déjà vu? Like, you see something and your mind does this kind of double take so that the first image, even though it happened only a fraction of a second ago, it's become part of your memory and you recall it like it was years ago or maybe in another life. Yeah?'

Looking hopelessly at Marcus and Cindy the Shaman

who'd kind of filtered into the room soon after Maiden left.

'I mean, listen, I'm ready to go with that,' Grayle said. 'I don't want you to believe me when I'm not too sure I believe myself, is what I'm saying.'

Marcus and Cindy looking at each other without a word.

'Hey, come on,' Grayle said. 'Help me out here, guys.'

The eyes of Annie Davies gazed solemnly out of a photograph over three-quarters of a century old. In the background was the church of St Mary, looking not much different from today.

A slow, icy shiver went right up Grayle's spine. A classic shiver, just as they were supposed to, just like in all the stories.

Marcus said, 'Do you know why they had her picture taken with the church in the background? For the same reason they sent her there every day for most of a year, to pray. For forgiveness. For her own soul. Can you imagine that? The indignity of it? Like a juvenile felon checking in with the probation officer. For the crime of seeing the Virgin Mary at a heathen burial place.'

He took off his glasses and wiped his eyes.

'It's true enough,' Cindy said. 'Just been quizzing them in the pub, I have. Still two sides in that village. Hard to credit. When I was about to leave, a very old woman caught hold of my sleeve.'

'*I* know,' Marcus said. 'Funny eye.'

'That's the one. Funny eye. You know what she said? She said, You want to ask yourself why it happened on her *thirteenth* birthday . . .'

'Bloody *hell*. People still saying that? You know, she never went to church again. A more Christian woman never walked this earth. But *her* holy place was High Knoll. The child in her, the healer in her, belongs to High Knoll.'

'It makes me wonder,' Cindy said.

'Wonder what?'

'What time did you see this, Grayle? Do you remember?'

'Well, I . . . I'd been to the centre, left there maybe around three. Three-thirty? I can't say for sure.'

'Half past three.' Cindy smiled thinly. 'As her coffin was being lowered into the earth.'

'What?' Grayle jerked like her chair was wired up. 'You're saying the woman who was buried today was—'

'She's gone back,' Marcus said breathlessly. 'Might be planted in the churchyard, but her spirit's up there. Liberated. And even bloody Falconer's taken down his fence.'

Grayle felt like her whole body was made of ice. 'You're saying—'

'And she's young again. That's the point, isn't it?'

'Oh gee.' Grayle stood up, backed off. The crazy world of Holy Grayle was coming alive all around her, too much, too quickly; she couldn't handle this. 'Listen, I'm kind of overtired. Could I get a ride back to the inn?'

'Wait.' Cindy moved to block the door, tall and straight. 'Young and free, Grayle? The apparition . . .'

Apparition. Jesus.

'Did she seem young and free to you?'

Grayle stared at Cindy, wanting out of here and fast, but Marcus's whisky had made her unsteady.

'Give it to us unexpurgated,' Cindy said. 'What did you feel when you saw this . . . child?'

Grayle held on to the back of her chair. The room swam out of focus.

'OK.' She breathed in, breathed out. 'There was no sense of freedom . . . no free spirit. Deep sorrow, real despair.'

Marcus looked sick.

'What I saw, it . . . *she* . . . she was like . . . how can I tell you . . . drained? Like a dried flower? Like a leaf at the end of the fall, you know, when all the richness of the colours have gone, and there's only the little stem things? Like the skeleton? And it isn't pretty any more? I'm sorry. It's what I saw. I'm sorry.'

'Thank you,' Cindy said. 'Thank you, Grayle.'

'I don't understand.' Marcus was on his feet, looking as unsteady as Grayle felt. 'I don't *understand*. What the hell are you saying?'

'You should have listened,' Cindy said. 'You never listened. To the local people who said the Knoll was a dark place.'

The camp Welsh accent all but vanished.

'The darkest evil will always gather round the perimeter of a holy place,' Cindy said. 'Sometimes someone lets it in.'

The lights were on in Abergavenny, under half an hour from St Mary's, as they passed through the town. Then there were long, dark hills against the evening sky like oil tankers anchored in a steel-grey bay.

'You must feel in a kind of limbo, down here, Bobby.'

'No more here than anywhere.'

Big hills – mountains, the Brecon Beacons maybe – were in all the windows now, sponging up what remained of the light.

'You could go abroad. Nah, forget that. What about the press? *Not* the *Elham Messenger*. Does the *News of the World* still do that kind of story?'

'Not got the tits for it,' Maiden said.

A bilingual sign came up on the left: *Hotel/Gwesty*.

Em ran the BMW into a gravel drive lit by small flood-lights in the lawns to either side. She parked in a stone courtyard enclosed on three sides by what seemed to be a very old and opulent country house. Wrought-iron lamps at the entrance. Golden light spilling from deep-sunk windows.

'Collen Hall,' Em breathed out. 'Thank Christ it's still here. Would have been a real drag if it had been turned into a home for rural battered wives or something.'

'You've stayed here before, obviously.'

'Just the once,' Em said.

'With Mr Curtis?'

'Would I do that to you? Or me, come to that. No, this was with Mr and Mrs Parker, actually. I was eighteen. We'd been to my cousin's wedding in Swansea, stopped overnight on the way back to London. I remember they had this gorgeous Italian waiter.'

'*Both* of them had him?'

'I'll rephrase that. An attractive Italian waiter was employed here at the time. None of us had him. Pa said he was probably a poof. Anybody good-looking, Pa always says that. And that's definitely the last time he gets mentioned tonight, if that's all right with you, Bobby?'

'Whatever you want.'

'You know what I want.'

With a lovely smile, Em stepped out into the courtyard.

'I won't have it,' Marcus shouted. 'I'm not fucking having it. I don't want your loony speculation. I don't want conjecture. Do you understand me, Lewis?'

'And do you want her spirit to rest, or to walk in torment?'

'Look . . .' Unease was crawling all over Grayle. 'We're getting carried away. I don't need this . . . this Gothic stuff. Not tonight.' Edging along the wall towards the door. 'Would it be OK if I just left it here? If you could like tell me the way back to the inn, I'll walk—'

Cindy said, 'You've come all this way, my love. You mustn't be frightened now. For your sister's sake.'

'My sister? What are you saying?'

'I . . . Perhaps your sister can help us throw some light on a . . . complex situation.'

'Complex? Jesus.'

'I'm sorry, Grayle.'

'You're *sorry*?'

'I want to help you—'

'Then *talk* to me, for Chrissakes. Don't I rate some answers? Like, who *are* you? Apart, that is, from some weird drag queen who says he has shamanic powers? Last night I asked you what you were doing here, and you were like *disinclined* to tell me, and now—'

'Drag queen?' Marcus roared. 'Fucking *drag queen*?'

'Shamanic tradition,' Cindy said weakly.

'This bitch is a *man*?'

'You didn't know? I thought you knew each other.'

Marcus sank back into the sofa, reached for the Scotch.

Cindy said to Grayle, 'I told you half of it. I told you there were two sides to that place . . . High Knoll and Black Knoll.'

Marcus poured an inch of whisky. 'You mean you've got bloody *balls* under there?'

'We discussed how the image of the rotting man in your sister's dream might have been the place-memory of some Druidic human sacrifice . . .'

Marcus sat up. 'What's this?'

'Show him the letter,' Cindy said. 'Take his mind off having a deviant in his house.'

Carved oak panelling, deep-set window sills. On the wall beside the slanting wooden stairs, lanterns of black wrought iron held electric candles expensive enough to fool you at first. Very romantic. And four stars. You wouldn't find many of those in Wales, Em said over dinner.

She was in a plain white frock, a gold locket around her neck, minimal make-up, no perfume. Blond wig gone, dark hair down. She shimmered. Took away his breath and most of his appetite.

This was better. This was close to real life.

Fiddling with a cooling Spanish omelette, he realized he knew almost nothing about her. What happened to her marriage? Did she have children? A job? A criminal record? To what extent was she still dependent on the

286

person they weren't mentioning . . . and on that person's business ventures?

Em frowned for a moment.

'Not at all. Not since I got out of university. Not since I found out what he was into. Before that, even. I mean, actually, that wasn't too long ago. It really never occurs to you that your kind, generous, loving parent might be a . . . businessman.'

'No,' Maiden said. 'I suppose it wouldn't. If, like Tony, you've been lucky and never had to go away for long holidays.'

'Anyway,' she said, 'over the years I've been . . .' Holding out her right hand, counting off on the fingers. '. . . an estate agent . . . a receptionist in a hotel in Devon – even posher than this one . . . a bit-part actor with walk-ons in *Inspector Morse* and a couple of soaps I absolutely refuse to name . . .'

'Which is where the lovely Suzanne came from?'

'Something like that. Then I was an English language teacher in the Dordogne . . . a partner in a small publishing house which we conveniently flogged to a *big* publishing house. Oh, and . . .' She grinned. '. . . and a prostitute in Bayswater.'

'And I have to guess which of those isn't true, right?' Maiden said. 'Estate agent. You couldn't have sunk that low.'

'Oh, Bobby, you're feeling better, aren't you?'

'How are *you* feeling?'

'I'm feeling all right, guv'nor. I'm feeling optimistic. Have some wine.'

'I don't need it.'

Because he was already high. Riggs was in another hemisphere. Cindy and the ley-line serial-killer fantasy, and the American girl who saw a ghost, that was in a parallel universe.

Above their table was another of those electric candle-lanterns with a glow-worm tip which flickered. Glancing at the tiny, pulsing filament, he caught an image of a blue-white streetlamp fizzling out and blinking on again.

Another woman. There'd been another woman in Old Church Street that night, under a faulty streetlamp. He couldn't remember anything about her except that she hadn't been Suzanne.

'Bobby?'

'Sorry.' He smiled uncertainly. 'Something came back to me.'

'In connection with what?'

'That night, before you came round the corner in Clutton's car . . .'

She sighed.

'Did you see a woman across the road, under a street-lamp?'

'Only you, Bobby. Strolling casually up the street. If there'd been a tin can you'd have been kicking it and whistling. What *were* you thinking about?'

'You.'

'Balls.'

'Are we sending for the sweet trolley?'

'I don't think I want the sweet trolley,' Em said. 'Do you?'

Marcus placed Ersula's letter beside him on the sofa. 'Look, she came to see me. Came here, to the house. With a briefcase, a personal organizer, a pocket tape recorder . . .'

'That's her.' Grayle felt tearful. On top of it all she felt tearful. *Get a hold.*

Marcus said, 'I found her, to be honest, rather pushy. As though she had a right to whatever information I could give her. You began to feel like a sucked lemon after a while, though you had to admire her persistence.'

Grayle said, 'Did you try to discourage her from sleeping at High Knoll?'

'No. Why should I? If it could bring out the healer in a naive thirteen-year-old girl, it couldn't be the evil, heathen place of local superstition and ecclesiastical prejudice, could it? And it . . . She was clearly doing it for her own research, nothing to do with Falconer's crowd-pulling schemes.'

'Did you see her again after she spent a night there?'

'No. I did ask her to let me know what happened, but . . . Well, she was looking for a scientific explanation of Annie's vision. Electromagnetism in the stone, low-level radiation . . . anything which might have stimulated the brain into hallucination mode or whatever she called it. I presumed she hadn't had any quantifiable results.'

'She didn't strike you as kind of . . . you know . . . unbalanced?'

'Absolutely not. Girl was a human database.'

'Did she say how she might follow through with all of this? Any other place she might have been planning to visit?'

'While she was here, she seemed to be focused entirely on High Knoll. The vision of the Virgin, all that.'

'The unknowable,' Cindy said. 'The ineffable light. Such things happen, lovelies. They do.'

'Ersula was drawn to that,' Grayle said. 'The whole Virgin-goddess thing. Ersula has always been a feminist, right from about age two.'

'Two sides,' Cindy said. 'The ineffable light and the unutterable evil. The question we should be asking is, what – or who – has tipped the balance towards the latter?'

'The black light,' Marcus said bleakly.

'Indeed.'

'Only mentioned it a few days before she died. If I thought of it, I suppose I regarded it as subjective. Psychological. A reflection of the state of her health.'

'Well, dear.' Cindy stood up, easing his feet out of the sensible walking shoes, gliding to the window and looking out into the nothingness of the night. 'Perhaps it was. If she was drawing energy, inspiration, call it what you will, from the Knoll and the energy there had been *negated* . . .'

'Then she'd be like a diver whose air pipe was blocked,' Marcus said.

'And if, the night she died, she went back there, determined to *unblock* . . .'

Marcus poured himself some whisky and drank it. 'And now she's dead and frozen out, just as she was for most of her life. Betrayed. Stuck in some sepia limbo. I can't bear it.'

Suzanne would not have worn it.

Suzanne's would have been short and black, possibly shiny.

This nightgown said, as explicitly as you could get, *no more Suzanne*.

She stood in the bathroom doorway, the light behind her. No lights on in the bedroom, where Maiden sat, still fully dressed, on the edge of the four-poster bed.

Out of place in a house this old, the four-poster was patently fake, with posts of 'antique' pine and dusky pink-frilled curtains. A bottle of house champagne, with a big, red bow, unopened on one of the bedside tables. A 'quaint medieval' sign warning, DO NOT DISTURB, hanging, undisturbed, from the door handle inside the room.

Naff trappings of the honeymoon suite.

But nothing naff about Em Curtis. Her hair was covering her shoulders, hiding the tops of her breasts. Her nightgown of magnolia silk, long enough to cover her feet, had long, wide sleeves ending in little ropes.

He stood up. He was shaking. She glided like some Tudor ghost down the two thickly carpeted steps from the bathroom and halfway into his arms.

'I'm not questioning it,' Maiden said hoarsely. 'I died. I'm *entitled* to go to heaven.'

A finger on his lips.

'Not another word, Bobby. Close your eyes.'

Bringing her lips close to his but not quite touching, except with her soft wine-breath.

Presently, he felt slender, ringless hands moving under his sweatshirt, skimming his skin.

Life after death. There *was* life after death.

XXX

A scarred moon hung diffidently outside the stone-sunk mullioned window of room five. A moon which had seen too much of this and didn't want to get involved.

'But it's OK,' Em said. 'Really.'

Maiden felt his hand would leave a filthy smut on her skin and he took it away.

She pulled it back. 'Don't.'

'I don't know what to do,' Maiden said.

'Hey,' she said, 'I was half expecting it, you want the truth. Christ, when I think of all the things that happened to you . . . knocked down, beaten up . . . it's a wonder you . . .' Interweaving her fingers with his. 'Anyway, it's OK, it really is OK, Bobby. All right?'

'I don't think . . .' He didn't want to talk about it; all the words were like cardboard cut-outs. 'I don't think you understand.'

'Come on, guv'nor, don't say it never happened before. There isn't a bloke alive it never happened to. Certainly not someone as messed up and threatened and . . . Bobby, *relax*.'

'I'm sorry.'

'And look, we're here. I'm happy. Believe it. When you went away – ask Vic, Vic knows – I wasn't functioning. I've thought about this a lot. I mean, I didn't want to get this wrong, because I've got enough things wrong in my life . . .'

'Listen, let me tell you, Emma, whatever else you got wrong was as—'

'And I kept on asking myself, could it have been the *excitement* of it? Because it *was* exciting, all that Suzanne stuff; you create a fantasy and you want it to go on. I wanted to tidy up your flat, put your pictures on the walls . . . Christ, they were so *lonely*, those pictures. So, you see, I wanted to be sure it wasn't the romance of all *that*.'

'Romance?'

'You don't see it, do you?'

'Sorry.'

'The loner? The misfit? Dark, good-looking, trapped in a world where he doesn't belong . . . Oh, God, *yes*. And now an *eyepatch*.'

Clutching his hand to her breast. The breast, surely, felt warm and wonderful; it was the hand that felt like dead meat.

'We're all Mills and Boonies at heart,' she said.

'That's why so many women get murdered,' Maiden said. 'Didn't you know? Fascination with the lone, moody . . . psycho.'

'Crime-prevention hint number 486. Thank you, Inspector.'

'No more inspector. That's all over.'

'I wonder if it is. Hey, listen, I think I want to meet your dad. I want to meet Norman Plod.'

'Christ.'

'I've been thinking about him a lot. I reckon he's probably got a secret. Something like the paintings, only different. Something he had to hide. He's your old man, after all, he can't be *totally* insensitive.'

'No?'

'All down to genetics.'

'You're wrong. He's profoundly insensitive. If he was here now, he'd be sneering.'

'I will never sneer. You know that, don't you?'

'Oh God, look,' Maiden said, wanting to cry. 'Piss off out of this while you can. Please?'

'No chance,' Em said softly. '*No* chance.'

'I thought it was going to be all right, I was convinced tonight . . . But it's not . . . going . . . to be . . . all right. I really want you to just, just . . . be out of it. Because—'

'You're full of shit, Bobby.'

'You don't know how much.'

'We can get rid of it.'

He said nothing. His lips felt dry and cracked. He was cold and without sensation. He thought he'd never felt as much hatred and contempt for anybody as he did for himself tonight.

'You want to sleep?'

'*No!* I mean . . . no. No, I don't want to sleep.'

'It's just, when I talked to your friend the Sister, she said head damage, you need a lot of extra sleep to get over it.'

'What else did she tell you?'

'Not much. It's a patient-nurse thing, I expect. How about I make some tea?'

'Don't go.'

He held her hard against the full length of his body. His body – but, tragically, not all of it – had gone rigid at the thought of what would happen if sleep swallowed him.

'All right. I won't.' She sounded just a little scared. 'I won't go.'

'Oh God, Em, I . . .'

'What?'

He rolled onto her. Inside what was left of his head, buried between her breasts, he begged for help. Silently screaming into the cold void.

'What were you going to say?'

'Nothing, really.'

'Say it.'

'It's very much the wrong time.'

'No, it's the right time. There'll never be a better time. Please, Bobby. I'm thirty-three, I'm getting too cynical. Say it to me.'

He closed his eyes on her, and something altered.

Something altered. He imagined her body damp and

cold under him like clay, her arms around him knobbly like roots, her breath turned brackish.

And that – *oh no, oh, please, no* – was when he became suddenly and sickeningly erect.

She said, not moving at all, as if she hadn't noticed, 'I love you, Bobby.'

'*No!*'

Almost exploding with self-hatred, he rolled out of bed and crawled away, in his shame.

'What are you trying to say? What are you walking all around on tippytoes trying, God damn it, to say?'

'We don't know what we are trying to say,' Cindy said. 'We are both of us in the dark. And, when it comes down to any form of remedial action, I am afraid, powerless.'

Grayle said, 'You're trying to say my sister is dead.'

'Of course not,' Marcus said gruffly.

'Or maybe she's insane, right?' Grayle shrilled. 'She got taken over by the goddamned Dark Forces of the Stones.'

'Now see what you've bloody done,' Marcus said to Cindy.

'See, maybe . . .' Grayle standing at the door, waving her arms. '. . . maybe the Ancient Evil of the Stones possesses everyone who sleeps there, right? And they're cursed for ever, and when they die their spirits hover around the stones and roam the dark hills and it's all . . . it's all Stephen King. Oh, you guys, you sure don't help a person just had their first psychic experience. Do I need this? Do I *need* an evening with the goddamned Brothers Grimm?'

She started to cry.

'I'll drive you back to the pub,' Cindy said.

'Thanks,' Grayle snuffled.

In the grounds, there was a wooden bench by a stone well-head, capped now, so that you couldn't see down below a couple of feet. Bobby Maiden sat on the bench beside the well, his leaden head in his damp hands.

Bare-chested, barefoot. All he'd grabbed were his jeans.

He lifted his head, looked up with his uncovered eye at the shambling façade of Collen Hall. Mostly dark now, except for a small peachy light, a bedside table light, in a first-floor mullioned window.

Room five.

As he watched, the light went out.

'No.'

So tell her. Go back and tell her.

Tell her? About the dreams of death? The body, your own body, rotting around you? Tell her about the fear of sleep?

Tell her everything. Tell her what she'd be taking on.

Yes.

Inside the clanky old car, Grayle apologized.

'Good heavens, child,' Cindy said, 'I think you were rather restrained under the circumstances.'

'All too much. All at once. Plus, with all our pre-conceptions of England, everybody staid and reserved and bowler hats and stuff.'

'Underneath it all, my love, we are a horribly weird nation.'

The old car chugged under the castle walls. 'But I'm gonna find her.' Grayle tried to settle in the torn and lumpy, sit-up-and-beg passenger seat. 'I mean it. I won't leave until I find her.'

'Leave St Mary's?'

'This country. She's somewhere in this country. See, I'm going to this wedding tomorrow, there'll be people there who know her. Maybe even . . . Jesus, maybe *she'll* be there. It's possible.'

'You are a determined girl.'

'Don't *patronize* me . . . Shit, I'm sorry, there I go again . . .'

'No, *I* am sorry. You must think we're all batty. Me, with my shamanic fantasies, my obsessions. Getting old is what it is, Grayle. Getting old and getting nowhere. An old queen in search of a stable throne.'

'And me? With my ghost fantasy?'

'Fantasy now, is it?'

'I couldn't begin to say. Is it all in the mind? The brain pulling some scam?'

'Is that what you feel?'

'No. I *feel* . . . I feel it really happened.'

'In that case, it really happened. You were a witness to the failure of the spirit of Annie Davies to return to the level from which she might go on. It's quite true what they say. A traumatic death . . . an unfinishing . . . a snatching away. Causes a blip. The term "earthbound" . . .'

'She . . . she's out there . . . ?'

'She is out there.'

'That's scary. And real sad.'

'*Terribly* sad, Grayle.' Cindy pulled in under the sign of the Ram's Head. 'Get a good night's sleep. Enjoy your wedding, regardless. And afterwards . . . perhaps don't come back. Marcus will look out for Ersula. Leave your telephone number and your address with Amy. We'll keep you fully informed. Get on with your life.'

Grayle put a foot out to the kerbside. 'Aren't you coming in?'

'I'm going back. I need to talk to Marcus while Bobby's out. Some things I haven't been told. This is no night for secrets.'

'Just in time, sir.' The night porter's keys swinging from a thumb. 'About to lock up, I was.'

'Sorry,' Maiden said. 'Left something in the car.'

'Should keep them in your wallet, sir.' The night porter eyed his bare feet, gravel between the toes, and winked.

'Right.' Maiden shuffled a smile.

'Very good, sir. Good night.'

'Good night.'

Bobby Maiden set off up the stairs. The thought of

warm, firm Em in the bed set off the old stirring, but that was how it had been before. It meant nothing.

All the artificial candle-lanterns had been switched off, except for one at the top of the stairs. Into his thoughts fluttered the image of a woman standing under it, like the woman standing under the streetlamp. Before he died.

He shook his head.

Opened the fire door to the first landing. Perhaps she'd locked him out. Liz, now, Liz, his wife, would have locked the door, attached the security chain and thrown all his clothes out of the window, everything except possibly the car keys.

Stood for a moment outside the door of room five, the honeymoon suite. The light was out. Ran fingers down the jamb; the door was half an inch ajar and a wave of something broke over him and it was something more than gratitude, and he knew that Emma Curtis wasn't going to be asleep. Felt her grin through the darkness. *Life gets complicated, don't it?*

Maiden padded into the room.

You didn't give in. You didn't *ever* bloody well give in. You came back. Whatever you left behind, you had to get *that* back too. You didn't let the grave win. You turned a deaf ear to the cold calling. In the end, love wins.

Love wins. In the darkness, he kicked away his jeans.

A wafer of moonlight lit Em's hair on the pillow as he slid between the posts and into the bed.

All right. This is a bed. It isn't a tomb. The mattress is soft. The four posts are not stones. The carpet is not earth. The smell is in your head; ignore it. You can love her, you can do it.

He slipped a hand under the nightdress, around a breast. Slid it down over a thigh, where she was wet.

'Em? Can I talk to you?'

She didn't reply.

'Em?'

Where she was *too* wet.

And cold.

He leapt out of bed and across the room and slapped on all the lights.

Smears on the switch as the lights came on.

And on his hands: dark wine-red.

On his chest, his arms. A trail of blotchy footprints from the bed to the switch.

The bed itself . . . like a waterbed which had burst.

Dark water.

XXXI

The Morris Minor took a bend on what felt like two wheels, Cindy grinding the arthritic gearbox to get out onto the main road ahead of a container lorry.

Marcus closed his eyes. 'Do you want to kill us both, Lewis?'

Cindy said. 'Do you want to tell me the truth about our friend Bobby?'

As Cindy was coming through the door, the phone had rung and Marcus had said, 'Maiden? Maiden, is that you?' a couple of times, before shaking his head and handing over to Cindy. 'Can't make make out what the hell he's saying.' And Cindy had listened gravely, for a long time, to a man sounding like someone teetering on the very edge of the abyss.

Asked Bobby precisely where he was, which sounded from his garbled description like Glangrwynne, between Abergavenny and Crickhowell. There was a bridge there, over the river, and Cindy had very calmly told Bobby to wait there, by the pub, and they would come and pick him up.

'All right,' Marcus said, resigned, as they crossed the Welsh border. 'Name's Maiden. Police detective. Got knocked down by a car in Elham. Died in hospital. Dragged back into the picture by a friend of mine. Anderson. Nursing sister.'

'Friend?'

'And, ah, spiritual healer. Initiated, as it were, by Mrs Willis.'

'Really?'

'At the Knoll,' Marcus said reluctantly. 'Anderson says she used the holy light to raise the boy's, ah, dormant spirit. They had one of those crash things going on Maiden's chest. Anderson threw the light into him at the same time.'

'Fusion of science and the Holy Spirit. Also the shamanic art of soul-retrieval, where the shaman takes a trip to—'

'Yes, yes!'

'Marcus, how experienced is she?'

'She's a nurse.'

'I didn't mean professionally. Could she have let something else in?'

'I don't know. How would I know that?'

'See, what we have here is a young man left with a terrible fear of death and prey to images which leave him – and me – feeling extremely cold. Fair play to the boy, he's only a copper, not going to give us a dissertation on site-specific negative atmosphere, is he? But he's sensitive. He's been telling us, pure and simple, what he feels. Been telling people ever since, I'd guess.'

'First time I met him,' Marcus said, 'was at the Knoll. As Mrs Willis lay dying. Kept urging us to take her down from the stone. I asked him why. Said he didn't *know* why.'

'Well, of course he didn't. Had a very negative death experience. Not wonderful for everyone, as you know. The nice ones are the only ones people like to talk about, feeling the others tend to reflect badly on what kind of life they must have led thus far.'

'Hieronymus Bosch demons clinging to their toes. Examined it in *The Phenomenologist*, couple of years ago. Several biddies complained.'

'No wonder he was in a state. He'd never been to the Knoll in his life before, but some part of him *knew* the place . . . intimately. And it was a place without happy memories.'

'You could be right,' Marcus said grudgingly. 'Had a head injury. Perceptions dulled ever since.'

'Plus, whatever he encountered during the minutes of his death was so traumatizing that he's blocking it. His subconscious erected a barrier. Made even more dense, as you say, by the effects of the head injury . . . which is also filtering ordinary, everyday sensory input to his brain. His whole experience of life is diminished. Like looking down a telescope from the wrong end. He feels he's in a murky dream. Desperate to wake up, he behaves . . . erratically.'

There was a short silence, apart from the choking noises emitted by the car.

'Erratically?' Marcus said warily.

Cindy sighed. 'Perhaps our friend Grayle's outburst was closer to the truth than she imagined. The virus in the stone seems to inflame dark emotions. I should tell you . . .'

'Yes. Perhaps you could tell me why we're picking them up.'

'Not *them*. He's alone. I wish I had known what he was doing. What he was proposing for tonight.'

'Merely proposing to get his end away, far as I could see.'

'Because the situation, I am afraid, is that Bobby seems to think he may have murdered the girl.'

In this dismal room in the Ram's Head, even in the dark, Grayle was finding it hard to relax, drift off. Too much had happened. All of it scary. And the worst thing kept rearing.

Ersula dead.

She'd never let herself even contemplate it.

Outside the window, in a village out of time, the wooden pub sign creaked on its pole. Grayle rolled over on the mattress which was surely no more comfortable than the top of some frigging burial chamber.

You never like to think of yourself as a *religious* person – *spiritual*, maybe, *sensitive*, sure – but religion, in the end, is what it came down to: I'm religous; I need something to lean on. I come over here to lose Holy Grayle and who do I find but Holy fucking Grayle?

She realized she was lying here in the dark, mentally cutting up fragments of Ersula's letter and fabricating that long conversation she'd been planning to have with her when they met up here in England. This made her feel even more lonely.

Believe it, Grayle.

I told you. I *do* believe it. I'm a half-ass, gullible, New Age goofball, I . . .

I mean, take it seriously, for the sake of all that's holy . . .

Ersula throwing back the hood of her dark parka and putting her face right up to Grayle's, her eyes burning with urgency.

'Jesus!'

Grayle's whole body lurched. She blinked in terror. The inn sign crashed back in a gust of nightwind.

. . . all that's holy . . . Ersula's voice echoing in the room.

Ersula, who didn't believe in holy. Who didn't believe in ghosts.

Who hadn't written, in her letter, half of the stuff Grayle just heard her say.

Eyes stretched wide, Grayle gathered the sheets and the eiderdown around her and shivered herself into dream-sodden sleep.

They found him, as arranged, a few miles north of Abergavenny, where the road narrowed into a clutter of white and stone cottages and a pub that was closed. He came shambling up from the darkness of the riverbank, head bowed, unsteady, looking like a man who'd been dragged by muggers into some alleyway and had the stuffing kicked out of him.

'All right.' Cindy throwing open the passenger door. 'Get in the back, Marcus. Bobby and I have to talk.'

Cindy plucked at a sleeve of Bobby's jacket as he got in, then inspected his fingers.

'Blood.'

Bobby did not respond; he sat silently, wrists crossed over his knees, as though they were already in handcuffs. He looked like a man who could imagine no future.

Cindy flung the Morris into gear, accelerated away in first, Marcus howling that he was going the wrong way, should have turned round on the pub forecourt.

'Scene of the crime,' Cindy said softly. 'I would like to see the scene of the crime.'

Bobby's shoulders jerked at this, but he said nothing. The old car made it to fifty mph with a horrible metallic shriek. Two minutes later, Cindy slowed at a sign which said *Hotel/Gwesty*.

'This the place, is it, lovely?'

'Look.' Bobby's voice parched as a ditch in August. 'I'm sorry about this. I panicked. Should've driven the BMW to the police station in Abergavenny. If you go back that way, you could drop me outside.'

Marcus leaned over from the back seat. 'Makes sense, Lewis.'

Cindy stopped the car just inside the hotel gates but didn't switch off the engine, which juddered, shaking the whole car. He reached up to turn on the feeble interior light.

'That way neither of you are involved,' Bobby said, pale as death. 'I'll just tell them I thumbed a lift into town. Drop me at the station, drive away, no risk of anyone—'

'All of life . . .' Cindy lowered the handbrake and the car lumbered a little further up the drive. '. . . is one delectable risk after another.'

An old house came into view, more stately, less rambling than, say, Cefn-y-bedd. Security floodlights shot emerald rays across the bowling-green lawns.

'You realize,' Marcus said, 'that if this engine cuts out, as it seems in imminent danger of doing, you'll never get it going again, and then we'll all be . . .'

'Sixteenth century at least,' Cindy mused. 'Probably older. Possibly much older.'

'Look, if you want to come on like Nicholas bloody Pevsner, let's make it some other time, shall we? Just turn this heap of scrap round and get your dainty little fucking foot down.'

The front door of the hotel opened. A man peered out towards them, shading his eyes against the floodlights.

'Night porter,' Bobby said. 'He'll get your number.'

'In that case, I hope you paid your bill, lovely.' Cindy put on the headlights, full beam, and you could see that the night porter's jacket was green and Marcus grabbed Cindy's shoulder from behind.

'Are you *completely* bloody mad?'

'Abergavenny police station,' Bobby said. 'Ten minutes.'

'So that you can confess to murder? Because, see, I really think you ought to confess to me first. I'm your fairy godmother. Talk to me, lovely.'

'Go, Cindy.'

'Turn the engine off, then, I will, if you want time to think about it.' Cindy leaned back and reached for the keys.

'At your fucking peril . . .' Marcus snarled.

The night porter was strolling across the grass towards them.

'Did I kill her? You want to know?'

'All the time in the world, lovely.'

The night porter took what appeared to be a notepad from his top pocket.

'No,' Bobby said. 'For what it's worth.'

'Worth the Earth, it is.' Cindy cut the headlights, slammed into gear, let out the clutch with a bang and reversed her in a long, orgasmic scream.

Bobby breaking down into dry sobs, poor dab.

XXXII

They'd walked up by the light of the stars and the cold, cynical moon. Cindy up front, carrying the canvas suitcase, followed by Marcus in an old naval duffel coat with a hiker's backback and Malcolm on a lead and Bobby Maiden, wearing a lumpy old tweed jacket of Marcus's over a white T-shirt and sweatpants.

Cindy bent to set down the candle-lantern at the end of the big stone, and the light shone out, as if from the prow of some fossilized sailing ship.

Maiden was unsure why they were here. He remembered going back to Castle Farm. Marcus throwing logs on the stove. Cindy giving him some herbal drink to calm him.

He did feel calmer. Calmer than he'd any right to feel.

'Why?'

Cindy straightened up, face gaunt and hollowed like eroded stone in the lonely light, and there was something about Cindy Maiden couldn't fathom.

'To sleep, Bobby. And perchance – as I was never considered suitable to confide to an audience in even the meanest repertory outfit – perchance to dream. You, that is. Not us. All right?'

'What was in the drink?'

He didn't remember changing. He didn't know what had happened to his bloodied clothes, but it was Em's blood and he wanted them back. To be stained with Em's blood for ever.

She thought it was me. She must have died thinking it was me.

'What was in the drink?'

'Nothing a doctor wouldn't prescribe, and with fewer side-effects. Relax, Bobby, you won't be seeing pink tigers. Right, then, children . . .' Cindy pulled from his case some kind of plastic sheet. 'Let's examine our situation.'

Cindy and Marcus laid the sheet on the grass and weighed it down with a couple of small stones and the suitcase. Cindy made them sit down, their backs to one of the huge supporting stones of the burial chamber, which looked bigger at night and less like a ruin. Maiden remembered Grayle Underhill and her ghost and that seemed a very long time ago.

'Been talking about you, we have, Bobby.' Cindy gazed beyond the small circle of light. 'On the basis that you know more than you have been able to tell us. More than you *know* you know, if I am making myself clear.'

Maiden hadn't realized until he sat down how tired he was. His head nodded, although he knew there was some reason he shouldn't sleep.

'Bobby!' Cindy's hands clapping his face. 'Not yet, lovely. Listen. Listen to me. We're going to take a leaf out of Professor Falconer's book.'

'Bastard borrowed the bloody book, anyway,' Marcus said.

'Sister Anderson told you, did she not, how she brought into play the light of High Knoll in the moments before your heart was restarted, yes? We believe that you were exposed, in those moments, to what we might call the *night* side of these stones. And something lodged in what, to avoid a more contentious word, I will call your subconscious mind. What I want to do now is take you back, using the dream techniques employed by the professor and his people. Are you familiar?'

Maiden shook his head.

Cindy explained simply.

'Whatever,' Maiden said, long past caring. 'Whatever.'

Cindy nodded, stood up, grabbed the suitcase from the plastic sheet and strode off into the darkness.

After a while, Malcolm howled suddenly, once, his wedge-shaped head inclined to the starry sky.

Marcus patted him. 'Settle down, old son. He's just a bloody old ham.'

'Where's he gone?' Maiden wondered.

'Fuck knows.'

Behind them, the chamber was a primeval altar on fat legs. It had cracks and fissures, filled with black shadow now, where the wan candlelight could not penetrate. Maiden put out a hand and touched the stone for the first time and recoiled. It really wasn't that cold. As though blood was pumping through it.

'Maiden, you—'

'Sorry, Marcus?'

'You couldn't have hallucinated the whole thing, could you? I mean, this woman. This . . . butchery.'

'Due to brain damage? And lack of sleep? And she's really still alive?'

Marcus said nothing.

'And the blood?'

'Sorry.' Marcus rubbed his eyes. 'Never had anything to do with anything like this before. Who do you think . . . ?'

'It was a kind of accident, Marcus. It was supposed to be me.'

In the blackness of his heart of hearts, even he *wants you popped now . . . Killed, then.* Killed. *All right?*

'Not this bent-copper nonsense?'

'Right,' Maiden said. 'The bent-copper nonsense.'

Some contract-psycho. Maybe the same inept out-of-town hardmen he and Vic encounted in the flat. In which case they'd better be *well* out of town when the news got back to Tony Parker. One way or another, they were going down, all the way down. There'd be another bloodbath.

And Riggs?

The trail of blood would make a big circle all around Mr Riggs, and he'd stand there in the centre, perfectly still and perfectly dry. As ever.

Into the circle of light came the bird of prey.

'Bloody hell,' Marcus said.

'Been consulting my guides, I have.' It hung over Maiden, wings spread wide.

'Dear God,' Marcus said cynically.

It was a full-length cloak made of some rough material like sacking with rows of feathers sprouting out of it.

Cindy also carried a drum. And a large bird made of some black and red fabric, with a curved beak and big, globular, spiteful eyes.

'Off-the-peg shamanic-wear,' Marcus explained to Maiden, with heavy ennui. 'The feathers are especially meaningful for Lewis. Kite's his totem-creature. Once wrote a piece for *The Phenomenologist* about spending three days and nights fasting in the Cambrian mountains, and on the last night, the great red kite flew down in a dream. The red kite, at the time, being almost extinct in Britain and more or less confined to that particular part of mid-Wales.'

'What a memory you have, Marcus.'

'Kelvyn Kite.' Maiden awakening to an old, fogged memory. 'That's Kelvyn Kite.'

Marcus looked up, but the bird said nothing.

'Kelvyn Kite. This big talking hawk. On telly when I was a kid.'

'You must be older than you look, Bobby,' Cindy said, sitting down, arranging the cloak.

A single, hollow drumbeat.

'This place is a special place. The lights down there are the little lights of England. The darkness behind us is the darkness of Wales. Above us, heaven. Below us, Earth. Duality. The Black Mountains: a sacred frontier.'

Cindy paused.

'Four leys cross here. From stone to tumulus to holy hill and ancient church. Lines of spirit. Soul-paths.'

Maiden saw that Cindy was holding the flat drum between his knees. Looked so much bigger in the cloak of feathers and yet less substantial. Shimmering in the unsteady light. But then, nothing seemed entirely solid seen through a single eye blurred with tears, drugs, fatigue.

'And, behind me, the stones themselves, set to the midsummer sunrise. Stones of light.'

On the drum, Cindy's hands had found a slow rhythm, regular as a hall clock ticking, and Maiden became aware of his heart beating, in time to the drum.

'And stones of darkness. Because, when times grew harsh and the land itself darkened into war and strife, the religion of the Celtic priesthood, the Druids, degenerated into blood ritual, animal sacrifice, human sacrifice. And the shaman no longer waited in the chamber for the blessing of the sunrise but stood, with sickle raised, under the full moon, and blood gushed over the capstone and trickled in rivulets down the fissures in the stone and so to the earth.'

Maiden flinched. The drumbeats speeded up; he thought of the thrumming of blood through veins. *Oh, Em, oh God, I'm sorry, I'm sorry you ever had to know me.*

'And so the Knoll became a place of fear and death.' Cindy's voice matching the rise-and-fall rhythm, acquiring the timbre of a chapel preacher. 'High Knoll, in effect, became Black Knoll.'

Bang on the drum.

'*High* Knoll.'

Bang.

'*Black* Knoll.'

Bang.

'*Du-al-it-y!*'

Bang-bang-bang.

'Think on it, children. Think on it, as we call upon the

guardian of this site to yield to us the images lodged in the soul of our friend Bobby. Ready, are we, Bobby?'

'What's going to happen?' Token question; he didn't give a shit.

'We take you back,' Cindy said. 'To the minutes of your death.'

'And you leave me there. No need to bring me out of it.'

XXXIII

We're mad, Marcus thought, still amazed at himself for going along with this bollocks. *Mad*.

Standing here like relatives around a bloody deathbed.

Insane. Or will be by morning.

Supposed it was the remains of the bloody teacher in him, but he liked a certain level of *order*. Liked his anarchy to be *structured*. Which was what *The Phenomenologist* was supposed to be all about: bunch of tweedy old academics and retired surgeons and vicars and bank managers whose hero was the immortal Charles Fort, collector of yarns about black rain and toads that fell from the sky. All right, it'd been taken over by the biddies now but it was still *respectable* people . . . breaking out of their social strait-jackets, daring to consider the absurd.

To *consider*. Not to be bloody *part* of it, for Christ's sake!

Maiden lay on the foam-rubber mattress from Marcus's backpack. The capstone, a little above chest height to Marcus, was on a slight incline, so that Maiden's head was higher than his feet. There was a small cushion under his head and they covered him with a travelling rug.

'All right there, lovely?'

'Fine,' he said dully. Poor bugger was half out of it. Staked out on the tomb like an offering – Lewis blatantly exposing him to the dark side of the Knoll. Maiden too low, too beaten down, to care. And *was* he a killer? Was he lying to them, to himself? Was he a *killer*?

And where the hell was this nonsense going to get

them? Falconer's dreaming experiment was designed to find out if human consciousness was affected in any quantifiable fashion by the location and composition of ancient sacred monuments. Whereas Lewis seemed to think Maiden's dreams could solve everything. Lewis ought to take over the damned magazine. Get on well with the biddies.

The first candle had burned three-quarters down and Cindy the bloody Shaman, in his ritual cloak, blew it out and Marcus heard him ramming another one down the lantern.

'We'll watch him in ninety-minute shifts, all right? You know what you are doing, Marcus?'

'Every few minutes, I check his eyes for REM.'

'And then you give him a few minutes more – no more than three, because the action in a dream happens very quickly.'

'Then I wake him up, poor sod.'

'Very gently. You want him talking about the dream almost before he is out of it. He may fall asleep again and awake with no memory of having spoken to you. We have to be able to play his dream back to him, make him face up to it. How is the recorder?'

'You have to shake it, hope the bloody light comes on. Haven't used it in years.'

'Hardly needs to be broadcast quality, Marcus. Switch on just before you wake him. Can you hear me, Bobby? Very tired, you are, yes? Now, I want you to empty your mind. I don't want you lying there thinking about what happened tonight. Just make yourself quiet inside. Watch the sky.'

Lewis lit the new candle.

Another two hours, it would be dawn. The miraculous dawn at High Knoll. Marcus was freezing, wished *he* had a bloody cloak of feathers. During Lewis's shift, he'd managed to doze intermittently, for about two minutes at a time, before the cold razored through his duffel coat.

He realized Malcolm had moved away, leaving another large cold patch. Aware of the dog standing a few yards away, growling uncertainly, and the voice of Cindy the bloody Shaman.

'Perhaps you could assist me, Marcus?'

Opening his eyes fully to see Lewis leaning over the stone like some Victorian granite angel over a grave.

''S wrong?'

Marcus stumbled to his feet and approached the stones. The lantern showed the sleeping Maiden's visible eyelid behaving like a moth trapped in a jar.

'Oh. *That* all?'

During his own shift, Marcus had spent too long leaning over the capstone, persuading Maiden to spill some irrelevant nonsense about a woman under a streetlamp, while Lewis sat on the groundsheet, legs folded under him, meditating or whatever they did. Not even coming out of it when Maiden had begun to weep, Marcus feeling obliged to take off his eyepatch to let the tears out, endless bloody tears, crying himself back to sleep, poor bastard. Marcus fighting tears, too, because all the worst nights of his life had involved females dying: Celia in hospital, Sally at home, Mrs Willis here at the Knoll. His adult life a series of bridges over rivers of death.

'No. That's not quite all, Marcus. Thing is . . . a little resistant, he is now, to awakening.'

'You can't *wake* him? Well, that's all we bloody need, isn't it?'

'And your cassette recorder is malfunctioning.'

The recorder lay on the capstone. Marcus snatched it up and hit it with the side of his hand. The red light wavered on then went out.

Maiden's face had that frozen effigy look. Still in REM, and thank Christ for that because if his unpatched eye wasn't moving you could think he was . . .

314

'Don't like the look of him. Come on, man, snap out of it.'

'*Softly!*'

'Bugger *softly*. Man's got bloody brain damage. Could be that stuff you filched out of the Healing Room. I did warn you.'

'Bobby.' Lewis shook Maiden's shoulder. The rug over him moved and Lewis pulled back, holding the candle high when one of Maiden's arms came out as if he was going to grab it.

'Bobby? Can you hear me?'

Maiden's hand went instead to his throat, dragging the rug away. His head started rolling from side to side. He began to cough.

'Come on now, Bobby.'

A dry, rasping cough. His head still rolling until it dislodged the cushion, which fell off the capstone and then his head was rolling on the bloody stone, you could hear it, and it must be hurting and even that didn't bring him out of it.

'Don't think I like this, Lewis. To put it mildly.'

Chest heaved weakly and the cough softened into a kind of hoarse breathing, as though there was something he wanted to bring up, but he was too weak.

'What if he bloody dies?'

'Again?'

'Yes, again. *Except*, Lewis, that this time there'll be no whitecoats, no crash team, no oxygen mask, no Scottish nurse with healing hands. Only a silly old sod who should know better and a lunatic in a bird-suit with a lot of bloody explaining to do. Maiden . . . wake the fuck *up*!'

Marcus pulled the rug away. Maiden's chest was throbbing weakly, like a sparrow's when it's been hit by a car and you know it's only seconds away from expiring.

'Oh,' the madman Lewis said. 'Oh dear.'

'Oh fucking dear, indeed! He wanted to go to the police

station. He *begged* you to take him to the fucking police station . . . but you had to be clever.'

'Because the police – fair play to them – would have been no help at all. Because, if that girl is dead, they'll never know why.'

'And you *will*?'

'I *do*, Marcus. I want Bobby to know. It's important Bobby *knows*.'

'It's more important he bloody *lives*.'

Maiden was making a sort of whooping noise in the back of his throat, as though there was some ghastly blockage there. He gagged. His fingers clenched. Back arched. Whole body tightened up, clenched, went rigid, his face convulsed in the lanternlight, swimming in sweat and tears.

Dead silence.

A moment of heightened reality. The reality, in fact, was almost searing. Marcus, holding the lantern now, was aware of all these delicate mosses and lichens and tiny plants stubbling the stone.

One of those crystal moments when you realized you were at the heart of a nightmare and you kicked a hole in the dream-membrane and woke up covered in sweat and trembling with relief and went downstairs and made coffee.

He heard himself say, 'I hope your famous shamanic training included the basics of first aid. Because I think this poor bastard's run out of air to breathe.'

'All right!' Lewis throwing off his stupid bloody feathery cloak, dragging himself up onto the capstone, extending a hand to pull Marcus after him. 'Help me.'

'Turn him over,' Marcus snapped. 'On his side.'

Both hands underneath Maiden's back, heaving him over so that one arm was flung out over the edge of the capstone.

'Marcus, no! Sit him up. That's it.'

Marcus pulling Maiden's body forward, taking the

weight, and Lewis bunching a fist and striking Maiden sharply in the small of the back, again and again and Marcus was utterly furious.

'You bloody bastard, Lewis. You knew something like this would happen, didn't you? *Didn't* you?'

'I thought it might be . . . rather unpleasant, and . . . you might make me . . . stop it before it was over, and . . . Oh dear. Oh *dear*. Take the light! Marcus . . . hold the blasted light . . . look.'

Maiden's body twitched violently, a spasm, and the dog let out a terrified yelp, eyes glowing at the foot of the burial chamber.

Something falling out of Maiden's mouth. Pink and grey in the candlelight. Coming out in lumps.

'Marcus, don't . . . don't touch it!'

Marcus froze. On the horizon, a thin, grey bar appeared, where the night was lifting like a roller blind.

Part Three

The nasty cruelties of slaying Cock Robin with an arrow, or of walling up poor Jenny Wren alive in a hole in a tree, were once celebrations of the passage of the year and offerings to the gods of nature, but when the magic necessity was finished with, the hunting of a few birds and their needless deaths were just ignorant savagery. Perhaps they released emotions from the unconscious minds of bigger children who took part in them; but in our world of repression and parallel outbursts of physical violence, the old rituals must assume a new meaning or we may drift into brainless cruelties on a bigger scale than the killing of wild birds. A return to pagan sacrifices, even of people, is not impossible.

C. A. Burland, *Echoes of Magic*.

XXXIV

First light, if you could call this off-white seepage light.

Andy prodded the car into the dull, redbrick street with the derelict furniture warehouse hanging over it like a half-expended curse. Doing the usual slow slalom between parked cars – some families had three or four beat-up wrecks; summer nights, the street would be full of hard-faced kids with spanners trying to make them go faster, sound louder.

Not much better at seven-forty-five on an autumn morning, even the kids at home.

Coming off nightshift, usually, you couldn't park within a couple of hundred yards of your own house. Today, though, Andy slotted in between a dark Rover and a rusting camper van, as if the space had been reserved for her. The Rover looking suspiciously new: either a visiting doctor, or the police were getting so apathetic the kids were bringing stolen cars home now.

Jesus God, she'd be glad to get out of here for ever.

Her mind almost made up now, just needing one more sign – OK, this was stupid, but it was that kind of decision: intuition over logic.

The air was white and bland and smelled vaguely of gas as she carried her shopping bag to the front door of the middle terrace house. Shoved her key in the Yale, slammed the flat of her left hand against the door where the wood had swollen. Making herself regard the place, however temporarily, as home again, this was the hardest thing. A place where she couldn't even make a safe phone call, until

Bobby Maiden, or whatever passed for him these days, came back to collect his life.

Or lose it.

Aw, come *on* . . .

For once, the door fell open easily. Due, maybe, to the other hand above hers on the panel.

'After you, Mrs Anderson.'

The big guy pushing her inside, shouldering the door shut behind him, flashing the credentials in her face.

'Police, Mrs Anderson. Superintendent Riggs.'

Marcus faced himself in the bathroom mirror, tying today's bow tie, the sea-green one. The considered formality of the exercise was supposed to give him a grip on the day. And, by Christ, this was a day that needed a grip.

He'd drunk four cups of strong tea and had a shower. Hadn't helped much.

Cindy the bloody Shaman was still on the premises. Supposed to be sleeping on the sofa in the study, but Marcus had awoken to hear the sound of the TV from down there.

Marcus looked out at the castle walls in the white morning. How those ruins had excited him a few years back. Now, just a crumbling pile of medieval dereliction you were legally obliged to keep from crumbling further. Age and erosion. Enough of that in the bloody mirror.

He went downstairs. It was strangely quiet. No sign of the appalling Shaman, but the sofa had its cushions neatly arranged, as only a woman or a raging poof would leave it.

Malcolm ambled over. 'All right,' Marcus said. 'Fair enough.' He put on his jacket and they walked out across the old farmyard. 'Come here, dog. Don't shit in the bloody ruins.'

Wanting it all to look pretty for the estate agent's camera.

The dog followed him over the stile onto the footpath through the meadow. Marcus kept his eyes on the grass a few yards in front of him. No longer wanted to look up at High . . . no, dammit . . . *Black* Knoll.

'You bloody idiot!' he bawled out suddenly. 'You bloody old fool!'

Couldn't *believe* he'd gone along with last night's bollocks.

Take you back . . . to the minutes of your death. The trick was the high drama, the scene-setting. The cloak and the candle. The senses fuddled by lack of sleep. Anyone would be hallucinating at the end of a night like that.

Marcus remembered all that buzz back in the seventies about the psychic surgeons of the Philippines or somewhere, who'd produce handfuls of intestines without the customary incision. Bollocks. A conjuring trick. Lewis had pulled off something similar last night: wake you up, get you into a panic thinking Maiden's dying, and then . . .

Conjuring trick.

'*Bollocks!*'

The mountains were hard as prison walls. He needed to be miles away. In a town. With traffic and fumes and the sound of kids he used to teach, now ram-raiding Curry's.

'Marcus?'

He stopped. Because he'd had his eyes on the ground, he hadn't noticed he wasn't alone in the meadow.

A still figure in white stood a few yards away. Unearthly, somehow, because it was so unexpected. The dog strolled over, tail waving.

'Get you some tea?'

'Thank you, Mrs Anderson, I don't think I can spare the time.'

'Busy man, huh?'

Riggs didn't reply. She'd seen him a few times at the hospital. Big guy who seemed even taller the way he carried himself: with dignity – whatever you heard about Riggs you'd never believe it to look at him. And – face it –

very few had heard anything, only the likes of Bobby and Emma Curtis and Vic Clutton.

He wasn't smiling and yet he was. There was one big, smug smile fizzing away inside this guy, she could feel the heat of it. Mr Riggs was on a roll. Mr Riggs was focused.

'Time to stop playing, Mrs Anderson.'

'I don't have time to play. I'm a working woman.'

Standing in the living room doorway in his bulky leather coat. An energy in him, all right. It made her nervous; she hated that.

'Let me come to the point, Sister,' Riggs said, loud enough for them to hear next door. 'I believe you know where my officer is.'

'Your officer?'

'Maiden,' Riggs said patiently. 'Bobby Maiden.'

'No my responsibility.' Andy wrinkled her nose. 'He walked off the ward. As was his right, but anything happens to the guy after that, it's no our problem.'

'My understanding is that you considered Bobby to be very much your problem.' Leather creaked, Riggs flexing his shoulders. 'My understanding is that you established quite a rapport.'

'You have to do your best. With Bobby, his senses were a wee bit fuddled. Wouldnae surprise me if he had no memory of me at all by now.' Looking straight up into Riggs's tawny eyes. 'Wherever he is.'

'Where did he go, Mrs Anderson?'

'Like he'd tell me?'

'If you were with him, he wouldn't need to tell you. According to Detective Sergeant Beattie, you were rather evasive about your own whereabouts on the night Bobby disappeared.'

'Aw, come *on* . . .' Andy spreading her hands, laughing. 'You think Bobby and me ran away together or something? Jesus God, his head was no that messed up. His eyesight was fine.'

'No.' Riggs smiled. 'I didn't imagine for one minute that you and he were . . . romantically connected. If so, he was two-timing you. With a woman named Emma Curtis.'

She tried not to react. Telling herself she didn't know an Emma Curtis.

' 'But it's over now,' Riggs said. 'I think I can say that.'

'Aye?'

'Last night, Bobby Maiden and Emma Curtis booked into the Collen Hall Hotel in South Wales.'

'Really?' Andy's brain racing. What was going on?

'Under the name Mr and Mrs Lazarus.'

'Neat,' Andy said. And why was Riggs on his own? Superintendents never went around without a sergeant or two in tow, maybe a couple of uniform guys. Bearing in mind what Bobby had to say about Riggs, how official was this?

'You heard from Bobby Maiden this morning, Mrs Anderson?'

'What the hell is this about? No, I haven't. Why should I? What's goin' on?'

Riggs's eyes were searching the room.

'Mr Riggs, I just got off shift, I'm very tired.'

'Does your radio work?'

'Why, you follow *The Archers* or something?'

'A little early for *The Archers*, as I recall. But we might catch the eight o'clock news. May I . . . ?'

Andy shrugged. Riggs fiddled with the radio. They heard some stuff about a row at the Labour Party conference. Riggs sniffed.

'I'll tell you this much, Sister Anderson. If you *do* know where Maiden is, and you fail to tell me while you have the chance, I'll have you in.'

'Have me *in*? Listen, pal, either you bloody tell me right now what this is about, or I'll have you *out*.'

'On suspicion of being an accessory,' Riggs said, as if she hadn't spoken.

'To what? Jesus God, you bust in here—'

'Ah!' Riggs lifted a finger. 'Here we are. I think you'd better sit down.'

The dog wagging his tail. Going right up to Maiden and Maiden kneeling down on the grass. Greeting each other like old friends after an unfortunate misunderstanding.

Tears in Maiden's eyes again. Both eyes exposed, the patch gone, the bad eye still purple. Maiden still in the sweatpants and the white T-shirt that said something about *Fun*.

'Time is it, Marcus?' White-faced, bloodless lips.

'Oh . . . Eightish. I suppose.'

Maiden stood up slowly. Looked like something that rolled off a mortuary trolley.

Poor sod.

In the dawn, he'd followed them down from the Knoll, hadn't said a word. Nobody had. Back at the farm, Maiden had gone directly to the cottage – he'd need to sleep the bloody clock round after last night. And then what? God knew, Marcus didn't.

'What's happened?' Couldn't have had more than two hours' sleep and here he was wandering the fields like a lost soul. 'What's happened, Marcus?'

'Don't ask me about it,' Marcus said. 'Just don't bloody ask me.'

Maiden looked slowly from side to side. As though he was seeing the place for the first time. As though he'd fallen asleep somewhere else and awoken here. Marcus was aware of his eyes. He didn't usually register the colour of people's eyes. But these were blue and clear and un-blinking. Once had these inane, born-again Christians at the door. Or maybe it was Mormons. Fanatics, anyway. They all had eyes like this.

'Better get some breakfast.' Marcus turned, unnerved, and headed back towards the farm.

*   *   *

The radio said, *Police investigating the brutal stabbing of a thirty-two-year-old woman in a hotel room in South Wales say they want to question a senior detective from the Midlands. Detective Inspector Bobby Maiden disappeared from the hospital where he was being treated for serious head injuries. Peter Tilley reports.*

Andy did sit down. On the sofa by the bookcase. She felt her face muscles go slack. In a framed black and white photograph on the wall opposite, the early sun came up between the pinnacles of the tower of St Mary's church.

On the radio, the reporter said, *Mrs Emma Curtis, daughter of a Midlands businessman, was found dead early this morning by staff at the four-star Collen Hall Hotel, near Abergavenny. She had multiple stab wounds resulting from what police have described as a frenzied and vicious attack.*

Police say Mrs Curtis, a divorcee, was staying at the hotel with thirty-six-year-old Detective Inspector Maiden, who was based at Elham in the West Midlands. Several days ago he disappeared from the town's General Hospital where he was being treated for head injuries following a hit-and-run incident near his home.

Police in Gwent and West Mercia have declined to expand on a joint statement naming Inspector Maiden as the only person they want to question in connection with the killing. Anyone with information about his whereabouts is asked to contact police but advised under no circumstances to approach Mr Maiden, who may be in an unstable state of mind. He's described as . . .

Riggs switched off. 'I think we both know what he looks like.'

XXXV

Malcolm the dog had eyes on different levels in his big, white face. They could give you the idea that Malcolm was unstable, dangerous even. Plus, he was part bull-terrier, with a mouth like a gin-trap.

But Bobby Maiden knew that Malcolm was basically innocent. Whatever was happening, he just wanted to be part of it, part of the pack. Bobby Maiden petted the dog and talked to him because this was simple and warming and it didn't make you cry.

He sat in the study, on a hard chair, with his back to the window. He didn't need ever to move. The study was lined with bookshelves separated by bricks. There were thousands of books.

Books about Big Mysteries.

Marcus said, 'What the hell's the matter with him? What have you done to him?'

'Not me.' Cindy had been back to the pub for a change of clothing. He looked neat and clean and powdered and coiffeured, his bangles jangling. But the eyes were blood-shot and the make-up extra thick to hide the lines of strain.

'He's like a bloody backward child!' Marcus said.

'He will be fine. Why don't you make us all some tea, Marcus. Feel free to take your time.'

They'd fed Bobby Maiden local honey on a slice of crisp toast. The honey tasted incredible. Probably nothing had tasted this good since he was a kid.

Which was wrong. Nothing should taste good this morning. Why did the honey taste good? Why did the air taste pure? Why was he aware of breathing? When, not twelve hours ago, he was sitting in the dark by a dry fountain wishing he was properly dead because of his inability to do the business . . . and the real horror only just beginning?

There was a clock over the fireplace, the only wall without books. The clock did not tick. It went *thock, thock, thock*. The clock said 8.40.

Malcolm yawned. His eyes closed tight and opened.

Maiden thought about Emma Curtis. He remembered awakening once and seeing her eyes in the haze around the candle on the stone, as clearly as he saw Malcolm's eyes now.

She was dead. He didn't know why she died. There was no earthly reason she should have died. Been killed.

Malcolm became a blur.

'Marcus is, I suppose you'd say, in denial.'

Cindy's left-hand bangle displayed amethysts; each stone had a vivid interior life.

'Like little Grayle Underhill, spent most of his life, he has, wanting to believe, and then something happens and he goes into denial. Seen it before. Happened to me, even. A long time ago. No, I'm lying, it still happens. There's always a part of us that doesn't want to believe, and sometimes it takes over and we get angry with ourselves for being so credulous. A phase, it is, that's all.'

Bobby Maiden was thinking about painting. One week, soon after Liz moved out, he'd painted only in white – acrylic, layer upon layer, different densities, all white.

Cindy held up a white envelope that bulged.

'Don't you want to know what's in this, Bobby?'

'Not just now, if that's OK with you.'

'Don't you want to ask if *you* are going through a phase?'

Maiden stroked Malcolm's ears.

'Yours isn't a phase, Bobby. You've got trouble. You can deal with it or you can run away. This is just a respite.

Thinking time. It isn't even denial. *Your* denial came after you were killed, and that wasn't even a conscious thing. Your inner self blocked it, and just as well, my love, or you'd be in a psychiatric hospital by now.'

'Go bloody mad,' Maiden said, in Norman Plod's voice. 'Cut their ears off.'

Hunched on the edge of her sofa, Andy felt her insides contract. Looked at her roughened hands.

Did these things bring back a killer?

Her eyes rose to the photo of the Golden Valley from High Knoll.

'A shock for all of us, Mrs Anderson.' Riggs had his arms folded. 'You think you know someone, but you never do, quite.'

How was a state registered nurse supposed to live with this? She found it hard to look at Riggs. A long second passed.

'Going to destroy his father,' Riggs said. 'I met him recently. At the hospital. Old-fashioned, letter-of-the-law copper. Very sad.'

'How can you be sure? How can you be sure this is down to Bobby?'

'Mrs Anderson, I'd give anything if it wasn't, believe me.' The guy looked bowed down with grief. 'We're waiting for forensics, obviously. But, ask yourself why, if he had nothing to do with it, did he leave the scene? And when does this kind of murderer ever strike in a hotel room booked for two?'

She felt Bobby's head between her hands. The incredible holiness of the moment less than two weeks ago. Oh Jesus *God*.

'Think about it,' Riggs said. 'Call me.' He placed a card on the top of the TV set. 'My mobile.'

'I can't help you,' Andy said. 'I'm sorry.'

She stood up. Riggs turned slowly and examined the picture on the wall.

'Mysterious.' Like this was a social call. 'You take this, Mrs Anderson?'

'No. A friend.'

'I'm trying to place it. Cotswolds?'

'Herefordshire,' Andy said, dry-mouthed.

'Welsh border. I see. Spend holidays there?'

'Once or twice.'

Riggs nodded, moved to the door.

'Look, if he was the kind to kill a woman,' Andy said desperately, 'then, my God, would that wee bitch Lizzie Turner be alive today?'

'Perhaps she was lucky.' Riggs turned at the door. 'Look, if it helps you, he won't wind up in Dartmoor. He's a sick man. He'll get the care he needs.'

'Soil, it is,' Cindy said. 'Earth.'

Shaking out the last crumbs on Marcus's desk.

'I don't get it,' Bobby said.

'This is what came out of you when you vomited on the Knoll.'

He rubbed his empurpled eye, as though he was only now waking up. Which perhaps he was. Awakening, perhaps, into a different world where there were different laws. *More crimes in heaven and earth* . . .

Cindy took a soil crystal and rubbed it to powder between finger and thumb. 'I'm not going to spend hours trying to convince you, lovely. I saw this come from your mouth onto the stone. Marcus saw it too, but Marcus is in denial. There we are.'

'OK,' Bobby said slowly. 'Say I believe it. How?'

'It seemed to have been in your mouth, your throat. Whether it was ever in your lungs is debatable. But . . .' Cindy wondered how to put this. '. . . it was certainly in your *mind*, Bobby, wasn't it? Deep, deep down. Because this is grave dirt.'

Bobby's hand at his throat.

'Well, yes, all right,' Cindy said. 'Dirt is dirt. But for

you . . .' He leaned back in his chair, hands crossed on his lap. '. . . the grave. Powerful night, see. Powerful place, powerful energies. Some of which were your own. We channelled them. It was a great purging. You feel better?'

'I feel kind of . . . white.'

'There speaks the artist. You're a blank canvas again. Stunning, isn't it? Knocks you back?'

'I don't want to move. Just absorb. Small things. Textures.'

'Good. It's like when a blind man regains his sight, the colours are brighter. You're seeing through to the levels you could always see, before your perceptions were severely filtered, courtesy of your subconscious. But perhaps those perceptions didn't fully register before it happened, because you were so used to them. You could become a *real* artist now, boy. It may never happen again. Relish it.'

'I can't.' Emotions fought each other briefly for control of Bobby's face. He started to cry again. For as long as it lasted, there would be no inhibitions, no embarrassment, no social pressures.

'Poor dab,' Cindy said. 'How long had you known each other?'

'Not long. She was in . . . the car that knocked me down. Old man's the vice king of Elham. Drugs, prostitution, that kind of thing.'

'And she knocked you down, this girl. She caused your death?'

'Indirectly.'

'Then you are bound together on the wheel of fate,' Cindy said.

Bobby smiled bitterly through his tears. 'Mystic Meg, huh?'

'Yes, an old Mystic Meg, I am. Mark my words. Now. Tell me what happened in the hotel. Why were you not there when she died?'

'I had a problem.'

'Kind of problem?' Cindy said, more brutally than he'd intended.

'Couldn't get it up. We talked about it. She was very kind.'

'Why couldn't you?'

'Nerves, maybe. I mean the nervous system. Nerves were damaged.' He rubbed his eyes again. A moment of self-discovery. 'I'm lying,' he said. 'I don't want to say it. Not even to myself. Whenever I got close, she . . . There was a smell of corruption. Decay. Death. Dead people.'

He fell back on the sofa, expelled a great, long breath.

'Thank you,' Cindy said. 'Thank you for that.'

'It wasn't from her, was it?'

'No.' Cindy bent to the desk and brushed the soil with his fingers back into the white envelope. 'I don't imagine it was.'

'Andy . . . told me I was carrying my own corpse around.'

'Yes.' Cindy put down the envelope. 'And the rest, Bobby.'

'Meaning?'

'Been listening to your dreams again, I have. On the tapes.'

'Do I get to hear that stuff?'

'Well, sadly, after you gave up your ghosts, as it were, to Marcus's old cassette machine, it now seems to have given up its own. Packed in, Bobby. Not a squeak.'

'I see. But you were there when it was recording.'

'So were you.'

'It's a blank, Cindy.'

'Ah.'

'So, you going to tell me?'

'Well, all a little confused, it is, Bobby. Awakened in the middle of a dream, few people give a fluid and coherent report.'

'The substance of it?'

333

'Well, it . . . it supports my feeling that you are close to *him*. You're the man, Bobby.'

'You still think—'

Cindy held up both hands. 'There was a moment . . . a moment when I thought you were, yes. When I thought you might *be* him.'

'Thanks.'

'I still think you're the man who can take me to his door. All the people who might have received that night . . . and it has to be you.'

'Received?'

'Oh, Bobby, if only you could see the world as I see it. Look . . . If the night is criss-crossed by radio waves, satellite transmissions, is it so hard to imagine other levels of communication, unseen media through which thoughts and feelings, passions, longing, curses . . . *essences* . . . are constantly travelling? Just because nobody invented it, it doesn't mean it wasn't there already.'

'And?'

'Part of him came into you. A policeman.'

'What a lucky break,' Maiden said distantly.

'Wheel of Fate, Bobby. Wheel of Fate.'

XXXVI

'I'm sorry, love.' Amy Jenkins wasn't looking too surprised at Grayle carrying her suitcase into the bar. 'I never did hold out much hope. If your sister was still here, we'd have known. That's a fact. A small place, this is. You can't hide people.'

'I guess not. Could I pay you now?' Not too much daylight made it into this bar, but what there was was painful.

'And what will you do now?' Amy was wearing another little black dress with a tiny, frilly apron.

'Play it day by day, I guess. See where the trail leads. I'm looking in on this wedding. In Oxfordshire. Friends of Ersula's.'

'Sometimes the strangest people turn up at weddings.' Amy pushed Grayle's bill between the beer pumps.

'Or, maybe, you know, she already went home, ahead of me. Maybe I just wanted a holiday. An experience.'

An experience. The kind that was better looked back on, from across an ocean.

'You look to me like you need a holiday,' Amy said frankly.

Grayle looked away. 'Where's, uh, Cindy, this morning?'

'You tell me, my love. Didn't come back last night. Room hasn't been slept in. An odd person, that Cindy, I feel.'

'An enigma. Like the pyramids. Hey, come on, this can't be right?'

'Too much?'

'Come *on*. In the hotel in Oxford, they charged—'

'A horrible little room, you had,' Amy said. 'I'm trying to do the place up, bit by bit, see. I can hardly for shame to charge you at all.'

Grayle discreetly added another twenty pounds to what it said on the bill and put the money on the bar. In a strange way, she was finding it hard to leave. Probably, she was going to look back at yesterday as the most shockingly awesome day of her entire life. The day her mind blew. The day she learned there was *more*. The night she called up her own, warped version of Ersula and terrified herself into sleeplessness.

Basically, the kind of memories that would attach her for ever to St Mary's.

'Well,' she said awkwardly to Amy, 'I hope you, like, get it together. Maybe I'll come check it out one day.'

'You be careful,' Amy said.

And somehow this wasn't the same as You Take Care Now, which was just another way of saying Have A Nice Day. Jesus, it was just too easy in this place to get into the state of mind that made everything appear sinister. Grayle carried her case to the baby Rover, parked out in the village street.

Brakes screamed. A big, green Land Rover pulled up lower down the street and then reversed until it was alongside Grayle's hire car, the driver's door swinging open before it stopped.

Adrian Fraser-Hale jumped to the ground.

'*Grayle?*'

'Oh. Hi.'

Adrian stood in the middle of the road. He looked severely startled, his haystack hair all mussed up. Maybe the way *she'd* looked when she saw what she saw in the rain at Black Knoll. Or maybe just normal, for Adrian.

'What . . . what are you doing here, Grayle?'

336

'I've been staying here. And now I'm leaving.'

'Staying . . . *here*?'

Uh-oh. It didn't support the cover story too well, did it? Hardly the kind of joint normally frequented by New York journalists on assignment. Not that it mattered any more.

'Local colour,' Grayle said. 'You stay in a big hotel, you don't get the same local colour.'

'Colour,' Adrian said. 'I see.' He had on a green army-type sweater with patches at the shoulders and elbows; there was a camouflage fishing hat in his hand. He looked kind of cute and jolly and vaguely out of it.

'Which is why I'm going to the Rollright Stones,' she told him. 'I figured, like, a New Age wedding . . . you know?'

'Great fun,' Adrian said. '*Great* fun. Which is why . . . I mean, I was looking for you, actually. We said we'd go together, didn't we?'

'Uh, right.' Well sure, kind of cute, but two more hours of this heavy-duty, hearty Englishness when you had a lot on your mind . . . 'Just, uh, as you see, I just checked out. That is, I won't be coming back.'

'That's all right. Actually, I . . . Well, I was actually rather hoping you could give me a lift to Rollright. I've got two iffy tyres on this thing and the engine's sounding more than a bit ropy. Fine for shunting around the lanes here, but I'd be rather anxious about the motorway. I mean, if you wanted to push on somewhere afterwards, that's no problem.'

'You mean, go in this?'

'I can easily get a lift back with someone. Look, if you want to leave soon, I could zoom down to Cefn, toss a few wedding sort of clothes in a bag, be back here in no time at all.'

'Isn't Roger going?'

'Oh gosh, you're *joking*. Nice people, but not *Roger*'s

337

type. I mean, you know, having them on the summer courses is one thing . . .'

'And taking their money.'

'Quite.' Adrian looked uncomfortable. 'You won't print that, will you? Golly, I'm so indiscreet.'

Grayle smiled. 'OK. How about I follow you down to the centre, get your stuff?'

'Super,' Adrian said. 'I'll buy you lunch somewhere.'

'That'd be real nice.'

And maybe it would.

A single red circle had been drawn on the 1:50,000 Ordnance Survey map (Sheet 161 – Abergavenny and the Black Mountains) spread out on the desk, and Cindy tapped it with his fibre-tipped pen.

'This is your Collen Hall, see?'

The name spelt out in Gothic lettering.

'Which suggests a site of antiquity,' Cindy said. 'Now, if we consult *The Buildings of Wales*, we find that Collen Hall is actually built on the site of a Norman Castle, destroyed during the Glyndwr rebellion in the fifteenth century. And the castle motte itself may well have been constructed around a prehistoric burial mound. Agreed, Marcus?'

'Seems feasible.'

'Indeed. So you see, Bobby, we have a site of considerable antiquity. Now if we look around for other evidence of ancient occupancy of this area, we find . . . ah . . . this is the rather phallic Neolithic stone outside the army camp at Cwrt-y-gollen . . . you see the recurrence of that name . . . Collen mutates to gollen in the Welsh. Probably a reference to the Celtic saint, Collen. Anyway a connection. All right, let's follow the line . . .'

Cindy encircled more spots on the map and then laid a perspex ruler along them and drew two straight lines.

338

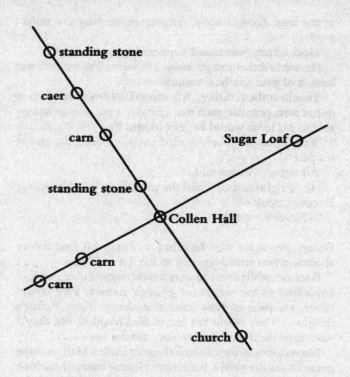

'*Caer* suggests a hill fort or enclosure. Often a holy hill, a place of veneration. The lines tend to cut across an edge rather than go through the centre. *Carn* is a cairn or mound, usually Bronze Age. And if we continue the line past Collen Hall we come to Llanwenarth Church, which I should imagine is quite ancient.'

Maiden peered down at the map. 'What you're saying . . . this is a ley line, right?'

'And here's another one connecting a cairn, another *caer*, and passing through Collen Hall itself to the very summit of the Sugar Loaf, which is the highest mountain in the area. Now, Bobby, do you see the way I'm thinking?'

'God, Cindy, what am I supposed to say to that?'

He wanted them to go away. He wanted to sit here and look at objects and hear sounds.

'Humour the creature,' Marcus said. 'He's been praying to his own peculiar gods that one day a policeman amenable to his ideas would be sent to him.'

'True enough.' Cindy smiled coyly, nibbling the end of his pen.

'All right,' Maiden said.

He straightened up. Said the most detective-like words he could think of.

'What've we got?'

Going over again why he'd had to dump his first theory about the two scumbags sent to the flat in Elham.

Because, while these insects would cut and dice a copper any night of the week, for enough money, they would never, on pain of slow castration, harm Tony Parker's daughter. They might tail her to find Maiden, but they'd wait until she'd gone before they did the necessary.

No way would they follow them to Collen Hall – maybe going in via the public bar before closing time, unlatching a window for later – with a view to doing the job on the premises. Unbelievably risky.

And awkward. The hotel rooms were self-locking from the inside. The obvious way would be to tap on the door, cough politely, announce yourself as hotel management come with clean towels, fresh soap, whatever. And then, when it opens, you come in fast and hard.

And noisily.

Dangerously unprofessional. And you leave covered in blood.

Besides which, whoever it was had gone in after Maiden had *left* the room to make himself an easy target in the grounds.

Which raised the unthinkable: that Emma Curtis was the intended victim. Putting Maiden in the frame. A set-up.

Too complicated. Too many potential pitfalls between arrest and a life sentence.

Surely.

The only other solution was Cindy's. A killer concerned less with the victim than the location.

'A human being,' Cindy said. 'Not a supernatural force. Not an energy. An ordinary human being.'

'Yeah, but does *he* know that? Because this is the thing with serial killers. They don't think they're ordinary.'

Maiden inspected the map, in a cursory way, focused, but not concentrating.

And it was suddenly incredible. The map was alive. Green hills flexing like muscles, bulging into brown. Roads and rivers wriggling. Black symbols translating themselves into groups of houses and telephone boxes and stone churches and Collen Hall in its neat square of tamed countryside.

A pale glow around it. Like the glow around caer, carn, standing stone, church, the pencil line joining them replaced by a taut wire of white neon.

He was tingling.

'This guy would feel . . . connected? Right? Wired.'

'Go on,' Cindy said.

'I mean, he would feel that because he knows this secret countryside of glowing . . . glowing things, he's . . . What am I trying to say?'

'In touch with the spirit countryside,' Marcus said.

'Which is what?'

'A can of worms. But if you imagine another layer of existence . . . a numinous landscape both within and around the one we can see. If you imagine Lewis's hypothetical assassin feeling himself to be somehow moving around in that separate country.'

341

'As the shaman does,' Cindy said.

Marcus groaned.

'But this *is* what the shaman does,' Cindy insisted. 'He or she . . .'

'Or in your case both.'

'. . . can move along the spirit-paths. Shamanic flight.'

'Fuelled, no doubt, by a mug or two of magic-mushroom tea,' Marcus said.

Cindy ignored him. 'This is what you are doing now, Bobby, in a limited way. You're looking at the map and putting yourself into the landscape. But the map is not the real landscape, the map is a pattern of symbols your mind is able to use to *create* a landscape. Which may be even more vivid than what we call the real one. Does this make sense?'

'In a way.'

The glow around Collen Hall was twice as intense as the others because it marked the confluence of two lines.

'This may be a naive question,' Maiden said. 'But why can't he just enjoy the buzz? Why does he need to kill people?'

'A policeman is asking this?' Cindy was running his hands over the bookshelves.

'I suppose what I'm looking for is something more meaningful. If this guy's educated enough to research history and folklore and what have you . . . he's not just a slasher, is he?'

'See what you mean.' Marcus sat astride an arm of the sofa. 'Well, these are ritual sites. Most of them, at some time or another, have seen sacrifices, human or otherwise. Blood sacrifices. Blood is the life-force. Blood was shed to fertilize the land. Goes way back in most societies.'

'We're looking for an educated, primitive savage?'

Savage.

Took a blade to her. Em. Went in, in the dark, and she's probably thinking it's me. Perhaps he climbs into bed with her. Whispering the odd endearment. A little heavy breathing. Finds her throat with his fingers . . . slashes . . . *and again and again again . . . until her head's almost off. And then . . . what? Pulls back the bedclothes, because there's blood everywhere by now and he can't see what he's doing. Sticks the knife into her exposed abdomen and rips upwards. Takes it out, puts it back and rips downwards, all the way to her—*

'Stop it, Bobby, you can't change it.' Cindy placed a book on the desk. Black. No dust jacket. Golden embossed title.

Pagan Images.

'I said you were close to him, Bobby. Look at his face.' Cindy opened the book.

XXXVII

It occurred to Grayle, as she waited on the forecourt at the University of the Earth, that she was going to have to come clean with Adrian.

Problem with this wedding was that the bride and groom both knew whose sister she was; no way it wouldn't get mentioned before or after whatever kind of ceremony this turned out to be.

At least there wouldn't be the embarrassment of having to admit to Roger Falconer that she would not be doing any kind of article on his project. Adrian had invited her in for coffee, but she said she wanted to get to Rollright in good time, get an idea of what kind of clothes people were wearing.

Now he came bounding out of Cefn-y-bedd, still in his army sweater. Looking like the son of the house, some young officer, played in the movie by – yeah, yeah – Hugh Grant. Only a little beefier and with Redford's hair. He was carrying his stuff in this ridiculous, sausage-shaped leather bag.

'What the hell is that?'

'It's a cricket bag,' Adrian said, and she started to laugh, because this guy would just *have* to carry his suit in a goddamn cricket bag.

Suddenly feeling better than she had since she arrived here. Adrian . . . well, he might be into dreaming on stones and recording EVP messages and all that Holy Grayle stuff, but he did it in this big-schoolboy way that was kind of infectious. Maybe the whole scene would be healthier if there were fewer stoned, wild-eyed beardies and more straight-up guys like this.

Reversing on the forecourt, she glanced in the driver's mirror and saw someone watching them from the porch. Falconer, with his ponytail and his denim shirt and his tight jeans. Some guy on the *Courier* had once said a ponytail was just a swinging dick you were allowed to wear outside your pants. Watching Falconer watching her, as she swung the little car out through the gates, she just knew that, at some stage of the game, this man had fucked Ersula.

No big deal, unless he also fucked her mind.

'The foliate face,' Cindy said. 'The Green Man. You saw one on St Mary's church yesterday and it frightened you.'

Maiden leaned over the book, hands flat on the desk. 'This is a different face.'

'Oh, they're all different. But substantially the same. An image which is half man, half vegetation. A woodland sprite, he is, or a fearsome giant, with leaves and twigs sprouting from every orifice. A personification of nature, with enormous energy and fecundity and . . . an absolutely ferocious life-force. He is a guardian of the earth, Bobby. A god of ecology, powerful and forbidding.'

Maiden closed the book. 'He doesn't look the kind of guy who helps old ladies with their gardens.'

'Looks inexplicably malevolent. Usually seen as a kind of mediator between man and nature who fertilizes the earth, but a woman called Kathleen Basford, who's written a study of the chap, suggests he's also a symbol of death.'

'Violent death?'

Cindy looked up. 'Aggressive enough for it, isn't he?'

Poured himself a glass of spring water, and Maiden saw how tired he was looking. Up all night too, and he was not so young. There were cracks in the face make-up, the bangles hung from knobbly wrists.

'Bobby, I asked if you'd seen the face in one of your unfortunate dreams and I don't think you replied.'

'Wasn't sure if it was a dream or not. Couldn't remember. I can now.'

H. W. Worthy's funeral parlour at the bottom of Elham high street. A wreath on a mock grave. A sombre, dark-leaved wreath.

'You know how you see things from a certain angle, and you sometimes make out a face. Clouds, coals in the fire, knots on the back of a door. I suppose, if you see a face in a wreath, it's going to look like this.'

Remembering when he saw the face in the wreath, what had happened to take his mind off the grotesque illusion.

You look lost, Bobby . . .

How good she'd looked in the back of the old Sierra, in the twilight, aglow in her orange sweatsuit, looking so happy to see him. Love-at-first-sight situation. Love at second meeting.

Love.

Life gets complicated, don't it?

He sat down again. 'Tell me everything about this bugger.'

And Cindy brought him the letter.

The letter was word-processed in Old English type.

'Came this morning,' Cindy said.

'Stick to the truth, Lewis. Post hasn't even arrived yet.'

'It was faxed, Marcus.'

'I haven't *got* a bloody fax!'

'No, but *I* have. I brought it in from the car while you were getting what sleep you could manage. And then I telephoned my friend Gareth, from *Crucible* magazine, and prised him from his bed.'

'*Crucible* magazine? What the hell is that?'

'It's a pagan periodical with a circulation no doubt approximating to *The Phenomenologist*'s.'

Marcus scowled. 'I'm going to make some more tea.'

'But less credibility among elderly ladies,' Cindy called after him. 'Read the letter, Bobby. You'll notice it begins, somewhat unusually for *Crucible*, with a polite "Dear Sir." The more usual term of address being, one imagines, something more on the lines of "Hey, listen, man." '

Dear Sir,

As a sporadic reader of your publication and other pagan periodicals, I must object to the assumption that those of us who believe ourselves to be more attuned to the living pulse of the earth must automatically be opposed to country sport.

By 'country sport', I mean, of course, blood sport. While I deplore the use of the appendage 'sport', I can understand why it is applied. By equating the ritual shedding of blood with such pursuits as football and tennis, it gains a certain social respectability in these anaemic times.

An essential element in the physical and spiritual equilibrium of a planet or country is the regular free-flowing of blood, in the open air.

As your readers ought to know, blood is the original creative and materializing medium. It is the physical substance best capable of interpenetrating the planes. It has been used (and sometimes misused) by magicians throughout history to assist in the manifestation of spirits and daemons.

It is also vital for the sustenance of the spirit of the earth. When a fox is killed, after the cumulative energy of the chase, it is a holy moment. The violent spurting of the blood equates with the climactic instant of orgasm. Both the energy and the blood itself are absorbed by the earth and converted to fuel both the planet and the human race.

There are, of course, places upon the surface of the

earth where the shedding of blood is most effective. And, for this logical reason, rites of sacrifice were practised by the oldest cultures of the earth. The insistence by many modern pagans that blood sacrifice is unnecessary and 'barbaric' is unbelievably stupid and damaging to all that your readers purport to hold dear.

Green is the opposite colour to red, and therefore it follows that these two colours represent the essential friction without which we shall all weaken and perish.

As long as it continues to embrace vegetarianism and oppose the killing of animals in the wild, the so-called 'green' movement, and the so-called 'pagans' who support it, is a dangerous sham.

Yours faithfully,
The Real Green Man.

'No signature, no address,' Cindy said. 'Gareth's excuse for not publishing it.'

'A nutter,' Maiden said.

'Oh no, Bobby. Sadly, not a nutter at all. A valid argument, it is, in theory. But hardly, as he implies, one that the blood-sport fraternities would use in defence of their rural pursuits.'

'OK,' Maiden said. 'Let's get this right. When you first told us about this, you said that some woman argued that when William II was topped in the New Forest, his blood . . .'

'Dripped all the way along the road from the sacrificial site in the New Forest to Salisbury Cathedral. According to Margaret Murray, the ultimate fertilizer for the earth because William was, as she put it, the Divine Victim. The god-king.'

'Human blood being more effective, in this guy's view . . .'

'In the view of every primitive tradition in the world, Bobby.'

'. . . than animal blood. So he's taken to hunting people.'

'Because he believes the Earth needs it.'

'Especially with all the threats to traditional blood sports, right?'

'I think you may have grasped the essential point.'

'He's mad,' Maiden said.

'No . . . as I keep saying, he is not. This man is not a conventional psychopath. He even prefers his victims to be people who, according to his philosophy, might well deserve to die. He is a man with a cause. He believes utterly in what he is doing. And he has some rather influential support.'

'What?'

'I'd like to show you a videotape on the television. Little Grayle Underhill gave it to me, bless her. We'll wait for Marcus to return. Be especially receptive to this, he will.'

But when Marcus came in from the kitchen he looked in no mood for TV. He was carrying a radio. He looked no less exhausted than Cindy and a lot more agitated.

'Maiden, they're giving your name out.'

'Who are?'

'The police. On the radio. Christ, they're as good as saying you murdered that woman. Say if anyone spots you they shouldn't approach you. They're saying you're bloody well unstable.'

'They're not wrong, are they?' Maiden sighed. Maybe the whole thing *was* a set-up. He tried to feel angry, but there was no tension in him, only a dark sorrow.

'Bobby . . .' Cindy put down his glass. 'How long, do you think, before they find out where you are?'

'Well, they probably suspect I'm still in the area. I don't know. They'll lean on Andy, maybe. Hard. So . . . Best thing is if I just walk into Abergavenny police station and—'

'No! Sit down. Do you really want to go to prison?'

'It'd give me a bit of time to think,' Maiden said heavily. 'Pending the trial. Pending the appeal.'

'While this man goes on killing?'

Maiden sighed. 'I don't know. I don't know what to believe.'

'We need you, Bobby. Look at us, Marcus and me . . . old men. An end-of-the-pier embarrassment and the editor of an excuse for a magazine dying slowly and ignominiously. Pathetic, we are.'

'Bastard,' Marcus muttered.

XXXVIII

'I, uh, I have a confession,' Grayle said.

They were through Hereford, headed for the Malvern Hills. Adrian Fraser-Hale had his long legs stretched out, the passenger seat pushed back as far as it would go. He beamed.

'You're going to tell me you're not really a journalist, your name isn't Turner and in fact you're Ersula Underhill's sister. Am I right?'

Grayle damn near hurled the car into the hedge.

'Hey, calm down, old girl.' Adrian folded his hands behind his head. 'Roger found out. He was bound to, you know.'

'Oh Jesus.' Grayle slowed down. 'He talked to, uh, Marcus Bacton, right?'

'You're *joking*. Roger absolutely can't *stand* Marcus Bacton. No, when you'd gone yesterday, he put in a call to the *New York Courier*. Roger is terribly paranoid. He thinks other academics are trying to steal his ideas or hijack his TV programme. The more powerful people seem, the more insecure they are. So anyone who shows up at Cefn-y-bedd, he wants to know who exactly they are and what connections they might have.'

'Pretty stupid of me,' Grayle said.

'Anyway, the *Courier* said they didn't have a Grayle Turner but they'd recently parted company with a Grayle *Underhill*. Wasn't awfully hard to put two and two together.'

'He's mad at me, right?'

'I suspect he isn't terribly pleased, to be honest. He'll get over it.' Adrian grinned. 'At least it means I won't have to watch what I'm saying any more.'

'The reason I didn't just come and say who I was, I had a feeling of . . . well, of maybe something going on between Roger and Ersula. People told me all this stuff about what a ladies' man he was.'

Adrian chuckled.

'Well,' Grayle said, 'if she'd, like, got hurt – and I mean, when it comes to men, being this kind of hard-assed intellectual isn't . . . you know what I'm saying?'

'Actually, yes. One always had the feeling that behind that cool façade she was really a terribly vulnerable girl. I'm an old-fashioned sort of chap and a bit of a sucker for a lady in distress and . . . Well, you know, what can one say? I did rather fancy her myself. I'm afraid.'

That amiable buffoon, Adrian Fraser-Hale . . .

Oh, Jeez, poor Adrian.

'Although it pretty soon became apparent that I wasn't, you know, quite . . . shall we say, cerebral enough . . . to compete.'

'With Roger?'

'Roger.' Adrian grimaced. 'He really is such a *frightful* bastard.'

The Great Pyramid.

Well, *a* great pyramid. The one arranged in steps. All pyramids looked the same to Bobby Maiden, except this one, with the steps.

Roger Falconer was halfway up, vaguely listening to a short guy with a beard, who was having to breathe so hard to keep up with him that it was taking the edge off the theory he was airing. Falconer would listen to his companion's stuff, with an occasional nod, and then do this expression that was nearer to a lopsided smile than a sneer but you got the idea, before sliding in some piece of superior knowledge like a stiletto, leaving the short guy spluttering.

'Wrong episode,' Cindy said. 'Flick it forward half an hour.'

'As we won't see the end,' Maiden said, 'who wins?'

The phone rang. 'Ignore it,' Cindy said.

'The little chap has a heart attack.' Marcus reached for the phone. 'But Falconer has to finish his piece to camera before calling for an ambulance, and so he dies. I'd better get it.'

'Might be the police,' Cindy said.

'Better we know about it than they just show up here with their Armalites or whatever they're sending the buggers out with these days.' Marcus snatched the receiver. 'Yes? Oh . . . Anderson.'

Oh God, Maiden thought. Really should have tried to call her at the hospital. She'll have heard it on the radio, seen it on TV. Or someone will. Be all round the General by now.

'. . . yes, I know that,' Marcus was saying. 'Absolutely not . . . If the bastard's saying that, it's a put-up job. Tell him where he can stick it . . . No, he's all right, he . . . What name? . . . Right . . . No, don't. Don't worry . . . Yes, call me tonight.'

Marcus put down the phone.

'Just reassure me that she was calling from the hospital,' Maiden said.

'Who's this bastard Riggs?'

'I told you about him.'

'Oh, *he's* the one. He's been to see Anderson. Told her it's an open-and-shut case and they need to put you away for your own good, that sort of thing.'

'She tell him anything?'

'Of course not. Solid as a rock, Anderson.'

'And she was at the hospital?'

'No, he came to her home. She waited for half an hour or so after he'd gone and then she went to a phone box.'

Maiden moaned.

'For heaven's sake, Maiden, they can't tap every bloody phone box in the town.'

'No. But what they *can* do is keep an eye on her. If she's seen to enter a phone box at, say, nine-fifteen, they obtain from our friends at British Telecom a computer print-out of the numbers dialled from that particular box around that time.'

'Oh.'

'Yeah.'

'How long before they get this address?'

'I may not stay for lunch.'

'Better get the hell out now then, hadn't you?'

'But not before we watch the video.' Cindy picked up the remote control.

'Video? Are you mad, Lewis? Sorry, bloody stupid question.'

'It's a video little Grayle was given. Of Professor Falconer's programme.'

'Lewis, I wouldn't watch that shit if the only alternative was *The Generation Game*.'

'Sit down, Marcus.'

Maiden looked over at the window and then at the clock. 'May be advisable to fast-forward where you can.'

'But, like, hold on . . . I thought you were buddies . . . OK, coming at it from different directions, pretending to despise each other's approach, but it's all good-natured banter.'

'That's just for the punters,' Adrian said. 'Roger and I really don't have much to do with each other. Don't have much in common.'

'But you live—'

'I live in a bedsit over the stables. Roger lives in the house. When he's here. Which isn't actually that often. He can only stand so much of the countryside. He likes dinner parties, that sort of thing. Also, he's very much of his generation. Sometimes smokes marijuana.'

Grayle stifled a laugh; he sounded so disapproving. Hard to believe England was still manufacturing men like this.

'We just sort of need each other,' Adrian said. 'He needs someone who can get on with people and knows all about earth-mysteries, but isn't otherwise terribly bright.'

'Oh, *Adrian!*'

'Well, it's true. I come from a long line of solid chaps who are not terribly bright, but pretty practical. I'm a useful guy to have around. Turn my hand to most things. I rigged out the Portakabins, laid Rogers's helicopter pad. Things like that.'

'I'm impressed.'

'It's a way of earning my keep when there's no course on. You see I need him, too. Who else would employ someone to take parties on outward-bound trips to ancient sites and supervise dreaming experiments, lie in stone circles all night with a tape recorder?'

'You love it, don't you?'

'It's my whole life,' Adrian said. 'I put up with Roger, for as long as it's necessary.'

'You said he was a bastard.'

'He uses people. He's unscrupulous. I don't think there's anyone he wouldn't use – or anything he wouldn't do – to put himself ahead of the field. *His* field. He has to be, you know, pre-eminent in his field.'

'Archaeology?'

'Bigger than that now, his field. Embraces anthropology, psychology and the more acceptable areas of *para*psychology. He's like one of these wealthy farmers who pulls out ancient hedges to develop this huge, private enclosure.'

'Sounds almost scary. Megalomania.'

'It's OK,' Adrian said. 'It helps if you *know* how you're being used.'

*　　*　　*

The wind is blowing Roger Falconer's hair into his eyes as the camera tracks him to the summit of the small hill, not much more than a bulge in the middle of a green field.

Falconer turns to camera.

'This Bronze Age round barrow is known, for no satisfactory reason, as Jed Balkin's Mump. Whoever Jed Balkin was, the farmer who has to plough this field rather wishes he'd stuck his Mump somewhere else. But why did those prehistoric surveyors choose to put it here? Well. If we look to the west . . .'

The camera, following his pointing finger, goes into a zoom.

'. . . we can see the tower of St Anne's Church. Which, as we noted earlier, appears to have been built on another prehistoric burial mound. And if we look east . . .'

Falconer, back in the picture, spins round, the same arm outstretched like a signpost.

'. . . we can see a small wood. Now . . .'

Close up on professional smile.

'If I were some species of spring-heeled sprite . . . and I were to take a mighty leap in a dead straight line . . .'

Falconer braces himself.

'. . . into the very centre of that wood . . .'

The screen fills with sky; Falconer's voice-over.

'. . . where do you think . . .'

A racing blur of greenery.

'. . . I would land?'

The picture jolting and then settling on Falconer standing in the centre of a circle of small, stubby stones, enclosed by trees.

'This is the Ninestones Circle – although, as you can see, there are only seven left. It's a key feature of what even I have to admit is one of the more credible of thousands of alleged "ley lines" connecting ancient sites all over Britain. Our New Age friends would claim that this invisible line marks a flow of terrestrial energy across the landscape. The life-force of the Earth. If they're right, I should be getting a stiff shot of the stuff through my system at this very moment.'

Falconer bending down to place his hands over a stone no more than two feet tall, smiling the kind of smile that says precisely what he thinks of this New Age garbage.

Close up.

'To the New Agers, Stone Age and Bronze Age person was a wise and civilized soul, very much into peace and love and celestial harmony. He or she would probably have sat where I'm sitting now, meditating and being at one with nature.'

Falconer stands up.

'Sheer nonsense, of course. The New Agers have reinvented the Stone Agers in their own image. In reality, words like "peace" and "love" would have meant nothing to these people. The key word for them would have been . . . "survival".'

Falconer stalking through the woods, now, like an explorer.

'Stone Age man – and perhaps Stone Age woman, too – moved through the landscape like a guerrilla. In tune with the Earth? Well, of course he was. He recognized that the Earth was his provider, that a relationship was crucial to his continued existence. But let's not beat about the bush. This was a relationship cemented . . .'

Tight into Falconer's savage grin.

'. . . with blood.'

A rustling in the undergrowth; the camera pans across the flight of a frightened rabbit into a bush. Falconer's voice-over.

'If anything sharpened the senses of Neolithic people, raised their perceptions, gave them an instinctive feel for the environment, it was . . . the hunt.'

Shots of familiar cave paintings showing lumpen, bovine creatures getting speared.

'Hunting . . . killing . . . was a natural, pivotal aspect of a Neolithic lifestyle which would, one suspects, thoroughly disgust our New Age friends.'

Full-length shot of Falconer holding a twelve-bore shotgun.

'Blood sports – hunting, shooting – are anathema to many supporters of the Green movement. But green and red are opposites which, throughout history, have been linked together. And there's little doubt that the original Green Man was a hunter, a stalker, who understood that the true, undiluted life-force was a flow . . . a gush . . . of lifeblood.'

Falconer emerging from the wood into the field where Jed Balkin's Mump swells like a boil.

'It's surely naive to deny the extent to which the religous beliefs and rituals of our remote ancestors were linked to violent death.'

Sound of hunting horn and shots of traditional hunt, red-coated men and women and yelping hounds.

'The ritual aspects of the hunt, as practised by some of Britain's oldest families, are inescapable. This is still the most dynamic example of a flow of real energy through the landscape.'

Cut to group of huntsmen. 'Oh yes.' *An old guy with huge sidewhiskers.* 'There's no doubt about it. The chase absolutely takes one over. I never feel more alive. Indeed, at the height of the chase, one feels . . . immortal. Godlike, I suppose. All I know is that when I can't hunt, it'll be time – ha ha – to put me in the ground.'

The old huntsman clambering onto his horse. Falconer's voice-over.

'So which is closest to the earth. This man? Or this woman?'

Cut to shot of flaxen-haired beauty in a cloak and headband sitting in Lotus position at the foot of a standing stone.

Cut back to Falconer, his back to a church wall, the tower rearing behind his head.

'There's now a body of opinion which maintains that, psychologically and sociologically, we took a wrong turning when we abandoned the spear and the bow for the plough. When we ceased to be hunter-gatherers and became farmers. Out of agriculture came urban life, a cauldron of constantly recycled energy. Out of urban life was born stress, frustration, crime, domestic violence. What we like to call civilization. Was this the Fall of Man? It's an issue we'll be debating in the studio in next week's edition of Diggers. Join us then.'

Credits roll. A University of the Earth production for Channel Four.

Silence.

Cindy switched off the set.

'Well.' Marcus sat up. 'No wonder he was guest of honour at the bloody Hunt Ball.'

'Interesting, isn't it, my loves?'

'Notice he said "the original Green Man". Not a million miles from the *real* Green Man.'

'Some of the phrases are almost the same,' Maiden said. 'That about red and green. Of course, the Green Man may simply have seen that programme. Television puts ideas into people's heads. This guy sees that programme, a week later he thinks it's his own concept.'

Cindy slid the videotape into its sleeve. 'The programme was transmitted, as far as I can make out, last July. The letter was received by *Crucible* nearly a year ago.'

'Could have been the other way round, then. Falconer saw the letter. It fitted the angle he was after, so he developed the idea for his programme. Academics are terrible magpies, isn't that right, Marcus?'

'Vultures.'

'It wasn't printed, Bobby.'

'Maybe somebody else printed it.'

'Possibly,' Cindy conceded.

'The other alternative,' Marcus said, expressionless, 'is that Falconer wrote the letter himself. Why he'd do that, I don't know. Maybe he was fishing for reaction.'

'Well.' Maiden stood up. 'Why don't we go and ask him?'

'Yes. Get you out of the house, wouldn't it, lovely?'

'Why not?' Marcus was on his feet. 'Personally, I wouldn't miss this for—'

'I don't think so,' Cindy said. 'I'd hate you to get overemotional.'

'Listen, Lewis, the bastard has some explaining to do. If there's any basis to your crackpot theory, at the very least he's going to have an idea of the kind of person stupid enough to be influenced by his ideas about the bloodlust of Neolithic man. Right?'

'But at best,' Maiden said, 'all it does is link the letter-writer to the programme. The rest is conjecture. You're both, in your separate ways, too close to this. *I'll* go.'

'Under what pretext, Maiden? As a copper? Or as the most wanted man in Britain, possibly unstable?'

'I'll have thought of something by the time I get there.'

'You be very careful, Bobby . . .' Cindy's eyes were hooded, watchful. 'In some ways, you are closer to this than either of us.'

XXXIX

She could picture the wounds all too clearly, and it didn't make her feel sick, just angry as hell. She was supposed to sleep now? Go on up to bed, get in six hours, awake refreshed for the Saturday slaughterhouse shift?

Oh, aye, the perfect sedative: two people you'd got fond of, and the police were saying one had killed the other and they needed to put him away for his own good, and the hunt was on, nationwide.

Marcus had said no, absolutely not, no way was Bobby Maiden a murderer, which, naturally, he would. Clearly wanting to get her off the line. Which suggested Bobby was with him or he knew where Bobby was. And she ought to go down there, not least because the whole scenario had started to unroll under her own hands in A and E that day at 2.37 a.m. But even getting to the phone box had felt as public as the first bloody moonwalk.

Andy kept looking out of the window for strange cars in the street, but it wouldn't be that obvious.

Sat down, with a fresh pot of tea. Closed her eyes, and there was Emma Curtis, a nice girl, a great girl, face up on some mortuary slab. She set down the cup and saucer, stood up and paced. If it wasn't Bobby, then who?

If the bastard's saying that, it's a put-up job, Marcus said.

To put Bobby in the frame? Somebody killed her to hang it on Bobby, protect themselves? Some big, megalomaniac copper had it done? Did such things really happen? Jesus God, it made your head swell just to think about it.

Made you want to drive down to Police HQ and accuse Riggs, very loudly, very publicly, of being bent as a coathanger. Pull the lid off the can of worms and hope the worms had wriggled all over town by the time they took you away. Get it in the *Elham Messenger*.

Sure. Two paragraphs, bottom of page nine. NURSE CHARGED WITH PUBLIC ORDER OFFENCES.

Jesus God, there had to be *something* she could do.

There was only one V. Clutton in the Elham phone book. There was no answer. After a few minutes, Andy decided to go and see Tony Parker.

They came out of Tewkesbury, in Gloucestershire, headed for the Cotswolds, the countryside looking milder, more ordered. Around twelve-thirty, Adrian suggested they grab some lunch.

'Can we afford to stop for lunch? Will we make it in time?'

'*Loads* of time,' Adrian said. 'Oh, but then, you wouldn't know, would you?'

'Huh?'

'Matthew rang last night. They've decided to put off the ceremony until late afternoon, early evening. The Rollrights are open to the public, so they realized they were going to have quite a few unwanted guests – tourists, people like that. It is Saturday, after all. Anyway, Matt thought it would be a better atmosphere if they waited till dusk. Candles and lanterns and all that. Frightfully romantic.'

'Right.' Grayle was dubious. It was a dull day, but not too cold; an evening wedding would be, well . . . atmospheric. In a sinister kind of way. 'You think that is a romantic setting? The Rollright Stones?'

'You don't?'

'Well . . . maybe it just wasn't a nice day when I went there. Seemed kind of a forbidding place. Which was odd, I guess, when you think how close it is to the road and all.

It seemed, I dunno, kind of mean. The way the stones are like curly and notched and knobbly.'

She snatched a glance at Adrian to gauge his reaction. Saw a look of concern on his young-officer's face. He said, 'You really didn't care for it?'

'Maybe it was just an emotional reaction,' Grayle said. 'Probably the way I was feeling that day. I'd hoped to get some hard information about where Ersula could be, and I didn't. Call it personal negativity. Nothing scientific.'

'Because, you see, Grayle, this is a *holy place*. It's not supposed to be . . . cosy. Any more than a great cathedral is. It's an integral part of a huge, sacred pattern. Nobody, not even Roger, denies that any more. It's another level. Another Britain. Which we're only just finding our way around again.'

'Right.' Maybe it's because Britain is so small, Grayle thought. If they want to discover anything new about it, it has to be on some invisible level.

'And what we don't understand, we naturally fear – people are just as primitive in that way as they ever were, they're just more shielded from the dark. It's a fear we're jolly well going to have to conquer, those of us who want to evolve. All kinds of fears, all kind of blocks . . . we're going to have to break through them. If we're going to get in tune with the earth again. Before it's too late.'

'Aw, gee.' Grayle pulled the gear lever to low, for a steep downward slope. How to *put* this . . . how to tell him she'd heard all this before. 'See, you guys, you come on like, We got to tune in to holy places, we got to recover our lost knowledge, our forgotten ancient wisdom . . . Jesus, I used to talk like this all the time.'

'And that's the problem, isn't it?' Adrian put his big, warm hand over hers on the lever. 'It's all *talk*. It's just a coffee table thing. So few people *do* anything. Imagine if the druids had simply . . . you know . . . theorized. Gosh, for them it was real life . . . life and death. So if the Rollrights feel sort of brooding, that's why.'

'Uh, why?' Grayle felt herself blushing, tugged her hand back to the wheel.

'Because it's been a working site. It isn't all manicured and prettified like some monuments. Some of the New Age people would be absolutely horrified if they actually knew what it was like in the ancient days. They all think it was some sort of Golden Age and perhaps it was, but it was a cruel age too. Or rather people today might think of it as cruel, but it was necessary.'

'You mean sacrifices.'

As they drove into the Cotswolds, the countryside was lightening up, the stone becoming golden against a white sky like the fluffy lining in a jewel box.

'People try to close their eyes to it, Grayle. They say, Oh, even in the degenerate period when the priests practised human sacrifice, they only sacrificed criminals who deserved it. Well, what kind of a sacrifice is that? That's not sacrifice, it's *execution*. Surely, it's only a *real* sacrifice if you give up the life of someone you don't hate, who hasn't done you any personal harm. And perhaps the ultimate sacrifice is to take, well . . . the life of a friend, I suppose.'

'But when would it be worth losing a friend for?'

'Oh, that's just a modern attitude. Look at the Bible. God tested Abraham's faith, his absolute conviction, by asking for the blood of his son. And off they went to a high place, a holy site, and they built an altar and Abraham took a knife . . .'

'But that was just a test, surely. God never intended him to follow through.'

'Depends how you look at it. Abraham was being shown that if he ever wanted true wisdom – to walk with the gods . . . I mean, people in several civilizations *did* sacrifice their children.'

'Plus, this was the Old Testament God. Pre-Christ. We progressed from that stuff.'

'But we *didn't* progress, did we?'

'In a lot of ways we did. Did *Christ* ask for blood sacrifices?'

'Grayle, Christ *was* a blood sacrifice.'

This was all getting a little heavy for Grayle. After yesterday, she needed to lighten up. She'd hoped being with Adrian . . . good-looking guy, for heaven's sake, rough-hewn, country-boy charm. Why'd he have to be so intense about all this? And who did *that* remind you of?

'You talk about all this stuff with Ersula?'

'Ersula understood. As an anthropologist. Oh yes, we'd talk for hours and hours.'

'And Roger? Would she talk for hours with Roger?'

'You're asking me if she had an affair with Roger.'

'You told me yesterday she left in a hurry.'

'Well, you know . . . I mean . . .'

Adrian looked uncomfortable. Jesus, he was fine talking about ancient blood ritual and sacrificing your kids, but you changed the subject to, like, contemporary sexual relations, he got embarrassed.

'. . . I suppose it's possible.'

'I know it's *possible*, Adrian, but did it *happen*?'

Adrian swallowed, and Grayle began to see how it might have been: Adrian majorly turned on by Ersula, by her intensity, her passion for the past, the very stuff that put most guys off. But Ersula finds Adrian a little raw and gauche, especially up against Roger . . . smooth, eloquent, experienced . . . the kind of man who could intellectualize his way right into your pants.

Perhaps Falconer had it right; you needed to hunt, you needed the friction, the wind of the chase just to keep on living.

Maiden had come on foot. Cefn-y-bedd was less than a mile from Castle Farm, along the path towards the meadow, but instead of going up towards the Knoll you detoured down a half-overgrown footpath, over a stile and into the woods.

He felt a sharp edge of purpose. The fresh air sang with sensation. There was a light rain of crinkling leaves. Birds, probably undisturbed for months, flew for the exits. A squirrel sped across the path in front of him.

It was a curious state of mind. Not at all happy, but hyper-aware, so alive it ached. He was hunting Falconer, a man with a lot of questions to answer.

And yet, he kept looking behind him.

Leaves rustled in his wake. Twigs snapped. It was probably wildlife. Rabbits, birds. Not many people came this way; the wildlife would be spooked.

But he kept looking over his shoulder.

Quite a heavy crunch this time, and he spun round and thought he saw a face framed in foliage, and thought, in shock, *Green Man, Green Man, Green Man.*

The Green Man hunting *him.*

And then there was big noise everywhere and he didn't know where to run as, with this huge, angry clattering, a helicopter, white and red, lifted up, apparently out of the centre of the wood, not fifty yards away, in a golden storm of October leaves.

Crows rose screaming. The helicopter hovered under the sheet of the sky, rotors churning. The helicopter was very hard-edged and real.

It meant that Roger Falconer was leaving.

Maiden breathed out slowly, in dismay. 'Thank you. Thanks a bunch, Roger.'

The machine was directly above him now, and he instinctively bent and moved forward in a crouch, through the trees, and found he was on the edge of a clearing, with a big slab of flat, flesh-coloured concrete at its centre. He walked around the clearing, keeping close to the trees, watched the chopper banking, heading off south.

The crows calmed down. His spirits sagged. What would he have done anyway? Flashed his ID and hoped Falconer hadn't heard the radio this morning?

It was all so flimsy, so fanciful. As the noise dwindled to

a distant drone, he sat on a mossed and slimy fallen branch, head in his hands, the way he'd sat last night by the well at Collen Hall.

So *convenient*. So conveniently timed. Just hours after Cindy airs his wild theory about the mystical killer who needs to spill blood at holy places, the killer strikes again. Under Maiden's nose.

A pigeon or something rattled in the bushes, like Cindy's bangles on those bony wrists.

Cindy. This ageing transsexual (probably) actor, reduced to the end of the pier. Embittered by sneers, pining for applause, living half his life in a fantasy dimension where kites talk and shamans fly.

Grabbing his chance for a final blaze of public attention, Cindy invents a bizarre solution to the murder of his landlady's daughter. Hampshire police kindly show him where the door is. He becomes obsessed. Any unsolved murder he finds in the papers, he works it into his theory. The police aren't laughing any more; he's become a nuisance. Finally, he's reduced to trying to involve the failed magazine editor Marcus Bacton by convincing him there's something unnatural about the death of his house-keeper. Only to find, conveniently staying with Marcus, another policeman. A sick, screwed-up policeman, ripe for conversion. But the policeman is sceptical. He needs to be shown the truth.

Maiden went cold. Was this it? Was this the truth? Had Cindy followed them in his old Morris Minor to Colleen Hall? Had Cindy given the performance of his life, casting himself in the role of the imaginary Ley Killer?

But he wouldn't have had time, would he? Would Cindy have had time, after slashing Emma, to get back to St Mary's to take the call from Maiden?

He'd been there all night. With Marcus.

No. You only *assumed* he had.

Maiden began to sweat with paranoia. He saw Cindy in his shamanic cloak of feathers, a giant bird of prey. In his hand a sacrificial knife. The theatrics, the melodrama. An actor manipulating reality.

A woman walked into the clearing from the other side.

Maiden dived back into the trees. She glanced his way just once. She was carrying a pickaxe. She hefted it, looked down at her feet. Swung the pick with both hands high above her head and brought it down.

So savagely that when the pick connected with the concrete all the breath came out of her in a sharp cry.

He watched her for several minutes. She was making a mess. Lumps of concrete spun across the helipad. Dust sprayed up at her flapping Barbour coat and into her dark, curly hair. She didn't care. She pushed one point of the pick into a crack and swung back from the handle, straining.

'*Damn* you . . .'

The pick prised out a slab about eighteen inches across and she fell backwards, the handle clipping her under the chin. She screamed and let go and rolled over into the rubble.

'*Shit!*'

Maiden walked out across the concrete. 'Can I help?'

The woman froze on the concrete, contracting like a caterpillar, a hand at her jaw, looking up at him. For just an instant, she looked as if she might be terrified. Then she coughed and grabbed hold of the pick and came up scowling.

'No. You can't help. Go away. This is private land.' She had the kind of voice that went naturally with words like *private* and *land*.

'Are you OK?'

'I'm fine. Piss off.'

'Could take you a while to chop up the whole pad,' Maiden said.

'Are you going, or do I have to call—'

He took a chance. Call it intuition; there was something

interesting here. He pulled out his wallet. It felt strange flashing the warrant card. Something the other bloke used to do before he died.

'Police,' he said.

She stared at him. This time the fear was real, but soon controlled. She was younger than he'd thought. Early thirties. She had a wide mouth, green eyes, the kind of take-it-for-granted, careless beauty that said *breeding* and then yawned.

He said, 'And you are?'

'Magda Ring. I work here.'

'As?'

'Admin manager. Controller.'

'And the professor's just taken off in his helicopter, and you're fixing it so he can't get back, right?'

'Don't be ridiculous. I . . . I was . . .'

Maiden smiled. She really couldn't think of an adequate explanation of why she was hacking up Falconer's helipad.

'Look.' Magda Ring rose up. 'You might be police, but this is still private land. You can either tell me what you want or bugger off.'

He overturned a slab of concrete with his shoe. Underneath, there was red soil, stone, grit.

'It's not very deep, is it?'

'Why should it be?'

'I don't know.' He borrowed the pick, shifted another lump. 'I don't know anything about helicopters. Are they very heavy?'

The pick snagged. He pulled it. It ripped through fabric. He bent and pulled out what appeared to be a sleeve; it was nylon, quilted. It smelled bad.

'Christ,' Magda Ring said softly. 'How did you know? How the *fuck* did you know?'

He bent and lifted out a weighty concrete cube. There was most of a nylon coat down there. When he pulled more of it away, a rich, putridly familiar stench started to pulse and wriggle out of the hole. The smell was a living thing.

As always, it was Islington, two heads fallen together on a sofa, flies and kiddy porn.

Maiden turned his face to the sky, swallowed a long breath, looked down.

What you could see of the body was partly liquefied. It lay in a soupy, brown sludge. Half the face was visible, features darkened, puffed, blistering.

Magda Ring cried out once, turned and stumbled away. Maiden gagged and bit hard on the sleeve of his jacket. When he found he was starting to shake, he, too, walked away.

From the edge of the wood, like some comical, gulping birdcall, came the sound of someone vomiting. Magda on her hands and knees among the autumn mulch: burnt sienna, yellow ochre and sour pink.

XL

He was hardly what you expected.

But come on, hen, what *did* you expect – black suit, slicked-back hair, white skin, Ronnie Kray rosebud lips?

Well, the black suit was right, very classy, but there wasn't enough hair to slick back and the skin was closer to yellow. He wore thick glasses, had the manner of an old-fashioned accountant. Distant.

Distant you could understand, today. The black suit, too.

'*Sister* Anderson?' His hand felt like the inside of a banana skin. 'You some variety of nun?'

Andy smiled. 'Nursing sister.'

'Oh. Right.'

He didn't look too well. Signs of high blood pressure, could be liver trouble, too. He was older than she'd figured, seventy maybe. How could a guy this old still be doing what they said he was doing? Young men, she could just about get her head around it – the lure of easy money, plus the illusion that you were invincible. This guy was well beyond all that.

'Thank you for seeing me, Mr Parker. Time like this.'

'Yeah, well.' Tony Parker motioned to a hard chair on Andy's side of the desk. 'You told them downstairs it was about my . . .' An eye twitched, dragging down loose skin.

'Daughter. Aye.' Like, how else would she have got in to see him?

'So, go on.' He nodded at the two black phones on his desk. 'I've told them to hold all calls. 'Cept for the wife.'

'If it rings, I'll go out.'

'No need. We ain't that close any more. She lives down in Essex. Got her sister wiv her.'

His voice was dry, his London accent trimmed. He looked like a man who didn't cry much but spent a lot of time thinking. In Andy's experience, crying was simpler, and much more therapeutic.

'I'm more sorry than I can say. I'd got to know her a little. Great girl.'

'Yeah.' He was slumped in a high-backed swivel chair. It was the only sign of luxury in the room. The desk was scuffed, old rather than antique. Looked like it had come out of one of the old Feeny Park solicitors' offices. There were no pictures on the walls. This was really Emma's old man?

This office was over Parker's town-centre nightspot, the Biarritz. Who the hell had clubs called the Biarritz and the St Moritz any more?

Only fading guys like this, in towns like Elham.

It had gone quiet. Tony Parker gazed past her, out of the window at the beauteous Elham skyline, the old parish church, the new tech-college building. He looked like he was already forgetting she was here.

Of course, Riggs would know, by now, that she'd come. Whatever she said here would get back to him, every word of it, and quickly.

'I also know Bobby Maiden,' Andy said.

'Really.'

'When he had his accident, I was with the team that brought him round.'

Parker looked at her. 'You'll pardon me if I don't recommend you for a medal.'

'What I wanted to say was, he's no the kind of guy would do this . . . thing.'

'That's it? You come here to say that?'

No, what she came to say was, *If anything should happen to Bobby Maiden there's me here, this big-mouthed Glaswegian*

372

harpy, who knows who it's down to. And, by coming here, parking out front, also indirectly conveying this information to Mr Riggs.

'You come here,' Parker said, 'to try and tell me that piece of fucking shit did not kill my daughter. Get out. Get the fuck out of my office, Sister Anderson.'

Andy didn't move. 'You're makin' a mistake, Tony.' Could feel her accent thickening like phlegm in her throat. Somebody came on aggressive, it usually happened.

Tony Parker didn't speak. Clearly couldn't believe she hadn't gone.

'Your friend Mr Riggs was round just now. Figured I might know where Bobby was hidin' out.'

'And you didn't, I expect.'

'No. I didn't.'

'You're a stupid cow. How many times the police name the man they're after? Not often, Sister, and if they fink it's a copper they'll sit on it till they can't sit on it no more. Martin Riggs, however, he's too straight for that.'

'Jesus God.'

'He knows one of his men's guilty, he won't cover it up. A good man, I'm telling you. Martin Riggs says the little shit did it, you can count on it. As indeed I *am*.'

'Do me a favour, Tony, don't patronize me. Riggs is as bent as bloody Quasimodo's spine. He's tryin' tae stitch Bobby up. I know that, and if you don't know it, you're more fuckin' decrepit than you look.'

Parker's eye twitched again, which made him angry; he controlled it.

'You know Jim Bateman, Sister?'

'Of Bateman and Partners? Aye.'

'You may be hearing from him.'

'You mean . . .' Andy almost laughed. '. . . you mean you didnae stay with your London lawyers? What a bloody loser you are, Tony. It's all Jimmy Bateman can do tae conveyance a hoose. Present him wi' a slander case tae prosecute, the guy'd go off sick for three months. Listen, I couldnae care less what you and Riggs are intae, I just don't want anybody doin' anything hasty in relation tae my friend Bobby Maiden, you got me?'

She watched Parker tighten. 'Like who, Sister?'

A phone rang. Parker picked up the one next to it. 'Yeah. Take her back. Say I'll call her. Who? All right. Yeah.' Hung up. Lifted his sick eyes to Andy. 'Who might act hastily, Mrs Anderson?'

'A few people might. Given the circumstances.'

Truth was, he didn't look capable of haste. He looked like a man on whom age had crept up like a mugger. Turned round and *thump*. Never saw it till it happened. Wakes up with no hair and thick glasses and he has to cut down on his drinking and his late nights, and London doesn't seem so homely, and Elham is a tacky wee retirement haven, in the care of kindly Superintendent Riggs. Sad, eh?

Parker said. 'You're from Glasgow, ain'tcher?'

'Aye, but I was educated at Roedean, as you can tell.'

'You people.' Parker shook his head. 'You're all barbarians up there. *Act hastily* . . . Jesus wept.' A digital timer on his desk bleeped twice and Parker took a gold-plated pillbox from his top pocket. 'Save us all from television.' He put a small white pill on his tongue and swallowed it.

'You should take water with that,' Andy said.

Parker looked politely contemptuous.

'You need to look after yourself, Mr Parker.'

'Why?' He put away the pillbox. He didn't look at all well. 'That girl was the only kid I had. I was gonna sell this lot, set her up nice. Whatever she wanted.'

'I think she wanted you to slow down.'

'Talked about me, did she?'

'A wee bit.'

He stared at her. He'd probably aged a couple of years since she came in.

Andy stood up, moved round the desk. Parker watched

her without much curiosity. She went behind him, placed both her hands on his forehead.

'What's this, Sister?'

'Reiki. Japanese therapy thing.' His skin felt like crêpe paper.

'Never heard of it.'

'Cost me damn near two grand for the courses.'

Parker grunted. Talking his language.

'Shut up. Close your eyes.'

She'd given him nearly ten minutes' Reiki when the phone rang. 'Unplug the fucker,' Parker said.

Andy's hands moved down his face. She didn't think about High Knoll.

After a while, Tony Parker fell asleep. When he awoke, there were tears drying in the hollows of his cheeks. He was maybe too relaxed to notice.

After a minute or two, he said, 'You want a job, Sister? Eight-fifty a week and a lump sum when I'm brown bread?'

He didn't seem to know he was crying. It could be powerful, the Reiki, if the patient was willing to disconnect.

'I'm no looking for a job,' Andy said. 'But you can do me one favour. Just tell me if you did anything hasty this morning.'

XLI

Following Magda Ring towards the mellow farmhouse home of the University of the Earth, Maiden felt a spasm in his chest.

A brief tightening sensation was all it was, and the other bloke would have ignored it. But the other bloke was only aware of surface things. And the other bloke died.

Magda almost fell at the door, shoving in a long key. As though she was desperate to put that fat slab of oak between her and the smell of corrupting flesh tainting the grounds of Cefn-y-bedd. He could understand that. But he also understood that the tightening of the chest was a response to a deep-down feeling that this house enclosed something darker and worse. And personal. As if he'd followed a preordained trail and the trail ended not at the grave in the concrete, but here, in this quiet old house.

He followed her into a big, square hall with a wide wooden staircase, several doors leading off, a deep window halfway up the stairs.

And, on the only blank wall, almost exclusively lit by this window, a picture. A picture which sent a weight slamming into his chest, like a wrecking ball fracturing some old factory wall.

Turner. He was transfixed. *J. M. W.* bloody *Turner*.

His heart seemed to crunch.

Adrian had steak, done rare. Grayle, compromising with a ploughman's lunch with cheese, was surprised.

'See, most of the New Age people I know are vegetarians.'

Adrian groaned. 'Oh . . . really, Grayle! An interest in earth-consciousness doesn't necessarily make one *New Age*. Those people are doing our subject so . . . much . . . *damage*. As the cave-paintings so amply demonstrate, Neolithic people were hardly veggies. They *hunted*. They hunted to live and they lived to hunt!'

Lecturing again. The didactic side of him taking over, changing him from schoolboy to schoolteacher. It was beginning to irritate her. Grayle shook her hair out of her eyes. And also . . .

. . . also, apart from placing his hand over hers on the gear shift that time, his interest in her as a woman seemed actually to be receding.

No problem. Sure, a good-looking guy, and she was unattached, but anything of a personal nature could only be a complication and right now she had enough of those. It was just that a little *recognition*, that's all, of mutual attraction, generally made things easier.

Ho-hum. Too late now. They'd soon be among a whole bunch of people, celebrating, having a good time. The pub was just outside Stow-on-the-Wold, and less than a dozen miles from the Rollright Stones. It was old, like the Ram's Head at St Mary's, but it had polished panelling and brass lamps, and it was full, suggesting a wealthier, more populous area.

'Well, all right.' Adrian sawing up pink steak, real efficient. 'A lot of the people on the courses are, naturally, New Agers, and it's my job to keep them amused. But, really . . . I mean, some of them are such incredibly silly, shallow, inconsequential people that it's a struggle sometimes to hide one's contempt.'

Jesus, was this Ersula or was this Ersula? 'What about Janny and Matthew? They're kind of New Age, aren't they?'

A shadow crossed his eyes. 'They're nice people. They're friends.'

377

Something here she wasn't getting. 'How'd you get into this stuff, Adrian?' Grayle abandoned onto a side plate the cob of squelchy, white bread that came with her lunch.

'Didn't get into it.' He pushed a piece of meat into his mouth. 'Got into me. You don't want that bread?'

'Sure, help yourself. *It?*'

'The Earth. Always aware of Her, of course.' He grabbed the bread, took a bite. 'Grew up in Wiltshire. Father was an army officer. Stonehenge was always there. Better seen from a distance, rather lost its magic with all the main roads and tourists. And the army, all manoeuvres, no real . . . Anyway. At least Avebury's surviving. Despite the undesirables it attracts. At Avebury, I had a sort of vision. A calling, I suppose.'

'In a church-minister kind of way?'

'In *exactly* that kind of way.'

'To go out and spread the word about earth-mysteries?'

'But that's not enough, is it? Everybody's just living *on* the Earth. We should live *in* Her and She in us. We should move with Her, *breathe* with Her.'

Sounded kind of sexual. 'Where'd you get this, Adrian? Where'd it come from?'

'From?' He looked surprised. 'From the Earth, of course.'

'No, I mean, which books, in particular?'

'Books?' He was almost shouting. Strands of steak clung to his teeth. 'I received it from the *Earth*, Grayle. I *received* it.'

'Yeah, sure, but . . .' Feeling herself going red. 'I mean . . . how?'

He looked at her for a long time, the way a teacher looks at the dumbest kid in the class when the kid reveals, by some inane answer, that it hasn't grasped what the lesson was even supposed to be about.

'The dreaming,' Adrian said.

'I'm sorry . . . You get guidance from dreams. Of course.'

'Guidance? Instructions! Look, you don't seem to realize, the dreaming *is* the University of the Earth. You're surrendering your consciousness to the oldest teacher of all. And when you've been doing it for so long, when you've shown you're ready to serve Her, the Earth will tell you what She wants from you.'

Ersula had written, *What you are dealing with here is the unconscious and that must be left to find its own route to what you would probably call enlightenment.*

'Adrian, how long you been doing this?'

'Oh, I don't know. Several years. Put it this way.' Adrian began to mop up the remains of his gravy with the remains of Grayle's cob of white bread. 'So far, I've spent . . . hold on, tell you exactly . . . seven hundred and thirty-eight nights in ancient sites.'

'*What?*'

'It was why I just had to have this job. I can take groups of students all over the country to sleep at sacred sites. Go alone, first, of course, to test them out.'

She had a picture of him, some big boy scout with his knapsack, leading a crocodile of well-heeled innocents in anoraks.

'The sites know me now. Most of the guardians know me. Of course, if a certain guardian has a particularly fearsome aspect, I won't take students there.' Adrian grinned. 'Wouldn't do to lose one of the poor punters through a heart attack or something.'

Grayle recalled Matthew Lyall talking of the grotesque hag-like guardians invading your dreams, barring the way. Also recalled what Cindy had said about the death of Mrs Willis at the Knoll. A stroke.

'Can be quite terrifying at first,' Adrian said. 'Mind you, it can also be a wonderfully *healthy* thing. Quite often, after a dreaming, you'll notice that the subject's health has improved.'

He looked past Grayle, at green hills through a window, his knife in one hand, the last of the bread in the other.

'Funny thing. When I spend a night in an ordinary bed, I feel quite disoriented. Dislocated, you know?'

Dislocated? Jesus, was this any wonder after seven hundred and thirty-eight nights inside prehistoric ritual temples? According to Ersula, just a couple of experiences could blow your mind. Well, it was clear enough now: what this guy did, he OD'd . . . *he OD'd on the dreaming.* Turned himself into a dream-junkie.

'But, Adrian, what happens when the dreaming experiment comes to an end? When all the stuff goes into the computers?'

Adrian threw down his knife. 'It will never end. It's already way beyond an experiment. Do you really think we can learn all the Earth has to teach us in a few years? In a lifetime, even?'

'Let me get this right.' *Oh boy, just when you think all the world's crazies are gathered in LA, with a small New York overspill . . .* 'You see the University of the Earth developing into some kind of channel . . . into like a universal planetary consciousness?'

'Already is. And one day I'll prove it. At present, She speaks to just a few of us, in our dreams. One day, quite soon, She'll speak to everyone. You'll hear Her. You'll all hear Her.'

'The EVP tapes? You think one day you'll get to record the voice of . . . ?'

'Perhaps we already have. We just can't understand it. Any more than we understand when She speaks to us in the wind, the sound of waves on the shore.'

'Well,' Grayle said. 'I guess he even convinced Ersula.'

'Who? Who convinced Ersula?'

'Roger.'

'Roger?' Adrian pushed aside his plate. 'What does *Roger* know?' He stood up. 'We'd better go. Do you need to use the loo or anything?'

*　　*　　*

Sky coming to the boil. Finger of lightning prodding languidly out of sweating clouds. Below, several sheep already struck down, a heavy tumble of bodies, milk-eyed heads flat to the plain.

A few yards away, the shepherd lying dead. His dog, back arched, howling a pitiful protest at the vengeful heavens.

Energy. The hideous energy of violent death. In this painting, only Stonehenge was truly in its element. Whitened, as though lit from within by electric filaments, the stones exulted in the storm.

Inside his tightening chest, Maiden felt he was howling like the sheepdog.

The print, gilt-framed, hung at the foot of the wide wooden staircase in the panelled hall at Cefn-y-bedd.

A phone was ringing somewhere then stopped when an answering machine collected the call. Maiden's chest felt bruised with memory. His mind rewinding at speed. The lightning striking again and again. Revelation. Big lights, a distant roar. Hospital smells. He remembered, the evening he walked out of Elham General, seeing Turner's painting of the angry sea around Fingal's Cave. Feeling that same tightness in the chest. It had not been the same image, but the style . . . the elemental rage . . . *that* was the same. What did it mean?

It meant this picture, this image, of stones and death, had been in his tumbling, dislocated dreams when Andy's hands were around his head and the defibrillator was smashing at his ribcage.

Part of him came into you, Cindy said. Cindy, the has-been, end-of-the-pier shamanic joke.

Cindy had it right.

More crimes in heaven and earth . . .

Cindy, Godalmighty, was *right*. The intensity of it all made it impossible to stand still. He walked around the hall, arms and legs tingling with electricity, unable to pull his eyes away from the Turner: stones and energy and violent death.

'It's his favourite.' Magda Ring glanced at him once, a flicker of uncertainty, as she shed her dusty Barbour on the hall floor. 'Turner's *Stonehenge*, 1828. You never seen it before?'

'Not on a wall,' Maiden said. 'I'm sorry. I like paintings. You ready to talk now?'

Letting her think it had been a deliberate ploy, him appearing hypnotized by the print. A digression. Subtle, like a TV detective.

'Prettier ones in here.'

Magda led him into a large, airy drawing room with a beamed ceiling and oak pillars, plush armchairs set out like a hotel lounge. And more Stonehenge prints: Girtin, Inchbold and Constable's impressionistic sketch of the rain-washed megaliths with the double rainbow.

'The sister called you in, I suppose.'

For a moment, he could only think of Sister Andy.

'Grayle,' Magda said. 'Listen, Inspector, I didn't know. I really didn't know she was there. I didn't know she was dead.'

'I'm supposed to believe that?' Detective-mode. 'Why did you dig the hole? How did you know where to dig?'

'Because . . .' Her eyes flashed. '. . . to satisfy myself it was nonsense. I didn't believe it for one minute, but I couldn't get it out of my head. And this was the first chance I had to check it out. Adrian gone to his wedding, Roger up to town for the weekend. When he goes off in his helicopter, at least you can tell when he's coming back.'

'You must've grabbed the pick before he was over the horizon.'

'Perfect time, I'm trying to tell you. Course starts next Wednesday. Staff – cleaners and people – start arriving this afternoon, get the place ready. No time to waste. Look, I had the pick ready round the back of the helicopter shed. I was going to allay my own fears once and for all. Oh *God*. I can't believe it. It's all destroyed, everything we worked for's *ruined*.'

'Magda, a woman's dead.' Before they left the scene, he'd placed concrete slabs back in the hole, covering the body. 'You do know who it is, don't you?'

'The hair.' Magda's face puckered. She tightened her jaw, looked down for a moment. 'Can I get a drink?'

'Course.'

She brought whisky and tumblers from a stripped-pine corner cupboard. 'You?'

He accepted a small one. Turned out to be the one which tasted of peat, damp and lonely, moorland meeting the sea, no visible horizon. It would be, today.

Sadness seeped through him. He saw Em, as Suzanne, sitting opposite, black hair, black eyes, mauve lipstick. The image crucified him.

Too much time passed and Magda was standing in front of him: tight black sweater, jeans with a spiked leather belt. Pale, but together.

'Sorry?'

'I said, What are you?' Magda said. 'You're not an ordinary policeman, are you?'

'No such thing as an ordinary policeman.'

'I mean, not local.'

'Serious Crimes Bureau,' Maiden lied. 'We . . .' He hesitated. 'We're investigating a series of murders linked to prehistoric sites.'

'Whaaaat?' Magda Ring was aghast. Sank down, involuntarily, into one of the armchairs. He observed her: she was loosened with shock, rather than relief at finally being found out; there was an obvious difference.

'Look . . .' Stared at him, green eyes wide, the colour scared out of her face again. 'For God's sake . . . this is nothing like . . . This isn't *murder*.'

'How long have you known she was there?'

'I didn't *know*, I keep telling you. I half thought it was fantasy. Everybody who comes here inhabits a fantasy world. It takes you over. The unseen Britain. The spirit-country. The whole earth-mysteries game. It's to do with romantic theories to make us feel . . . connected.'

'So whose body is it?'

'Ersula Underhill. I thought you knew. The sister—'

'Grayle. Sure. I've spoken to Grayle.'

'Inspector, I believed . . . I swear to God I believed Ersula had gone back to the States. Because of Roger. And then the sister shows up, incognito, and obviously Ersula *didn't* go back, and the sister suspects . . . something. Look, shouldn't you be making phone calls? Summoning your forensic people. Whoever. Shouldn't this place be buzzing?'

'She'll come to no harm down there.'

'I want her out of here.' Magda shuddered. 'I want her safely stashed away in some path lab. I never liked her when she was alive. One of those . . . lofty, know-it-all Americans. Roger thought she was wonderful because she was so damn serious all the time, tons of extra gravitas to bluff the punters. Brings out the worst in me, though, that kind of attitude.'

'That a fact?'

'Look.' Magda frowned. 'If I'm going to have to watch every bloody thing I say, I want my solicitor here.'

Maiden sighed. 'I've got no witness, you're not in an interview room, you're not being taped, and it seems unlikely to me that you killed her. All right?'

'Delirious.' Magda sniffed. 'I've got to start looking for a job. It was good here, for a while. Until it got stupid.'

'Why did it get stupid?'

She offered him more whisky; he shook his head.

'Greed.' Falling back in the chair, crossing her legs, the bottle on her lap. 'Always bloody greed, isn't it? He was the country's most respected Neolithic archaeologist. Honorary fellow of Christ Church, etcetera, etcetera. And then he started doing TV. Wouldn't think it could turn the head of a guy that educated, would you? Let me tell you, they're the worst. Especially someone with a libido off the Richter scale who's had to worry about the career risks involved in shafting too many students. Now, suddenly he's getting fan letters on funny-smelling paper. Dear Professor, that shot of you stripped to the waist in the Roman villa just haunts me, so if you've got a spare place on any of your digs, I'd be happy to accommodate your trowel.'

'The University of the Earth began as a supply-line for non-stop totty?'

'Partly. Well, the big angle's money, obviously. Roger wasn't slow to pick up on the fact that a large proportion of the people writing in to the programme were New Agers and earth-mysteries fanatics trying to convert him. That's where the real money is. People don't want digs, where after six months you've uncovered some boring foundations and a few bits of pottery. They want the Ark of the bloody Covenant. So . . . he starts to compromise. The reason I know all this, by the way, is I was his producer at the BBC. Before he realized he could quadruple his income overnight by making his own programmes for Channel Four, and I went with him, naturally, because who wouldn't?'

Magda looked defiant, drank some whisky.

'And, no, he wasn't fucking me. Needed me too much. Doesn't sleep with anybody he might need in two months' time.'

'As the abrupt termination of a loving relationship often offends,' Maiden said wryly.

'Quite. Which is also why he didn't sleep with . . . her . . . Ersula. Woman after his own heart, you see. Talked crap in a very learned, intense way. Everything she said sounded like a balanced argument resulting from years of study. He loved that. He wanted to employ her. He wanted her mind. I mean, on the payroll. Whereas – this was the problem – she wanted *him*. Body *and* mind.'

'Was she . . .' All he could see was the puffed-up, blistered, decomposing face in the concrete tomb. '. . . good-looking?'

'Not good-looking enough. Anyway, she was throwing

herself at him. Where's the fun in that? Where's the *hunt*? Sad. Like an undergraduate going for her tutor. Except this was a grown woman. Brilliant mind, sexual age of twelve. And she sets her sights on *Roger Falconer*? Save us! I mean, really clever woman, but not clever enough to realize what a sham he was. Have you seen his programmes?'

'Just been watching one. About hunting.'

Magda nodded. 'Good example. *Very* good example. That's the one where he puts the esoteric case for blood sports?'

'Linked to ley lines. Hard to tell whether he was serious or he'd just concocted it to take a poke at the New Agers. Interestingly, that same argument, about . . .' He struggled to frame it.

'Hunting feeding the earth?'

'Mmm. It had been aired in a letter sent to this little pagan magazine some months earlier.'

'God,' Magda said. 'You've really hit the spot, haven't you? How long've you been looking into all this?'

'Long enough.' Sorry, Cindy.

Magda's green eyes didn't blink. 'You're right. It's not his theory. He got it from Adrian. He gets everything from Adrian. It's almost funny. I mean, have you *met* Adrian?'

'No.'

'He seems quite ludicrously harmless at first. Minor public-school idiot. Caricature. Sort of chap you see in old black and white films. I mean, you know, a *hunk*, for heaven's sake, although he doesn't realize it. Too engrossed. You can imagine him, as a child, collecting pictures of standing stones like other kids collected stamps.'

Magda uncrossed her legs, started to uncork the whisky then changed her mind and put the bottle on the floor.

'He's somehow not of this . . . not of this *age*. Very polite, very . . . courtly. He paid *court* to Ersula. In awe of her. Supervised her dreaming sessions. And when she became obsessed with all that, he mistakenly thought he was going to be part of the package.'

'He was pursuing her and she was . . . ?'

'Pining for bloody Roger. I don't know how Adrian didn't realize that from the outset. But, as I say, he's not of this age. Poor sod belongs in Jane Austen, you know what I mean?'

'OK.' Maiden thought they were wandering from the point. 'What happened to Ersula?'

'Vanished.' Magda said. 'Well, sort of. I mean . . . not unexpectedly is what I mean. One night, near the end of the summer course, she was closeted with Roger in his study for a long time, over two hours. I stayed out of the way, I could guess the kind of things being said. Fairly self-evident when she didn't come down to breakfast next day. She was due to go with Roger and a group of students in a couple of minibuses. He sent me over to the stables to see what was wrong with her. Too professional, surely, to let a little emotional hiccup . . . etcetera, etcetera. Bastard. So I'm knocking on her door, she's shouting, Go away, leave me alone, sob, sob, etcetera. So I had to go and shepherd the idiots around. When we got back, it was after dark. I didn't see her, but the following morning she'd gone. Suitcases, everything.'

'You didn't try to find out where?'

'How could we? Where would we start? She was American. She probably went back to America, to nurse her broken heart in the family's Long Island beachhouse or wherever. Anyway, we had to see all the punters off the premises, and we were all pretty knackered.'

'While you were away, where was . . . ?'

'Adrian?' She pushed both hands through her dark, curly hair, exasperated at her lack of perception. 'Good old Adrian was otherwise engaged that day. Taking delivery of a few truckloads of ready-mix concrete for Roger's new helipad.'

'Oh.'

'Adrian's terribly practical. Laid it all out, himself. You see, there's a very significant ley line in that area. Goes through the woods, connects eventually with St Mary's churchyard. Adrian said the helicopter shouldn't come down on the ley because the Earth wouldn't like it. So only one edge overlaps the line – don't tell me how he worked out precisely where it goes, he just *did*. And he marked it with a row of crosses raked into the surface of the concrete, so we'd know where the ley went and Roger could avoid it when he landed.'

Magda stood up and walked to the biggest window, overlooking the courtyard.

'So, naturally, that's where I went to hack it up.'

'Just like that?'

'Listen, I know the guy. It's what he'd do. The ritualistic side of him. He was besotted with her. He'd want to put her in a place where her spirit could fly.'

'And?'

'And what?'

'And how do you think she died?'

'She obviously killed herself. Someone that serious, that single-minded . . . and he spurns her, he says, Sorry, old girl, but you're really not my type, have a drink . . . I don't know how she did it. Pills or something. That's for you to find out. Jesus, the stupidity of men.'

He waited.

'This is Roger. This is the way he is. I *know* this is what happened. Wasn't going to have a silly, hysterical girl's suicide destroying his enterprise. I mean, the scandal, the publicity. You see, he has big expansion plans. More land – Castle Farm, when he gets old Bacton out. Wants that castle so badly, he's drooling. A *real* little university. So he needs every punter he can get now, especially rich Americans.'

She stopped for a moment, working it out. She was an intelligent woman, Maiden thought. But she was wrong.

'And they just buried her? Without a thought for the relatives?'

'This is Roger Falconer we're talking about. Of course he wouldn't think about the relatives. And Adrian would do as he was told. He needs this job.'

'What about her possessions, her cases?'

'There's an old forge out at the back. Adrian restored it last winter. Likes to make himself useful. Perhaps they burned the cases there, I don't know.'

Maiden stood up. 'I use your phone?'

'Table in the hall.'

Maiden called Castle Farm. Cindy answered. Maiden said, 'Cindy, get over here. Wear trousers.'

XLII

Outside, the Morris Minor spluttered indignantly.

Marcus felt that way, too. He glared resentfully at the front door as the Morris chugged away.

The bastard hadn't explained. Other than to say he'd been summoned to Cefn-y-bedd, suggesting Marcus hold the bloody fort. Which made Marcus furious, because if anyone was going to tackle Falconer it should have been him.

To make it worse, Lewis, the smug bastard, had buggered off upstairs, bracelets jangling, and come down five minutes later looking not entirely unlike a *normal man*. He was going to Cefn-y-bedd to play it *straight*.

And whatever was happening there, Marcus Bacton was being excluded. On grounds of age and infirmity . . . and the likelihood of his causing a scene, no doubt.

Bastards.

Irritable and unsettled, Macus slumped back to the study. Amid the clutter on the desk were the cup-stained maps with leys drawn in, the book displaying an illustration of the Green Man. And the Edwardian photo album.

He opened the album at the picture of Annie Davies, from which Grayle Underhill had identified her ghost. Annie's eyes, in the sepia picture, looked aeons old. He tried to see in them the birdlike eyes of Mrs Willis and couldn't.

If Underhill hadn't reacted to that photo, he would have chanced his arm with another one. In colour. Girl in a deckchair, wearing her mother's sunglasses and a very sad and knowing smile. Sally's last summer. Marcus blinked away the tears as the phone rang.

'Marcus,' Andy Anderson said. 'Listen to me. Don't argue, all right?'

'Haven't the strength to argue with you, Anderson. Where are you?'

'I'm . . . doesnae matter. Marcus, you take Bobby and the dog and get the hell out.'

'. . . bloody hell . . . ?'

'Just do it. You may have visitors, know what I'm saying?'

'Maiden's not even here. I'll simply tell them I've never heard of him.'

'I'm no talkin' about the police. All right? Y'understand what I'm saying? This is bad guys, Marcus. Won't take no for an answer.'

Marcus was suspicious. 'How can you possibly know about this?'

'Doesnae matter. I know. This is no a scam. These people, they won't want any witnesses. That means you, Marcus. This is very, very bad guys, y'hear me?'

Marcus pondered a moment.

'All right,' he said. 'I get the message.'

'Thank Christ. Act on it. I'll call back in ten minutes' time, I don't expect an answer.'

Anderson hung up.

Marcus didn't move for a whole minute. He looked out of the window at the empty yard. The castle ruins firm against a white sky. He remembered how excited it had made him feel when he first saw it, when he realized the castle came free with the house.

From his inside breast pocket, he pulled the colour photo of his daughter in the deckchair. The sunglasses with diamante frames, too big for her.

Malcolm stuck his bucket head round the door and then wandered in, tail waving nonchalantly.

'Wants us to get out.' Marcus placed the photo on top of

the picture of Annie. 'Very bad guys.' He went down on his hands and knees, put his nose up to the dog's. 'Very, very bad guys.'

Malcolm growled.

'Englishman's castle is his bloody castle,' Marcus said. 'Get out for good when I sell this place and not before.'

In the stable block, Maiden pushed at Adrian's door.

'You're the law.' Magda watched, a little hostile now, but made no attempt to stop him. 'I suppose you can do what you like.'

The door was made of old pine boards. It wasn't even locked. Maiden stepped back, let her go in first.

'But I don't know what you think you're going to find.' She stood in the middle of the small, wooden room, as if she knew she was by far the most interesting item in the whole place.

Which was true enough; conditions here would have made a Spartan recruit feel underpampered. Single wardrobe and a bed. No clock, no books. The bed had been stripped to its boards, the mattress up-ended against a wall.

Maiden raised an eyebrow at Magda. 'Some kind of fakir, this bloke?'

'I didn't realize it had gone quite this far. He spends so many nights on stones, his body probably revolts against an orthodox bed. Or he's educated it that way, more likely.'

Maiden was going through the clothes in the wardrobe. Shirts and trousers – army trousers, tweed trousers, not jeans. One suit. He thought, It's a soldier's wardrobe. An *old-fashioned* soldier.

'What's his background?'

'Small-time country-gentry. Military family. Hunting-shooting. Father's a retired colonel, lives near Salisbury. Came over once. Nice man. Quiet.'

'What did he do before he came here?'

'Some form of youth-worker, I think. VSO, perhaps.

He's just a big boy scout. I really don't see why you're doing this. Why aren't you raiding Roger's quarters? Too influential, is he? Too well connected?'

'Actually,' Maiden said, 'difficult though it may be for you to understand, that really doesn't worry me a lot right now. But, if Ersula was murdered, she was probably murdered while you and Falconer were away. Which leaves Adrian in the frame. Where was he last night, do you know?'

'I don't see him come and go. I have a three-room apartment in the granary across there, and it has nice, thick walls. I mean, he was around, I assume. Messing in his workshop, up at the Knoll, doing his EVP tapes. He's always *around*.'

'EVP?'

'Electronic Voice Phenomena. Recording so-called spirit voices. Some people claim to pick them up between stations on the radio. Adrian left cassette recorders in ancient sites. He says you can sometimes hear voices.'

'Like the Yorkshire Ripper heard voices?'

'That's ridiculous.'

'All right. You said Falconer got his ideas about hunting generating energy and feeding the earth and all that . . . from Adrian.'

'*Through* Adrian, I ought to have said.' Magda sat down on the wooden bed-frame. 'Through his dreams.'

'His *dreams*?'

'Keeps tapes of all his dreams at ancient sites. He's become so practised at it now, he doesn't need anyone with him. Wakes up promptly at the end of a dream and talks it into a recorder. Sometimes – increasingly, in fact – he has, you know, *prehistoric* dreams. He'll dream about tribal rituals and ceremonies and sacrifices and—'

'Sacrifices?'

'All kinds of things. Sacrifices were part of life then.'

'*Human* sacrifices?'

'I don't know. I don't listen to them. I mean, Roger was deeply cynical at first. Then he began to see information and descriptions that Adrian couldn't possibly have learned from books . . . not that he ever *reads*. He hardly ever reads anything any more. And yet, possibly because he's such a simple soul, he seemed far more in tune with Stone and Bronze Age thinking than Roger could possibly be. I don't, you know, think Roger believes he's getting psychic messages or anything like that. But the points he makes seem to gel. Trigger off ideas which somehow germinate into programmes. There's going to be a book, too, on the mind of Neolithic man. That's an ongoing thing.'

'But you don't listen to these tapes.'

'I listened to a couple. I didn't like them much.'

'Why not?'

'I don't know, it . . . it was somehow like listening in to one of these sex chatlines. A sort of . . . gloating tone. I didn't like it. It wasn't like Adrian. I have to work with the guy. It's bad enough working for Roger.'

'Why do you stay?'

'Because I was divorced and not too well off and now I've been able to buy a lovely town house in Hay, which I shall move into quite soon. And because we're producing some wonderful TV programmes, and one day . . . one day, it's . . . it *was* . . . really going to take off. The University of the Earth. That's why we started with such an ambitious title. There'd be a lot of people working here . . . not just here, we'd have places all over the country. It wouldn't always have to be so . . . intimate.'

'Adrian ever make a move on you?'

'God, no. Not *connected* enough. Has to be the full deep-and-meaningful for Adrian. And not deep and meaningful, necessarily, in the way you'd expect. Until Ersula, I don't recall Adrian ever showing much interest in women. Some of the students were *very* interested, but he's always the gentleman. I sometimes thought – this is strange – that he

394

was more attracted – I mean in an almost erotic way – to the Earth. His idea of the Earth.'

A sharp, soily smell stabbed at Maiden's senses, and he wanted to run out into the fresh air and keep on running.

'Where does he keep his tapes?' he asked her.

In the mirror in the pub's ladies' room, Grayle saw herself, really *saw* herself for the first time in what seemed like months.

She was shocked.

Tried to flatten down the bunches of hair. Jesus, this wasn't a grown woman's hair, this was goddamn *teenage* hair. Didn't go too well with the puffy eyes and the lines. Lines? Were those *lines*? Back home, there weren't lines; there were *never* lines back home. See, the hard lights in these British bathrooms seemed designed to condition you to the idea of your own mortality. *You'll die*, the light on your face said. *Sooner than you can imagine*.

'I'm out of here,' Grayle said aloud.

She wouldn't spend too long at the wedding. Tonight she'd check into a good hotel, where the rooms had phones. She'd take a long, hot shower then spend a small fortune calling home. Call her dad, who, for all she knew, had news of Ersula. Call Lyndon McAffrey. Maybe she could get a new column someplace, and one thing was sure, it would be a different kind of column; it would deal with the same stuff, but this time it would be responsible, it would recognize this was *serious* stuff. Stuff that could screw up a person in a big way.

Adrian was waiting out in the parking lot. Beyond him, fields of light green, cottages and barns of golden stone under the whitewashed October sky.

'Super,' he said.

Asshole.

She looked into his bland, smiling face and saw the other face. The face with meat fibres in its teeth.

Dream-junkie. Fanatic. He was immature, this was the problem. He hadn't learned how to live in the real world.

Jesus. Here was Holy Grayle thinking this?

'What should we do, then?' Adrian looking at her across the car, chin resting on folded arms on the red roof. 'Should we go straight to the stones and acclimatize ourselves, or join the others in Chipping Norton?'

'Maybe I need to change. My clothes. I oughta check out what the others are wearing.'

'OK. You're the driver. Chipping Norton it is.'

When they were on the road, he said, 'I say, look I'm sorry for getting so . . . preachy.'

'Oh. Well. I, uh . . . it was all fascinating stuff, Adrian. Really.'

'I get sort of carried away.'

'It's enthusiasm, is all. People today, uh . . . not enough people have enthusiasm. It's become a very bored society.'

'Do you think so?'

'Sure. Folks just staring at the tube for hours. Listening to the same old Guns 'n' Roses albums.'

'What's that?'

'It's a band, Adrian.'

'Oh.'

'You aren't into music?'

Adrian considered this. 'It's unnecessary. It diverts us. Stops us listening to natural sounds. If we pollute our ears with music, we can't hear the Earth breathe. My father listened to Mozart all the time when he was at home. Blaring through the house. You couldn't *think*. Worse now he's retired. Believes he needs to educate himself on the finer things of life. What does your father do?'

'He's uh, he's an academic. At Harvard. Didn't Ersula talk about him, ever?'

'To Roger, I expect.'

'Yeah, well, Ersula can be kind of hurtful sometimes. She doesn't mean to be that way, she's just a little impatient of, uh . . .'

'People who weren't as brainy as she was?'

'I guess. I'm sorry. This included me, too. To Ersula, I was just . . . just crazy Grayle . . . and she's younger than me.'

'Brains aren't everything. She needed to find her spiritual side, she knew that. She did recognize that I could help her in that direction.'

'She did?'

'Thought at first that she could get what she needed from Roger, but I showed her how wrong she was. How utterly wrong.'

'How did you do that— Hey, what's wrong here? I'm losing . . . What's wrong with the car?'

Loss of power. Keening noise.

'Don't rev it like that. Pull in. Pull in here.'

'What's that noise mean?'

'Better switch off.' Adrian opened his door. 'Do you know how to loosen the bonnet?'

'Huh?'

'To get at the engine.'

'You wanna look under the hood? You know what you're doing?'

'I'm a practical sort of chap,' Adrian said.

They came back out the front way. As Maiden followed Magda towards the small Gothic door in the side wall, a venerable Morris Minor creaked into the forecourt.

'Who on earth is this?' Magda said, strained. 'I'll get rid of them.'

'Don't do that, it looks like the local CID chief. It was, er, politic to bring him in. Case like this, the local guys need to be seen holding your hand.'

'In *that* thing?'

'You never watched Columbo, Magda? Afternoon, sir.'

Cindy strode towards them. *Strode*. He was wearing slacks and a blazer and something that might have been an old school tie. His hair was slicked back, the mauve area so faint it might have been an effect of the light.

'This is Detective Superintendent Lewis,' Maiden said, very slowly and clearly. 'Sir, this is Ms Ring. She's in charge here in the absence of Professor Falconer.'

'How are you?' Cindy turned to Maiden. His voice had deepened and seemed to have acquired a coarse London accent. 'Sincerely hope this isn't a waste of my time, sunshine. Got an armed blag in Hereford on me plate already this morning. Plus a floater in the Wye.'

Maiden said to Magda, 'Would you excuse us a moment?' Cindy followed him into a corner of the forecourt, under trees.

'Not overdoing it, am I, Bobby? Played a detective in *The Sweeney*, in the seventies. Shot dead before the first commercials.'

'And not a minute too soon,' Maiden said bitterly.

'I shall temper my performance. Good of you to make me your superior, Bobby.'

'It was your age. Listen. We're going to hear some audiotapes of ancient-site dreams recorded by one Adrian Fraser-Hale. If they answer any of your Green Man questions, try not to show it. You might also have to look at a body.'

'Oh dear God.'

'An American woman. Ersula Underhill. Grayle's sister?'

Cindy closed his eyes briefly. 'I wish I could say I was surprised. She was killed?'

'And buried inside the concrete helipad, round the back.'
Cindy winced.

'On a ley line,' Maiden said. 'As it happens.'

'Yes,' Cindy said heavily.

. . . and the smell . . . No, I don't suppose the smells are stronger as much as the air itself is cleaner and keener. One can smell smoke from . . . oh, miles away. One can see, in the air, all around, a

rainbow of colours, although far more than a rainbow, and each colour is represented by a smell . . . the auras from different kinds of vegetation and wildlife . . . and stones, rocks. The rocks are very much alive. There's distant smoke. And blood. The blood is the keenest, sharpest smell of all and it's coming from . . . I think it's a chicken or something. Killed by a fox, I expect . . .

'Are they all like this?' Cindy said.

'More or less.' Magda Ring flipped the tape out of the machine. There were scores of cassettes on metal shelves above the tape decks in the Portakabin. The spine of each plastic box had a reference number.

Bobby had stopped talking as soon as the voice began and he hadn't spoken since. Something was disturbing him; the poor dab probably could not identify it. Although he'd be closer, after last night, much closer.

It was not a particularly dramatic voice. Educated, to a point. Certainly well brought up. Amiable, but bland in itself. There was a zest here, but it seemed relatively innocent. The enthusiasm of a trainspotter. But still . . . the voice of the Gloucester mass-murderer Frederick West was, apparently, matter-of-fact and almost jovial about his murders.

'Certainly a man with a mission,' Cindy said.

'It gets incredibly boring after a while,' said Magda Ring. A rather beautiful woman, if somewhat sullen. Feeling slighted, perhaps, that this Adrian seemed oblivious of her charms. And oblivious he would be. If he was the Green Man.

If . . .

'Where does he sleep?'

'In a room above the stable.' Bobby blinked, as if waking up. 'On bare boards. I've checked it out. Nothing.'

'Nowhere else?'

'He doesn't have much baggage,' Magda said. 'Travels light. Roger admires that. The itinerant hunter-gatherer. There's his Land Rover . . .'

'Worth a look, I suppose.'

'Oh, and the forge. He restored an old blacksmith's forge. Nobody else goes in there.'

'Let's see it.' Cindy held open the door for her. She led them to a building very much on its own, part concealed by laurels and leylandii. A squarish, stone building with a chimney and castle-like slits for windows. A cast-iron bar ran the length of each slit. A rough, thick door of oak had no handle, only a large keyhole. Cindy pushed it; it didn't move.

'Well, Maiden, what do you suggest here?'

Magda said, 'Don't you people need a warrant for this?'

'With a woman's body out there,' Cindy said menacingly, 'do you really think it would take us long to get one? Let's not waste time. Kick it in, Maiden.'

But the door resisted the flat of Bobby's foot.

'All right. I'll get you a crowbar,' Magda said dully. As if she also knew that this was the place.

They found the tapes behind some loose bricks at the back of the forge itself. Maiden thought they wouldn't have found them at all if one of the bricks hadn't been left half out, as if it had been replaced in a rush. The cassette cases were numbered one to six, in Roman numerals. Except for one, which had been placed on top of the others in the cavity.

'So he's been here recently.'

'So it appears, Bobby.' Cindy opened the unnumbered cassette case; it was empty. 'Safe to handle these? Fingerprints?'

'If it's his voice on the tapes, we'll hardly need prints. Sir.'

'Quite. Maiden. Just testing.'

Cindy gathered up the tapes. Maiden looked around. There were cinders in the forge.

'What's he do here?'

Against the wall opposite the door was a small lathe,

metal shavings on the cobblestone floor. An acrid tang in the air.

'Turn his hand to anything,' Magda said. 'Made those bars for the window slits, for instance. As I said, Roger loves this in him. His self-sufficiency.'

'He do much hunting?' Maiden said.

'He goes out with the local hunt sometimes. And I believe he belongs to a gun club in Hereford.'

'A gun?'

'There's a cabinet in the house, a couple of twelve-bores in there. Roger goes with him sometimes. Roger says he's just an extremely balanced person, which is why he's so affable most of the time. No stress, Roger says. A simple man. We all have a lot to learn from Adrian.'

'I suppose . . .' Cindy picked up a strip of black metal. '. . . if he's so practical, he could manufacture such a thing as a crossbow. How long did you say he had been here?'

'Just under two years.'

'Ah. Not relevant then. Shall we play these?'

Back in the Portakabin, Cindy took out the cassette marked I, handed it to Magda.

Maiden discovered his mouth was dry. Magda put the tape into the machine.

A swishing sound issued from the speakers.

'Rain,' Cindy said.

The voice began, hesitant at first, but a certain swelling excitement beneath it. The voice was distorted and tinny.

No-one can see me. I feel almost invisible . . . a part of . . . of everything. So utterly relaxed. So fused. I've never felt like this before. I . . .

There was a squeak.

'Wind that back again,' Maiden said. 'It's different. It's not the same machine . . . you hear that? That's one of those little hand recorders. The squeak is when he pushes the pause button. I'd guess this is not the kind of gear you'd use on the dream project?'

'We use Marantz. Or Sony Pro-Walkman. With a microphone, with a windshield.'

'No windshield on this. You can hear the wind banging against it.'

'Which suggests?' said Cindy.

'That when he made this particular tape, he didn't have access to the equipment here. Maybe the original was on a mini-cassette and he transferred it. Roll it, Magda.'

The rain noise again. But when the voice came back, it was stronger. As the tape continued, it became more confident, more fluent, more insistent.

. . . he is invisible in the greenery.

The Green Man.

The very oldest Guardian of the Earth, whose face one sees carved in stone above church doorways, his hair luxuriant with leaves, the leaves bearing fruit – stone nuts and stone berries. More leaves sprouting whole from the grinning mouth, foliage gripped between stone teeth. The grin that says, I am the Earth.

There was a crash. Cindy had slumped against the metal shelves, collapsing one.

'It's all right.' He picked himself up. 'Don't mind me. Slipped. Clumsy. It's all right . . . Maiden.'

Nobody spoke until the crackly, distorted tape was over.

The speakers hummed. Magda made no move to remove the cassette. Her hands were squeezed tight together.

'It . . .' Her voice cracked. She coughed. 'It doesn't sound like a dream.'

'It wasn't,' Cindy said. 'I can assure you of that.'

'Christ, that's why you asked if he could make a crossbow.'

'Play the last bit again,' Maiden said.

. . . broken the convention.

And wasn't it easy?

'His first kill.'

'His first *human* kill,' Cindy said.

402

'The convention. The *convention*.'

Magda said, 'Excuse me,' and went out into the yard. They heard the slap of vomit.

'She dug up Ersula's body this morning,' Maiden said. 'She's seen what he can do.'

'Ah, me . . .' Cindy took out the cassette tape, held it up between two fingers and dropped it in the box, as if it was radioactive. 'Can you imagine anyone more despicable?'

'And like all of them, like all serial killers, he doesn't believe he's doing anything wrong. He's broken a convention. He's feeling alive for the first time, the cunt.'

'No . . . me, I meant. *I* wanted . . . so much to believe it. I wanted to be proved *right*. Can you imagine anyone more contemptible than that?'

'Shut up, Cindy. If it hadn't been for you . . .'

'Maria. I knew that girl so well. She could talk to me. Damn. If I was any kind of shaman, I should have seen the danger, should have been able to warn her. I'm no bloody shaman, Bobby.'

'Cindy, this was random, in its way. He just wanted a hunt saboteur. Someone he believed the Earth would be better off without. He thought it might be difficult, so it'd be better starting off with someone he expected not to like. It could have been any one of them.'

'And it wasn't difficult at all, in the end, was it, lovely? *Wasn't it easy?* he says, *Wasn't it easy?*'

Maiden walked to the door. He could see Magda Ring with her back to the perimeter wall, gazing nowhere.

'What I find disturbing is the way he starts off saying "I" and then he switches off the recorder. We don't know how long he's sitting there. Could be a few seconds, could be an hour. Longer. But when he switches back on, he's become "he". He's created this character. The Green Man.'

'He hasn't created him. He exists. He's an ancient archetype, almost a god. Our friend Adrian is taking on his magic, his charisma.'

'His voice changes. He's immediately stronger, more fluent. He tells the story without hesitation.'

'With an absolute belief in himself and his mission. A refuge, too. He can slip into the persona of the Green Man whenever . . . whenever it's called for. This man is unbelievably dangerous. Do we know where he is now, Bobby? Could he, I mean, come back any time . . . ?'

'Not imminently. Gone, apparently, to a wedding.'

Cindy froze.

XLIII

Magda Ring was up against the wall, Cindy practically shaking her.

'Where is he? How long ago did he leave? Whose wedding is it? Come on, girl!'

Bobby Maiden pulled him away. 'Cindy, this guy performs quietly. He isn't going to do it at a bloody wedding.'

'You don't understand.' Cindy whirled on him. 'Little Grayle. Grayle Underhill was going to a wedding. You might believe in coincidences, Bobby, but in my world they don't exist. Where's the wedding, my love?'

'What's happened to his accent?' Magda, looking scared by now, began to slide away from Cindy along the wall. 'Why's he gone Welsh? You two . . . you aren't police at all, are you?'

'*I* am,' Maiden said. 'I promise you. I'll show you—'

'I don't want to see your damned card again, I want to know what the hell's going on.'

'All right . . . look . . .' Maiden held up one hand. 'This guy's a friend . . . contact . . . of Marcus Bacton's. He's suspected for some time that several murders in various parts of the country were down to one man, and the police didn't want to listen. I've been listening. End of story.'

'Where's the wedding, my love?' Cindy said insistently. 'Which nice old pre-Reformation-church-on-an-alignment are we talking about?'

'It's not a church. It's some sort of New Age nuptial thing. It's at the Rollright Stones, in Oxfordshire.'

'Oh, my Christ.'

'Janny Oates, Matthew Lyall. They're the couple. I don't know where they live. They'll be on our books, if you can wait. They did a course here, which is where Adrian—'

'How long ago did he leave?'

'Couple of hours . . . three hours . . . I don't know. He didn't take his Land Rover. Rushed in this morning, grabbed some things, said he had a lift.'

'We *can't* wait.' Cindy rocked, tearing at his face with his fingers. 'Bobby, we're going. We're going now.'

'What about the rest of the tapes?'

'Listen to them in the car.' Cindy began to run across the courtyard, pulling car keys from his blazer pocket, shouting back over his shoulder. 'She's given him a *lift*. Bobby, she's got this psychopath in her car!'

'You're not leaving me here!' Magda clutched at Maiden's jacket. 'Not with that bloody open grave.'

'Do you have a car?'

She nodded frantically, all sophistication abandoned.

'Anywhere you can go?'

'People in Hay . . . my new house . . .'

'Do it. Don't speak to anyone about this. Especially the police. No . . . Listen . . . give me a phone number. If you don't hear from us by, say, seven tonight, call the police yourself. Tell them everything. Tell them where to find Ersula's grave. Tell them . . . tell them DI Maiden, Bobby Maiden—'

The Morris Minor was clattering towards them, its passenger door flapping open.

Magda grabbed his wrist. 'Pen.'

He found a chewed-off Bic in his pocket; she scribbled a phone number on the back of his hand.

'She said her sister was in a, I think she said, *dislocated state*. When she met some people at the Rollright Stones. *They're nice*, she said. *The people, not the stones*. I remember that.'

Cindy swung the car between the trees into the drive,

406

almost scraping a Land Rover parked under a willow tree's browning umbrella.

'You need to know about the Rollrights, Bobby? I shall—'

A memory had kicked Maiden in the head at the sight of the Land Rover. He was in another passenger seat, a woman in a blond wig driving.

'Cindy, stop . . . let me out. Half a minute.'

The Land Rover's doors were unlocked. Maiden jumped in, rummaged around. Ordnance Survey maps, a thick paperback guide to stone circles of the British Isles, much thumbed. A hand lamp, pair of wellingtons and . . . He found the recorder wrapped in sacking underneath the driver's seat, a cassette inside it, half wound. He slipped the cassette out, took it back to the Morris.

'Ah . . .' Cindy pulling sluggishly away before the passenger door was shut. 'Rather hoping, I was, that you wouldn't find that one.'

'How do you know what's on it?'

'I think that he wouldn't be able to rest – would not be free of the Green Man – until it was done. Out of his system. The other one he recorded in the rain, before he left the scene, presumably.'

'Sure,' Maiden said quietly. 'It's also occurred to me why he may have done this. How it came about. Why he killed Em.'

'Perhaps you won't need to hear it then.'

'Put it on.' Maiden said.

When the Green Man started speaking, it was deliberate, unhurried, a voice full of an awful, calm, precise, relentless certainty.

. . . the energy at Black Knoll is having a most interesting effect on the woman. She is clearly reluctant to enter the precincts of the burial chamber. She stands there, her unruly blond hair pushed down by a cap and by the rain, and then all at once she cries out.

'Oh come on, you're fucking crazy!'

She begins to sob . . . standing on the Knoll, soaking wet and sobbing . . . before at last going to sit on one of the flat stones in the short avenue approaching the chamber itself.

The stones amplify her thoughts . . .

. . . so that the Green Man, lying snugly, invisibly, between two gorse bushes, knows at once that she is crying out for release.

It's really quite astonishing. She has walked the line precisely, from the clearing, from stile to stile, the old sacrificial path. She has walked through the darkening rain, this woman who has crossed an ocean to present herself to the Earth.

And to the Green Man, Her servant, Her lover.

The woman whispers, 'Ersula?'

And rises, screaming 'Ersula!' into the rain.

It is all that the Green Man can do to restrain himself from leaping to his feet in euphoria at this joyful union, across the Veil, a union which cries out to be complete.

How, then, should he facilitate the completion of the union? With his hands around the tender flesh of her throat?

Yes, she is begging now for deliverance. Her hands are clasped, she is swaying, her breath coming faster, in great gulps. The Green Man feels his fingers pulse. He begins to rise from the bracken, in his majesty.

And then, all at once, she rears up, her arms wide.

'Oh God,' she whispers. 'Oh . . . God.'

And then turns and runs away, taking the castle line, looking over her shoulder, once, as if to say, Follow me, follow me!

'Oh, Grayle,' Cindy whispered. The voice broke off and there was only the sound of breathing in the night.

'This is when she saw whatever she saw,' Maiden said. 'And then came running down to the Castle, looking shattered.'

'Though not as shattered as perhaps she would have been if she had known how close she had come to death.'

It is dusk when the Green Man returns to the castle, in his vehicle this time, driving into a field and parking, without lights, behind a hedge almost opposite the entrance.

When the woman was taken into the house, earlier, he was

408

baffled. Was it to be done here? And what of the man? Him too? It occurred to him that now, in the absence of the old witch, the castle would at last be fully open to him . . .

Cindy stopped the tape. 'Mrs Willis, you see. He could not have killed with Mrs Willis present. And now she's dead he demonizes her, he calls her a witch.'

'Why? Why couldn't he . . . with her around?'

'He perceived too much power around her, too much light? I don't know.'

'But you said he killed *her*.'

'And now I am unsure. We do know that he drew her out in the only way that would work. He approached her and asked her for healing. The one thing Mrs Willis could not deny him. This gift she believed she had received from the Holy Mother at High Knoll. She could never refuse healing, see? Couldn't refuse at least to try. Thus are saints martyred.'

'This is getting too apocalyptic for me, Cindy.'

Cindy didn't reply, but put on the tape again.

. . . and when he returns at dusk, he knows the identity of the woman.

Full circle.

He has realized – everything is for a purpose – that it must be done in the knowledge of who she is and why she is here.

Sent.

Yes.

But what if she is no longer here? He does not even know where she is sleeping.

You fool, he tells himself. Have you no faith?

And as he is telling himself this, a car turns into the castle gateway.

The Green Man alights silently and follows on foot, waiting in deepest shadows, under the castle walls.

He sees a man leave the house and get into the car. As the door opens, the interior light identifies the woman and, before the car emerges from the castle gates, the Green Man is back in his own vehicle, searching, without lights, for the field entrance.

This time Maiden switched off.

'He thought it was Grayle. He thought Emma was Grayle. Because of the blond wig.'

'And he was locked into it by then,' Cindy said. 'It was ordained. From the moment he saw her on the Knoll he knew what he was going to do.'

'He nearly ran into the back of us once. Em slammed on the brakes and this Land Rover nearly went in the ditch. And yet didn't protest. No horn-blowing, nothing. I should have known.'

'How could you possibly have known?'

They were off the single-track roads now, passing stone farms, paddocks.

'Can you go any faster?' Maiden said.

It's a new experience for him. He does not normally use the modern roads which brashly thrust across the old straight ways. He wonders occasionally, now, if this is right and tells himself to have faith.

And his faith is amply repaid when they leave the road and enter a wooded enclosure whose antiquity is immediately apparent to the Green Man. He does not need his map. He knows from the contours of the landscape and the ancient sanctity of this area, between the Black Mountains and the Brecon Beacons. Here rise some of the tallest and finest standing stones in the land. He is at once at home. His spirit burns.

It is an inn. The sign says, Open to Non-Residents. He is gratified to note that his is not the only all-terrain vehicle in the car park. Through a ground-floor window, he can see into the bar, which is quite full of people who, from their clothes, he can tell are mainly local. He does not see the woman there.

He must be careful not to bump into her; she will recognize him at once. But he is beginning to feel secure and protected. He enters the bar, speaks to no-one, passes through to the toilets and then to the reception area.

It seems that they are staying the night. There's no-one at the reception desk, which is fortunate. The keys to the rooms are on a board on the wall. Three are missing. Rooms two, five and ten. There is no-one to see him as he casually ascends the stairs.

On the first landing he tries doors. Only one room is accessible: room seven, at the very end, which has no lock or handle, only a freshly drilled hole.

His footstep echoes in an unfurnished room. There is a smell of sawdust. He switches on the light to discover that room seven is presently undergoing refurbishment. There are scattered tools and heaps of plaster and some paint-stained overalls.

He hears voices from the landing and creeps back to the door.

Because of the age of the house, the passage is narrow, and the two people are in single file, walking away from him towards the stairs, the woman obscured by the man, whose back is turned to the Green Man until he half turns to make sure he has locked the door of room five, and the Green Man recognizes him at once, from Castle Farm. He's probably the nephew of Marcus Bacton, and he poses a slight problem. For the Green Man's human quarries, to date, have all been hunted singly.

Well, no hurry. They're obviously going for dinner. Now that he knows, the Green Man emerges and takes a leisurely look around the upper rooms of this pleasant old house. He finds two ugly metal fire escapes, geomantically disastrous for such a building, but obviously useful to him tonight. In fact, he uses one to effect his exit, wedging the door open just a slit, using a chisel he has found in room seven.

Who knows? The chisel may be useful later. At the bottom of the fire escape, he finds himself in near-complete darkness amid trees and bushes, but, when he emerges onto a lawned area, the moon emerges too, from behind a cloud, and he can see the lie of the land as far as the mass of the mountain called Sugar Loaf.

He walks round the perimeter of the building and arrives on the other side of the fire escape, where he discovers a narrow path leading through bushes to higher ground.

A mound, in fact. A distinct mound! Elation blossoms like a golden flower in the Green Man's groin.

Not yet.

The mound is flat-topped. A tumulus, surely! A holy place. A *small area has been dug, where some fool has attempted to plant flowers.*

The Green Man sits on the mound, in meditation, for some time, perhaps hours. He sleeps. The moon is in his eyes. In his dream, the moon becomes a Druid's shining sickle. He awakes and, for a moment, it seems that the moon is finely rimmed with blood. When he comes to his feet and stretches, he is cold but braced. And certain in his mind. At last, the Earth calls to him.

He removes his clothes. He stands in his majesty atop the holy mound, lifts his arms to the shadow of the Sugar Loaf. He is not at all cold now. He feels the flow of energy through the land . . . he knows instinctively that this is a crossing point. The Earth calls again to him, and he lies down upon the area of attempted culti-vation, and he penetrates Her.

'Am I getting this right, Cindy? This guy *fucks flowerbeds*?'

'And probably rubs damp soil into his skin.' Cindy didn't look at him. 'And eats it, of course. He sees the Earth as his lover. He wants to be a part of Her and Her of him. In Her, in him. Think about it. But resist, at all times, any temptation to regard this man as ludicrous.'

'Unlikely,' Bobby Maiden said grimly.

And thought about it. Thought the unthinkable. About the smell and the taste of the grave. About the smell and the taste as he lay with Em. And his reaction to it. It made him want to put his shoulder against the car door and hurl himself into the road.

'Calm yourself, Bobby.'

'What are the chances,' he said tautly, 'of him being impotent with women?'

'Considerable, I would say.'

'And what Magda says about him being besotted with Ersula Underhill? Do you think he was perhaps more besotted with the idea of getting close to someone he knew he was ultimately going to kill?'

Cindy waited to pull onto the main road that would take them into the city of Hereford.

Maiden pushed in the cassette.

Returning by the fire escape – fully dressed, of course – he enters room seven. He sees it with new eyes. At one end of the room lies a roll of carpet. And the retractable knife used to cut it. In a cleaner's cupboard in the bathroom, he has found a pair of ladies' rubber gloves which he somehow manages to stretch over his hands. He dons the paint-splashed overalls, which also are a little tight, but not too much of a problem.

He waits in room seven, but not for long. He knows he must act before the earth-energy dissipates in this filthy secondhand atmosphere, this central-heating smog.

Rage takes him. A sort of internal thunderstorm. His fingers tense and tremble . . . not tremble, vibrate, his fingers vibrate.

He picks up the retractable carpet knife and pushes out its steel blade. Unfortunately, it protrudes less than an inch. Hardly a Druidic sickle! Impatient now, he gets down on his hands and knees and scrabbles around until he finds a screwdriver, and he takes the thing apart, empties the spare blades on the floor. He examines them. One is longer than the rest and has a curved end, a sort of hook thing. It is previously unused and when he tests it with his gloved thumb it slices cleanly through the rubber.

He rises. Very well, he will release both spirits. The Earth has decreed it. He will open the window immediately afterwards so that even if the blood cannot soak into Her, its essence will be carried into the night air.

He wrenches open the door of room seven, and, almost simultaneously, another door opens.

The lighting in the passage is dim, but if Bacton's nephew had glanced to his left there would have been enough light for him to see the Green Man in his majesty. And all would have been ruined. But the Earth is with him tonight . . . the nephew, with a bundle of clothes under his arm, walks directly to the bathroom.

The Green Man steps back into room seven and waits to see what will happen.

In a short time, the nephew emerges, half dressed, and walks, with his head bowed, towards the stairs.

It is the sign.

The Green Man moves into the passage, flicks out the short, curved blade – like the moon . . . another sign! – and walks to the door of room five. Only then does it occur to him that these doors self-lock from the inside. Oh, he thinks, he should never have come here! His is an outdoor pursuit!

But even as he's thinking these defeatist thoughts, he notices that the door is not fully closed. A garment has been inserted around the catch of the lock to prevent it engaging.

Presumably to facilitate her lover's return, the woman has enclosed the lock in the cup of her brassiere. The Green M—
click.

'I think that's enough,' Cindy said. 'Take out the cassette, lock it in the glove compartment. It represents your freedom. Lock it away, don't think of personal revenge. Think what . . . what a fine girl she was. Cry for her. And then put it behind you and clear your mind for what is to come. Do you hear me, Bobby?'

He couldn't see Bobby's face for his hands.

Cindy pulled alongside a phone box. 'I'm going to phone Marcus. Put him in the picture.'

There was no reply at Castle Farm. Gone for a walk, perhaps, to think things out.

When he returned to the driving seat, Bobby looked composed again.

For now.

XLIV

The circle was looking even more chewed up today, as if the stones had some degenerative disease.

Or maybe, once again, it was just the way she was feeling.

'Limestone,' the Reverend Charlie said. 'This is what happens with limestone. They'll still be here in another two thousand years, count on it.'

He didn't look a lot like a reverend. He had on this really old fringed leather jacket and frayed, off-white jeans and sneakers with a hole in one toe, through which you could see he wasn't wearing socks.

The sky had cleared now, late afternoon, or maybe this was a different climate zone or something. In the east, purplish clouds were forming like a mountain and the sun had a dull, dirty sheen.

'Going to rain at some stage.' Charlie had a mild, London accent. 'Nothing surer. Always rains at my weddings.'

He grinned, showing teeth that were uneven, chipped and brownish.

A lot like the Rollright Stones, in fact.

Grayle had come out here, ahead of the party, because Charlie had to come get his stuff together. She'd gotten talking to him, told him about Ersula, and he seemed like a nice guy, and he'd offered her a ride over, in his van.

She'd explained to him what had happened. How the hire car had broken down and Adrian couldn't fix it, but said he'd run back to the pub and call up the AA, and when he returned it was in a car with this couple who were headed for Chipping Norton. Made sense, Adrian said, if she went along with these people and he'd stay and wait for the AA, who sometimes took *simply for ever*, and he'd bring the car along to the Stones once it was fixed.

On the one hand, Grayle didn't like to leave the hire car. On the other, she'd had enough, for one day, of Adrian and his lectures. And it *was* kind of him. So she'd unloaded her case and gone with the people in the car and Adrian had stayed with the Rover and his cricket bag.

In the hotel in Chipping Norton, not surprisingly, there was no sign of Matthew or Janny, and Grayle obviously didn't know any other guests. Which was how she'd homed in on the individual with the dog collar.

'You conducted weddings here before, Charlie?'

'Actually, no.' The reverend massaged one of the taller stones with both hands. 'Weddings here tend to be of the pagan variety. Handfastings, that sort of thing. I'm here by way of a compromise. Friend of the family. And also just about the only ordained clergyman they could find willing to conduct an open-air wedding in a place this notorious.'

The last tourists, two spinsterish ladies in golfing-type checked trousers, walked out of the circle and didn't look back.

Grayle said, 'Notorious?'

'Been some fairly unpleasant goings-on at the old Roll-rights over the centuries.' Charlie leaned against the stone. 'Well, over this century, particularly. It's because it's so relatively accessible from Oxford and London.'

'What kind of goings-on?'

'Oh, you know, satanic rites. Sicko stuff. For instance, a spaniel was sacrificed here some years ago.'

'That's awful. What kind of people would do that?'

'No-one I'd care to break bread with, Grayle, but these are difficult, desperate times. Everyone searching for a quick, cut-price spiritual fix. Could you help me with my altar?'

Charlie's altar was a small wooden picnic table. They set it up at the far end of the circle, where the pine trees reared. It looked flimsy and lonely.

'You have your church hereabouts, Charlie?'

'Don't have a church at all. I'm a sort of embarrassing Anglican mendicant. Travel around, begging for scraps. Wedding here, two-week locum post there. Few rock festivals in the summer. They're great. Sunday morning worship . . . surprising how many crawl out of their tents for it, even if they're too stoned to read the hymn sheets. No, poor as the proverbial, but then so was JC.'

Charlie took out a tin box, placed it on the altar and began to roll himself a cigarette.

Grayle said, 'You think these are, uh, bad places, generally?'

'Course not. Terrific places, some of them. Wild and spectacular, like Castlerigg in the Lake District. Awe-inspiring like Avebury. Just not awfully sure about this one. Feels polluted, somehow. But, then, these are the places we should be bringing a little light down on, don't you think?'

'You think they still have power?'

'Absolutely. Why else would we have built most of our churches on the same sites? You can feel it while you're working, you really can. When you stand in front of the altar in some tiny little country church and raise your arms . . . vroom!'

'And maybe you see . . . things?'

Charlie's eyes narrowed. He looked her up and down. After inspecting the other guests at the hotel in Chipping Norton – nothing formal, but lots of floaty stuff – she'd changed in the ladies' room into a long print skirt and a scoop-neck blouse, thrown a woollen wrap around her shoulders.

'What sort of things?' Charlie said suspiciously.

'Kind of . . . unexplained phenomena things?' She pulled on the tassels of her wrap. 'I think I may be a little crazy.'

The Reverend Charlie invited her to sit on his altar with him, offered a cigarette. 'Good stuff. Only the best from a man of God.'

Grayle blinked. 'Uh, not right now, thanks.'

He nodded. 'You know, Grayle, it's an odd thing, but I never saw a ghost. Problem with ghosts – and I believe in them, sure – they never seem to appear to people who really want to see one. Strange, eh?'

'Oh, I *always* wanted to see one. Back home. When I had this New Age newspaper column. But when I came over here, to find Ersula, when I was really alone in a strange place, no I did not want to see anything I couldn't explain.'

Grayle sighed and found herself secondary-smoking the reverend's dope.

Andy had dozed for a couple of hours on the sofa. Woke up feeling lousy and gave herself some Reiki. Called Marcus back. Wouldn't put it past the old sod to stay away a couple of hours and then return. Too meek, come to think of it, the way he'd accepted the idea of danger.

But no answer from Castle Farm, so she made herself some soup and got ready for work. Having agreed to call in on Tony Parker on the way. Dispense more laying on of hands.

She'd asked him could he not just call them off, these bad guys.

'If somebody sent them,' Tony Parker had said, 'if . . . hypothetically, and from my limited knowledge of such matters . . . some operatives had been *contracted* . . . then the hirer would not expect to hear from them again until completion of the contract. That's the way of it. As I understand it.'

'I'll leave you to your grief, then.'

His colour was improved, no question of that. Jesus God, Andy thought, the things we wind up doing.

'Well, Sister, whatever it was, I appreciate it,' Parker had said as she stood up. 'And that offer stands.'

Had to admit she'd never treated anybody – or at least any *man* – more receptive. Mostly, they were a wee bit nervous, or trying too hard. Tony Parker, both emotionally drained and entirely confident that nobody would mess with him in his own office, had submitted totally, and so had realized immediate and immense benefit. Better than pills, clearly, and no side-effects. So he wanted more, and he thought he could buy it.

'You flatter me, Tony. Only, private nursing's no my thing. I prefer to put it about, you know?'

'You'll come around. And we didn't have no conversation, mind.' Suspicious now. Wondering if the treatment hadn't been some form of hypnosis to promote indiscretion.

'No,' Andy had said. 'We didn't. Listen, I'll come back tonight, on my way to work, see how y'are.'

He'd brightened at that. She pitied him. A hard-looking young guy had peeked in on them earlier. Parker would be surrounded with people like this and the older he got the less he'd be able to trust them. Half of him would have wanted to bring smart Em into the family business, the other half to keep her the hell away from it.

'Sister,' he'd said as she left, 'I ain't decided whether I believe what you say about Maiden, but I'll do what I can to suspend things meantime. Just that other parties got to be consulted.'

This didn't entirely make sense. Who? Riggs? She'd ask him about it again, after giving him another treatment. She was out of her depth. Felt useless. Needed to be hands-on again.

Parking the car on a pay-and-display up the street from Parker's club, she contemplated ringing in sick and driving down to St Mary's. Like, she'd go to work as normal, park at the hospital, vanish into the building then out through the ambulance doors and away to the border. She'd know if they were tailing her. Wouldn't she?

'Mr Parker, please,' she told the girl in the office next to the Biarritz Club. It was five p.m.; she could spare him half an hour. 'I have an appointment.'

The receptionist looked at her with recognition. 'You're a bit late, Sister,' she said without much feeling either way. 'Mr Parker collapsed at his desk this afternoon. We've just heard from the General he died a short time ago.'

Andy just stood there, and her healing hands felt like dead meat.

'He hadn't been a well man, anyway,' the receptionist said. 'But you'd know that.'

Cindy pulled out tape III, switched off.

'Let's give it a rest.'

Maiden had no argument with that. It was starting to make him feel sick. Tape III recounted a killing even Cindy hadn't discovered in the papers. Victim was a seventy-year-old church verger, near Worcester. His skull smashed on the edge of the twelfth-century stone font. The Green Man had learned in a dream that the medieval font had begun its working life as a Druidic sacrificial stone.

'Seems to me, Cindy, that his dreams have become increasingly literal.'

'Yes. I had noticed.'

'Does this happen much in your experience? Where you actually dream about the place you're sleeping?'

'Oh, yes. Site-specific imagery is quite common. You also have an increasing number of lucid dreams – that is, dreams where you know you are dreaming. And then you might gradually learn to *control* your dreams. Which is when it gets complicated. Where is the borderline between a dream and a self-induced fantasy?'

'So he could be dreaming what he wants to dream. Or convincing himself when he wakes up that his dream was significant to whatever nastiness he's got in mind. What I'm really asking is, what effect is the sleeping on powerful energy . . . points . . .'

'Nodes. Energy nodes.'

'Whatever. What effect is that going to have on the mind of a psychopath?'

Cindy urged the grumbling Morris Minor past a tractor and trailer.

'That's an interesting point, Bobby. And a most disturbing one. If we go back, see, to the first killing, poor Maria, in the New Forest, you'll recall he's operating almost instinctively. In killing Maria, he's attempting to please the Earth, to get in tune, but he's a little frustrated that he can't have *confirmation*. He says something like, If only there was a way of speaking directly to the Earth and listening to Her instructions . . .'

'So when he hears about this dreaming experiment . . .'

'Which began, as I recall, in the eighties, with an earth-mysteries group called the Dragon Project Trust. If he read about this, he would try it for himself. It's a free country. You can spend a night at virtually any prehistoric site you like, except Stonehenge. He would believe he had found it. A channel of communication with the Earth itself.'

'And then, when he goes to work for Falconer, he introduces the idea. Which became very popular among the punters. Maybe he thinks they're all going to start—'

'God forbid! No, I think . . . I think he believes they will be educated. By the Earth . . .'

'The University of the Earth.'

'. . . into accepting the Old Ways.'

'Seeing how he's already influenced the great Falconer.'

'Which I doubt the good professor would admit under torture. No, I don't think he believes they will all become serial killers. He believes that to be a great honour. He is a chosen instrument. One of the Elect. You notice how he refers to himself—'

'The Green Man "in his glory", "in his majesty".'

'Exactly!'

'It's not untypical, Cindy. I've never heard of a modest, unassuming serial-killer. Delusions of superiority, uniqueness . . .' Maiden leaned back as far as the seat would allow, which wasn't far. He breathed out.

'I think this is called assembling a psychological profile, is it not, Bobby?'

'Yeah. Though what good it's going to do . . . How far now?'

'Tewkesbury and then the back road into the Cotswolds to Stow. Say an hour.'

'And then what? What do we do when we get there?'

For a while, he'd felt like a copper again, the big jigsaw interlocking in his head. Yet the more he heard of the Green Man tapes, the less he felt up to it. Killers on this scale had absorbed CID teams from four, five divisions, heavy uniform back-up, incident rooms, the works. A damaged DI with a personal angle and an ageing actor-ventriloquist with dubious shamanic powers in a thirty-year-old Morris Minor for which sixty mph was a distant memory . . .

'We find Grayle,' Cindy said soberly. 'If it's not too late.'

'I wonder what the bastard's reaction was when he found out he'd killed the wrong woman.'

'Bobby,' Cindy said, 'after the initial shock, I doubt if he'd consider your poor friend to have been the wrong woman after all. For him, everything is ordained. Collen Hall, on its energy node? However would he have been led to this magical place otherwise?'

'In the end, the identity of the victim is not important?'

'He believes the Earth will choose. This is underlined for him by the killing at Avebury, when he discovers his victim is a hairdresser, thus providing a link with the famous medieval Barber-Surgeon whose skeleton was found beneath one of the stones after, presumably, trying to damage it. A reverberation, through the ages. Vindication.'

'You notice, how, although he might know his victim – Ersula . . . Grayle – as soon as he sets out to kill them, as soon as they become the quarry, he depersonalizes them. They become "the woman". Like "the fox", "the pheasant". He's not a murderer, he's just a hunter.'

'Not just *a* hunter, Bobby.'

'Cindy, I'm going to have this cunt.'

'Of course you are, lovely, of course you are.'

Marcus made himself a cheese sandwich and shut Malcolm in the kitchen with a bowl of water and four Bonios to keep him quiet.

He was a good dog, a brave dog. But *very, very bad guys*?

'Stay,' Marcus said.

He went out of the house and prowled the tumbledown buildings, in search of weapons. The best he could find was the head of a scythe, which he couldn't hold without it biting into his hand, and a wooden-handled pitchfork with rusted tines, so badly eroded, in fact, that it was hard to tell if there was actually any metal beneath the rust.

Marcus straightened his bow tie and climbed over a short, broken wall to the remains of the only serviceable tower, the highest part of the castle. It was no more than about half of a sundered tower in the remains of the curtain wall. Possibly part of a gateway. Perhaps there'd been a portcullis here.

Could have used one now, all right.

Marcus climbed a treacherously narrow, dangerously worn spiral staircase inside the tower. Hadn't done this in years; bloody steps would be beyond repair soon.

He turned a corner and came out in the sky. Always a surprise, the way the steps simply ended, broke off. A sycamore tree had grown up next to the tower, partly obscuring the view in high summer, but there was still quite an extensive vista of the Black Mountains, for once living ominously up to their name, filling the western horizon, like the massed tents of a dark army.

Once, raiders had come down from the mountains, from the poorer country into the lushness of the Golden Valley. The reason the castle had been built. But now the threat, presumably, was from the east. The only way to reach this place was by road from St Mary's. From the tower, the road was visible for nearly half a mile before it dipped between the high hedges and the hills.

Marcus sat on the top step, adjusted his glasses and unwrapped his sandwich. Might as well go out on a full stomach. Joking, of course. Maiden and his urban thugs and his bent coppers. Nothing would happen.

The jagged walls of the castle sawed into a sky of sickly yellow, like tallow.

XLV

This was the tape Cindy had found himself dreading the most.

Ersula Underhill.

They'd been playing them at random. Realizing that, with perhaps six hours of Fraser-Hale's boastful ramblings, there wasn't going to be time to hear all of it before they reached Rollright. Snatching out a cassette if it didn't appear to be going anywhere, opening another.

Ersula's was, as he'd feared, the worst death of all. Worse than Maria, worse than Emma Curtis – that would have been terrifying for her, but it would also have been relatively quick; he was in a hurry that night, frantic almost.

With Ersula, he'd had time to plan.

When he goes to find the woman, he has already prepared her tomb.

And she is prepared for it.

She's weary of her life and its limitations. Her dreams have shown her better. She has found a fulfilment in sleep . . . in sacred sleep and dreams surpassing, in their intensity, all her waking achievements. Which, in the superficial world of scholarship and academe, have been considerable.

But such so-called learning, lies passed from book to book, is nothing. A waste of life. Even Falconer admits this now.

As a follower of the Green Man.

Falconer is a weak man with no original thoughts. She is his superior, but he has betrayed her, and she turns at last to the Green Man. When he enters her room at dusk, she is crying. And bitter.

She asks the Green Man to lie with her.

On the tape an owl hooted.

'Where's he recorded this one, do you think?' Bobby Maiden hit the stop button.

'Same place as all the later ones. When I tire of his mock-heroic ramblings, I study the background. You notice that, although it's obviously exterior as shown by noises like that owl, there's also a hollow sound. A *vault-like* sound. We should have realized. It's High Knoll itself.'

'He wouldn't fit inside.'

'His tape recorder would. And his head and chest. I think he's lying in the entrance. So proud of this, he is, that he's giving his voice some resonance, making sure the Earth hears, telling it in Her temple. And he's letting the chamber absorb it too. Stone records, see.'

'Thinking, maybe, that one day some EVP enthusiast will capture remnants of the Green Man himself. That it?'

'Imprinting his life's work upon the great earth-memory. Been missing the obvious, we have, the final link. We hear him talking about a place, we assume that's where he is. But he isn't. The Knoll has become his psychic confessional. He's been bringing as much as he can back to the Knoll. Storing it all there, abomination upon abomination.'

'Like a database?'

'If you like. And also restoring a tradition, which he sees as having been damaged by the holy vision of Annie Davies in 1920. It's become a vaguely acknowledged "healing place". Which he would see as feeble and womanly. It needs to be reinstated as *Black Knoll*. Now let's hypothesize, Bobby, that he was dictating to the stones a chapter of his memoirs . . . say this very chapter . . . on the night of your death. He sleeps at the Knoll – *on* the Knoll, laying himself out like those corpses of criminals – night after night. He dreams of the time when it was a sacrificial stone, a hunter's stone. His dreams are running with blood and steaming with putrescence. And by now, see, he's developed a certain amount of control. He's *conditioning* his dreams. And, at the same time, consciously feeding into the Knoll his accounts of such blood and darkness as it has not known in many centuries. This . . . all this . . . the foul contents of the tapes . . . is the *black light* perceived by Mrs Willis. This happens, Bobby, don't look unconvinced, these places have been, for thousands of years, the receptors of the Earth.'

She disgusts him. Once, he was attracted to her . . . to the power of her spirit, the intensity of her longing to know. But now, as she lolls about on the edge of her bed, with her skirt plucked up to her thighs, he sees that underneath she's little more than the rest of modern womanhood, flawed and weak and unstable, a prey to lower desires.

She has been drinking. There is a brandy bottle on the dresser, three quarters of its contents consumed. She can hardly stay upright. She's repulsive, a disgusting mess.

'You want me,' she says, 'I know you want me. You've wanted me from the start. So go ahead. Have me.'

And yes, he thinks, yes, I will have you. In spite of it all, I'll help you. I'll free that deep and questing soul from the squalid desires of the shell. I'll free it to rise up and pursue its finer goals.

'I'll make some tea,' he tells her.

She giggles. 'How profoundly, goddamn English of you.'

'I'm proud to be English.'

'Well, listen to you.'

'Yes. You should.'

The Green Man puts the kettle on the electric ring. She giggles and lies back on the bed, her eyes closed and her skirt ridden up. The Green Man turns away in revulsion. From a pocket he takes a screw of paper containing the mixture he has prepared including the sedative herbs from the healthfood shop in Hereford and the psilocybin mushrooms he has picked at the foot of Black Knoll.

When the herbal tea is made, he sits on the bed and lifts her up to drink it, tolerating her sweating face against his shoulder. She grimaces. He tells her it will help her. Soon she is rambling. She insists that the Knoll is a place of utter, profound evil.

Talking nonsense.

'Magic mushrooms.'

'Britain's best natural hallucinogen. Used by generations of witches. Magic mushroom tea, with God knows what else in it. After all that drink.'

'A more merciful death than any of the others got.'

'It's not over yet, Bobby, I'm very much afraid.'

'*Grayle!*'

'Oh, hi.'

'Gosh, I'm *delighted* you came!' Matthew Lyall, to her surprise, wore a morning suit, with tails. Traditional English wedding outfit. OK, maybe the white T-shirt underneath was a *mite* irregular . . .

'Compromise.' He fingered the white rose in his lapel. 'Everything's a compromise today. My parents are both here, with their respective spouses. And Janny's mother. They all wanted a traditional old church wedding, and we said, well, you won't find an older church than this one! And Charlie's the real thing, so where's the problem?'

The relatives, stiffly obvious, stood outside the circle, near the hut where you left your courtesy-donations to animal charities. In memory of the poor, sacrificed spaniel maybe.

Matthew said, 'Er, have you . . . ?'

'No.'

'Oh gosh, I'm so sorry. But there are loads of people here who might've run into her.'

'I already asked around,' Grayle told him. 'A little.'

'No luck?'

'Uh huh.'

'Suppose I get Charlie to make a special appeal after the service. How about that?'

'That would be kind. You haven't seen Janny today?'

'No, that's another compromise. We wanted to spend the night here in the circle . . . in a chaste sort of way. In spiritual preparation. And to see what our dreams might tell us about our future together. But Janny's mother . . .'

'May be better not to know,' Grayle said. 'Maybe marriage should be an adventure.'

'That's one way of looking at it. Could be quite an adventure today, actually. Just look at that sky.'

'It'll hold off, Matthew. After all the favours you did for Mother Earth, it's the least She can do.'

It is nearly two a.m. when he carries the woman to the organic tomb. She falls to sleep in his arms and still slumbers as he brings her, perspiring freely and smelling disgustingly of drink, to the place.

A cloudy night, but sufficient moon. It glitters in the fluted tin roof of the helicopter shed, which screens the place from the house.

His night-vision is pretty remarkable by now and he can see the egg-shaped hole from twenty yards away, on the edge of the freshly concreted base. Soon after dark, he lined the hole – three and half feet deep and oriented east to west – with alternate layers of moss and gravel, and then added a bed of soft grass-cuttings, warmly mulching. Beside the hole lies the mound of excavated soil and a heap of local gravel. Between them, a spade.

The Green Man places the woman in the hole, on her side. She awakes and giggles and reaches out for him and he forces himself to caress her and she moans and drifts back into sleep. She needs to be awake, but not yet.

It came to him, as always now, in a dream. He dreamed of a green land of mounds and standing stones and gaily dressed people horse-trading, racing, making merry.

While, in the Earth, not far below the merrymaking, a woman screamed for all eternity.

Next day, in the university library, he found an account of a burial at a place called the Curragh, in County Kildare, where gypsies and tinkers traditionally gather for their fairs. In a henge there, about fifty years earlier, an oval grave was found, less than four feet deep and packed with gravel. In this grave was the skeleton of a young woman, on her back, facing towards the rising sun, the skull pressed hard down upon the chest and the arms tight against the sides of the grave. The bones were in a contorted and unnatural posture, suggestive of writhing.

In the hole, the woman whimpers, rolls onto her back and wiggles her fingers, in the throes of some hallucinatory semi-dream.

She seems to be beckoning.

It is the sign.

The Green Man loads his spade with good, red border soil, the flesh of Her body. The woman chokes as the soil enters her mouth and her eyes open – fear pushing through the psychic membrane of the drugs – to meet the second spadeful . . .

Cindy had to slam on the brakes and pull over onto the verge, and Bobby Maiden almost fell out of the car, rolled over in the grass, producing enormous dry heaves, mouth open fishlike and hands at his gut.

He'd be fine. Cindy watched him through the windscreen and the tape played on, the unbearable details only half registered. What *did* register was the tone of voice. On top of everything the Green Man remained the most insufferable prig.

After a minute, Bobby rolled over onto his back below the car's weak, yellow headlights, and Cindy got out under a spreading fungus of dark brown clouds. It was a dull country lane, open fields and hedges, not a house nor a steeple in sight.

Cindy stood where Bobby had been. Nothing but dented grass. No evacuation. It had all come out last night. It was in an envelope. Nothing left other than what remained in Bobby's head. And now it was in the manageable part of his mind, no longer buried deep.

Why then, bearing in mind the circumstances of its entry there, had his subconscious mind not seen it from Fraser-Hale's side of things, letting him experience the perverse ecstasy of unspeakable, self-righteous cruelty?

Because of what he was. He had experienced it only from the side of the victim.

Bobby held on to a signpost to pull himself to his feet. The sign pointed left to Long Compton and straight ahead to Great Rollright: two miles.

Which meant they were less than half a mile from the Rollright Stones.

Cindy thought of the day when, back home in the caravan in Pembrokeshire, he'd let the pendulum dangle over the map and asked the question: *Where will it happen next?* The pendulum had gone into a violent anti-clockwise spin not where it was expected to go, among the Black Mountains, but over the area where Oxfordshire met Gloucestershire and Warwickshire, and Cindy, hoping for the Welsh border, had dismissed it.

'Sorry.' Bobby produced a smile which contrived to be both bashful and bitter. 'Something went down the wrong way.'

'When we see Grayle,' Cindy said, 'don't tell her, will you?'

'You're joking.' Bobby brushed grass from his jacket.

'For what it's worth,' Cindy said, as dispassionately as he could make it, 'it was another of his failures. She was supposed to have been buried alive, like the woman in prehistoric Kildare. But when the soil went into her eyes, she came out of it and began to scream. At which, our man felt obliged to finish her off. With the spade. In her throat.'

'He can't get anything right, can he?'

Bobby's face as rigid as a mask, his bad eye livid in the last, unhealthy light. Dealing with it now. He said, 'I remember, in one dream, I saw his face shadowed by the spade. That is, the Green Man face. Twigs sprouting. And again, in a wreath in the front of a funeral parlour. And yet we don't know what he looks like, do we? Except he's a big lad with corn-coloured hair. Harmless-looking. And we don't know if he has anything in mind for today. He can't do much in front of an entire wedding party. Crowds aren't his style, unless—'

'Surely, Bobby, that's the problem. Doesn't *have* a style, does he? He responds to the location and the prevailing conditions. And he watches for *a sign*. Which could be anything. He's pretty free with his interpretations.'

Bobby was looking up into the east, where the sky was darkest.

'What is it, boy?'

He shook his head.

'Tell me.'

Bobby shrugged, and Cindy listened without interruption as he described a painting by Turner, showing Stonehenge lit by a vivid storm.

'Maybe another of your archetypal images,' Bobby said. 'But I just had the feeling that was the bolt that hit me. When I was dead. They've got a print of it at Cefn-y-bedd. Knocked me back, seeing it. Magda said that was *his* favourite painting. I assumed she meant Falconer.'

'But that was Stonehenge?'

'But the public isn't allowed into Stonehenge any more. Security guards and everything. It's the one place he can't get to.'

'No, indeed.'

'There're dead lambs in the picture,' Bobby said. 'And a dead shepherd. It's like the storm's been drawn to the circle. This break in the clouds, like the eye of the storm's just opened over Stonehenge. It's a scene of violent death and there's a sense of inevitability about it. See, if I was him, and that was my favourite painting and I just happened to be in a stone circle during a thunderstorm, even *I* might see that as some kind of *sign*. You know?'

Cindy said, 'Know much about meteorology, do you? How long, for instance, before this one arrives?'

'Surprised we haven't heard it already.'

Cindy looked into the hard, tight sky. 'And how many dead lambs?'

432

XLVI

Marcus knew it was them by the speed the van was travelling.

You'd think the drivers who would race along these lanes would be those who knew them best, had negotiated them all their motoring lives, could anticipate the angle of every treacherous bend.

Not so. The locals knew, from bitter experience, that if they crashed it would be into a neighbour. Or a neighbour's wife. Or a neighbour's second cousin who was pregnant. Or the midwife on her way to deliver the second cousin's child.

The locals knew that if they crashed and it was their fault and someone died, then the crash would live with them, even unto the third and fourth generation. No, the locals took it easy, pulled into the verge for oncoming tractors, exchanged polite waves.

So Marcus could tell by its reckless speed in the dusk – and because it was an anonymous white van and because it drove past the castle entrance and then returned the same way within a couple of minutes – that it was them.

He discovered that he had wedged himself against the highest, most concealing part of what now constituted the battlements of the tower. He found himself hunched up, his hands gripping his knees.

He recognized what fell onto the left sleeve of his tweed jacket as a droplet of sweat. Truth was, he hadn't really expected anyone to come at all.

It had occurred to him that in not leaving the farm-house after Anderson's call, he had been spectacularly stupid. If Maiden and Cindy the bloody Shaman had returned, he'd have told them about Anderson's message and they'd have urged him to go with them; he'd have refused, naturally, at first, but might conceivably have backed down.

It occurred to him, as he noticed how rapidly the sky was darkening and curdling, that he might actually be rather frightened.

Some of the families, Grayle saw, were dubious about going inside the circle. They hung around on the fringes, a couple of feet behind the stones. Grayle moved back, too, hearing their whispers.

'. . . must be drab enough on a *nice* day.'

'. . . ought at least to have the union blessed in a proper church.'

'. . . and I'm sorry, Chris, but if it starts raining I shall have to go back to the car. Not going to get much shelter from those pines, are we?'

Sure won't, Grayle thought. The pines stood tall and ravaged, strung out behind the circle, even more witchy, somehow, than the stones.

The people inside the stones, making another circle, were mostly young and casually dressed, though with a flourish, most of the women in long skirts like Grayle's. A couple of guys wore sixties-style caftans and there were bright gypsy scarves and vests – New Age, earth-mysteries chic.

Charlie had brought his altar out over a bald patch in the grass, close to the centre of the circle. He was talking to Matthew. Apparently there wasn't going to be a best man; Matthew said there should be just the three of them at the heart of it all, himself, his bride and the priest.

She wondered where Adrian would stand when he arrived, which group he would feel he belonged to, the

New Agers or the establishment. Strange guy. Not what you first thought he was. She wondered how he was getting on with the car.

There was a ragged cheer from the New Age contingent as three men and a woman arrived with a couple of guitars and one of those Irish hand drums and set up under a tall, thrusting stone in the eastern part of the circle.

'I can see we won't be having hymns, then,' a relative observed sourly.

Charlie had placed two candles on his altar, with glass funnels round them to prevent the wind blowing them out. There was no wind. Looking at the sky, they'd need all the light they could get.

'Grayle?'

She turned. It was a voice she knew, a face she didn't, not at first. Grey-haired guy in a jacket and tie.

'Thank God,' he said.

'I'm sorry?'

'Cindy Mars-Lewis.'

'Oh God. What are you—'

'A word, Grayle.'

He wasn't smiling. He walked away, not a single bangle jangling, into the wood between the circle and the road, and she followed, with a sense of dumb foreboding. Behind, on the edge of the circle, the band had started playing an English folksong about its being pleasant and delightful on a midsummer morn, and that sounded about as wrong as everything else here this evening.

Two of them. One was thickset, almost chubby, his head shaved close; he wore jeans and a short denim jacket. The other had a longer, looser jacket, one hand inside it. He was a longer, looser man all round; he had spiky red hair and a seemingly permanent smile.

They must have left their van in the lane. Marcus hadn't heard it stop. He kept very quiet at the top of his broken tower. It was dark enough for there to be lights in the house and there were none. They'd surely reason it out that there was nobody at home and bugger off.

Or perhaps go back to their van and wait for someone to return.

When they had a slight struggle opening the five-barred gate, he saw they both wore short leather gloves and the squat man had a leather wristband with brass studs.

There was no creeping about; they walked in as if they owned the bloody place. Marcus was furious.

'Whassis? Fucking castle?'

'Think of it as a new experience, Bez. Life's rich tapestry. We never done a castle.'

Birmingham accents.

'All I'm saying, he never said nothing about a fucking castle.'

'He said Castle *Farm*, you twat!'

'So? We lived in Castle Close, but there weren't no fucking castle there. And the next street up was called Palace Place, but there weren't . . .'

'Are yow gonna shut the fuck up? It's only a fucking ruin. Be no fucking men at arms up there with fucking crossbows.'

'Just fucking hate old places. Got rooms where they shouldn't've got no rooms. Bits of wall sticking out, fucking slits yer can't see what's the other side. What's the fucking use of it? Knock 'em down, I would.'

'Yer scared, yow, en't yer? Yer fucking scared. Yer *spooked*.'

'Fuck off.'

They were standing now directly under the tower where Marcus sat. They were perhaps mid-twenties. Kind of youths he used to teach, used to have for breakfast. Ten years on. Marcus felt a sense of outrage.

The squat, shaven-headed one cupped his hands around his mouth and bawled out. 'Anybody in?'

'Anybody comes out,' the other one said, 'tell 'em we broke down up the road and can we use the phone, right?'

The squat one walked out into the middle of the yard. 'I said 's there any fucker in?' Turned back. 'Deserted. What y'wanna do, Bez?'

'Not going back without. No way. We fucked up once. Fuck up twice, you get a reputation. We'll wait. I'm not staying out here, neither.' Bez looked up. 'Gonna rain. Yow go'n do a door, I'll just check the outbuildings. In case. And the castle, case Dracula's in. Eh? Gallow?'

'Fuck off.' The squat one, Gallow, jerked up a forefinger and walked off towards the house.

'Hey!'

' 's up?'

'Just in case . . .' The red-haired one, Bez, took his hand out from inside his jacket. Something gleamed. 'Which one you want?'

'Gimme the sawn-off then. Might be a few of 'em in there, keeping quiet sorta thing.'

A gun? A sawn-off bloody *shotgun*? Marcus's whole face seemed to explode with sweat. They were assassins. They were here to *kill*. When you thought about professional killers, you somehow imagined serious, sinister, taciturn individuals. Not mindless young cretins, egging each other on, taking the piss. What was happening to the world?

Bez turned away and looked up and around and Marcus saw his face between the stones, through the branches, saw that Bez was old beyond his years, his face hard and flat, his smile stamped on, his eyes small and bright and compassionless.

Marcus cursed Maiden. Clutched the jagged stone that stood up like a single battlement and wished that Maiden might never have a night's sleep for the rest of his miserable second life.

When Gallow reached the front door, Malcolm barked.

'Shit. Fucking dog in there, Bez. I hate it, me, when there's a fucking dog. En't scared, dogs en't. Can't threaten a dog. Gotta shoot it, then y'gotta fuck off case it made too much fucking noise and some fucker phones the filth.'

'Get fucking real, willya, man. No problem, place like this. No neighbours, shotguns going off the whole time, rabbits and things, nobody gives a shit. Nobody even notices. Now, go on. Do a door, do a window. Any problem, shout.'

'I hate the fucking country. Everything's too big.' Gallow began to kick the front door, looking for weak points. In the kitchen, Malcolm barked and barked.

Marcus hugged his jagged stone for support. The bastard would get in. Start kicking open door after door, until he reached the kitchen, and then, when the door was open, Malcolm would go silent. Observe the newcomer through his unbalanced eyes, wondering if there might be a chocolate biscuit in this. Come waddling towards him, a dog that wouldn't go in his basket at night without his teddy bear, but unfortunately looked like a complete psycho, an animal you wouldn't ever argue with. Especially if you happened to be tooled-up and nervous.

Meanwhile, Bez, the one with no fear of spooky old buildings, would probably be unable to resist investigating the one stone, spiral staircase in the ruins.

Bez was prowling the buildings and he was tooled-up.

He was supposed to do . . . what? Stand up on the battlements, boom out, You, *boy*! Threaten them with five nights' detention?

Could've been out of here two hours ago, the dog too. And why hadn't he gone? Because he didn't really believe it? Not precisely. It was because Maiden and Cindy had buggered off to face up the delightful Falconer with evidence that his ideas had inspired a madman. Leaving old man Bacton to hold the fort, make the tea, attend to a few senior citizen's chores.

Marcus looked round for his eroded pitchfork.

*   *   *

'OK, we had a breakdown,' Grayle said. 'Adrian organized a ride for me into Chipping Norton, and he said he'd call up the AA and wait for them and then he'd bring the car later. Why do you need to know this?'

They were standing out in the lane, across from a big, twirly-shaped outlying stone surrounded by railings. Cindy – looking even more bizarre, somehow, in men's clothes – had with him Bobby Maiden, *sans* eyepatch and grilling her like a cop.

'What's the car?'

'It's a Rover. A small, red Rover something.'

'And you haven't seen him since you left him at the roadside, with the car?'

'No.'

'You're sure he's not here?'

'He's not here. Where could he be? Hiding out behind the pines?'

Still suspicious of these guys. All this shamanic stuff, the way Cindy found a supernatural dimension to everything. She hadn't needed it last night after her experience at the stones; it had surely caused that awful dream of Ersula. And she sure as hell didn't need it at the Rollright Stones on the edge of a thunderstorm.

Except that Bobby's questions were clipped and urgent and entirely prosaic.

'When you picked him up, he have anything with him?'

'Change of clothes was all.'

'In what? A case? A bag?'

'Yeah, he had . . . he called it a cricket bag.'

'Big, long, leather bag, two handles?'

'We couldn't fit it in the trunk, had to stash it across the back seat.'

'Did you feel there was anything in it, apart from clothes? Did it seem heavy when he picked it up? Was it bulging out anywhere?'

'I don't know! What else could be in there?'

Cindy said, 'Perhaps a crossbow?'

'Jesus, what's all this about?'

'When you broke down,' Bobby said, 'what do you think was wrong? What happened?'

'I don't know cars. We started losing power, the engine kind of whined.'

'Fan belt? Could it have been that?'

Grayle shrugged. Cindy said, 'What would be the significance of that?'

'Was there any time Adrian was with the car and you weren't there?'

'Not really. I was driving. Oh. After we ate, I, uh, went to the bathroom and when I came out he was waiting in the parking lot. At the car.'

'And you were in, what, five minutes?'

'Jeez, you wanna know what I did in there? Well, I took a pee, I washed my hands, tried to make my hair look normal . . .'

'And how long after the pub did the car start playing up?'

'Not long. Half a mile?'

'Right. See, while you were in the bog, he could've slashed the fan belt, so it'd snap soon after you drove away.'

'Why?'

'I don't know. Most likely to get you out of the way and get himself some wheels. We should all be bloody glad it worked. He might have done something more drastic.'

Cindy said, 'He would never do that unless it was a sacrifice. Where killing is concerned, he has his rules.'

Grayle said, voice faltering, 'What is this? Just what is this about?'

'All right,' Cindy said. He held her shoulders, looked into her eyes. 'You remember when we spoke the other night, in my room at the inn, of the contrasting aspects of the Knoll, male and female? And the male element linked to blood, slaughter . . .'

Grayle shook herself away. 'Before you go any further, what's your angle? Who are you?'

Bobby brought out his wallet. Grayle had never seen British police ID, but it looked straight. Also, he sounded right. He looked all wrong, but an undercover cop, the whole point was he should look all wrong.

'And you?'

'Me?' Cindy said. 'A concerned member of the public.'

'And Adrian?'

'Someone who kills people,' Bobby said.

It was kind of a hollow moment, the words repeating themselves in her head.

'And why?' Grayle asked, her head somewhere up there in the curdling sky but her voice down here and surprisingly calm. 'Why is he killing people?'

'Because he believes that's how we should be living,' Bobby said. 'Hunting and hunted and feeding the earth with blood. We think he's killed about half a dozen people.'

'Including my sister, Ersula, right?' That scarily calm voice giving verbal substance to what she'd instinctively known before she even left New York, that Ersula was dead and had been dead for weeks.

'We think that's possible. I'm sorry.'

'How did he kill her?'

'We don't know,' Cindy said. Too quickly.

'We think . . .' Bobby said '. . . we think he may be planning to do something today.'

'Here?' Her voice still calm, still grounded. How was she doing this?

'Here seems the obvious place.'

'Why would he want to take my car? Why not just stick along with me?'

'We don't know. Maybe he needed the car for something and he didn't want you around. He'd replace the fan belt, no problem . . .'

'Practical guy,' Grayle said bitterly. 'Comes from a long

line of *solid chaps* who are *not terribly bright*, but good with their hands. Rigged up the Portakabins, laid down the helicopter pad.'

She saw Cindy wince. Ersula's death hung in the air between them. Either she could haul it down and go some place to weep or she could leave it suspended there until this was over. If it would ever be over.

'I think . . . maybe . . .' Something dawning on her. '. . . he didn't want to be seen to *be* here. Didn't want to come in his own truck. Made some excuse that it wasn't road-worthy. I thought he was just grabbing at the chance to be with me. I thought maybe he, uh . . .'

'When was this?'

'Early morning. I'd just checked out of the inn, he pulled up in the street. Seemed . . . surprised. Yeah. Real surprised to see me there.'

'He would be,' Bobby said. 'He thought he'd killed you last night.'

Grayle drew breath, felt a weakness behind her knees. Fifteen, twenty yards away, a metallic blue Jaguar melted into the side of the road and a guy in a dark suit climbed out the driver's side, came round and opened the pass-enger door. Performed a theatrical bow, extended an arm . . . and Janny Oates stepped out in a long, plain white dress, a golden circlet in her hair. She saw Grayle and waved, all flushed and excited, looking about six-teen, and Grayle waved back and forced an encouraging smile.

'He followed someone last night,' Bobby said. 'We're sure he thought it was you.'

'And he . . . he killed her?' Janny was luminous against the sky.

'Yes.'

'OhmyGod.'

'I'm sorry to unload all this on you, Grayle.'

'We have to find him, don't we? We have to find him right now.'

'We do,' Bobby said.

'Just tell me. Who else did he kill?'

'Just people. You wouldn't know them. *He* didn't know them.'

'Except for Ersula.'

'Yes.'

'A friend,' Grayle said. 'She was his friend. Listen, he talked about sacrifices. He said people would be horrified if they actually knew what it was like here in the old days. He said . . . sacrifice . . . he said it was cruel but it was necessary.'

'He said that to you?'

'On the way here. He said the best sacrifice, the only *real* sacrifice was if you did it to someone who hadn't done you any harm. He said the ultimate sacrifice was to take the life of a friend. And . . . and . . .'

'Go on,' Cindy whispered. 'And?'

'He doesn't like New Age stuff. It's like they're wimps. He said they'd done real damage to the traditions.'

The wedding march was being played on a violin, ragged and a little out of tune, with guitar backing. Some people were cheering.

'And I said – a couple times I think I said this – I said Janny and Matthew – because those guys are real New Agers, as you can see – I said, you know, what about them? Like, how come, if you hate all these people, you're going to their wedding? And he goes, he just goes . . .'

Through the trees, she could see that Charlie had lit the candles on his altar. It was close to dark.

'. . . they're my friends.'

Marcus coughed.

It had taken him a while to build up the cough, and now it was out there wasn't much to it. But it was quiet in the castle precincts now that Gallow and Bez had split up. Malcolm had given up barking. There was just the sound of Bez kicking open the barn door, the more distant thrust and rattle of Gallow unsubtly forcing the rear door of the house.

So the cough was distinct.

It brought Bez out of the barn into the darkening yard.

A splintering sound from behind the house meant Gallow was in. Gallow . . . loose . . . in the house.

Malcolm barked once.

Bez said, 'Gallow?'

He stood in the yard looking over towards the castle walls. His hand went inside his jacket, came out with a pistol, a big one, automatic. They were completely bloody mad, Marcus thought. Drove halfway across England with an automatic pistol and a sawn-off shotgun in the van? What would they do if they were stopped?

Well, they probably never had been and so it wouldn't happen, and if it did they could always shoot it out. The mad, brutal arrogance of young men. No animal more dangerous.

Bez said, 'Gallow? That yow?'

Marcus smothered his second cough in his handkerchief. It was the cough of a man desperate not to cough, crippling himself to keep quiet.

It was enough.

Bez didn't say, 'Who's that?' or 'Come out.' Bez just wore his smile. The cough had made him happy.

At the top of the spiral, Marcus tensed, his arms so tight around the jagged stone that it rocked, and that stone must weigh more than the average anvil. Marcus closed his eyes as Bez put a foot on the first cracked stone stair. There were eleven steps before the stairs broke off. Seven before the final curve.

Come on then, bloody well get it over with.

Bez came up slowly. One foot on a step, then the other foot. Bez was, God forbid, some sort of bloody professional.

In the house, Gallow would be walking up the hall, being careful because he didn't know where the dog was.

Bez reached the fourth step. Gallow would have discovered the old treatment room. Three more doors to the kitchen.

Please, Malcolm. Under the table, you cross-eyed bloody idiot, stay quiet until he arrives outside the kitchen door and then he'll know you've been shut in and he'll simply turn away.

Unless he thinks there's someone in there with you.

God.

Fifth step.

Two and a half years he'd had Malcolm. Ugliest pup the RSPCA kennels ever took in. Poor old Malcolm.

Six. Bez stopped, listening. He'd see there was a curve ahead; he'd have his gun out in front of him. Marcus backed up the broken wall where the branches of the sycamore tree overhung. Sat on the top of the wall, leaning back into the branches which dipped under his weight. He was breathing hard, his glasses half misted. Braced himself against the biggest branch, holding on to it with both hands. Both feet wedged against the great stone that looked, from the ground, like a single battlement.

The yard was about thirty feet below. Break his bloody neck quite easily if he fell. And he'd rather fall than be shot by a moron.

And so Bez arrived on the seventh step and saw Marcus cowering on the edge of the tower, half into the sycamore tree. He relaxed.

'All right, pal,' he said. 'I'm looking for Maiden.'

'Sonny,' Marcus said, through gritted teeth. 'Be bloody lucky if you can find a maiden over the age of twelve between here and Chepstow.'

Bez didn't laugh. 'Funny man, eh?' Bringing the pistol into view. 'This oil yer memory, Grandad?'

'I've got an excellent memory, you cocky little bastard.'

'Good. Yow gonna tell me where Maiden is?'

'Don't know what you mean.'

'Then *yow* . . . are fucking dead.' Bez brought up the pistol. '*Old man.*'

Marcus stared into the pistol's small, black hole and pushed both feet into the battlement stone.

The gun didn't even go off. It clattered down, from step to step, quicker than Bez as the stone toppled onto his chest and he clutched it to him with both arms as he fell backwards, half spinning. And when his head hit the stone lintel on the curve of the spiral, there was a very delicate, genteel little crack, like the sound of two crown green bowls meeting in the stillness of a summer evening.

Marcus stood on the top step for a moment with both hands over his face.

Then he heard Malcolm yelp and he snatched up his pitchfork and staggered down the steps. At the bottom, his eyes met Bez's eyes and Bez looked astonished, both eyes wide open, his mouth too.

Bez was dead.

'Oh lord,' Marcus said, shocked into moderation. 'Oh *God*.'

And then stumbled across the dark yard to the house, edging round the building to the rear door, the pitchfork out in front of him.

The light was on in the passage. Doors either side were flung open. In the Healing Room, bottles and jars had been swept from shelves; some were still rolling on the stone floor, and two clicked together, reminding Marcus of the appalling sound of Bez's skull smashing.

His back to the wall, his pitchfork pointed upwards, he slid round the L in the passage. The kitchen door came into view. It was still closed. From the other side of the panels, the dog growled.

Marcus saw Gallow's gloved hands around the sawn-off aimed at the kitchen door. As he edged round the bend, trying not to breathe, he saw the whole of bulging-eyed, shaven-headed Gallow, backed up, the shotgun at groin level, the way he must have seen Sylvester Stallone or some other movie oaf doing it. Gallow's lips were pulled back over his clenched teeth.

'Come and fucking get it, then!' Gallow kicked the door.

Which remained shut. There wasn't room in the passage for anyone to get in a decent kick. As Gallow's foot came back again, Marcus hurled himself round the corner. *'Baaastard!'* Pitchfork out in front, aimed at the shotgun.

Gallow spun round and the pitchfork missed. When it connected with the wall at the end of the passage, both its corroded tines fell off.

Marcus stood there, holding a wooden shaft. Looking into a double gun barrel.

'. . . the fuck are *yow?'*

'Might ask the same question,' Marcus said gruffly. 'My bloody house.'

'Back up.'

Marcus stood his ground.

'I said *back up, y' old fuck!'*

'All right. All right.'

Gallow prodded him back along the passage to the open rear door.

'Out. Slowly! Don't turn round.'

As if he could. As if he could take his eyes from those two black holes.

Gallow bawled, 'Bez!'

Marcus said nothing. Stepped out backwards into the yard. The only sound was Malcolm barking, way back in the kitchen.

'Yow on your own?'

Marcus raised his eyes to the snarlingly familiar, horribly dangerous face of the Boy with Something to Prove. Gallow was perhaps a couple of years younger than the late Bez, blotches of acne still fighting the stubble on his chin.

'I *said* . . . yow on your own?'

'Not necessarily,' Marcus said belligerently, and Gallow's arms swung out, and several things happened

447

almost simultaneously. With sickening force, the shotgun barrel smacked him in the jaw and left cheek. His glasses fell off. Something crunched into his left leg, just below the knee. He crumpled. The yard blurred up at him.

He couldn't move.

'Bez! Where the fuck . . . ?'

He was kicked in the stomach.

'Where's my mate?'

He retched and tried to curl into a ball, but his knee wouldn't bend. He heard the crunch of his glasses becoming powder under the heel of Gallow's boot. He was wrenched up by the lapels, dragged a few inches in the dirt. Flung back, his head and shoulders meeting stone. The house wall.

He could make out Gallow's shape against the light. Gallow with his legs splayed, his shaven head like a hard-boiled egg.

'Yow move a fucking inch, I'll smash yer eyes out. Got that?'

Couldn't, if he'd wanted to. Marcus moaned over the sound of Gallow's feet skidding away.

'Bez? Don't shit me, man. Bez!' The shouts echoing between the house and the castle, fading off.

The world had turned into a dark expressionist painting, full of violent blotches. Marcus gave up trying to focus on it, and consciousness slipped away like an ebb tide on a long beach. Along the beach skipped Sally, following a big, coloured ball, laughing, the laughter echoing.

'Bez!'

Marcus's one coherent thought was that Maiden and Lewis couldn't be far away. Maiden knew what these people were like. Only one of them left now, anyway. One man. And a gun.

Out of it again. Footsteps along the sand.

Sally?

Darkness. Then he couldn't breathe. His nose flattened under a great, flat weight.

'Dead.'

The weight lifted. He snorted some air.

'Fucking *dead*.'

The boot came down on his mouth this time. Slowly enough for him to catch a brief, blurred, zigzag flash of rubber.

'*He's fucking dead!*'

Smell of metal. Two endless, black, metal-smelling tunnels under his eyes.

'And so are *yow*.'

There was a brief moment of total awareness.

An absolute knowledge of who he was, why he was here . . . why he was here on this Earth.

No pain, only this brilliant crystal clarification of the Big Mystery.

Marcus closed his eyes and never heard the big bang.

He saw two smiling girls running hand in hand across a golden hay meadow. One girl was in sepia, the other in bright, glowing colours.

XLVII

The King Stone, nearly eight feet tall, was like a caged beast inside its iron, schoolyard-type railings. To Maiden – standing in an open field behind it, now – it seemed like a huge head and neck attached to feet or claws, half sunk into the worn grass, clutching at the ground, as if it was preparing to spring out of there.

'Known as an outlier, this is.' Cindy set down his suit-case outside the rails. 'We often find them in the vicinity of stone circles, but set apart. For astronomical reasons usually, or it gives you a line on the rising sun. Not sure about this chap, never having worked here before.'

Maybe once, the King Stone and the Rollright circle had been part of the same prehistoric observatory or whatever it was, but now they were separated by a road and a hedge and part of a wood.

Cindy opened the case, brought out a rolled-up woollen mat. Maiden opened the gate in the railings and Cindy carried the mat through and spread it out next to the King Stone. The mat displayed an interwoven Celtic design, such as you saw on ancient crosses.

'Far as I'm concerned, Bobby, if they call this the King Stone and the circle's known as the King's Men, then this old chap has to be the boss. Getting better feelings, I am, from him, certainly. He hates these bars, but he's kept his distance from some of the bad things that've happened in the circle. Hasn't been tampered with much. Kept his integrity, see. I think I can work with him.'

Maiden and Grayle watched him in sceptical silence.

Against a luminous backdrop of the most malign combination of dusk and stormclouds Maiden ever recalled, every hole and hollow and crevice in the King Stone was clearly defined.

This seemed crazy, time-wasting, probably irresponsible. Logically, Maiden thought, what they should be doing was simply calling the police.

Who would send two cars. Maybe three, if they were informed that the murderer Bobby Maiden was here. And then what? They'd arrest him, and he'd try to explain in the little time they had. It was impossible. Convincing even sensitive, reborn Maiden had taken many hours, plus the discovery of a woman's body in a concrete grave.

'So what's going to happen?' He was tense, restless, the impending storm getting to his nerves. Desperate to *move*, flush out Fraser-Hale. Needed to *see* him. To know the disease.

'I'm going to talk to the storm,' Cindy said.

'I see,' Maiden said.

'Do you?'

'No.'

'All right, Bobby. Very quickly: weather control. Marcus knows more about the scientific side of this than me, and I wish we had him with us. But the electrical storm is a terrific source of energy, the most powerful phenomenon in nature's bag of tricks, and there is evidence that Neolithic people sought to control storms – using megalithic circles – and perhaps to store the energy so that rain could be summoned when it was needed.'

'How would they use stone circles?'

'Because they're invariably sited at places where underground streams intersect, places which are likely to attract bolts of lightning seeking to discharge themselves in the earth. Grayle, this cricket bag of Adrian's, could it have contained, for instance, rods of iron, or copper?'

'I guess.'

'When you were in or around the circle, did you see

anything of that nature sticking out of the ground, anywhere?'

'I don't recall . . . I'm sorry, what would they be for?'

'Lightning conductors, perhaps? Bobby, if you remember, when he is discussing the circumstances of the killing of the birdwatcher, he talks of dismissing clouds and also *creating* them. By willpower and meditation, yes? So we know he's studied weather control. Suppose he's convinced himself he can bring about, by force of will, an electrical storm, like the one in Mr Turner's picture? Suppose he's been working on this for quite a considerable time . . . with this little gathering in mind.'

Grayle backed off from the King Stone. 'At a wedding? That's what he meant by sacrificing friends?'

'I don't know. This is speculation. Adrian's view of our remote ancestors has them as rather less practical and scientific and agriculturally minded than we would perhaps like to think. A storm, as your picture demonstrates, is a dynamic killing-force.'

'Aw, come on,' Grayle said. 'He's just a guy.'

'Practical guy, though,' Maiden said.

'And, at the risk of sounding religious,' Cindy said, 'history has shown that individuals who wish to do evil can seemingly attract to themselves an element of, shall we say, back-up. But I don't want to talk like this. I don't want to court your scepticism. Let's just say that if there's a grain of truth here, we can do three things. We can find Adrian Fraser-Hale and . . . constrain him. We can stop this wedding. And we can try to hold off the storm meanwhile. Do you see?'

Maiden didn't see, not really. Adrian was not like Cindy; he was a nuts-and-bolts man; he was practical. 'Still,' he told Grayle as they crossed the road between a couple of dozen parked cars, to get back to the circle, 'you learn not to dismiss anything Cindy comes up with.'

When they took a final look back at the King Stone, there was a big red thing on top with wings and bulbous eyes you could see even from this distance. Cindy must have stood on his suitcase to prop it up there.

'What the hell is that, Bobby?'

'I think it's Kelvyn Kite. His, er, shamanistic totem creature. Something like that. Don't think about it, you'll only lose confidence.'

They turned left into the small wood which hid the entrance to the circle. The congregation was hushed. The two candles flickered innocently.

'OK,' Grayle whispered. 'I'm gonna be straight with you. I don't know what to believe.'

'Like I said, a problem you tend to have, around Cindy.' Maiden dropped behind the wooden hut.

'No. Listen to me,' Grayle said. 'Ersula. Do you *know* she's dead?'

Her lower face was in shadow. Her eyes, through a soft tumble of hair, were bright with pleading.

'I . . .'

'Bobby, I just need to hear what you believe is the truth.'

'Well. A body's been uncovered at Cefn-y-bedd. In the ground. It's a young woman. Very light, blond hair.'

'Oh . . . OK . . .' Steadying her voice. 'That's . . . that's . . .'

'I don't know her, do I? But he says he killed her.'

'You talked to him? When?'

'He left tapes. He talks all the details into a recorder. At the High Knoll burial chamber. Laying down his own EVP for posterity. That make sense to you?'

'Like a confession.'

'More like a celebration.'

'Friends!' From the circle, the minister's voice rose up, loud and relaxed. 'We're gathered here today in the sight of God – Oh, yes, it is! . . . whatever some of you might think about stone circles . . .'

Laughter.

Grayle said, 'And the woman . . . when he thought he'd killed me?'

'Was called Emma Curtis. She was my friend. Close friend. She was the woman who collected me last night at Castle Farm, while you were there. It was going dark like now, and she had . . . light hair, and he thought it was you. He'd followed you down from the Knoll – that was your mistake, the Knoll is *his* – and he climbed into his Land Rover and he tailed us. To a hotel. And later . . . when she was on her own . . . he . . . he killed her. After he discovered the hotel was at the crossing point of two leys. Serendipity.'

The minister said joyfully, 'To join together this man and this woman in holy matrimony!'

'How did he kill her?'

'With a carpet knife.'

'Jesus. And Ersula?'

'We . . . can't be sure. It'll take a post-mortem. But . . .' He waited.

'The cause of death may be . . . a kind of suffocation.'

She shook a little. She didn't want to hear any more. 'You're not lying to me, are you?'

'I swear to God I'm not lying to you.'

'Now,' said the minister. 'It says here, in this little prayer book, that marriage is an honourable estate, instituted of God, in the time of man's innocence, signifying to us the mystical union between Christ and his church. I want us to think about that, about what it means.'

'Close friend, huh?'

'Almost,' Maiden said, and there must have been a fissure in his voice because Grayle suddenly clung to him, for just a second, then let him go, stepped away, blinking hard.

'Bonding of the bereaved,' she said. 'Jesus, he could be in these woods. He could be just yards away from us now.' She didn't look around. 'This shamanic stuff of Cindy's. You believe he can intercede with nature, head off that storm?'

'Do I hell,' Maiden said.

Grayle nodded. 'So we need to stop the ceremony.'

'No need to make a drama out of it. We just get everybody together in one place, well clear of the circle, for safety.'

'I know,' the minister said, 'that some members of Janny and Matthew's families must think a stone circle is a highly unsuitable place for a wedding.'

'I'll do it,' Grayle said. 'I'm from New York. Everybody knows how crass and crazy we are. I got nothing to lose.'

'Just don't start a panic. Be playing into his hands. Be discreet.'

'Sure. What will you do?'

'If he's here, I'll find him. I *have* to find him.'

'How?'

He didn't reply.

'. . . and what do we think of when we think of a wedding?' the minister asked. 'We think of a ring. And here we are, all of us, inside one of the oldest rings in these islands. Joining together, in our faith – perhaps our various faiths – to celebrate love. So I'd like us all to join hands . . . no . . . come on . . . there's nothing pagan about this, we're all decently dressed . . .'

'If you're gonna be alone,' Grayle said, 'you make sure he doesn't find you first.'

'I know.'

'Or Cindy. He's alone too.'

'If you don't include the spirits of the air.'

'I could get quite fond of that old weirdo,' Grayle said. 'But spirits of the air I can live without. You take care.'

I have to know, Cindy said deep inside himself. *Is it blood you want? Is it the lifeblood of mammals? Is it our terror? Do you thrive on the fear of the fox before the hounds tear it apart? And do you suck the life-force released in the blood of a woman or a man at one of your shrines, at the crossing of energy lines and ghost roads? I have to know, or this is useless.*

From the top of the King Stone, Kelvyn cackled contemptuously.

You old fool, you don't even know who you're talking to.

It was true. He'd never known. The Welsh were a contradiction, they both worshipped nature and feared the God of the Old Testament, in whose honour they built, in place of standing stones, all those grim, grey, monolithic chapels.

Shrines to cruel nature, a cruel God.

And yes, there were times when that Old Testament God would have struck down the guests at a wedding with hardly a thought. In the Old Testament, people died for being in the wrong place at the wrong time in the wrong company.

'Cindy?'

He opened his eyes. On the other side of the railings stood Bobby Maiden.

'This is a bit hard,' Bobby said, 'if you want the truth.'

He'd taken off his jacket, stood there, his T-shirt brilliant against the sky, torn at the left shoulder.

'Tell me, lovely.'

'Grayle's trying to stop the ceremony, I'm wandering around like a spare prick. And . . . what I thought . . . anybody can find him, it's got to be me, right?'

'It's an argument.'

'Only I don't know how to go about it.'

'And?'

'Possibly, you can help.'

'I see.' Cindy rocked a little on his shaman's mat, working this out. 'You want to go back into the darkness. Into the cold.'

'Whatever.'

'Remembering that the whole point of last night was to get you out of there. And to get it out of you.'

'The way I see it, for a few seconds, me and him . . . I may be losing it a bit here, but I feel some part of him collided with some part of me.'

'So it seems.'

'Maybe they need to collide again.'

Cindy deliberated, taking several long, pensive breaths. Kelvyn cackling nastily in his head.

'Don't think about it too long.' Bobby folded his arms. 'I think I can hear the cold calling.'

'Hmm.' Cindy stood up. Couldn't spring up, these days, like he used to; old age catching up, what a bind it was. 'I helped to bring you out, see, but I can't ask you to go back. You have to ask me, isn't it? This is how it's done.'

'Shamanic etiquette.'

'Bit more than that, lovely. Do you really want to ask me?'

'I think I just did.'

Cindy made him sit on the mat – forget the shamanic posture, no time for that, sit however was most comfortable – and then blindfolded him with a black woollen scarf, pulling it tight, heedless of the bruised eye.

'Don't fight it, don't try and see through it. Submit to it. Steady your breathing. Empty your mind.'

From the suitcase he brought the envelope. *That*, envelope. He emptied the pieces of dry soil into his palm and crumbled them into dust. Whether this had come out of Bobby didn't matter; it was what they had found on the capstone when he stopped vomiting. And it connected directly with the worst of all deaths, the choking, in the earth, of Ersula Underhill.

'Don't worry about time. There will be time.' Cindy sprinkled the soil in a thin circle around both Bobby Maiden and the King Stone. 'Step out of time. And think dark. Think cold.'

Lifting his drum from the case, fingers finding the rhythm.

'After me . . . dark.'

'*Dark*.'

'Cold.'

'*Cold.*'
'Dark is cold.'
'*Dark is cold.*'
'Cold is dark.'
'*Cold is dark.*'
'Cold is *Earth* . . .'

It was a pity. Even the older, family guests were getting into it, resistance breaking down. Charlie had charm, he had style. It was a friendly, participatory wedding. He was making more of it than most of these guys did, in Grayle's experience, most likely spinning it out because he was having fun too. And because of the dope, maybe.

They were all holding hands, even the relatives, and now the band was leading them in a hymn. Charlie was facing where the sky was darkest, so that Janny and Matthew, the other side of the picnic table altar, could look into the last light, not that there was much of that.

See, Charlie could have had it all over by now, the ceremony part at least. Not that this would get everyone out of the circle, someone having erected another picnic table out by the pines, this one more secular, bottles of champagne on it, towers of paper cups. Getting their money's worth out of the Rollrights this black Saturday.

While they sang the hymn, *All Things Bright And Beautiful*, Grayle wandered quietly among the guests, looking into their faces, fearful that one would be the rugged, corn-topped visage of Adrian Fraser-Hale.

He was not here. Neither were there any stakes or rods protruding from the earth inside the circle. What would she have done if she'd found one? Pulled it out? Would that have made everything fine, made the dark clouds disperse?

Sure, and brought Ersula back to life.

Earth is dark.
Earth is dark.

Earth is cold.
Earth is cold.

When Bobby started shivering, Cindy stopped drumming, reduced his chant to a whisper, brought out the cloak of feathers and hung it round Bobby's shoulders.

It was 6.30 p.m. and almost night. But not cold; this night was as close as October could get to humid. Only cold, apparently, where Bobby was, which was how it should be, but Cindy wasn't happy about this. It was unknown country, a level of being he'd had no experience of, a harsher, more elemental place, kept in motion by the energy of slaughter. And it made no difference at all that this was, in all probability, an entirely imaginary country which had never existed outside a single, disturbed psyche.

The chant had taken its own direction, Bobby no longer responding to Cindy's words. Which, again, was how it should be, but also rather frightening. It meant that Cindy no longer had a measure of control. He prayed for assistance, without knowing quite to whom the prayer was addressed.

Earth is dark.
Earth is cold.
Earth is grave.
Earth is grave.
Earth is dark is cold is grave.

Bobby stopped chanting. He was utterly still, did not even appear to be breathing. Face as pale as his T-shirt.

Cindy heard a humming. Not heard exactly, he was *aware* of a humming. It was coming not from Bobby but from the King Stone. The stone blurred before his eyes and seemed to swell, then came into sharp focus; despite the paucity of light, he could see every smear of mould and liver-spot of lichen.

Bobby Maiden's lips parted, as if to resume the chant, but all that came out was a hiss, a sibilance, a rustling, in more than one tone. As though one hiss was communicating with another, a whispered conversation.

A whispered conversation between huddled figures. Identifying the location.

Cindy shook him, yelling in his face. *'Stop. Get up. Get up!'*

They could have got through this. It could have been over.

But then, just as Charlie came to that routine stuff about how if anyone knew of any just cause or impediment why these two fine young people should not, right this minute, be declared man and wife, then . . .

. . . then, in the east, over towards the city of Oxford, came a small but vivid flaring in the sky.

Christ.

Pushing people's hands apart, Grayle ran out towards the altar. Reaching it about half a second before the distant punch of thunder.

'Listen, I'm sorry . . . I'm sorry . . .'

The Reverend Charlie broke off, half turned to her. Another faraway fan of lightning briefly lit up his creased surplice.

'Grayle?'

'Charlie, listen to me, we have a problem. No sweat, but we need to suspend this ceremony. Until the storm passes. We have to get all these people out of here.'

Laid-back old Charlie, a dope-haze over his senses, he just looked at Grayle, kind of curious. But Matthew Lyall – a bulge in his top pocket that anyone could see was a ring box – was cold-sober and angry.

'Who says?'

'Me. I say. Please. You saw the lightning. That's bad news, Matthew. That is very seriously bad news. See, I was hoping it was gonna pass, but it didn't, and that's real bad news, I'm sorry.'

'Grayle, what on earth are you trying to do? This is our *wedding*.'

'I, uh . . . Listen, I got a bad feeling about this whole thing. I'm a very sensitive person, Matthew, OK?

Holy . . . Holy Grayle, right? In the States people listen to me. You should listen to me.'

'I'll listen to you as long as you like when Janny and I are married. Which would probably have been by now, if you hadn't—'

'You saw that lightning? Up in the sky? It's gonna come closer. My feeling . . . I get feelings, OK, you should listen to my feelings . . . and my, er, strong, deep-down psychic feeling is you should not be getting married in a storm. It's bad luck. It will overshadow your whole married life. Cause instability, and in . . . uh . . . infertility. Your marriage will be barren.'

In the third, slightly brighter flash, Janny Oates's face crumpled like a paper bag, and Grayle felt like a piece of shit.

The slow, rolling thunder seemed to set off mutterings everywhere. 'Who the hell is this woman?' demanded some deeply offended, deeply Oxford-English man's voice among the congregation. 'She on drugs?'

A fourth flash lit a stone which was knotted and eroded – *good Christ* – into the shape of a hunched-up, grinning, winged demon, with a long neck and a bony crest on top of its head. Jesus, it was just a stone. They were all just stones. Like Adrian Fraser-Hale was just a guy.

'I'm someone who *knows*,' Grayle cried, 'OK?'

XLVIII

Maiden moved quickly but circuitously across the field. *Don't use the path*, Cindy had warned. *It's too straight. And don't, whatever you do, put yourself between the circle and the Knights.*

The Whispering Knights.

The Whispering Knights was the name given to another collapsed dolmen, once a kind of High Knoll-type structure, but taller, and the stones had folded in on one another, and now they were like giants conspiring.

The monument was in a fairly vast, open field on the opposite side of the road from the King Stone and about a quarter of a mile from the Rollright circle.

You can't miss them, Bobby; there's nothing else in that field.

Only a sprinkle of trees on the horizon, a line of hedge marking a field boundary – all briefly shown to him by the sheet lightning, some miles away yet, but closing.

And, unfortunately, anyone inside those stones, they can't miss you.

When the lightning came again, like a revolving search-light, Maiden dropped into the short grass. The image of the Knights burned into his mind. They were surrounded by railings, like the King Stone but far bigger, more like big birds than men, black hooded crows, huddled.

Rising.
Earth release me.
Clouds cushion me.
Sky receive me.

Cindy felt himself looking down on the bone-hard Cotswold Ridge, imagining his body growing lighter than the clouds, in all senses of the word, his cloak of feathers coming alive, becoming wings. And the wings, when he spread them, all aglow.

The Fychans had taught him this. The Fychans, father and son; there had been a grandfather, too, and two more generations before him, taking the family tradition back into the eighteenth century. And farther back, to the days when the family house of rubble was a house of skins. The word *shaman* never used, no specific Welsh word for shaman. *Dynion hysbys*, they called the Fychans. The Men who Know. When a Christmas show in Llandudno had been abandoned following a fire at the theatre, Cindy had wandered south into the mountains around Cader Idris, happened to stop at the Fychan farmhouse for a night's bed and breakfast, which turned into two nights, then three weeks and several years, on and off – the Fychans forever saying, in their sly, North Walian way, that he'd never make a proper *dyn hysbys*, not being born to the Welsh language.

But he would be . . . well, *something*.

It was an inner way, a discipline; it did not exclude Christian ethics, it harnessed the imagination in a practical way. Now Cindy made himself go walking in the unstable sky, into the nervous system of the storm, imagining every charcoal cloud he touched being softened by his incandescence.

When lightning came at him, he opened himself to it and the electricity hit him in a great, sizzling spasm of agony, but he walked on, playing with the storm, taunting it like a lion-tamer with a whip.

Only it wasn't a whip, not really; Cindy suspected that it was no more than a piece of string, that he was not a great and powerful shaman but very possibly an ageing sham.

*   *   *

Less than thirty yards from the Whispering Knights now, and Bobby Maiden was wriggling along the ground on his stomach, because there was nothing in that flat, spacious field but him and the Knights. And anything which the Knights might enclose.

If Fraser-Hale *was* here, there wasn't going to be much of an element of surprise, but advertisement wouldn't help.

Something inside him started quivering like a very thin wire. Trepidation. He'd never seen Adrian Fraser-Hale, only his blood-washed leavings. Trepidation, where there should have been hatred. He wondered how his dad would handle this. Wondered what had *really* happened the night Norman Plod took on Harry Skinner and his lads in the old paint warehouse at Wilmslow.

The daft things you thought about when you were terrified.

Aw, come on, he's just a guy.

Just a guy who killed and killed and killed again and was never even suspected to exist because his motivation was beyond the accepted parameters of criminal behaviour.

Out of the darkness, out of the old stones, the Green Man spoke.

'Hullo there?'

'Sheet lightning showed him leaning over the railings: flop-haired, boyish.

Maiden didn't move.

'Don't come any closer, will you, old chap?' the Green Man said. 'I wouldn't recommend it. Rather tense to-night.'

Maiden didn't reply. The darkness settled back around him like a security blanket. He couldn't believe the voice. Together with the flash-image, the voice – so clear in the still, taut air – had brought up a ludicrous picture of some cool young World War Two airman, leaning against his Spitfire, smoking a pipe and wondering, in a desultory way, what Jerry had up his sleeve for tonight.

'Except you might stand up. Quite like to take a look at you next time there's a flash.'

So Fraser-Hale couldn't see him, didn't know how close he was. Perhaps had heard him moving across the field. *Hadn't* seen him in the lightning.

Which made him seem less of a threat, less of a fine-tuned, hawk-eyed, all-sensing Stone Age stalker, half man, half Will o' the Wisp woodland sprite.

'So let's have you on your feet, shall we? See who you are.'

Maiden said carefully, 'Who do you think I am?'

Barely a pause. 'Someone the woman told I suppose. Made a mistake there, but we broke down in the wrong place, you see. Engines are man-made. Imprecise. I can't be doing with things I haven't made myself.'

'What woman's that . . . Adrian?'

'Oh . . . blond hair. American. Someone's sister.'

Green Man Psychological Profile: when they lost their identity, became 'the man', 'the woman', it meant they'd been consigned to the mental file marked *Sacrificial*.

'You mean the place you broke down, it would have been wrong to kill her there? Nowhere near a ley, or a sacred site?'

'Who are you?'

Maiden kept his voice steady. 'I'm your shadow, Adrian. I was with you in the New Forest. Under the pines near Avebury. And last night. At Collen Hall.'

'Who are you?' Plain curiosity.

'It doesn't matter. You wouldn't know me.'

'No,' Adrian said. 'It certainly doesn't matter to me. For the moment.'

'But we know you. Quite a few of us.' Tip the scales a little; make him feel exposed, analysed, possibly surrounded. 'We've been watching you for quite a while.'

'With what purpose? To learn?'

Bloody hell, the arrogance.

Think.

Remembering, while he was with the Met, being sent on a siege-negotiators' course. Not the full course, a weekend primer, play-acting. Learning to relate to the hyped-up nutter at the upstairs window holding a blade to his former girlfriend's throat, the fugitive on the eleventh-floor balcony with the baby. Keep them talking. Become a friend, the only friend they've got.

The course had been short on advice for dealing with a passionately motivated assassin perfectly at home among Neolithic stones with a storm on the way: his ideal killing situation, but you didn't know quite who he was planning to kill or quite when or quite how, only how he'd killed the others, no specific MO – apart from being governed by earth-forces which might not exist outside the labyrinth of his mind.

Maiden rolled onto his side. Over to the right, there was a tiny, twin glow. The candles on the wedding altar, over four hundred yards away. Were the people all still there? Had they moved away, leaving the candles?

And don't, whatever you do, put yourself between the circle and the Knights.

'Adrian,' he said. 'The thing is, you've quite impressed us. We don't think there's ever been anyone precisely like you.'

'Then you must be pretty stupid, if you think that. There was a time when everyone was like me.'

'Hunting?'

'Hunting to live. Living to hunt. Feeding the organism, feeding the Earth. The great energy cycle. It's the big secret.' Adrian laughed, a full-bodied ha ha ha sort of laugh. 'Killing makes the world go round.'

'Terrific.'

'What did you say?'

For once, Cindy was wrong. The storm might be a psychological trigger, but he wasn't expecting the storm to do his killing for him. Too random. The Green Man liked to be in full control. The Whispering Knights was a perfect, strategic observation post, a little island. Was he waiting for someone here? Would someone be *sent*, like the birdwatcher? Had Maiden fallen into that role?

It wasn't enough.

Pull him out of the abstract. Tie him down. A name.

'I gather Roger Falconer's been using your ideas.'

'*Ideas?*'

'Well, you know what I mean.'

'We were going to write a book together.'

'That's what he told you, is it? You and Roger, both names on the front?'

'Not sure. Not sure he deserves it.'

'Worried he might rip you off?'

A pause.

'Rip? I may rip his throat out. I may give him to the Knoll. Have to leave the Knoll something when I go. Could be Roger. What do you think?'

Talking to Maiden as someone who, having studied the Green Man, was expected to grasp the point.

'Where are you going, Adrian?'

Pause. 'Who did you say you were?'

'You wouldn't know me. My name's . . . Robert.'

'You're right. I don't know anyone called Robert. What do you do?'

'I'm a painter. Like Turner.'

'I don't know much about art.'

'But you know what you like. And you like the picture of Stonehenge. In the storm. That's a Turner.'

'*No!*'

'Yes . . .' Watch it. 'No. Sorry. Must be thinking of another one.'

'Don't be stupid, I know which one you mean. The lightning, called into the circle. And the sheep waiting to die for the Earth. And the shepherd. One of the world's greatest works of art. A message. From the Earth. I mean, it doesn't matter who daubed the paint on; it's a spiritual work, a coded message to mankind. They're all willing

467

sacrifices. I mean, for heaven's sake, a shepherd *knows* when there's a storm coming. A shepherd on Salisbury Plain – and I was born near there – he knows to avoid the stones, because, when it happens there, it's going to be a big one. I mean, not *now*, perhaps, because Stonehenge is pretty useless now, with all the tourists, but then . . . when was that painted?'

'About 1820?'

'Gave himself up, that shepherd. And a few sheep. I'm glad you spotted that, Robert. You're starting to understand.'

'And what's the message, Adrian? What's the coded message?'

'You'll see. You'll know.'

'That's why we're here. Right?'

No reply.

'You said Stonehenge was pretty useless now . . . that's why you've come here, right?'

Laughter. 'These stupid railings. What do they think they're keeping out?'

'Or keeping in?'

'Very good, Robert. Very perceptive. Are you standing up, Robert? I want to see you. So do the Knights.'

Maiden lay still. Thought he heard shouts from the circle. They were still *there*? What was she *doing*?

Adrian laughed. 'Why don't you come closer, Robert? Come and watch. It's like an army. It's regrouping. Gathering its forces. Conserving its energy, and it's coming. It's coming. It's very close.'

The storm?

'And what's going to happen when it comes?'

'I like you, Robert,' Adrian said. 'But you ask too many questions.'

Something came then. The first fork lightning, a jagged, white crack in the sky and it was close, speared the trees on the horizon and—

'Told you!' Adrian cried, splashed with ice-milk light,

arms raised in euphoria, amid the Knights and the *whump* of thunder. 'Told you, told you, *told* you! The next one – that's the sign – the next one will be *it*.'

No talking this one down.

'All right, Adrian.' He stood up. 'I'm coming over.'

'See?' Grayle screamed, and she wasn't the only woman there who did when all the stones lit up. 'I thought you knew all *about* this stuff! Stone circles attracting lightning and all, on account of the streams crossing. You stay here, you're gonna get blasted.'

'Oh, let's go,' Janny sobbed. 'It's all ruined now, anyway. It was a stupid idea.'

'No!' Matthew shouted. 'Grayle, I can't believe you're doing this. This is the most wonderful thing that's ever happened to me. It's a blessing. Tell her, Charlie!'

'Well,' Charlie said, 'they do say an electric storm's an Act of God, but whether . . .'

'It's a blessing! It's absolutely tremendous.'

'It's *ruined*!' Janny shrieked.

'I can get you a church,' Charlie said. 'Phone call should do it.'

'I think you better had.' People pushing forward. 'I'm the bride's father, and I think she's had just about enough of this nonsense.'

'I don't want a bloody church!' Matthew shouted. 'Just do the business, Charlie. Tie the knot.'

'No! You don't understand . . . There's a killer out there.'

With Janny's father, Grayle saw, was Duncan Murphy, the professor from Oxford; hadn't noticed him before. 'Come on, Grayle,' he said, 'I think you've made your point.'

'Duncan, you have to listen me. There's a mad guy . . .'

Duncan Murphy and some other man, they took an arm each and lifted her off her feet and back into the congregation.

469

*　　*　　*

He could see the Knights, but no Adrian.

No telling how much time he had. The only way he'd know what they were up against was to get inside those railings, step inside the tiger's cage.

And then? Would he still be Robert then, when the energy exploded, when the shit hit the fan? Or would have become 'the man'? Maybe 'a poor specimen'. And later tonight, the Green Man would be talking his storm-lit death into the burial chamber at Black Knoll.

'OK. I'm here, Adrian. Adrian?'

Walking those last few paces, his head was clearing. Pleasanter now, the night a bit cooler. Hands in his pockets, the essence of peat coming back to him. Damp and lonely.

A dodgy streetlamp flickering on and off and, even when it was on, it wasn't fully on, so you could almost see the filament in the bulb, a worm of blue-white light. She was standing under the lamp and seemed to be going on and off like the light; you saw her and then you didn't.

'Emma?'

He saw the face of the woman under the lamp. It wasn't Em's, though she was about the same age. Her hair was in a bun. She had a case at her feet.

She disappeared in the lightning.

It came down, against all the earth-mystery rules, not in the circle, but in the pines, those skeletal, stalky pines.

But it lit the circle. Seemed as if it lit up every one of the seventy-plus cheesy, pockmarked, weathered stones. So savage and so bright was the lightning that it seemed you would have had time to walk round and count them all one more time before it faded.

Except that Grayle – and possibly she was the only one of them – was not looking at either the stones or the pines, a couple of which had caught fire, but at Janny's wedding

470

dress, the only thing here which was, conspicuously, not an unnatural, blazing white.

Janny's wedding dress, from the waist to the prim, high neck, had grown a sunburst of deepest, rosiest red.

No . . . Jesus.

Grayle stood transfixed, feeling the hands of Duncan Murphy and the other guy dropping away, and then, spinning round, saw a small flash across the big, flat field and there was also a *crack*. Not the thunder, surely, because the thunder was almost directly overhead, like an avalanche in the sky, and Grayle wasn't sure of the order any of this was happening because so many terrible things were happening.

But that was a shot. That, God damn it, was a gunshot.

At some point, Janny finally screamed, and maybe it was at the thunder or maybe because she saw that she was soaked with blood or maybe – in the light of the burning pine trees – she saw Charlie sinking slowly to his knees, as if he was praying for deliverance, with a hole the size of a fist in the front of his surplice and everything emptying out.

Several people saw Charlie fall and there were screams of incomprehension that the lightning could *do* this. A guy rushed forward, and a woman shrieked, 'Don't touch him . . . he could be *live!*'

But Grayle Underhill knew there was nothing live about Charlie any more and she found herself walking purposefully out of the circle and into the big, flat field where she'd seen the flash and where, by the light of the burning pines, she could now see some stones, hunched up like gloating old men.

'Well, as you see,' Adrian said, 'it's an old Mauser. Nothing fancy. 1941, bolt action. Had it since I was a boy. Used to be my grandfather's, bit of a wartime heirloom. Super old thing.'

Maiden had been struggling to find the gate in the high

railings surrounding the Whispering Knights. Could have tried to climb over but he'd never have made it, and Adrian would have shot him and left him bleeding there on top of the iron spikes.

But nothing like that. Adrian had opened the gate for him, peering at his face in the faint, sparky light from the blazing pines four hundred yards away. Adrian beaming. 'Come in, Robert. You can come in now.'

Proudly showing him the set-up.

'The sight . . .' He detached the rifle from a metal frame wedged between two of the Knights. 'Well, I simply bought that at a gun shop in Worcester. Utility stuff. The support I made myself.'

'People say you're very practical.'

'One tries.'

Sharp screams of terror spattered the sky like sparks over the Rollright Stones. He must have killed or wounded. Two shots.

'Energy,' Adrian said. 'Look at those flames. That's confirmation. Oh God, Robert, feel the release. Feel that glorious, glorious release of pure, terrestrial energy. The fusion of the Earth and the sky and . . . *whump!*'

Adrian was sky-high. In his army sweater and his camouflage trousers, he looked strong, swelling with power. You could smell his sweat, like engine oil, feel his heat. He caressed the rifle in his arms. Even without it, he wouldn't have regarded Maiden as any kind of threat or any kind of sacred, chosen target because Maiden's approach had been along no known, or even suspected, ley.

Everything in Adrian's world was completely straightforward, rigidly aligned.

He grinned from a summit of self-belief.

'Must've got two, Robert.' Like some country-sport enthusiast talking pheasants. 'Do you think two?'

There was a smell of burning in the hellish, rosy night.

'Three would've been better, but I was only given the light for two, so . . . One has to go with the surge. When you're working together, *breathing* together.'

'Better than sex, Adrian?' Maiden recalling the Green Man's long, liquid, shuddering moan as the lightning flared and the gun went off.

Wrong. Adrian stiffened. He made a contemptuous noise. Adrian was a moralist. Adrian had strict ethics. Adrian did not like dirty talk.

'So who *are* you?' Adrian said, unfriendly again.

Maiden felt dog-tired, used up. Whatever energy had been generated it wasn't accessible to him.

'I *said* . . .' Adrian placed a hand in the centre of Maiden's chest, pushed him hard against the rails. 'Who . . . are . . . you?'

Adrian was bigger, heavier, swollen with self-righteousness. Close up for the first time, Maiden could see his eyes glittering with the mindless joy of the bully. Seen it, so many times, in his dad's eyes, when Norman brought the slipper out. Norman didn't wear slippers; he only had the one, used for disciplinary purposes. Discipline. Authority. Adrian would know all about that.

OK then. Maiden drew a hard breath.

'I'm Detective Inspector Bobby Maiden.' He paused. This was ridiculous. 'Adrian Fraser-Hale, I'm arresting you for the murder of Ersula Underhill. You do not have to say anything, but it may harm your defence if you fail to mention, when questioned, anything you later rely on in court. Anything you do say will be taken . . .'

'Oh.' Adrian retreated to the railings, the rifle in his arms. 'I see.'

This would be the first time anyone had applied the word *murder* to Adrian's continuing programme of sacrificial bloodletting. Maiden took a determined step towards him.

'Further charges will be made later. Hand me the rifle, Adrian.'

'*Adrian?*' a faint, subdued voice said from the other side of the railings.

'Oh shit,' Maiden said.

She stood in the grass, fifteen, twenty yards away. A small figure in a torn skirt, hair sweated to her cheeks.

'Come on, Adrian . . .' Maiden held out his hands for the rifle.

But really the hands were out there in prayer.

'Do the sensible thing, eh?' Maiden said, just like the old man would've said.

Grayle Underhill said, 'Oh.'

Feeling Fraser-Hale's attention waver, Maiden went for him, went for the gun.

And felt the air pulse as Adrian moved with a swift and shocking grace, bringing up the rifle, half turning as Maiden went for him. That fixed, opaque glaze of madness in Adrian's eyes, his teeth bared and parted. You could almost see the twisted, fibrous roots and stretched tendrils in the Green Man's feral smile, as he brought down the wooden rifle butt hard into Maiden's eye, the left one, the one that was still half closed.

As Maiden sank, in agony, to his knees, the world was divided into blurred segments by the railings, through which he could see the pale, wavering shape which would, by now, be sharp and tight in Adrian's line of fire.

'The woman's on the line, Robert.' The voice of the Green Man quivering with euphoria and a kind of wonder at the gloriously unexpected magic of the situation. 'I said it should be three, didn't I? The woman's *on the line*.'

XLIX

Never occurred to Andy to be scared until she was inside the castle walls and there was no light.

Never been here before, at night, when there weren't at least a couple of lights in the house. So Marcus wasn't here. Well, good. Good – probably. Where would he have gone? Down to St Mary's, most likely, into the pub. Andy would turn the car round, go check out the pub. OK. No problem.

She curved slowly round under the castle wall. Taken her over three hours to drive down from Elham, through the rush hour and then another damn rush hour and then foot down, but not too hard because it would be pretty stupid if, having driven twice round the suburbs to throw off any pursuit, she was nicked on some bloody cart track in the Black Mountains.

There'd been no pursuit, anyway. She'd have known. Would have been easy enough for Riggs to put out her registration to every force in Britain. It was clear enough, now, that Riggs had done no such thing. That the other person Tony Parker had felt obliged to contact with a view to calling off the bad guys was Mr Riggs himself.

And that Mr Riggs had said no. Or that Tony had died before he could even get round to asking him.

The bad guys, presumably, had been. But had the bad guys gone? Best to stay in the car a while. Andy checked the doors were locked. Leaning across to the passenger side, glancing out of the passenger window, she saw the body.

Marcus . . .

Backed up in a frenzy, turned the car round so that the headlights were on the face. Breathed again when it turned out not to be a face she knew: some young guy with dark brown, dried blood around a deep dent in his forehead, one arm skewed out with a hand upturned, clawed. A block of stone beside him big enough to mark his grave.

If he needed one? Wasn't moving, looked all twisted up, but . . . The hell with this. Andy got out, checked for vital signs.

Cold. Dead a good while. What *was* this? This one of the bad guys? Way he was twisted, it was pretty clear he'd come crashing down the tower steps. Treacherous, those steps, particularly in the dark, but why the hell would he go up there in the first place? Andy looked around. Dead silence.

And then the house door opened.

'Sister Anderson.'

Guy in a bomber jacket was walking across the dark yard towards her. She knew the voice, but then she knew a hell of a lot of voices. Whoever it was, he'd been in the house. If anybody was in that house, it ought to be Marcus.

Not so much scared as seriously apprehensive, she waited right where she was, within reach of the car. Until his face was in the headlights.

'Well,' she said. 'I didnae think it'd be you. Bloody Judas, eh?'

It began to rain. Big, hard, vertical bullets.

With a lot of difficulty, Grayle raised her eyes from the rifle barrel, which didn't move so long as she didn't. Which was pointing steadily at her breast bone.

'This is where I . . . I get to die . . . right?' She tried to see his face. She thought how Charlie had died. Not even crying out. Never knew. Poor Charlie. Came to conduct a wedding and he died.

Adrian said, 'Don't talk. Rejoice.'

'Rejoice?' Grayle flared up. 'That what you told Ersula? When she . . .'

'The bitch was unreceptive at the end.'

She heard Bobby Maiden speak, though she couldn't see him. He sounded weak, he sounded hurt.

Adrian said, 'Be quiet, Robert.'

'. . . bloody coward, Adrian. But that's hunting, isn't it? Essence of a great British tradition. Guys with guns against animals that only run. Guys on horses with packs of hounds against one exhausted . . .'

'Shut *up*!'

'Natural balance, isn't it? But, hell, Adrian, yours don't even get a chance to run . . .'

'I'll kill you . . . You miserable piece of town-bred vermin. When this is over I'll take you away to somewhere less sacred and I'll kick the life out of you. In the meantime, you'll shut your drivelling mouth and—'

'*You* don't kill.' Bobby's voice battling against the rain singing on the stones. 'The Earth kills, remember? You can't do it on your own. And the moment's gone. The lightning's over. Storm's past. It's raining. You've lost it. You can't do it without the lightning.'

Please God, Grayle thought, no more lightning. Please God . . . Please Cindy . . .

'Also . . .' Bobby said from somewhere down on the ground between Adrian and the back rails. 'Also, this is Grayle . . . You killed her once. And it wasn't her. You blew it. Got it wrong . . . Grayle's bad luck for you, Adrian.'

'*I do* not *get it wrong!*'

'You're *always* getting it bloody wrong. What about the barbed wire in Wales? Put it out for a man, you catch a young lad. But he didn't die, did he? You screwed up.'

Silence. Other noises behind the spattering on the stones. The smell of smoke from the pines. Grayle felt the rain pouring down her face, blurring her vision. Her clothes like a second, sodden skin. She was afraid to blink.

Adrian said, 'How do you know about that?'

'Ah,' Bobby said. 'Didn't tell the stones, did you? Didn't tell the stones you screwed up.'

Distant sheet lightning, no more than a veil. Grayle cringed. The barrel twitched. Oh Jesus. Involuntarily, Grayle squeezed her eyes shut, screamed, 'Adrian, do you know who you shot down there. You shot Charlie . . . shot the goddamned minister!'

'Well, good!' he screamed back through the torrent. 'Charlie was a disgrace. Charlie *took drugs*!'

'And what the fuck did you give to Ersula?' Bobby yelled.

'You watch your filthy, vermin *mouth* . . .'

'Maybe Grayle would like to know what else you don't tell the Earth. Hey, considering where we are, considering how stones *record*, maybe the Earth would like to know what happens when you . . . when you take a sacrifice . . . when you pull the trigger . . . bring down the rock . . . sink in the knife . . . shove . . . shovel in the gravel and the concrete . . . When the earth-energy floods into your system like golden light? and you feel this . . . *blinding joy*? Maybe Grayle and the good old Earth goddess . . . your mother . . . your holy bride . . . would like to know what happens then, how you always come in your pants, when . . .'

'*You filthy . . . swine . . .*'

Grayle's eyes jerked open to the sight of Adrian up on the lone recumbent stone, screaming, holding the rifle by the barrel, smashing it down on Bobby Maiden, Bobby shouting, 'Get off the line, Grayle, *get off the fucking line* . . .'

And then it was all lights.

L

'. . . that supposed to mean?' On the edge of the headlight beams, the guy looked worn out, two days' grey stubble.

'Tony sent you, right?'

'Kind of.'

'Nothing to do with Riggs, like.'

'I don't work for Riggs.'

'Oh, aye. Well, nobody does, do they? Nobody works for Riggs, *officially*.'

'Look, Sister,' Vic Clutton said. 'Time's getting on. I've got a bit of cleaning up to do before I leave.'

'I hope that doesnae include me, pal.'

'Oh, don't be bloody daft.' Clutton pulled a gun, a black pistol, out of his jacket pocket, tossed it into the dirt. 'Pick it up. Feel safe.'

Andy ignored the gun. 'What happened to your oppo over there?'

'Shit, Sister, you gonner let me get a word in? Parker . . .'

Andy took a breath.

Clutton said, 'Parker had me down here to keep an eye on Em.'

'Didnae do a great job there, Victor.'

'Look!' Avoiding her eyes, talking rapidly to his shoes. 'I was to watch her. Getting into bad company – policemen, this kind of business. He wanted to know how far it'd gone. I follow her down here, she picks Maiden up and I tail her and him to this hotel.'

'You were in that very same *hotel*?'

479

'Leaving them to get on with it. Well, I mean, that's her business. She's a free spirit. I've got no objection to a swish B and B on Parker's tab, even if I've got to stay out of the bar and the dining room and that. And yeah, yeah, to my shame, I didn't know nothing till next morning, when the premises are crawling with filth, and . . .' A glint of tears. '. . . I have never been so shattered in my life, Sister. That girl . . .'

'I know.'

'Plus, I *liked* the guy, in spite of he was filth. He was *clean* filth, you know what I mean? I couldn't handle it. I pissed off, building up the courage to phone Parker – hardest call I ever made. I start gabbling, I say, I don't care what you want, Mr Parker, but, with all respect, me, what I want, I want Maiden . . .'

'You're saying you came down after Bobby on your own? So who's this other guy?'

'Yeah, I come back here. I'm gonner hang around till he come out. I'd've hung around a week . . . longer. But he come out, all fresh and clean, and he's off over the fields, down the wood, and I'm straight in there after him. Woods? Fine by me. Good a place as any.'

'Just like that, eh? Regardless of he didnae kill the girl. And you with that gun?'

'No way.' Vic Clutton looked at his hands. 'That's not mine, anyway. Way I was feeling, I didn't need no shooter. I was gonner take him apart. When he meets up with this posh tart, I'd've took 'em *both* apart. Only, this tart, she's got a pick and she's hacking up this concrete, sorter thing . . . and . . . Well, there's a fucking *stiff* down there.'

'You *what*?'

'Yeah. I'm thinking . . . what? He done another one? What's occurring? You know? Next thing, they're off up this big house and then this other bloke's arriving in this crappy old motor, and after a while him and Maiden drives off, and I'm on foot, aren't I?'

'What time's this?'

'Two . . . three . . . I dunno. Afternoon. I figure maybe they've come back here or they're gonner come back here, so I trudge back and I'm laying low, and it's getting dark and no Maiden. Then this white van pulls in and out jumps these blokes and . . . shit, I *know* 'em. Last seen in Maiden's flat . . . you remember that business?'

'Just a minute.' Andy walked over to the corpse. 'Who is this guy? And where's—'

'Name's Bez.'

He was shambling across the yard, a short, fat guy in a tartan dressing gown. The big, stupid bull terrier trotting alongside like this was big walkies time.

'Don't ask me what kind of bloody name that is, Anderson. And he's fucking well dead, and I'm merely dying, so if you happen to have your little nurse's outfit with you . . .'

Vic said, 'Mr Bacton, I thought I told you to lie down.'

The cops came in from all directions almost simultaneously.

In force. Four cars and a van. The van was directly into the field, all these guys tumbling out with automatic rifles. The whole place surrounded. Portable lights. The stone circle cordoned off, armed guys around the back of the pines – some of them still smouldering in the hard, vertical rain.

A helicopter hovered above the Whispering Knights with a searchlight in case Adrian Fraser-Hale should overpower the three detectives and the four Armed Response blokes and make a break for it across the fields.

Seemed Adrian wasn't in the mood. When he saw the van coming, he'd stopped hitting Bobby with the gun and he'd turned it round and Grayle had thought, Jesus, he's gonna put it in his mouth. But Adrian had just looked at the gun in dismay, like checking the barrel wasn't bent or anything, and then the cops were screaming at him, ordering him to lie down. Grayle too. Also Bobby, except the poor guy already was.

Adrian, handcuffed, was looking kind of affronted. Offended. The way he'd been a couple times on the journey from Cefn-y-bedd.

'In the van,' the senior-looking white-haired cop said. Bobby knew him, called him Ron.

As the back doors of the van flung open, Adrian turned, looked at them, didn't seem to see anyone.

'It was all so absolutely *right*,' he insisted. 'I couldn't get over how *right* it was.'

They shoved him in. The doors were slammed.

'What did that mean, Bobby?' Ron said.

A hand over one eye, blood oozing between the fingers, Bobby demonstrated to Ron how the Rollright Stones could be perfectly viewed in the gap, no more than a foot wide, between two of the Whispering Knights. Now, with all the lights in the circle, it looked almost too easy a target, far closer than four hundred yards.

'One megalithic site to another,' Bobby said. 'Bang.' He sighed. 'How many? He got two shots off.'

'Killed the vicar outright,' Ron said. 'One through the back. Another bloke caught one in the thigh, so he'll be OK. Ambulance on its way. Better take you, too. After we charge you.'

'That a joke?'

'Let's bloody hope so. Stupid bastards. Whoever decided to put your name out, they should be for the jump.'

'Riggs.'

'Still need a good explanation. Bloody hell.'

'He'll have one. He always has one. So who called you out?'

'Message from West Mercia. Woman reported a body buried in concrete down near the Welsh border, Hay-on-Wye area. Funny name . . .'

'Magda Ring.'

'Yeah. After they see that body, they start taking her a bit

482

seriously. Mind you . . .' Ron smiled ruefully. '. . . if she hadn't given West Mercia the name Fraser-Hale and a photograph, we'd probably have let him go and pulled you for the lot, Bobby. Yes, David . . .'

A uniformed sergeant came over. 'Sir, there's a bloke . . .' He coughed. '. . . a bloke in a bird-suit.'

'Of course there is,' Ron said. 'This is the Rollright bloody Stones. Tell him to piss off.'

Grayle saw Bobby Maiden grin. It looked like it hurt.

Two cops took her back to the circle. Nobody was allowed out of it, despite the downpour. Just about everybody got searched. Charlie's body had been covered up. There were some cases of latent hysteria. Janny Oates, still unmarried, was not among them. Two policewomen were with her under an umbrella. She was entirely silent, deep in shock. Drenched with blood and all of it Charlie's.

Jesus. Grayle could only feel numb.

Andy took Marcus back inside, made him lie on the study sofa, Malcolm across his feet. Checked him over for broken bones, but Marcus carried plenty of padding. Cheekbone was a possibility. It was hard for him to talk, which was a mercy for all of them. He should be in hospital; some chance.

Round the back of the house, Vic showed her the body of a man called Gallow. Some of his head had been blown away.

'You're looking at contract boys,' Vic said. 'The hiring's always done through a third party, sorter thing, maybe even a fourth party. Riggs wouldn't touch 'em with coal-tongs. These boys would never even've heard the name Riggs.'

Vic and Andy both wore gloves for this. Vic did most of the carrying; he'd found some sacking in the barn and tied it round his waist with orange baler twine.

Andy said, 'So when Riggs found out where Bobby was,

thanks to my foolishness, he took no steps at all to bring him in. He just made a phone call.'

'Prove it,' Vic said.

'Word has it,' Andy said, 'that if you yourself turned Queen's Evidence, or whatever they call it, enough stones might get turned over to open up a path direct to Riggs's door.'

'I helped fit up several small operators, sure. Including Dean, my lad, God rest him. But that was for Parker. I won't drop Parker in it.'

'Of course,' Andy said, 'you wouldnae've heard, would you?'

They put both bodies in the back of the white van. They put the guns in too – the sawn-off and the pistol Vic had found near Bez's body and used on Gallow when he was about to kill Marcus.

Vic found the keys to the van in Bez's pocket. He said he'd probably drive down the Wye Valley and dump the van somewhere near the Severn Bridge. There was a mess of link roads around a half-built industrial estate. He'd walk to the motorway services, get himself a lift with a lorry driver to anywhere. Stay out of sight for a week or two. Maybe grab a holiday, Minehead or somewhere.

'And you'll think about what I said?' Andy said.

'I'll think about it.'

Andy walked back to the farmhouse and wondered, not for the seventeenth time, what it would really be like living here.

LI

Cold. The stones prickly with frost. She had to touch, just once, before she walked away, dug her hands into coat pockets.

Hallowe'en, night of the dead, didn't seem like a good time for this. But, then, it wasn't Hallowe'en any more. What did they call the day after Hallowe'en? Was that All Saints Day or All Souls Day? Anyway, the Celtic New Year, Cindy said, so that was OK. And a new moon, too. Must count for something.

And I'm still here, Grayle thought. What am I doing still here, waiting for the start of some stupid ceremony to rehabilitate a pile of rocks?

The pre-dawn wind was kicking at the grass, rattling the gorse bushes. There were no bad vibes around the place, but no good vibes either.

Just some old stones and a bunch of dysfunctional fruit-cakes.

After two days of questions and statements and assuring them that she'd return in good time for the trial, Grayle had left Oxford in a fresh hire car. They'd found the little red Rover up against a field gate, couple of hundred yards from the path to the Whispering Knights. Backed up, ready to go. Another sign that Adrian had seen no reason why he wasn't going to walk away from this.

At Duncan Murphy's place, Grayle had spent a half-hour on the phone to her father. She told him Ersula was dead, murdered by a clean-shaven, nicely groomed, old-fashioned, well-spoken, all-round decent guy who loved his country. Then she burst into tears. Her father had not asked when she planned to return. Her father only ever had one daughter.

Precisely what Adrian Fraser-Hale had done to Ersula, Grayle did not, at that time, know.

Soon, the whole world would know.

Somehow, without quite figuring out why, Grayle had found herself driving west again. Tuesday night, she was back in her depressing old room at the Ram's Head in the village of St Mary's. Along the passage from an even crummier room occupied by one Sydney Mars-Lewis.

'I should go home,' she said to him in the bar that night. 'But I feel so restless. So dislocated. So . . . so goddamned angry.'

'A hundred years ago . . .' Cindy was wearing his insouciant smile. '. . . he would have been hanged and his body brought back and laid out on the capstone at Black Knoll so that everyone damaged by him could walk up and watch him rot. Would that have helped?'

'Get outa here,' Grayle had said.

Now she looked at the High Knoll burial chamber and thought maybe this was what they were about to do. Kind of.

Someone put an arm around her waist. She looked up into an eyepatch.

Bobby Maiden hadn't been back to Elham. He'd been in Hereford for two weeks, engaged the whole time on the Fraser-Hale case. Sitting in on the days of interviews with Adrian, who was co-operative and expansive and some-times – although never quite, for Maiden – almost charming.

Different people kept listening to the tapes. 'Load of balls,' Armstrong would say periodically. 'Whichever way you look at it, the feller's bloody mental.'

Armstrong being the detective superintendent in charge

now. Because Adrian was so polite and co-operative, Armstrong didn't hate Adrian.

He hated Cindy instead.

'I don't understand where that mad Welsh poof comes into it,' he'd say every time Maiden strongly suggested they consult Cindy about some arcane issue relating to earth-magic. Armstrong hated having Cindy in the same room. Seymour, the forensic psychologist inflicted on the team, hated having Cindy in the same county.

'Don't worry about it, lovely,' Cindy said. 'How would I have coped with all that fame at my age?'

He did send one letter to Superintendent Armstrong. It suggested they should never become blasé or loosen the security around Adrian Fraser-Hale. That they should be very careful about which police stations or remand centres he was to be held in, which courtroom was to be used for his trial, which prison or unit for the criminal insane was to house him for perhaps the rest of his life. Cindy advocated the use of an Ordnance Survey map and a ruler.

Armstrong showed Maiden the letter before he shredded it. 'Tell this old toerag if he pesters me again I'll nick him for wasting police time.'

Maiden wondered whether he was going to quit the Job, officially, before or after the court case.

But he still wanted Riggs.

One night, he had a call from Mike Beattie to say his car had been found in Telford Avenue, jacked up on bricks, all four wheels gone, what did he want doing with it? Oh, and had he heard old Tony Parker was no more?

Sure. He'd heard it all from Andy, who'd given herself either two weeks' holiday or a nervous breakdown, depending how Elham General wanted to play it. She was staying in the dairy cottage at Castle Farm to care for Marcus, who, in Maiden's view, was playing weaker than he actually was. But not too weak to keep ringing Maiden up in Hereford, asking if they'd arrested Falconer yet.

Unlikely. Falconer was coming over dumbfounded.

After all, just look at the chap, would you think he was capable? Does he look like a Peter Sutcliffe, a Charles Manson, a Jeffrey Dahmer, a Fred bloody West?

'The University of the Earth will quietly fade away,' Magda Ring predicted over a lunchtime drink in the Ram's Head. 'I'm expecting a lump sum from Roger. What I think is called a Golden Gag. Of course, I could probably equal it, were I to write the full story of Roger and Adrian for one of the Sundays.'

'You really think he knew?'

'How *much* did he know is the only valid question. I think he kept Adrian like zoologists keep apes. Do you know what I mean?'

'They were going to write a book together.'

'You mean Falconer was going to write a book about the Adrian Phenomenon. And may still, when he's had time to disentangle himself completely.'

'I'll swing for the bastard first,' Marcus said.

'Ah. There you are, lovelies.'

Cindy wore a long, double-breasted coat and a tan fedora.

'No feathery cloak?' Maiden said.

'Too cold. Brrrr.' Cindy shook his arms. Bangles jangled. 'Oh . . . while I remember.' He slid a small package into Maiden's jacket pocket. 'There you are. You've got everything now, lovely.'

'What is it?'

'It's the cassette we recorded on the Knoll, when you slept on the stone. Your dream tape.'

'Do I want to hear it?'

'Well,' Cindy said, 'the truth is, most of it didn't come out. I lied.'

'What, that whole dream session . . .'

'You can call it a psychological placebo if you like, but I am a shaman and I collected the soil, and I believe . . . Anyway, recorders and cameras and such items often do malfunction when something really quite significant is happening. Someone up there laughing at us. There is, however, something about a lady. Under a street-lamp.'

'Oh, wow,' Grayle said.

Maiden smiled. 'That was my mum.'

'Interesting,' Cindy said. 'Do expand.'

'Well, actually, the truth of it came to me – bizarrely – when the fork lightning was coming down in the pines and Fraser-Hale was firing and I was struggling to find the bloody gate in the railings and failing. I didn't think about it again until last night.'

'Your mother's death, perhaps, in the hit-and-run?'

'My dad told me – and the inquest – that she obviously ran out to push me away from an oncoming lorry. While he was at work and someone left the gate open. Not quite how it happened.'

'How old were you?'

'Two. I . . . feel . . . that what happened was that my mum was finally leaving the old man. Because he'd hit her once too often.'

He'd dreamt about her again last night. A sputtering lamp in Old Church Street. Coming on, going off. A woman beneath it, lit up for a strobing second: a small woman in a light cardigan over a summer dress with bulls-eyes. A small, pale face, curly hair held back with clips that often fell out.

'Claimed he wasn't there at the time, but he was. He came back, maybe suspecting something, and she was waiting at the bus stop, with a small case. And me. She was taking me with her. It was a very quiet lane, almost in the country, no immediate neighbours. He got very angry. He hit her. She stumbled. And that was when I ran out in the road.'

'How do you know this, Bobby?'

Bobby Maiden gave him back the brown paper parcel containing the cassette tape.

'How the hell should I know? You're the bloody shaman.'

A pale band had appeared in the eastern sky.

'How you gonna handle this?' Grayle wondered.

Cindy seemed a little despondent. 'I'd hoped for more people, actually. We need to demonstrate that things have changed. Six of us, and all outsiders . . . Still, we can but try.'

'So, how—'

Cindy tapped his chin and his bangles rattled. 'Well, for a start, I thought it would be nice if one of us could go inside the chamber.'

'It's collapsed.'

'Annie managed it. And, of course, the good Sister Anderson. Replaced a little weight since then, fortunately for her. I wonder who is the smallest of us now.'

'Uh-uh. No way,' Grayle said. 'Let's forget this right now.'

'I should never have even suggested it. My apologies. I simply thought that, as only one of us has been permitted to *see* her . . . '

It was 6.50 a.m. A thin, amber line over the Malvern Hills.

'Hullo,' Marcus said. 'What's this?'

A chain of lights coming up the rise. UFOs maybe, Grayle thought. Something for *The Phenomenologist*. She'd been thinking a lot about *The Phenomenologist*, what a piece of crap it was, although it didn't have to be a piece of crap. With a little more cash behind it, a redesign. Some real journalism.

Stupid, a pipe dream. She didn't belong here.

'Quite a few of the buggers,' Marcus noted.

Andy said, 'Probably the entire hospital trust come to drag me back.'

*　　　*　　　*

They came up the path taken, Cindy understood, by Annie Davies herself on a morning when the castle ruins hung damply in the mist around the yard, Annie sliding through the scabbed and knobbly remains towards the pinkening light. Not this time of year, of course, there would have been no chill then; it would be another hot day.

There were not a great many, fewer than there'd been at the funeral. By the light of the torches, Cindy recognized several of those who had been in the pub when Amy Jenkins had broken the village's silence. Cindy spotted the old man in the flat cap, the fat woman with the hat and the old woman with the funny eye. And Amy herself, of course. Who would have rounded them up, badgered, cajoled, blackmailed, offered to wipe slates clean . . .

Cindy met her at the edge of the Knoll.

'Amy,' he said. 'If I were a *real* man, I should ask you to marry me.'

Bobby Maiden spotted a familiar shabby figure looking slightly uncomfortable amongst all these yokels.

'The lady in the pub said I'd find you here, no other police around,' Vic Clutton said. 'We need to talk, Mr Maiden.'

'Always happy to talk with you, Vic. Saved my life, as I recall.'

'Yeah,' Vic said, like this had only just occurred to him. 'I did, didn't I? You heard about me saving anyone else's life at all?'

'Wouldn't surprise me. But no.'

'Really no?'

'Really no.'

'Or any other . . . incidents?'

'Don't know what you're on about.'

'So there's no question of any of these . . . incidents . . . raising their ugly heads, sorter thing, in the future.'

'Wouldn't be because of me. Because I haven't heard of them.'

'Right . . . right. Erm . . . that time you suggested Riggs had Dean strung up . . .'

'Mmm,' Maiden said. 'I don't see us standing that one up either, I'm afraid. But there are other . . . issues . . . on which Riggs might be put away. And Beattie. And one or two others. Once you take away a few bricks . . . in a jerry-built place like Elham . . . you know what I mean?'

'Got you. All right. I'll be in touch.' Vic nodded and turned away. 'Be seeing you, Mr Maiden.'

'Don't go,' Maiden said. 'Stay for our little rustic ritual. Illegal drinks afterwards at the Tup. All nice, decent people. Oh . . . except for Marcus Bacton. The murderer.'

With the capstone only inches above her, the supporting stones on all sides and all the gaps between them blocked by the legs of the thirty-plus people standing in a circle around the monument, it was dark as hell in here. Ersula was right.

The claustrophobia can be intense. You start to scream inside. All you want is out of there. But, like I said, you have to stop your conscious mind getting a hold of you. What you are dealing with here is the unconscious and that must be left to find its own route to what you would probably call enlightenment.

Scary fun, huh, Ersula?

However, even without her coat, she found it curiously warm. She laid her head on her folded arms. Cindy was leading some kind of chant out there and it was kind of soporific. Maybe she fell asleep. Maybe she dreamed; maybe she didn't.

When she awoke (or didn't) her left hand was like on fire. And when she inched forward, it was suddenly so bright on her face that she had to shut her eyes.

In a long, long moment of amber radiance, Grayle's body was suffused with a startling warmth.

Now, OK, this was crazy. By all the laws of prehistoric science this should not be happening, because this was 1

November and the chamber was supposed to be oriented to the *midsummer* sunrise.

The warmth settled around her like a fleece, but very lightly. And then she felt it inside her, in the lowest part of her gut like good brandy. She kept her eyes tight shut and lay very still. This was no hardship. In the closeness of the burial chamber on High Knoll, she felt she never wanted to move again, that she'd be quite happy to die here, in this long, ecstatic moment, at the age of . . . goddamn it, nearly thirty, and what had she done that was in any way worthwhile?

When she opened her eyes, she found herself at the very end of the tunnel, and what had seemed like a slit . . . well, because of the positioning of the stones and the people's legs, it was now wide enough to be almost a doorway. She guessed that what had happened was that the capstone, having collapsed, had collapsed some more and the sun was coming in through some other slit.

Whatever.

The sun was a glorious deep red, made all the more intense by the frosty air, the starkness of the trees. You'd swear it was coming down.

Like just for her.

And Annie Davies.

'Bullshit,' Grayle whispered. Uncertainly.

Feeling, somehow, that she was not alone in here.

HALE QUIZZED OVER PRISON KILLING

The serial killer, Adrian Fraser-Hale, was being questioned last night by police investigating the murder of an assistant chaplain at Dartmoor Prison.

The Rev. Paul Campion, a 29-year-old father of two, was found with a peeling-knife lodged in his throat in one of the prison kitchens.

Hale, 31, who has been described as 'a model prisoner' since his arrival at . . .

The Times, May 17

Notes and acknowledgements

The ideas in this novel arose from established research into the paranormal properties of prehistoric monuments. The dream survey has been carried out, more or less as described, by the Dragon Project Trust. Details can be found in back copies of *The Ley Hunter* magazine and in Paul Devereux's book *Secrets of Ancient and Sacred Places*. Theories about prehistoric weather control are aired in Tom Graves's *Needles of Stone* and more about Cindy's shamanic heritage can be discovered in *The Celtic Shaman* by John Matthews and *Shamanism and the Mystery Lines* by Paul Devereux. Aubrey Burl's *Rites of the Gods* discovers what ancient sites have to tell us about the religion of Neolithic peoples.

Sightings of the Virgin Mary, incidentally, are not unknown in the Black Mountains.

This book would not have worked without Bill Scott-Kerr's unique combination of faith and ruthlessness, the tireless, even more ruthless, but inspired editorial overview of my wife, Deborah, and the help of the following: Pam Baker, Paul Devereux, Paul Gibbons, John Grant, Andrew Hewson, Wendy Isle, Derek Ivens, Mike Kreciala, Laurence Main and Lofty Wiseman. Many thanks to them all.

A LIST OF SELECTED FINE WRITING
AVAILABLE FROM CORGI BOOKS

14168 2	JIGSAW		Campbell Armstrong	£4.99
14169 0	HEAT		Campbell Armstrong	£5.99
09156 1	THE EXORCIST		William Peter Blatty	£5.99
14353 7	BREAKHEART HILL		Thomas H. Cook	£5.99
14518 1	THE CHATHAM SCHOOL AFFAIR		Thomas H. Cook	£5.99
14377 4	THE HORSE WHISPERER		Nicholas Evans	£5.99
13275 9	THE NEGOTIATOR		Frederick Forsyth	£5.99
13823 1	THE DECEIVER		Frederick Forsyth	£5.99
13990 4	THE FIST OF GOD		Frederick Forsyth	£5.99
13991 2	ICON		Frederick Forsyth	£5.99
14512 2	WITHOUT CONSENT		Frances Fyfield	£5.99
14293 X	RED, RED ROBIN		Stephen Gallagher	£5.99
14472 X	CONFESSOR		John Gardner	£5.99
14223 9	BORROWED TIME		Robert Goddard	£5.99
13840 1	CLOSED CIRCLE		Robert Goddard	£5.99
13839 8	HAND IN GLOVE		Robert Goddard	£5.99
13678 6	THE EVENING NEWS		Arthur Hailey	£5.99
14622 6	A MIND TO KILL		Andrea Hart	£5.99
07583 3	NO MEAN CITY	A. McArthur & H. Kingsley Long		£5.99
14302 2	LITTLE BROTHER		David Mason	£5.99
14136 4	THE WALPOLE ORANGE		Frank Muir	£4.99
14478 9	AUTOMATED ALICE		Jeff Noon	£6.99
14392 8	CASINO		Nicholas Pileggi	£5.99
13094 X	WISEGUY		Nicholas Pileggi	£5.99
14541 6	AMERICAN GOTHIC: FAMILY		William T. Quick	£4.99
54535 X	KILLING GROUND		Gerald Seymour	£5.99
14143 7	A SIMPLE PLAN		Scott Smith	£4.99
10565 1	TRINITY		Leon Uris	£6.99
14555 6	A TOUCH OF FROST		R. D. Wingfield	£5.99
13981 5	FROST AT CHRISTMAS		R. D. Wingfield	£5.99